The Courier's Wife

BOOK ONE | SECRETS OF THE BLUE AND GRAY

VANESSA LIND

A heartrending novel of courage and resilience
based on the true story of a female Civil War spy

September 1862. Hattie Logan is a restless young woman with a strong will and an effervescent spirit. When war ignites, she escapes her privileged family and prim finishing school to join Allen Pinkerton's spy agency, burning to make a difference for the Union. As one of Pinkerton's mailroom girls, she uncovers secrets that could change the course of the war. Still, she longs to do more. Dispatched as the courier's wife, she ventures behind enemy lines, where her passion for the man posing as her husband deepens. But from the shadows of Hattie's past, a secret threatens their plans and their lives. A sweeping story of courage and resilience, with rich historical detail and unforgettable characters who will tug at your heart.

ISBN eBook: 978-1-940320-18-2

ISBN paperback: 978-1-940320-17-5

Contents

Chapter One

SEPTEMBER 2, 1862

Not yet nine in the morning, and the September day already promised sweltering heat. South of the nation's capital, storm clouds piled along the horizon, teasing the promise of rain that never came. Directly overhead, the Washington sky was brilliant and cloudless, the air still and humid. Hattie Logan felt perspiration beading around her collar. Like a July day back in Indiana, Hattie thought, then immediately banished the idea, wanting nothing more to do with where she'd come from. Forward. That was the only direction for her.

She and Anne approached the Treasury building, a massive stone structure that towered over the path, casting a welcome shadow. "It's been three days," Anne said. "We should check the casualty lists."

"Two days," Hattie corrected. "And if we stop, we'll be late, and Lucy will run straight to Miss Warne." Lucy Hamilton was the self-appointed supervisor of Allen Pinkerton's mailroom girls, who opened letters the courier brought, searching for Rebel secrets that would aid the Union cause.

"Miss Warne won't mind," Anne insisted.

Of course Anne would say that. She was on good terms with the woman who oversaw their work for Mr. Pinkerton. "Maybe she won't mind about you," Hattie said. "But she doesn't like me."

"That's not true. It's just that you clam up whenever she's around."

"I'm only being discreet," Hattie said. It was a nice way of saying that the less she said, the less she'd be asked about who she was and where she came from.

Anne rolled her eyes, having heard this excuse any number of times. Of all Hattie appreciated about her friend, Anne's willingness not to pry was at the top of the list.

Crinolines rustling, they reached the wide marble steps of the Treasury, where the Sanitary Commission posted lists of whichever casualties had happened to filter in, often long after the battles were over.

"It will only take a few moments to check," Anne said, worry shining in her gray eyes.

Reports coming in from Manassas, where a second battle had ended only days ago, suggested casualties in the thousands. As usual, the soldiers' families would likely be the last to know. Especially in hasty retreats, there was no time to identify who'd been injured or killed. The wounded might or might not get carried off in stretchers. The dead might or might not be buried. A mother might learn of her beloved son's death, if she learned of it at all, from a letter published in her hometown paper, sent by a surviving soldier in the regiment. Anne longed to spare her mother that shock.

"All right," Hattie said, swinging toward the steps. "I know it'll bother you all day if we don't look. And hot as it's going to get, you'll need to keep your wits about you."

Ever gracious—she'd absorbed the finishing school lessons Hattie had decidedly rejected—Anne smiled gently. "There might be word of George too."

Hattie had last heard from her brother, George, back in May, a few weeks before she and Anne had come East. At the time, he'd said his regiment was preparing to march to Fredericksburg.- Like Anne's brothers, he'd seen heavy fighting and by all accounts was continually on the move. But Anne's concern for her mother steeled her in ways Hattie couldn't comprehend. Besides Hattie's grandma, George was the only family she cared about. If he lay dead on some forlorn battlefield or bloodied in a makeshift hospital, she'd rather not know. She'd rather remember him as she'd last seen him, freckles dusting either side of his nose, a wide grin hiding whatever fear he must have felt as he went off to fight.

The day their parents disowned George, the day they sent Hattie off to finishing school to stop her wailing after him—that was the day Hattie had decided the big house on Cherry Street, the finest in La Conner, Indiana, was no home of hers. At least as a girl, her mother had sniffed, there would be no worries about Hattie joining the fight against the good people of the South who only wanted to preserve their way of life. But Hattie had found a way, even if it wasn't as meaningful as she'd like

George was out there somewhere, she told herself, stuck on some distant battlefield without mail service, or wounded and unable to write. Or he was here, in Washington, and she'd run into him one day. Only yesterday, she'd spotted a Federal soldier with George's square shoulders and broad back. She'd run to him, heart thumping. But when he turned to face her, she'd had to mumble an apology about mistaking him for someone else. Whisky on his breath, he'd tried to grab her by the arm, and she'd fled from his reach.

The sun beat down as Hattie and Anne neared the top of the steps. Beneath the tight bun Hattie wore at the base of her neck, she felt a trickle of perspiration. Under the bodice of her navy dress—a poor choice in the heat, but her other two work dresses needed washing—her chemise stuck to her skin. Though the day had only just begun, she already felt exhausted, and she suspected Anne did too. They'd both lain awake half the night in the attic room they shared at Mrs. Sullivan's boarding house, listening for the booms of mortar and cannons. Yesterday, the streets had teemed with bloodied Union soldiers. All around the city, there was talk that General Lee's Rebel army was closing in on the capital.

Hattie brushed a damp curl from her forehead. At least the Treasury's broad colonnade shaded the portico at the top of the steps, offering welcome relief from the September sun. As in most parts of Washington City, persons of all different types were coming and going from the building. Some, like Hattie and Anne, had flocked to the city to help with the war effort or to search for loved ones. Others were formerly enslaved Negroes who'd fled north over the Confederate border to freedom. Still others were government officials helping to orchestrate the massive war effort. The rest were soldiers assigned to defend the capital from Rebel troops. General Lee's forces, headquartered only ninety-five miles to the south in Virginia, were a constant threat.

By September 1862, the War of the Rebellion had already dragged on months longer than most anyone, Reb or Federal, had expected. Every week, it seemed, a contingent of bedraggled Federal soldiers staggered into Washington, stunned by yet another defeat. The lucky ones flocked to the saloons, though no amount of drink could erase the shell-shocked gazes of the battle-weary. The unlucky ones were carted off to provisional hospitals where they would breathe the fetid smell of death and wince at the screams as doctors sawed off arms and legs.

Standing half a head taller than Hattie, Anne was first to spot the new casualty lists, tacked to a strip of wood. Skirts rustling against their petticoats, she and Hattie crossed the portico to the west side of the building, near the president's mansion.

Six lists were posted in two columns. Written in a hurried hand, the ink—already fading in the sun—detailed names and regiments, most from the recent fighting at Manassas. Hattie ran her finger along the names in one column while Anne scanned the other. Wounded. Deceased. Missing. It felt disrespectful to look so quickly. Every name represented a family forever changed.

Anne's finger reached the end of the names. "No Richard. No Henry."

Hattie shook her head. "No George either."

They turned, heading back across the portico to the stairs. "They're still alive," Anne said.

"Still fighting," Hattie said.

It had become a ritual, reciting these words, an invocation of good fortune, as if by speaking them, they could make them so. Still alive, still fighting, though they both knew their brothers might well be among the thousands of unnamed soldiers whose names never made any lists, the ones who just never came home.

They descended the steps, Hattie moving twice as fast as Anne, as if the sun couldn't catch her. "A descent unbefitting a lady," Anne said when she'd caught up with her, mimicking the prim tone of Miss Whitcomb, Ladygrace's headmistress. "Back up you go, dearie, and try again."

"Back up your arse," Hattie said under her breath, and they both laughed.

"I wonder what Miss Whitcomb would have to say about us opening other people's mail," Anne said as they started for the War Department building.

Hattie dipped her chin, pretending to look down her glasses as Miss Whitcomb did. "Wartime or no, one's curiosity must be restrained."

"But it's for the Union cause," Anne said.

"You always did think you could reason with her," Hattie said. "Even when everyone else knew it was hopeless."

"You can always reason with anyone," Anne said. "Or at least you should try."

Spoken like someone who's been raised among reasonable people, Hattie thought. But this wasn't the sort of thing she'd say aloud. Even with Anne, her best friend in the world, Hattie was careful not to say anything that revealed the past she was determined to forget.

Ahead, a carriage pulled up in front of the War Department building as it did every morning at nine o'clock. "Told you," Hattie said. "We're late."

Secretary of War Edwin Stanton got out, prompt as usual with his nine o'clock arrival and wearing his usual frock coat despite the heat. Hattie had heard him described as having a piggish face, and from the time she'd spent around hogs, the assessment didn't seem far afield. A retinue closed in around him. Several were young assistants Hattie recognized from the War Department's hallways, but an equal number, she knew, were people haranguing Stanton about government jobs.

Hattie and Anne slowed their steps. Late as they were, they'd have to wait until Stanton's entourage shuffled into the building before they could enter.

"Lucy must be squealing with delight, now that we're truly tardy," Hattie said.

Anne laughed. "And run off to tell Miss Warne."

"Oh, but I'm so *concerned* about Anne and Hattie," Hattie said, imitating Lucy's affected British accent. "They *clearly* haven't grappled with the fact that in our most *valuable* work, every moment counts." Lucy Hamilton had a high opinion of herself. Her father was a prominent New Hampshire politician who'd brought his family to Washington so they could all be well positioned for any wartime advantages that might come their way. Lucy was forever reminding the mailroom girls of how important her father was, and how she did her work not for money but for the cause.

From near the top of the War Department building, hammers rang out, a cacophony of pounding as carpenters framed in the third and fourth stories, which were being hastily constructed to accommodate the hive of activity under Stanton's purview. Hattie shielded her eyes, looking up at the scaffolding. That was where George should be, overseeing a big building project instead of risking his life in the battlefield. From his earliest years, he'd dreamed of becoming an architect, sketching plans and piecing together models of projects he envisioned.

"Those workers will bake out here in the sun," she said.

"No worse than in the Little Oven," Anne said, referring to the tiny, windowless storeroom behind Stanton's suite of offices. "At least those men have fresh air to breathe."

Hattie wrinkled her nose at the swampy odor that had hung over Washington City all summer. "Not what I'd call fresh."

The reply came not from Anne but from a man's reedy voice. "Not by a long shot."

Hattie turned. The first thing she noticed was that the people who'd been milling around the path had drawn back, making way for the tall, gangly man who'd spoken as he strode firmly in Hattie and Anne's direction. The long face with high cheekbones, upturned chin, large nose, and a rather woeful looking beard brought instant recognition, as did the black stovepipe hat.

Anne clapped her hand over her mouth.

"Mr. Lincoln!" Hattie had seen the president once before, from a distance as she passed the Executive Mansion. He'd stood on the balcony, gazing over the city. His boys had run to him, one on either side, and he'd smiled broadly, circling a long arm around each of them. Hattie had smiled, seeing a father who genuinely loved his children. She'd never imagined the president might speak to her. Not being one to let an opportunity pass, she held out her hand.

"A pleasure to meet you," she said with propriety that even Miss Whitcomb could not fault. "I admire you so for leading our country through these dark times."

He shook his head, and a gloomy look overcame him, his face darkening. "I did not think these times would be near so dark or last so long."

Hattie glanced at Anne, wanting to allow her a chance to speak. Her hand had dropped from her mouth, but she only stared, dumbfounded, so Hattie went on. "Our sacrifice will be validated when the Union is restored and the slaves emancipated."

The president's hands, clasped behind his back, fell to his side, and his face relaxed into a smile. "Well, there are two of us, then, who believe both results can be accomplished."

"Oh, but of course they can," Hattie enthused. "If we all do our part." She straightened, shoulders back in the posture Miss Whitcomb had taught. "My friend and I assist in Mr. Pinkerton's efforts. With the mail."

As soon as she'd spoken, she realized how foolish this sounded. What did the president know of their labors in the mailroom, or for that matter, care?

But his grin widened, and he said, "Spies, are you? I take heart in knowing that such lovely ladies are about such important work on the Union's behalf. And now, I must be about mine." He dipped his head slightly, first at Hattie and then at Anne. "Good day."

They stood, dumbfounded, as Mr. Lincoln strode ahead of them, entering the War Building through a side entrance. Heart thumping, Hattie took in the scene, wanting to impress it forever in her memory, the bright blue sky, the clatter of carriage wheels, even the stench and the stifling heat

"He goes every day to the Telegraph Office," Anne said as they began walking again. "To read the telegrams that come in from the battlefronts. But it's usually at night." She turned to Hattie. "I can't believe you chatted with him like an old friend, telling him what we do with Pinkerton's."

"He said it was important work," Hattie said. And it was, she told herself. Still, she wanted more.

Chapter Two

Entering the War Building brought temporary relief from both the odor and the heat. The marble floors and stone walls would be chilly in winter, Hattie knew, but for now, they lent a delightful coolness to the air. Above the grand staircase, a big clock overhead read a quarter past nine. After stopping to check the casualty lists, their encounter with Mr. Lincoln had slowed them even more. Lucy was sure to make a fuss.

Hattie and Anne edged along a far wall, headed for the mailroom where the Pinkerton girls opened letters brought by the agency's couriers, searching for information that would prove useful to General McClellan and his troops. When Anne's father had arranged for the two of them to work for Pinkerton in Washington, Hattie had thought they'd be doing real detective work. That's what the Pinkerton Agency was known for, after all—sleuthing out criminals.

But as it turned out, what they did felt more like ordinary snooping. Each day, the girls carefully opened and read the letters, then sealed them back up for delivery. Most of the messages were dull as dirt, but occasionally one mentioned a crucial military action the Rebels were planning or described the activities of smugglers who ran the Union's blockades. When a message was truly important, it was written in code. Those they were supposed to pass along to Pinkerton's decoders, a team to which no woman had ever been assigned.

But Hattie sometimes took a crack at the coded messages before passing them on. She'd always loved a good puzzle, and she'd convinced one of Pinkerton's decoders to show her how the work was done. Her favorites were the messages that required using an alphabetic table called a Vigenère's Square. She had a knack for it, the Pinkerton man told her. Childless, he seemed to take fatherly pride in watching her use the Vigenère's, telling her she cracked the codes twice as fast as some of the men he'd trained.

They reached the mailroom, and Anne opened the door to a blast of hot air. The room, a large closet converted for the secret operation, lacked the cool marble of the War Department proper. It held its heat overnight, generated by six women working in close proximity, not to mention the stove that heated the kettles they used for steaming envelopes open and the hot irons they used to reseal them.

The girls all looked up from their work when Hattie and Anne entered. Lucy and Agatha sat at the rectangular oak table, each with a stack of letters. As usual, Lucy held herself regally, her dark hair coiffed in a coil of braids at the back of her head. She wore a walking dress that could have come from Godey's Ladies Book, of gauzy grenadine embroidered with stylized figures, the skirt trimmed with plaited flounces bound on the edges with blue silk. In a simple cotton dress, a pale brown plaid, Agatha stood at the stove, shoulders stooped as she held an envelope over the steaming kettle.

"Look who's decided to join us," Lucy said. Her affected speech grated on Hattie. Lucy's mother might be British, but Lucy's accent seemed forced.

"Blazes, it's hot in here," Hattie said, ignoring Lucy's remark. She pulled out the empty chair nearest the door, and Anne took the seat across from her.

Lucy crooked a finger at Agatha and Constance, who was at the ironing board, pressing an envelope shut. With a wardrobe half the size of Lucy's, Constance rotated among three working dresses no matter the weather. Today she'd made the unfortunate choice of a heavy white cotton gown with brown leaves and branches twining from hem to collar.

"As luck would have it, my dear Constance and Agatha, your shifts have ended," Lucy said. "Hattie and Anne are at fire today."

Constance set down the flat iron and wiped her brow with the back of her hand. Agatha backed away from the stove. Looking relieved, they started around the end of the table, making their way to where Anne and Hattie sat.

"We were at fire yesterday," Anne objected.

Lucy crossed her arms at her waspish waist. "You come late, you're at fire. That's what Miss Warne said."

"Since when?" Hattie said. "You were late last week, and no one put you at fire."

"That was different. I was detained on important business."

"As were we," Hattie said. "We were conversing with Mr. Lincoln."

Lucy laughed. "The president speaking with the likes of you? Not a chance."

Hattie jutted her chin. "He did, whether you choose to believe it or not. And who tasked you with running off to tell Miss Warne we were a few minutes late?"

Lucy's green eyes bore into Hattie. "No one *tasked* me with anything. I was *concerned*, that's all."

Anne looked down, and Hattie knew she was stifling a smile.

"Concerned you'd get to punish us with an extra turn at fire," Hattie said.

"Shall I go fetch Miss Warne?" Lucy said. "So she can convey the directive in person?"

Anne's chair grated on the wooden floor as she scooted back. "That won't be necessary. Come on, Hattie."

Hattie hated backing down, especially to someone as arrogant as Lucy. And she hated the idea that Miss Warne had such power over them. Not that their supervisor was unreasonable. In fact,

Hattie admired her calm demeanor. Nothing seemed to ruffle Miss Warne. Still, she could be intimidating, and it took a lot to intimidate Hattie.

Pick your battles, she reminded herself. Unlike Lucy Hamilton, she needed this job. It was her livelihood, and having just turned nineteen, she wasn't about to go crawling back to her parents.

She pushed back her chair with such force that it nearly toppled, keeping her eyes locked on Lucy's. "I hadn't realized you and Miss Warne were so close. Perhaps you can put in a good word for me when a field opening comes around." Field openings—going out to do real spy work, as Miss Warne herself did—were coveted at Pinkerton's, though by the time word of them reached the mailroom, they were already filled.

Lucy stiffened, and her gaze bore into Hattie's. "I shan't put in a word for you when I can do the work better myself."

Constance and Agatha slid quickly into the vacant chairs as if they might vanish if not quickly occupied. Lucy sat motionless as a statue, refusing to scoot in her chair as Anne and Hattie squeezed past. Hattie lifted her skirt, trying to ease it around the chair, and a bit of fabric caught on the top rail. Bending to free it, she jabbed an elbow purposely into Lucy's shoulder.

Lucy started, then turned and glared.

"Mother always did accuse me of being all elbows," Hattie said, moving on to her post.

The wood in the stove crackled pleasantly, oblivious to the discomfort it generated on this warm September day. Using a hot pad, Anne took up the flat iron and started in on a stack of envelopes ready for sealing. Hattie plucked letters one by one from the stack that needed opening, holding them by the fingertips over the kettle while the steam did its work, undoing the seals. Her hands glistened in the heat, and her auburn hair, curly by nature, corked into tendrils around her face. When the paper began to wrinkle, she slipped a letter opener beneath the envelope's flap, then wriggled it across slowly, so as not to tear the paper.

The seated women chattered as they worked, hashing over gossip Lucy shared. But at fire, the extra effort of talking felt draining, and so Hattie worked in silence, as did Anne. They moved in a rhythm, steam and press, steam and press. Besides fixing their minds on all things cold—icicles, snowdrifts, a winter wind—that was how they had coped with being at fire whenever their turns came around.

"I have it on good authority," Lucy chirped from the end of the table, "that Mr. Pinkerton intends to address us today."

Every bit of gossip Lucy shared originated in good authority, or so she claimed. Some days, Hattie challenged her to reveal her sources, but today was simply too hot, and she needed to get her stack of envelopes opened without the distraction of bantering. Lucy leaned toward Constance, Bridget, and Agatha, who as usual gave her their rapt attention. Hattie had never visited a medium who called up spirits, but she suspected they operated much as Lucy did, demanding the full attention of everyone in the room, then leading them along a path of suppositions that became farther and farther removed from reality. Still, once in a while, Lucy's gossip bore out as true.

"Miss Warne and Mr. Pinkerton intend to choose one of us to go into the field." Lucy paused, looking from woman to woman. When she seemed satisfied that all were listening—and with this new assertion, that now included Hattie—she added another detail, dropping her voice to conspiratorial effect. "The person they choose will work directly with Mr. Welton, posing as his sister."

Seated beside Lucy, Constance straightened. "I'd be most honored if they chose me, and I should accept without hesitation, regardless of the risk."

"Who wouldn't?" said Bridget, seated across from her. "It's Mr. Welton, after all."

Of all Mr. Pinkerton's couriers, Thomas Welton, who ran letters between Baltimore and Richmond as a cover for his spying, was far and away the favorite of the mailroom girls. His soft brown eyes and gently furrowed brow made him seem intently interested in whichever of the girls was vying for his attention. This was part of what made him a good spy, Hattie knew, gaining the full trust of people who should know better. And unlike the other couriers, who were all business, dropping off and picking up letters, he never seemed in a hurry.

A silence fell over the room, and Hattie suspected each of the women was thinking as she was—if Lucy's rumor was true, she wanted to be the lucky one to do real spy work alongside Thom Welton. As the chatter resumed, Hattie stayed quiet, passing one envelope after the other over the steaming kettle. The more she thought of it, the more she wanted the assignment, if in fact there was one. She loved the idea of posing as someone other than herself. Asked about her past, she could give whatever details suited, and no one need ever discover that her parents supported the enemy.

Just as Hattie thought she might swoon from heat—and all her life, she'd made a point never to swoon—she and Anne finished with the stacks before them. Now they could sit in the two empty chairs, closer to the stove than they'd like but at least not directly in its blast, and go through the letters as the others were doing, looking for the ones that warranted deeper attention.

Relieved to be off her feet, Hattie plucked an envelope from the top of the pile she'd unsealed. She removed the letter, addressed to a Miss Sally Generoux, Richmond, Virginia. Noting the tidy script, similar to what she'd been forced to practice at the Ladygrace School for Girls, Hattie scanned the letter. At first glance, it seemed innocuous, its sender commiserating with her cousin over wartime shortages. A hall lamp needed replacing, its neck broken. She'd made requests for fresh vegetables but had received none. There was a daughter turning twenty-five, but no sugar for a cake, and with prices going the way they were, a pound of sugar would soon cost thousands of dollars, if the men who rationed it could be believed.

Nothing of importance to the Union Army. Hattie refolded the letter and was about to return it to the envelope when she felt a slight bump beneath her thumb. She unfolded the page and held it up to the light. The bump was in fact a pinprick above the word *hall*. She ran her finger along every line, feeling for more pinpricks. Besides the one above *hall*, she found them above *necks, requests, twenty-five, thousands,* and *men.*

"Hall necks requests 25 thousands men," she read aloud, stringing the words together.

Anne snatched the page from her. "Where do you see that?"

"Run your finger over the spaces above the lines. Feel the pinpricks?"

Anne ran her fingertip over the page. "Hall necks. I'll bet that's General Halleck," she said, naming the general who'd recently been appointed General-in-Chief of all Union forces. Anne read the war news religiously, and she knew the specifics on every general, every battle. "This person's found out that Halleck wants 25,000 more men." She glanced at the envelope. "I'll bet Miss Sally Generoux of Richmond, Virginia, would love to deliver that little tidbit directly to Robert E. Lee himself."

"Old Brains," Lucy said. "That's what Mr. Pinkerton calls General Halleck, you know. I sincerely doubt he means it as a compliment. How rich, that Halleck wants more men, after refusing McClellan the men he needs."

Lucy also never missed a chance to defend handsome Union General George McClellan, who led the Army of the Potomac in the ongoing struggle to keep the Rebels from Washington. Others were much less fond of McClellan, including Mr. Lincoln. According to Anne, who kept tabs on such things, the president was growing increasingly frustrated with McClellan's indecisiveness.

Hattie was hardly an expert in battle strategy, but she could not abide inaction and so was inclined to side with Mr. Lincoln and his allies who intimated that the war would be over by now if

"Young Napoleon," as McClellan's detractors called him, had half the confidence of the South's General Robert E. Lee.

"What matters," Anne said, "is that this letter is going no farther now that Hattie's found its meaning. It would've helped the Rebels immensely had it gone through."

Lucy sniffed. "The Rebels scarcely need more help, what with Halleck and Lincoln conspiring against General McClellan."

Hattie disregarded much of what Lucy said, but she felt protective of the president, and even more so now that he'd spoken with her. "Leave Mr. Lincoln out of this," she said.

"Look who Old Ape's got in his corner," Lucy said, using the derisive variation of the president's given name. Constance snickered. "A fellow bumpkin from the West."

Hattie rose from her seat. She'd learned a good deal about responding to meanness at Ladygrace, and it had little to do with either ladies or grace.

Anne stood, setting a hand on her shoulder. "Let it go."

At that moment, the door opened, admitting Allen Pinkerton and Kate Warne. Behind them came Thomas Welton. Lucy beamed, her attention fully on Mr. Welton, as Hattie and Anne took their seats. Mr. Pinkerton stood at the head of the table, near Lucy. Short of stature and not especially handsome, with a receding hairline, deep set eyes, and a graying beard, he reminded Hattie of an old farmyard goat putting on airs.

Miss Warne stood a step back from him, off to one side. As usual, her thin brown hair, parted in the middle, was pulled back in a simple bun. Her eyes, heavily lidded and attentive in the way of a faithful dog, softened the severe effect of her hair. She was not especially pretty, and she dressed plainly, in a gray morning dress, but there was an honesty in her appearance that inspired trust. Mr. Welton, dressed in a black waistcoat, stood apart from them. Leaning against the wall, he nodded in greeting to the girls at the table, with a smile that each likely thought was intended for her.

Mr. Pinkerton squared his shoulders, then cleared his throat, gazing pointedly from one woman to the next. "I've come to remind you all to have courage." After years in America, he still spoke with a Scotsman's lilt in his voice. "There's much confusion in the city, I know."

Confusion indeed, Hattie thought.

"But as we speak, General McClellan is organizing his troops for battle," Mr. Pinkerton continued. "No harm will come to us on his watch."

Lucy looked smug as a fly in a honey pot, her hero getting his due.

"I will be accompanying the general into the field." Mr. Pinkerton's chest puffed out like a bellows. "As he puts the screws to the Rebs, you can expect the volume of letters to increase. They'll be desperate to gain any advantage, and their allies in Baltimore will be passing on any scrap of information to aid them. While I'm away, Miss Warne will remain here, directing your work." His eyes softened as he gestured for their supervisor to come forward. "She has an announcement for you girls."

Miss Warne stepped forward. She stood half a head taller than Mr. Pinkerton, hands clasped at her waist, a smile teasing at her lips as she nodded his direction, making Hattie wonder if there was any truth to Lucy's rumor that Mr. Pinkerton and Miss Warne were romantically involved.

Directing her attention to the girls, Miss Warne spoke in a schoolmarm's voice, clear and direct. "Mr. Pinkerton and I applaud the work you ladies are doing." Miss Warne always addressed them as ladies, not girls, though the oldest among them, Constance, was only twenty-three. "I know this heat makes it especially uncomfortable, on top of the worries you must have over the security of the city. Rest assured that your efforts are vital and appreciated."

Even by Mr. Lincoln, Hattie thought.

"As you know, the Pinkerton Agency is aiding our government in a multitude of ways," Miss Warne continued. "Much of that effort is in the field. Couriers like Mr. Welton risk their lives with each Rebel contact they make."

Hattie glanced at Thomas Welton to gauge his reaction to this praise, but from his expression, Miss Warne might have been speaking of a stranger.

"Our courier work has become increasingly dangerous," Miss Warne said.

"As you ladies know," Miss Warne said, "Mr. Welton poses as a Secesh sympathizer, so others of that persuasion, whether in Richmond or Baltimore or points beyond, entrust their letters to him. Some of his most valuable work involves befriending men who know a good deal about Rebel plans. Some of these men—"

"And women," Mr. Welton said, his soft British manner of speaking a contrast to Miss Warne's plain-spoken speech.

"That's right," Miss Warne said. "We mustn't underestimate the dangers posed by female spies who side with the Confederacy."

"We caught Belle Boyd," Mr. Pinkerton interjected. He sounded proud of the effort, though Hattie had heard him criticized for bungling the arrest.

Thomas Welton shook his head. "Plenty more like her in Richmond. Smugglers, saboteurs, spies."

The thought of this thrilled Hattie. Where were the Union's women, doing such work for their cause?

"Until recently, Mr. Welton's claims of being a secessionist living in Baltimore were accepted without question," Miss Warne said. "But of late, there have been incidents of concern. May I mention some specifics, Mr. Welton? These ladies know how to keep a confidence."

With the sheepish grin of a boy caught in a good deed, he nodded. "As you wish."

"You tell them, Thom," Mr. Pinkerton said. "About what happened in Memphis."

Thomas Welton scratched the side of his head, the sort of folksy gesture that Hattie thought must endear him to the people he spied on. "A few weeks ago, I crossed at the Kentucky border, headed to the Tennessee line, hoping to rub shoulders with some of the renegades who claim to operate independently of the

Rebels, terrorizing the good people of Tennessee who support the Union cause. Some folks suspect these guerilla efforts are more coordinated than they appear, with support at the highest levels of the Confederacy."

Hattie caught Anne's eye. Only yesterday, she'd read a newspaper article to Hattie about these bands of highwaymen accosting innocent people after dark, not just in Tennessee but also in Kentucky, where the official stance of neutrality sat poorly with southern sympathizers. It was the sort of effort Hattie's parents would wholeheartedly endorse.

"The rigors of my work demand that I spend a fair amount of time frequenting saloons," Thomas Welton continued, cracking a wry smile. "I hope you ladies won't think the less of me for it. In Memphis, I took up with three Rebel officers at a place called the Dog and Pony, and for the price of three whiskies, I gained three new—"

"The train," interrupted Mr. Pinkerton, looking annoyed at how Mr. Welton was drawing out the story, entrancing the mailroom girls.

"Right. There was another man in the saloon, you see, sitting off in a corner. Long hair, wide-brimmed hat. I recognized him from the train. He sneered when one of the officers removed his gray cap and fitted it to my head, pronouncing me a comrade in arms. The next day, on the train, I spotted the long-haired man again, in the company of a big burly friend. I sneaked off at the next stop. They tried to follow, but I jumped the express to Louisville before they could catch me."

"So you see, ladies, this work is not for the faint of heart," Miss Warne said. "Mr. Pinkerton has noted the need to enhance Mr. Welton's standing with the Rebels."

Mr. Pinkerton cleared his throat. "A spy's credibility hinges on making a full person of him. He has origins, family, friends. The more convincing we make him, the better his cover."

"What we're seeking," Miss Warne said, "is a woman to pose as his sister. Mr. Welton occupies comfortable quarters in Baltimore.

Whoever goes there with him will have her own room, tended by the household staff that looks after Mr. Welton's needs. It will all be quite proper."

Lucy smiled like the proverbial cat who'd swallowed the canary. "I assume you'll want a woman accustomed to dealing with servants," she said, using her best British accent. "Someone who can pose believably as having crossed the Atlantic to live with her well-to-do brother who happens to sympathize with the South."

"Precisely," Miss Warne said. "We also want someone who can fold easily into the circles Mr. Welton has penetrated. That means one of you ladies. You have read countless letters. You know the thoughts and concerns of those who send them. That will be invaluable in winning their trust. Tomorrow I'll begin inquiries to determine which of you will be best for this assignment. Not that you would be obligated to accept if chosen. But I want to alert you to the possibility so you can be weighing the risks if the position is offered."

"Risks which do not, by the way, require you to smoke cigars or drink whisky," Mr. Welton said. "Those weighty responsibilities shall fall solely on my shoulders."

Too bad, Hattie thought. She'd often wondered what it would be like to pose as a man and partake in such activities.

Miss Warne offered a faint smile. "Well, then, ladies. We shall leave you to your work."

As they started for the door, Anne called out to them, waving the Generoux letter in the air. "Miss Warne, Mr. Pinkerton, there's something you should see."

They turned, and Mr. Pinkerton started toward her, with Miss Warne and Mr. Welton following.

"What is it?" Mr. Pinkerton asked, looking slightly annoyed.

"There's a coded message in this letter. About General Halleck wanting more troops."

Pinkerton snatched the letter from Anne. Hattie could tell as he read that the code eluded him. Drawing attention to this would anger him, she knew. What Mr. Pinkerton lacked in stature, he made up in ego. But Miss Whitcomb's lessons about holding her tongue had never quite taken. She leaned in, pointing at the word *hall*. "Look closely, and you'll see a pinprick."

Mr. Pinkerton squinted at the page. "Yes, yes, of course," he said, still looking confused.

"And another above *necks*, and then *requests*. Run a finger along the lines, and you'll feel them."

Mr. Pinkerton swung the letter from her view. "Confound it, girl! I've been at this business since before you could talk."

At the end of the table, Lucy smiled primly.

Mr. Welton stepped alongside Mr. Pinkerton. "If I may, sir."

Mr. Pinkerton relinquished the letter. "Locate the sender," he barked. "And the recipient."

Mr. Welton tucked the letter and its envelope in his jacket pocket, then made a little bow toward Anne. "Well done, miss."

"It wasn't me that found it, sir. Hattie did." She pointed across the table.

"Ah. I should have known." He bowed toward Hattie, more deeply than he had toward Anne.

Should have known what, she wanted to ask, flushing at how he'd singled her out.

Mr. Pinkerton clapped once, a percussive cue that indicated he'd spent more than enough time in the mailroom, evidenced by the trickle of sweat running down the side of his face. "Back to work, girls!" It was the sort of command Hattie supposed one would hear in a sweatshop—fitting enough, given that the temperature had to be nearly a hundred degrees in the former closet.

The detective chief made his exit, Miss Warne a step behind. Thomas Welton lingered a moment. "Keep up the good work," he said, winking. Hattie knew full well that she wasn't the only one who thought his wink was directed at her, but it felt good all the same.

With a flick of her hand, Lucy selected an envelope from the stack Hattie had steamed. She seemed desperate to make eye contact with Mr. Welton as he turned toward the door. At the same time, she seemed determined to impress him with how deftly she could open an envelope.

"Ouch!" she cried as the letter opener slipped. She held up one finger, examining it for injury, though the opener was far too dull to draw blood. But by then, Mr. Welton had taken his leave.

Hattie tried but failed to suppress a smile.

Chapter Three

By day's end, Hattie's bodice was damp with perspiration, front and back, and her auburn curls were tight as corkscrews from the humidity.

"Remind me again why we put ourselves through this," Hattie grumbled as she and Anne followed the other women out of the mailroom and into the relative coolness of the high-ceilinged War Room.

"Because it got us out of Ladygrace," Anne said. "Because we're doing something for the cause."

Ladygrace had been only a slight improvement from living with a father who'd long ago lost any inclination toward kindness and a mother whose standards were impossible to meet. When Anne had mentioned offhandedly last April that her father, a friend of Mr. Pinkerton's, could secure positions for them in one of the Pinkerton Agency's spy operations, aiding the Union cause, Hattie had jumped at the opportunity. Anne had been less certain, but by badgering her almost daily, Hattie had worn her down, and by May, they'd become mailroom girls.

Each day, Hattie thanked her stars that Mr. Pinkerton had trusted Anne's father, asking nothing about her past, and that Anne's father had in turn trusted his daughter, whose vague explanations about Hattie's background were all she knew. But on days like this when the mailroom was stifling and Lucy grated on her nerves, she wondered if she couldn't have found some other means of escape.

"We should have given more thought to nursing," she said. "At least we wouldn't be stuck in a closet all day with a fire blazing in the stove."

"I thought you couldn't stand the sight of blood."

"I could acclimate myself," Hattie said as she pushed an oaken door to the outside. At five o'clock, the sun had relented some of its hold on the sky, angling low over the horizon. She breathed deep, taking in air that was, if not entirely wholesome, at least somewhat cool. The scaffolds were empty, the hammers silent, the workers having gone home for the day, and the sidewalks were half as crowded as they'd been in the morning.

Anne lifted an eyebrow. "You'd truly rather be changing bandages than intercepting coded messages?"

"One coded message out of how many? I had no idea folks could write such mundane letters in the midst of a war, for heaven's sake."

"That one coded message might be reason enough for Miss Warne to send you to Baltimore."

At the prospect, Hattie's heart quickened. They started down the steps. "I don't know about that," she said. "Mr. Pinkerton seemed more annoyed than anything, and if he doesn't want me, Miss Warne won't either."

"On some matters, perhaps. But she's got a mind of her own. And Mr. Welton seemed duly impressed."

"He's a master of disguises. It's what he's paid for"

"But you want it, don't you? The Baltimore assignment?"

"Who wouldn't? A chance to do actual spy work. And to breathe actual air."

"I don't know that I'd accept if Miss Warne chose me."

"Whyever not?"

Anne shrugged. "It seems a lot of work, pretending to be someone else."

"Not really. All anyone knows about you is what you tell them, and you only tell them what suits you."

"But you might have to cut off contact with everyone, even me. Wouldn't that give you pause?"

"I'd teach you to use the Vigenère's square, and we could send coded messages. I'm sure Mr. Welton would be happy to deliver them. And Lucy would be happy to open them."

"If it's what you want, I hope you get the Baltimore assignment," Anne said. "But I'd miss you horribly."

"You'd have Julia, inviting you to tea every day." Julia Taft was Anne's cousin. Her father ran in Washington's highest circles. For her, meeting Mr. Lincoln was an ordinary occurrence. "You'd have a suitor in no time," Hattie continued. "Before you know it, you'd be married."

Anne stopped short, and her hand flew to her mouth. "Oh no. I quite forgot—I promised Julia I'd join her at supper today. Something about Aunt Patty's friend on the Sanitary Commission coming to supper and trying to enlist Julia." She clasped Hattie's arm. "Come with me?"

Hattie shook her head. "Your Aunt Patty has done enough for me already."

"It's no trouble to set an extra place. Aunt Patty likes you quite a lot, you know."

"She tolerates me because she adores you. Truly, Anne, I'm simply exhausted. I want to strip down to my chemise and fall asleep before the artillery starts up again."

"And dream of Baltimore?" Anne teased.

Hattie punched her lightly in the arm. "Get going. Your Aunt Patty's turtle soup must be getting cold."

"You don't mind walking home alone?" Home was only a room they shared in Mrs. Sullivan's boarding house, but it felt more like home to Hattie than her parents' big house.

"I'll be fine." Hattie waved her in the direction of her aunt and uncle's stately home. "Just don't wake me when you come in."

Anne peeled off toward the north, following 18th Street. Hattie continued west toward the boarding house, but her thoughts were in Baltimore. She'd never been there, but from what she'd gleaned from reading thousands of letters, it was a place big enough to get lost in. And while she didn't care about servants or fancy lodgings, she suspected Mr. Welton would be tolerable company as long as he refrained from asking too many questions. In fact, the more she thought about the position, the more she wanted it. She hoped Anne was right, that finding the coded letter would tip the scales in her favor. But she was wary of getting her hopes up. There were Miss Warne's inquiries to contend with, inquiries that were sure to include questions about Hattie's family and background which, if answered truthfully, would disqualify her immediately.

She was about to cross the street when a wagonload of wounded soldiers rumbled toward her. At the sight of their torn uniforms and bloodied bandages, she wanted to turn away, but she forced herself to examine each smudged face for George. The men stared back at her. Some looked utterly despondent. Other faces looked vacant, as if in their minds they'd gone off to some better place where their bodies were whole and their skin intact.

A worse fate awaited them at the hospital, she suspected. Lucy talked of stacks of limbs behind the hospital at Armory Square, cut off by saw-wielding surgeons. Hattie wasn't convinced Lucy had personally witnessed this carnage, but she feared the gist of the rumor was true. Passing by the hospital one day, she'd heard a man's screams, and she'd known an amputation must be underway. She hated to think how many soldiers left the hospital limbless or, worse, in a pine box.

One man on the wagon—a boy, really, from the looks of him—locked eyes with her. It was the same look she'd seen in the eyes of a fallen horse on her grandfather's Louisiana plantation, right before her grandfather pulled the trigger, pronouncing it worthless. She'd seen that look, too, on an enslaved man her grandfather's overseer was lashing because he'd begged not to be taken from his wife and baby. Anne wondered why Hattie refused to say much about her family, why the prospect of reinventing herself in Baltimore was so appealing. The answers were many, and some too horrific to speak aloud.

Now, Hattie held the gaze of the boy until the wagon passed, hoping it meant something to him to be noticed in his suffering, if only by a stranger on a street corner. So many dead and wounded. So much sorrow. It seemed impossible that she got up every morning and carried on as if life was unchanged by war. But what else could she do?

"Miss Logan?"

She turned, and to her surprise, she saw Thomas Welton. At his side was Lucy, her arm crooked around his. She nodded curtly, acknowledging them. "Mr. Welton. Lucy."

Lucy smiled sweetly. "My father was detained. Mr. Welton kindly offered to escort me home."

Mr. Welton held out his arm, an invitation. "Thankfully, I'm well equipped to escort two ladies, if you'd be so kind as to join us, Miss Logan."

Hattie straightened, meeting his gaze. He stood a head taller than she, and he smelled faintly of tobacco. If his opinion factored at all into Miss Warne's decision, she could not afford to be rude. But the last thing she wanted was to be subjected to more of Lucy's blathering, and at any rate, they weren't going her direction.

"I appreciate the offer," she said, hoping the flush she felt rising in her cheeks would be perceived as the effects of heat, not embarrassment. "But I haven't far to go."

"All the more reason I should see you home." He crooked his arm, leaving ample room for her to take it. "Truly, you'd be doing me a favor, Miss Logan. My reputation improves when I'm seen in the company of one pretty woman, let alone two. And Lord knows, it can use some improving."

Hattie shifted foot to foot, uncertain how or why he even knew her name. It reminded her of what he'd said earlier, upon learning she'd been the one to discover the pinpricks. *I should have known.*

It's his business to know things, she reminded herself. Still, it made her uneasy. What else did he know about her?

If she'd learned nothing else at the Ladygrace School for Girls, it was that getting the upper hand sometimes required rubbing shoulders when you weren't otherwise inclined to. "Very well," she said, slipping her arm through his. "If it helps the cause."

"I do so hope the tide is turning," Lucy said as they started down the sidewalk, Mr. Welton setting an easy pace. "Papa fears Mr. Lincoln has made some poor decisions."

"Haven't we all," Mr. Welton said.

"It must be so much more comfortable in Baltimore," Lucy said. "Without the continual press of troops upon the city."

"Baltimore has its share of troubles," Mr. Welton said.

"I should like to see for myself," Lucy said.

"And what about you, Miss Logan? Intrigued by the Monumental City?"

There was something in his broad face that made her want to be fully honest. *It's his job,* she reminded herself. *Show him you can play it as well as he does, inspiring trust while deflecting questions you'd rather not answer.*

"There's a great deal of the world to be seen," she said, evading a direct answer. "I suppose that's what brought you here from England, Mr. Welton?"

If he noticed her dodging his question, his face didn't show it. "In a roundabout way. Fresh start and all that."

She wondered if he meant to draw out her thoughts on fresh starts. If so, she wasn't going to take the bait.

"You must have had so many adventures since coming here," Lucy said, and her grip on Mr. Welton's arm seemed to tighten. "Thank goodness you're so good at what you do. Papa says we need more men like you."

Mr. Welton's gaze shifted, and for a moment Hattie thought his expression that of a loyal hound sniffing trouble. Then his face relaxed, and he said, "Mr. Pinkerton speaks highly of your father."

"They are likeminded in their devotion to the cause. As are you, Mr. Welton. Oh, but here's my turn." Lucy stopped at the corner, stately homes lining the street to the west.

Hattie let go of Mr. Welton's arm. "I'll take my leave here, and you can see Lucy to the door. I've only a short walk from here," she said, though in truth it was several blocks. "Goodnight, Lucy. Goodnight, Mr. Welton."

Before he could object, she strode purposefully away from them, relieved to get some distance from Lucy and feeling more tired than ever. Anne might have a point. It took some effort to carefully consider one's words while trying to appear casual in their delivery.

She'd not gone half a block when she heard footsteps behind her. She quickened her pace. The evening was young, and there was plenty of light, but caution was in order once you left the finer parts of the city for Mrs. Sullivan's neighborhood, which was why Anne's uncle would insist on taking her home in his carriage after dark. If not for Hattie, Julia's parents would surely have invited Anne to live with them, a far more gracious living arrangement than what she had. But Anne insisted that she liked their little attic room. And she was quick to say she wouldn't have had the courage to come East without Hattie, so it only made sense for them to stick together.

The footsteps behind her quickened. A man's footsteps. From the stride, Hattie could tell he'd soon overtake her.

"Miss Logan!"

To her relief, it was Mr. Welton's voice, deep and soothing. "You might have made yourself known," she scolded as he fell in step beside her. He did not, she noticed, offer his arm.

"I didn't mean to alarm you."

"I didn't say I was alarmed," she said coolly. "I was referencing manners."

"Of which I admit to fewer than my dear mother would have liked. I pray you'll forgive me."

"There's nothing to forgive, Mr. Welton. But Lucy may feel otherwise if you've abandoned her to chase after me."

"I don't expect Miss Hamilton would stand for being abandoned. We happened across her father. His affairs had concluded early, so I entrusted her to his care. But I didn't suppose your father would be coming after you, so I thought I'd best see you home safely."

There he was again, probing ever so gently at circumstances she was not inclined to reveal. "As I said earlier, I appreciate the offer, but I'm quite capable of getting myself home."

"You seem quite capable in a number of ways, Miss Logan. Or may I presume to call you by your given name—provided, of course, you call me by mine?"

She was not entirely sure she should welcome this familiarity. But if she was chosen to pose as his sister in Baltimore, she certainly couldn't be calling him Mr. Welton. "You may, Thomas," she said.

"Thom," he said. "No one calls me Thomas unless they're angry or hauling me before a magistrate."

She recognized this for what it was, dangling a bit of tantalizing information about his past so he could go tit for tat about hers, a tactic he likely used with much success in his spy work. Ignoring the bit about the magistrate, she said, "I've no cause to be angry. I scarcely know you."

"Ah, but you know of my work, and I of yours. I was sincere in my praise of what you noticed in that letter." He tapped the breast pocket of his shirt, where he'd stashed the envelope. "With the efforts you ladies go through—and the conditions you endure—I suspect it's hard to spot anything out of the ordinary, especially something as subtle as a series of pinpricks, visible only when held to the light. It's almost as if you've had training in subterfuge."

"I assure you, Mr. Welton—"

"Thom," he said, interrupting.

"Thom," she repeated. "You may rest assured that subterfuge was not part of the coursework at the Ladygrace School for Girls. Unless of course you count lessons in the comportment of an unattached female, which I must confess involves a good deal of masquerading of one's intentions."

"Ah," he said, as if she'd revealed a great mystery. "So that's what makes a woman good at this game."

"You sound quite confident on that point. But there can't be many women doing what you do, at least not on our side. I know only of Miss Warne. And of course the one she'll be choosing to go with you to Baltimore." It can't hurt, she thought, to let him know she'd taken note of the possibility.

"There are more women than you think doing secret work in this war. On both sides, though I admit Rebel women have a special knack for charming their way into places and information a man can't get at. And those skirts! It's amazing, truly, what one can conceal beneath hoops and petticoats. Letters, quinine, even ammunition. Almost makes me wish I were of the gentler sex."

"Spoken like a person who has never had to endure a hooped skirt."

He laughed heartily. "Point taken."

They arrived at her corner. The neighborhood was bad enough compared to where he'd left Lucy. She didn't want him to see the ramshackle Sullivan house, with its weedy yard and peeling paint. Only so much a widow can do to keep up, Mrs. Sullivan always said.

"You've come far enough out of your way, Mr....Thom." It felt odd, addressing him like a friend. "I'll be quite fine from here."

He rested a hand on her elbow, steering in the direction she'd inadvertently gazed, toward the Sullivan house. "You'll find I'm not one to give up on a project before I've finished, Hattie." He spoke her given name with the familiarity of someone who'd known her from childhood. "And neither do you, I'll wager. I understand you've mastered the Vigenère's square."

She turned to him sharply. "Who told you that?"

He shook his head. "Can't reveal my sources. But I am a detective, after all."

She'd throttle Carl Cunningham, the spectacled Pinkerton operative who'd shown her how to work the Vigenère's, the next time she saw him. He'd sworn her to secrecy, and she'd assumed the same from him.

"The decoders are overworked," she said. "And as you've indicated, the work of unsealing and resealing envelopes gets tedious."

"You prefer a challenge," he said.

"I suppose I do. I never hold a letter for long," she added quickly. "I take it home overnight, and unless I can cipher it out, I put it back in the stack that goes to the decoders."

His expression shifted. Alarm, concern—she couldn't tell which. "You take the letters home? The coded ones?"

She felt the shame of having been caught at a prank, which wasn't at all the situation. "Only two of them. I tried staying late in the mailroom to work the code, but the watchman insisted I leave. I felt I was on the verge of breaking through, and I didn't see the harm in carrying them home with me and returning them the next morning. They never left my person," she said, and then blushed, realizing she'd directed his thoughts toward her undergarments.

"Did you succeed? Work the code?"

She shook her head. "I got close, I think. But as I said, I didn't think I should try for longer than overnight. And a person has to sleep, best as she can amid the artillery fire."

He smiled, and she relaxed a bit. "The Vigenère's is tough. I've seen men wrestle for days with a single letter. I'd be no good at it, that's for certain. Lack of patience. But don't take any more letters home, no matter how close you keep them. There's always a chance some harm would come to you."

"I don't fear for myself," she said, straightening.

He tipped his head, gazing at her, and she resisted the urge to look away. "Fear can be a healthy thing."

"It can also be crippling," she shot back.

"True enough. At any rate, keep at your work if you can do it in the mailroom. The Rebs only use the Vigenère's with the most secret information. The more people who can crack their code, the better positioned we'll be to bring this war to a quick end. I wish we had a whole team of women with your intelligence and persistence."

She could have hugged him. Other than George, few people had ever praised her persistence or her intelligence. Her mother, in particular, called her stubborn and too smart for her own good.

"Thank you," she said. "That means a good deal to me."

And it would mean a good deal to Miss Warne, she thought, if Thom Welton put in a good word for her.

Chapter Four

SEPTEMBER 3, 1862

At the boardinghouse, Hattie went straight to her room. She stripped to her chemise and crawled into bed, pulling back the coverlet so that only a sheet lay over her. As she was thinking of various ways she might respond to Miss Warne's inquiries without saying too much about her past, she fell soundly asleep.

She woke to the creak of the door's hinges. Beyond the window, the sky had turned a dusky shade of blue that seemed to darken by the second. To Hattie's delight, a cool breeze came through the opening, prickling her skin with goosebumps.

Silhouetted in the faint light, Anne slipped through the doorway. "Sorry," she said, bending to undo her boots. "Aunt Patty's friend is quite a talker. I was about to enlist with the Sanitary Commission myself just so she'd quit jabbering and Uncle Joe could take me home."

Hattie folded over her pillow, lying on her side so she could talk with Anne without having to get up. "I must've slept through dinner."

"You did," Anne said. "Mrs. Sullivan said she didn't want to wake you. Now she's worried you've come down with the break-bone fever, and if you don't get some nourishment, you'll die before morning. She insisted I bring these up." Anne unfolded a napkin she'd set on the dresser, revealing two of Mrs. Sullivan's fresh-baked dinner rolls.

That was worth sitting up for. Hattie reached for the rolls, ravenous. The rolls were still warm. Slathered in butter, they almost melted in her mouth. She gobbled them down as Anne shut the curtains and undressed.

"So are you ready to give up Pinkerton's for the Sanitary Commission?" Hattie asked, licking a drip of butter from her fingers.

Anne laughed. "Not a chance. But Julia seems interested. It would do her good to get out instead of tending her brothers all day. And of course Aunt Patty would approve, being as it's for the cause." Anne's aunt was protective of Julia, her only daughter, who had suffered a series of illnesses as a child.

"Does your aunt realize what it's like, volunteering in the hospitals?" Hattie asked.

"I doubt Julia would do any actual nursing. More like rolling bandages or helping raise funds for supplies."

Through a gap in the curtains, a half-moon was rising, casting a pool of light that silhouetted Anne's slim figure. For the first time in days, the artillery was silent. Hattie lay back, her stomach happily filled with Mrs. Sullivan's rolls.

"Open those curtains a bit, please," Hattie said. "That breeze feels so refreshing."

At the window, Anne drew an audible breath. "It doesn't even smell of the swamp. Perhaps the season's turning."

"We can only hope." Hattie had begun yearning for autumn almost as soon as they'd arrived in Washington City. Indiana summers were hot, but not with the heavy, stinking pall that hung over Washington.

Anne lifted the sheet and slid into bed. It had taken Hattie some time to get used to sleeping in the same bed as her friend, but now she craved the comfort of it. Growing up without a sister, she'd felt her loneliness most acutely at night. Alone in bed, listening to the creaks and moans of the cavernous house, she'd imagined cozy homes filled with mirth and love.

On good nights, these were the images that filled her dreams. On bad ones, her dreams filled with her mother's bickering, her father's stony silence, and classmates taunting her for her family's wealth. Even worse had been trying to sleep in Louisiana, during the summers her mother insisted on spending at the plantation where she'd grown up. There, Hattie's dreams were haunted with the sharp sound of lashing and the anguished cries of women begging not to be carted off to the slave market, where they'd be separated from their children. The proper order of things, Hattie's mother said. An abomination, Hattie thought.

Beside her in bed, Anne lay staring up at the ceiling. "I'll miss you, you know. When Miss Warne sends you to Baltimore."

"She won't choose me. Not when Lucy wants it so badly."

"You think Lucy's father would let her go?"

"Of course. It's not as if she'd be in enemy territory. She'd just be a prop, seeing guests in the parlor."

"And that's enough excitement for you?"

"I'd make more of it."

"Doing what?"

Even to her best friend, Hattie wasn't ready to share the scenes that had played through her mind after bidding Thom Welton goodnight. Stealing secrets, poring over coded messages, sneaking off trains. Instead, she said vaguely, "Thom would assign me tasks as I proved myself capable."

Anne rolled to her side, smiling. "Thom now, is it? When did you come onto such familiar terms with him?"

Hattie trusted the darkness to hide the color that rose in her cheeks. "After you left for Julia's, I came upon him and Lucy, arm in arm."

"Don't tell me he's sweet on her."

"I don't think so. He was just walking her home because her father was detained. But you can be sure she was making the most of it. After leaving her off, he walked me here. Well, almost here."

"So he's sweet on you."

She punched Anne's arm playfully. "He's considerate, that's all. And maybe a little curious."

"What did he ask?"

"Not so much, really. We chatted, that's all."

"Do you think he's helping Miss Warne? With the Baltimore decision?"

"I'd think so. He'll have to live with whomever she chooses."

"I hope he sees Lucy for what she is, all fluff and hot air."

"Maybe that's what they're after," Hattie said. "Fluff and hot air don't draw much attention."

Anne rolled to her back. "If they're smart, they'll choose you. Now get some sleep, or you'll end up saying something outrageous when Miss Warne makes her inquiries."

During her months at Ladygrace, Hattie had made a reputation for herself with her outrageous statements. There had been the time in etiquette class when she'd point out that Miss Whitcomb's hoop was askew. Another time, during a supper of roast squab, she'd mused aloud about what had become of the chicks of the hens they were eating.

There was also the time when Miss Whitcomb had noted rather pointedly that even in a town as small as La Conner, a lady must be expected to comport herself with a modicum of grace. Hattie had retorted that she didn't give a rat's arse how anyone in La Conner judged her comportment. As punishment for this inappropriate language, the headmistress had made her polish every piece of Ladygrace's silver. Still, the look on Miss Whitcomb's face, hearing one of her ladies-in-the-making utter the word *arse*, had been worth every bit of the toil.

It wasn't as if she had no control of her mouth, Hattie mused as Anne's breathing slowed into sleep. After leaving La Conner, she'd managed to avert nearly every inquiry that would have revealed her connection with the town's wealthiest and most reviled family. But now, as the blessedly cool air prickled her skin and moonlight beamed through the window, she considered that deflections about her past would not sit well with Miss Warne, whose manner was cordial but direct. Widowed at age twenty-three, it was said that Miss Warne had barged into Mr. Pinkerton's Chicago office one day and declared her intent to become a detective.

A cooper by trade, Mr. Pinkerton had built his detective business by ferreting out criminal activity that the local police ignored—or worse, assisted. He ran an agency as tight as the barrels he'd made in his former trade, forbidding his employees from drinking, smoking, playing cards, or frequenting establishments of the lower sort—unless, of course, an assignment required such activities, as Thom's did.

A woman had other ways of gaining the trust of those she spied on, as Miss Warne had demonstrated more than once during her time at Pinkerton's. Once, she'd posed as a fortuneteller, convincing a suspect to admit to murdering her brother. In another case, she posed as a businessman's wife and helped catch a man who'd embezzled funds from a shipping company. Her best-known escapade had been last year, when Mr. Pinkerton caught wind of a plot to assassinate the president-elect in Baltimore, on his way to his inauguration. Disguising Mr. Lincoln with a shawl and cane, Miss Warne had posed as his sister, shuttling him to a train that whisked him from the would-be assassins in the middle of the night.

All told, Hattie expected Miss Warne was too astute to cotton with Hattie's evading questions about her past. What she needed, she realized, was a different background than her own, a story solid enough to convince her employer of its veracity. A father who traded with the enemy and a mother whose roots and sympathies lay entirely with the Rebels—any whiff of that truth would surely disqualify Hattie from becoming a real spy.

Whatever story Hattie devised would have to be foolproof. In the moonlight, pieces began to come together in her mind, an imagined upbringing that would prove her a loyal devotee of the Union cause. But the devil was in the details, as the saying went. These began to come to her, bit by bit, as she drifted into sleep.

~~~

"You're walking stiff as a board," Anne said as they walked to the mailroom the next morning. "Relax. You don't want Miss Warne thinking you're prone to nerves."

Hattie let go of the tension in her shoulders and softened her stride. "Anne, what will you say if she asks about me? She knows we're close—your father was the one who recommended us to Mr. Pinkerton, after all."

"I'll say you're a complete ninny who can't get by without your fainting salts."

Hattie jabbed her with her elbow. "Some friend you are."

"I'll tell her the truth. That I'd trust you with my life."

"And if she asks about my past? My family and such?"

Anne shrugged. "I'll say you're intensely private, and I respect that."

"Fair enough," Hattie said.

Anne lifted an eyebrow. "But I don't see why you won't tell even me about your family. It's like they're monsters or something."

"In a way, they are." Hattie swung open the mailroom door.

The other women had also arrived early, likely for the same reason Hattie had insisted on it. Only Lucy was absent. Every day, her father escorted her to the War Building on his way to his congressional office, arriving at precisely five minutes of nine. Leaving Lucy at the door, he sometimes positioned himself for Mr. Stanton's arrival, lingering about the War Department so he could learn the latest battlefront news.

The welcome drop in overnight temperatures had yet to fully reach the mailroom, but at least it was no longer sweltering. Constance had taken up her turn at the stove. "Beautiful morning," she said, more cheery than usual. Practicing for Miss Warne, Hattie thought.

"Indeed," Anne said, slipping into the seat Constance had occupied yesterday. "Not one inch of clothing has stuck to my skin."

"Oh, but it will," Hattie said. "Winter can't come too soon." She seated herself at the head of the table. It was Lucy's turn at the iron, and she wasn't about to allow for any wavering on that.

"Careful what you wish for." Constance added another unsealed letter to the stack. "Washington City suffers some bad storms in winter. Snow, ice, wind. But maybe by then you'll be in Baltimore."

"Or maybe you'll be." Hattie worked the opener gently beneath a steamed flap.

"I have the qualifications," Constance said, ever bent on impressing. "I've shown myself to be discreet, and I'm attentive to details. I'm confident I'd be an asset to Mr. Welton."

She'd been practicing for her interview, too, Hattie thought. "Any one of us would be."

Constance stared at her, looking surprised. "Even Lucy?" she asked. All the girls knew there was no love lost between Hattie and Lucy.

Hattie swallowed back a retort. "I suppose," she said. At her side, Anne smirked.

Direct and polite. That was how Miss Warne presented herself, and Hattie had vowed to emulate her, at least until she'd made her selection for Baltimore. The directness came more readily than politeness, but she could manage both if she put her mind to it.

She eased the letter from the envelope. *Dearest Brother,* it began. She thought longingly of George. She wondered if, from his many contacts, Mr. Welton might have some inkling of where George's battalion was headed next. But if she were chosen to go to Baltimore, she supposed she would not be allowed to write to him, even if she knew where he was.

If she were chosen. As Hattie started on the letter, some mundane gibberish about the sister preparing for her coming-out in Baltimore, Lucy entered the room. She always dressed more elegantly than Hattie, and today was no exception. The frock, mint-green and adorned with darker green ribbons, was not one Hattie had seen before. It was the sort of dress a young woman of a certain class, visiting from England, might pack in her trunk. Hattie had owned such dresses, but she'd left all but one behind at Ladygrace. Now she wondered if that had been a mistake.

"Good morning, ladies." Lucy's British accent had shifted a bit to match Thom Welton's, who'd come from Yorkshire. She, too, had spent the night practicing, Hattie thought.

"Good morning," Hattie said. A woman of her upbringing—that is, the upbringing she'd chosen for herself—would greet everyone, regardless of how distasteful they might be.

Lucy looked mildly surprised, but she gave Hattie only a moment's glance as she glided gracefully to take her place at the iron.

Hattie returned her attention to the letter, addressed to a lieutenant serving with Virginia's 18th Infantry. Having dispensed with the details of the dress she'd be wearing at the Coming Out, the sister wrote of the Federal Navy's ships now crowding Chesapeake Bay and the city's mills that produced steam engines and armored plating. Nothing suspect there—ever since last year's riots, the Federals had made Baltimore a staging area for their naval activities, all the better to keep an eye on the subversives. The sister also mentioned a neighbor who'd been apprehended and imprisoned at Fort McHenry on what she said were the flimsiest of charges. But that, too, was not so unusual.

Thank heavens for the trusted couriers who deliver our letters, the sister wrote in closing. *I pray daily for your safety, and I trust that God will see fit to reunite us soon.*

So many families divided, with state lines now drawn as national borders. Not Hattie's, though. Not the family she'd invented.

Within minutes, Miss Warne came in. Gracious as ever, she walked around the table, addressing each of the women individually and commenting on her work. She was a master at conversing while revealing little, Hattie realized. So much had to do with paying close attention to the people around you while drawing as little attention as possible to yourself.

Completing her circuit, Miss Warne asked Constance if she might have a word. No mention was made of Baltimore or a new assignment. The room tensed with their leaving. At the iron, Lucy hummed "The First Gun is Fired" and "Battle Cry of Freedom," as if to remind everyone, including Miss Warne, when she returned with Constance, of her devotion to the cause.

Hattie had read through five more letters, none of them noteworthy, by the time Constance returned, resuming her work at the stove. Her fingers trembled as she picked up an envelope, and she kept her eyes low. Perhaps the interview had not gone as well as she'd wished.

Confident. Intelligent. Firm but gracious. Those were the traits Hattie had determined Miss Warne would be seeking, and she intended to prove she was right for the part. She even had the background, invented last night as she lay awake in bed, to prove it.

Miss Warne summoned Charlotte next, and then Agatha. Each returned looking less rattled than Constance, but not by much. Miss Warne was a professional, Hattie reminded herself. Someone to be respected, not feared. Still, she felt a surge of anxiety each time the door opened.

When Miss Warne entered next, it was Anne she summoned.

"I appreciate your willingness to consider me," Anne said. "But I'm not interested in going to Baltimore."

Only Miss Warne's eyebrows, lifted slightly, registered her surprise. "Very well, Anne. Miss Hamilton, I trust you have an interest?"

Lucy set down her iron and made a little curtsy. "Indeed I do, Miss Warne," she said, prim as a schoolgirl.

Hattie wanted to think Miss Warne disliked such kowtowing. But in truth, she had no idea.

A near-perfect distraction showed itself after Lucy left with Miss Warne. The next letter Hattie read was entirely in code. Not a simple word substitution code like the one Mr. Pinkerton reportedly used, where "whale oil" meant "Federals," "barley" meant "Washington," and "rooster" meant "Tuesday." This had been coded with the Vigenère's, jumbled letters arranged in five-letter blocks. *GYAAC MCQBL*, it began.

Heart quickening, she nudged Anne beneath the table. Anne looked up and saw the message. Her eyes widened. She shook her head, a warning. "Hand it over to Miss Warne," she whispered.

But for a sender to use the Vigenère's Square, the message had to be important. If Hattie handed it over to Miss Warne, she would be showing herself no different from the other girls.

She looked down the table. Charlotte and Agatha were each bent over a letter, reading. Constance was at the kettle, her back to Hattie. Satisfied that none were paying her any mind, she slipped the Vigenère's square, penned on a single sheet of paper, from her cinched purse and unfolded it on her lap.

At first glance, the square was dizzying. The alphabet ran along the table's top row and left column. Letters repeated along diagonals. A row of Zs divided the table from the top left corner to the bottom right. Above the Zs, the diagonals ascended to A. Below, the diagonals started with As and descended to Zs.

The success of a Vigenère's message lay in its receiver knowing the keyword, which was conveyed separate and apart from the message itself. To encode the message, the sender ran a finger along the row corresponding to each letter of the key to arrive at the column headed by the letter being encoded. The key was repeated until it reached the length of the message the sender wanted to convey, and then each letter was changed using the square. Then the entire message was broken into five-letter blocks.

Receivers could decode the message by using the same method, but working in reverse. They wrote the keyword—if they were lucky enough to have intercepted it—above the ciphered letters. Then they located each ciphered letter in the row matching the keyword's letters. Easy enough, provided you knew the keyword.

Carl Cunningham, who'd taught Hattie to use the Vigenère's square, assured her the Rebels were unimaginative—or perhaps arrogant—about their keywords. Many Pinkerton men working many hours had used a factoring method to discover that "Manchester Bluff" was among the Rebels' favorite keywords. So was "Complete Victory."

Bent over the letter, Hattie started with Manchester, glancing back and forth between the coded message and the Vigenère's square. Quickly, she saw that the decoded letters formed no words, so she tried Complete Victory. G standing for C led to I. Y standing for O led to M. A standing for M led to M. I-M-M.

She was tracing backward from the next ciphered letter, another A, when the door opened. Sitting up straight, she saw that Miss Warne was looking directly at her. Hattie waited for her to ask what she'd found so fascinating in her lap, but her lips were pressed in her usual enigmatic smile. Lucy came up behind her, skirt swishing as she returned to the iron. Judging from her smile, Miss Warne's inquiry had apparently gone well.

With her supervisor staring right at her, Hattie couldn't hide the coded message. She held it out to Miss Warne. "This one needs to go to the decoders."

Miss Warne took the letter, holding it by its edge. "Thank you, Miss Logan. And now, I'd like a word with you, if you're interested in the Baltimore assignment."

"Yes, Miss Warne." Hattie started to rise from her chair, then remembered the Vigenère's square in her lap. *Don't look down*, she told herself. *Let it slide to the floor, and with any luck, it will be there when you return.*

She stood abruptly and followed Miss Warne out the door. As she closed it, she glanced beneath the table. The floor where she'd sat was empty. Anne caught her eye. She winked, and Hattie relaxed, knowing she must have picked up the paper.

Miss Warne led her to Mr. Pinkerton's office, tucked at the end of a long hallway. Hattie had not been inside the office since her first day at the War Building, at the end of May, when she and Anne had been shown to the office for introductions. It smelled as it had then, of old leather and lemon polish. Hattie had been nervous that day, hearing only half of what Mr. Pinkerton and Miss Warne told her about the mailroom, but at least Anne had been with her. Today she was alone, and she stood before Miss Warne without a glowing note from Anne's father to recommend her as it had then.

Today, the desk was entirely clear of papers except for the ciphered letter that Miss Warne deposited there. She settled into the big leather chair where Mr. Pinkerton had sat the first time Hattie met him. She looked more at ease there than her employer had, or perhaps it only seemed that way because of her demure smile. But there was a weariness in her eyes, Hattie observed. It must be true, what Lucy said about Miss Warne working late into the night, playing the part of a Secesh-sympathizing socialite at Washington gatherings. No wonder she came and went through a back door at the War Department.

"Please, Miss Logan. Have a seat." Miss Warne indicated the straight-backed chair beside the desk.

Hattie sat, then smoothed her skirt. "I appreciate you considering me for the assignment in Baltimore. I believe you'll find me a quick study."

Miss Warne put a finger to her cheek but said nothing. Hattie considered reminding her of the pinprick letter. But that had only been yesterday. A reminder would insult Miss Warne's intelligence.

"I've done some acting as well. I can speak the part of an English woman," Hattie said, demonstrating with an accent every bit as convincing as Lucy's. "Or a southerner," she said, switching to a voice that sounded disconcertingly like her mother's.

Miss Warne moved her finger from her cheek to the arm of the chair. She drummed it lightly, not with impatience but more like the slow, steady rhythm of a metronome. "Impressive," she said, but her expression remained unchanged. "These acting opportunities—they came at school?"

"Yes. I've always loved the stage. When I was younger, I read every one of Shakespeare's plays."

"Is that so? You must have had quite a library at home."

"We did." This felt like safe territory. There was no reason why Hattie's made-up parents couldn't have had a love of literature. It seemed more believable, actually, than the truth of her real parents having an expansive collection of books in a private library that was only for show.

The narrowing in Miss Warne's eyes was barely perceptible. "You come from a small town in Indiana, as I recall. It's heartening to learn that even in such a burg, there are those who concern themselves with furthering their education."

"Like Mr. Lincoln," Hattie said, for the president had fared well enough from his isolated Indiana upbringing.

Miss Warne's expression warmed, her smile more genuine than before. "Yes, our Mr. Lincoln is quite the lover of books. Your family—do they go back far in the state?"

Hattie breathed deep. She prided herself on truth-telling. Even to her parents, she rarely lied. But this wasn't lying. This was playing a part to secure a desired outcome, no different from Miss Warne pretending that Mr. Lincoln was her ailing brother in order to keep him safe. "My parents are—were Quakers. They left North Carolina when I was young. Many Quakers did, abhorring slavery. Sadly, my parents lost their lives in a house fire while I was away at school."

Parents who led peaceful, unassuming lives that came to a sudden, tragic end—that was the background that best suited, she'd decided last night. People tended not to probe into the details of such tragedies, and Miss Warne proved no exception. "I'm sorry to hear that," she said. "That was in—what was the name of the town?"

"We lived in La Conner, but the fire was in Kansas, where my parents had gone to visit my mother's sister. She was ill and doing poorly. They used what little savings they had for the train fare." This had to be said, in case Miss Warne decided to check the veracity of her story by looking up probate records, a method Hattie thought detectives must use when circumstances required it.

"You'll be wondering how I could have afforded the tuition at Ladygrace," Hattie continued, wanting to lay the whole story on the table. "An older woman from the Society of Friends was generous enough to sponsor me. But then she passed on, not long after my parents died. It was fortunate that Miss Duncan's father was able to put in a good word for me with Mr. Pinkerton."

Miss Warne shifted in her chair. To Hattie's relief, nothing in her expression suggested she questioned any of this. "Mr. Welton tells me you've had some informal training in the Vigenère's square."

So he'd spoken to Miss Warne about her, as she'd suspected he would. What else had he told her? Miss Warne didn't necessarily look impressed about her ability with the Vigenère's, but neither did she seem to disapprove.

"I enjoy a challenge," Hattie said.

Miss Warne folded her hands on the desktop. "The Baltimore assignment will have its challenges," she said, launching into what Hattie assumed was the explanatory portion of the interview. "That is not to say it will be exciting. The number one priority for our women in the field is to inspire trust. We do that primarily by watching and listening. The less attention you draw, the better." She paused a moment. "Can you do that, Miss Logan?"

"If you've ever been to a Quaker meeting, you know that watching and listening and not drawing attention is the whole point," Hattie said, hoping she didn't sound too defensive. Thank heavens the Duncans were Quaker, so she knew something of their habits.

"Good." Abruptly, Miss Warne stood. "Thank you, Miss Logan. It has been a pleasure getting to know you a bit better."

"The pleasure is mine," Hattie said, invoking words that Miss Whitcomb had instilled in all her Ladygrace girls. "I hope you'll grant me the opportunity to aid my country. I want to see the Union restored. It would be a tribute to my dearly departed parents to assist in the cause of liberty and justice for all." The more she spoke of her imagined parents, the greater her affection for them grew.

"From what I've seen, they'd be proud," Miss Warne said.

This was the closest Miss Warne had ever come to praise. Hattie left the room glowing. Whether she had Mr. Welton to thank or her own ingenuity, she'd made a favorable impression. Life would bring Lucy Hamilton plenty of opportunities. Hattie had to take hers as they came, even if it required some invention.

Chapter Five

H attie said little about her interview when she returned to the mailroom. Discretion, after all, was what she'd need in the new assignment. She could read the curiosity in Anne's eyes, but she was reluctant to share anything with Lucy in the room.

When their work ended and they were leaving the building, Anne grabbed her arm. "Enough of your clamming up. Did you get the assignment?"

Hattie shrugged. "I have no idea. But she knew about me using the Vigenère's square, and she didn't seem to mind. Maybe it even impressed her."

"You told her?" Anne asked as they turned toward the Treasury building to check the casualty lists.

"No, I think Mr. Welton did."

"You mean Thom?" Anne teased, her gray eyes dancing.

Hattie willed herself not to blush. "I just wish I could've kept decoding that letter. The key was Complete Victory. I'm sure of it. *I-M-M* was the start of the message."

"Immediate," Anne said.

"Imminent," Hattie said.

"Immobilize."

"Immune."

"Immodest," Anne said.

Hattie laughed. "Immodest generals headed for Richmond? At any rate, I hope the message doesn't go to some lackey who labors over it for days on end."

The afternoon light was waning, and in contrast to yesterday, there was a chill in the air. Hattie almost wished she'd worn her cloak. Soon the leaves would turn, and winter would blanket the city. By then, she hoped to be in Baltimore. However cold the wind might blow there in winter, it couldn't possibly be worse than what she'd endured on the prairie.

As they'd hoped, the lists had been updated since yesterday, with two new columns added. Anne took the one on the right, Hattie the one on the left. *George, George.* She repeated his name to herself as she ran her finger down the list as if she might conjure him onto the page.

Anne clapped her hand to her mouth, then released it. "Henry! He's here!" She pointed to a spot midway down the column. Under *19^(th) Indiana,* there was the name of her older brother: *Henry Duncan, Wounded, transfer Ind. Hosp.*

Hattie hugged her. Pressed to her chest, she felt Anne's heart race. "Ind. Hosp," Hattie said, letting go. "Does that mean he's back in Indiana?"

"Not if he was fighting at Manassas," Anne said. "I'll bet he's here in the city, at Indiana Hospital."

"There's an Indiana Hospital here?"

Anne nodded. "The woman from the Sanitary Commission mentioned it yesterday when I told her I was from Indiana. Federal employees from Indiana set up a hospital to care for wounded soldiers from back home. It's in the Patent Office Building."

A hospital in an office building. It made sense, she supposed, with the number of wounded being brought to the city. She pointed east. "The Patent Office—it's over there, isn't it? Near the Castle?"

"I think so." Anne grabbed her hand. "Let's go."

Thoughts of Baltimore vanished as they hurried down the steps. Hattie's immediate concern was her friend. Henry was alive, or he had been at the time of the casualty posting. But what shape was he in? Generally, little ruffled Anne, but there was no telling what they'd find at the hospital.

They followed the street east, passing in front of the big Executive Mansion where the Lincolns lived, and headed toward the turrets of the building known as the Castle. A wealthy Englishman, James Smithson, had bequeathed his substantial fortune to the United States for the purpose of creating an institution of science and learning. Built with funds from his endowment, the Smithsonian Castle had opened only a few years ago. Hattie had heard that a corps of young men, many from the West, were at work within its walls, identifying new species and building the museum's collections.

As they turned south, Hattie grabbed Anne's arm and pointed toward 7th Street. "There it is," she said. "The Patent Office."

They veered toward the stone structure, more massive even than the Treasury building. Someone must have been anticipating a lot of inventions, designing such a large facility to accommodate the approval process. On either side of the portico were wings four stories high. Like many Federal buildings, it was still under construction. Hattie recalled Carl Cunningham saying it was one of the slowest building jobs he'd ever seen.

When they reached the building, they found three teams of horses and their empty wagons tied to hitching posts out front. A promising sign, Hattie thought. But the front doors were locked.

Anne's bright expression crumpled. "They've all gone home for the day."

"Hospitals never sleep. There has to be another entrance." Hattie started around the side of the building, Anne keeping pace with her. They tried door after door of the side wing, which with its own portico looked identical to the front. Finally, a door in the building's back corner yielded.

It closed behind them, echoing in the quiet. Ahead, a large interior space fanned into corridors lined with offices. To their right was a set of stairs.

"Nothing that looks like a hospital here," Anne said. "Let's check the second floor."

They climbed the stairs. The large apartment before them held dozens of tall glass cases. Inside were what looked like models of various inventions for which patents had been issued. Between these cases were rows of men, crowded close on narrow cots. An eerie quiet pervaded, broken only by a groan now and then as Anne and Hattie crept among the cots, searching for Henry.

Halfway down the first row, Anne stopped in front of a cot. She leaned close, studying the man, his eyes closed, his head wrapped in a bloody bandage. "Henry?"

The man's eyes fluttered open, and she shook her head. In the lamplight, Hattie saw the tears that welled in her gray eyes. "Sorry," Anne said. "I thought you were my brother."

As she turned to leave, the man lifted his arm, groaning with the effort, and reached for her. Where three of his fingers should have been, there were only bloody stumps. "Water," he said, his voice raspy. "Please."

Hattie looked about but saw only an empty pitcher. "We'll bring some," she said.

The man's face relaxed. He dropped his arm to the bed and closed his eyes.

As Hattie and Anne slipped away, Anne wiped her eyes with her sleeve. "We should bring the pitcher," she said. "You promised him water."

Hattie steered her by the elbow, moving her along the row of cots. "We'll come back for it once we find where there's water. Right now, we need to find Henry."

At the end of the row, they came upon a man so still and ashen, Hattie thought he'd passed on. Then he drew a shuddering breath. Not dead, but not long for this world. He had all his limbs, and there were no bandages indicating wounds, so he must have been suffering some illness. Chickahominy Fever, maybe. McClellan's troops had succumbed to the disease by the thousands in the swamps along the slow-moving Chickahominy River near

Richmond. Or maybe he had typhoid or another of the summer fevers that had stricken the troops.

They moved among three alcoves of makeshift beds, Anne's expression growing grimmer by the minute. Hattie suspected they were thinking the same thing— within a matter of hours, a wounded man could become a dying man and then a dead one, especially if gangrene set in. The smell rising from one poor soldier was so fetid that Hattie clapped her hand over her nose as they passed. He would not last the night, she thought.

It was hard to be among the wounded and dying, and yet it felt wrong to just pass them by, with all in need of comfort and not a single nurse or doctor to attend to them, at least that Hattie had seen.

Not finding Henry in any of the alcoves, they pressed on to the next apartment. There they again checked cots that were crowded in double rows between glass cases. Again, no Henry.

In the next alcove ahead, they finally came upon a woman and man that Hattie took for a nurse and a doctor, standing beside one of the cots. The nurse glanced up at the click of their boots on the marble flooring, then looked back at the patient. Neither she nor the doctor seemed to be rendering any sort of assistance to the poor fellow.

As she neared, Hattie saw why. Glassy-eyed and ashen, the man was on the verge of dying. This would be his only comfort—not his mother or wife, but two strangers pausing in their grueling work to bear witness to his passing. *Please, don't let this be Henry,* she thought.

Anne paused, looking at the dying man. Then she turned away, as did Hattie, thinking he would not want strangers gaping at him in his final moments.

They turned into the next alcove, Hattie more worried than ever that they would not find Anne's brother. Then, from the third cot in the row, a man turned at the sound of their footsteps, his arm wrapped in a bandage nearly soaked through with blood. His foot was bandaged too. His face was streaked with dirt, and a bruise covered most of one cheek.

He raised his good arm to scratch at a head of unkempt hair. "If I didn't know better, I'd swear one of you lovely ladies was my sister."

Anne threw open her arms. "Henry!" She knelt at his cot, hugging his neck and planting a kiss on his forehead, dirt and all. She crouched alongside the cot, stroking his hair. "It's you, really and truly."

"Really and truly," he said, "though I'm told I'm a bit worse for the wear." Hattie remembered him as a freckle-faced boy who didn't look old enough to fight, much less be felled in battle. Here he was, grown into a war-weary man. His half-smile, much like Anne's, was nearly all Hattie recognized from when she'd met him at the Duncans' house in Indianapolis, right before he went off to fight.

"I'm so glad they brought you here where I could find you," Anne said. "Manassas—is that where you were wounded?"

Henry nodded, but only a little, as if moving his head pained him. "Wily old Stonewall Jackson was waiting for us, up on a ridge. He came charging as we crossed over a farm field, then took up position along a railroad grade. We came along his right flank, and the Johnny Rebs began lobbing artillery. I've seen a few battles, sis, but I never saw nothing like that. We fought back hard, but they got the best of us."

With his good arm, he reached for Anne's hand, blinking back tears. "I don't know what's happened to Richard. We were..." His voice trailed off. "We stuck together, best we could. But there was fire all around, and so much confusion. A blast went off behind us. He pushed me to the ground, and then I lost track of him. I stumbled around, looking for him, and then got caught in a round of muzzle fire, which is how this happened." He indicated his bandaged arm. "I got hit in the foot, too, but not so bad as the arm. I was calling and calling for Richard. No answer. I'm sorry, sis. I'm afraid he's—"

A quiet sob. Tears ran down Anne's face. "Richard wouldn't want you worrying about him," she murmured. "He's a fighter. He might have gotten away."

Hattie rested a hand on Anne's shoulder.

Henry's face contorted as he struggled with his sorrow. "I wish I'd talked him out of enlisting instead of tagging along."

"I'm sure you took care of each other as best you could." Anne wiped the tears from his cheeks with her thumb. "Wherever Richard is now, he'd want you to focus on getting well."

He gripped her hand, then let go. "I do feel encouraged, knowing you're here. And looks like you've brought an angel along with you." He nodded at Hattie.

Anne brushed a lock of hair from his forehead. "This is Hattie Logan. You met her once when she came to the house. She's a dear, but she's no angel, I assure you." Anne offered a weak smile. "We attended Ladygrace together. Father got us positions here in Washington City, so we could do some good for the cause."

"You're doing some good for this soldier, that's for certain," he said. "A sight for sore eyes don't begin to describe it."

Footsteps sounded from the main section of the apartment. Hattie turned and saw a woman approaching, or at least someone who appeared to be a woman, judging from the style of her hair, held back from her face with a slender black band and falling in ringlets to her shoulders. Her attire, however, was nothing Hattie had ever seen a woman wear. The white shirt was ordinary enough, in Jenny Lind style, named after the singer people called the Swedish Nightingale. The shirt was sewn into the waist of a gray skirt that fell not to the floor as a proper lady's skirt did, but to just below the woman's knees. Beneath the skirt, she wore trousers. A Bloomer costume, Hattie thought. She'd read of such outfits, mostly in accounts that derided the women who wore them, but she'd never seen one in person.

In her manly outfit, the woman approached Henry's bed. "You must be one of the new arrivals," she said.

"I was just talking of angels," Henry said. From where he lay, he could not see how odd she looked from the waist down. "Judging by that sweet face of yours, I'm guessing you're sent from heaven."

The woman's lips turned in a smile as she encircled her hand around the wrist of Henry's good arm, feeling his pulse. "Where I come from does seem like heaven, compared to what goes on in this city. I'm Dr. Greenfield."

Henry gave a low whistle. "You don't look nothing like the doctor that came by earlier."

She let go of his wrist. "I don't suppose I do. Did he have a look at that arm?"

"Glanced at it. Told me it would come off tomorrow."

Anne drew a sharp breath. "Come off? He can't mean—"

Dr. Greenfield glanced her direction. "To amputate. I'm afraid he does. There's a good deal of eagerness with the saw among army surgeons. May I have a look?" she asked Henry.

"Sure. But it's an awful sight, from what I'm told."

Gently, the doctor unwound the bandage. Henry winced each time she moved his arm.

"It must hurt something awful," Anne said.

He managed a weak grin. "Just reminding me it's there."

As the doctor reached the end of the bandage, Hattie forced herself to look. The wound was jagged and gaping, blood oozing at the edges of the torn skin, muscle showing beneath.

"Those Minié balls." Dr. Greenfield shook her head. "They do so much damage. Someone ought to hang Mr. Minié up by the thumbs for inventing such dreadful ammunition."

She bent close, examining the wound. She pressed a finger to its edge, and Henry stiffened. Then she took a fresh bandage from the table beside his bed and began wrapping his arm. "You say the other doctor glanced at it. Did he remove the bandage?"

Henry's shoulders relaxed now that the worst of the examination had ended. "No, ma'am."

"It looks to me like a flesh wound. A nasty one, to be sure, and I expect there's some injury to the tendons. You may never regain full use of your arm, but I don't see that it needs to come off.

"His arm can be saved?" Anne asked.

"I can't guarantee anything, but if it were me, I'd watch and wait. A few days should tell whether he truly needs an amputation. There are far too many done unnecessarily, in my opinion."

Henry's countenance relaxed. "I prefer your doctoring to the other one."

Dr. Greenfield patted his good shoulder. "You're allowed your preferences, of course. But I must ask you to promise to mention my advice to no one. When they come for you with the chloroform, kick up a fuss. Swear at the doctor if you have to."

"You hear that, Henry?" Anne said. "She's giving you permission to swear."

"If necessary, tell the surgeon that if he forces the operation without your consent, you will not rest until you return with a gun to shoot him dead. That generally gets his attention."

"I should think it would," Hattie said.

"Anything you need before I go?" Dr. Greenfield asked.

Henry clasped hands with Anne. "I've got more than I deserve, right here."

Hattie remembered the water. "There's a man in the first apartment. Second alcove, third cot. He's desperate for water."

Dr. Greenfield nodded, seemingly unperturbed that Hattie's request was better suited for a nurse. "I'll see to it," she said, and proceeded in that direction.

Gazing on the brother and sister, fingers entwined, Hattie felt a twinge of envy. Despite his wounds, Henry was alive. She had no idea whether her own brother was.

"I need to send Mother and Father a telegram." Anne let go of Henry's hand and brushed back a tendril of hair that had fallen across her face. "They've been desperate for news."

Henry's pained expression returned. "You'll tell them about...about Richard?"

Anne nodded. "Better coming from me than a report they read in the newspaper."

"Mother will be devastated."

"Yes." Anne straightened. "But she has Father there. Sally and Roger too," she added, naming their younger sister and brother. "They'll comfort one another."

Hattie pictured the Duncans in their home in Indianapolis, more modest by far than the Logans' house and grounds, which took up an entire block in the center of La Conner. But what it lacked in elegance was made up in love. Hattie had witnessed that for herself on the occasions when Anne had brought her to visit.

Warm, welcoming, unassuming, and without a trace of bitterness at any circumstances—Mrs. Duncan was everything Hattie's mother was not, and Mr. Duncan was as jovial as Hattie's father was mercenary.

As Quakers, they were peace-loving people, opposed to wars in general. But as Quakers, they were also devoted abolitionists, determined that no person should hold another in bondage. Many Quakers, including Mr. Duncan, aided the Underground Railroad, helping escaped slaves on the treacherous journey to freedom.

From what Anne had told her, Hattie knew her brothers had struggled with the decision of whether to go to war. In the end, they'd decided it was their moral duty. Explaining why he'd enlisted, and Henry with him, Richard had told Anne, "I know the Bible says thou shalt not kill. But I'll be serving my country and standing up for those who've been wronged."

Their parents had given their blessing. Small wonder Hattie had thought of them when fabricating a set of Quaker parents for herself. Not fabricated, she reminded herself. Invented, to further the cause, that the war might end swiftly and spare men like Henry—and George and Richard, if by some miracle Richard had survived—any further pain and suffering.

Chapter Six

A nne would have stayed at Henry's side through the night, but she needed to send a telegram home. When Henry began nodding off, clearly in need of rest, she and Hattie took their leave.

"Aunt Patty and Uncle Joe need to know too," Anne said as they left the building. "But that will have to wait, seeing as how the telegraph office is in the other direction from their house."

"If you don't mind going to the telegraph office on your own, I can stop by and tell them," Hattie said, wanting to be helpful.

Anne squeezed her hand. "You're a dear. They've been so kind to me, and to Henry and Richard, too, when they came through the city with their regiment. I'd hate to feel as if I've slighted them."

"Don't give it another thought. Get going. You'll probably have to wait in line, and you should try to get back before dark." The streets were well-lit and mostly safe, but in certain parts of the city, drunken soldiers came out like fireflies after dark.

"You too," Anne said, waving as she turned north. Hattie continued west, the evening light spreading like a golden blanket over the city. In the months since she and Anne had come to Washington, the streets had become familiar. She'd grown used to regiments of soldiers coming and going, and to the sounds of the drum and bugle calling them to reveille and morning drills. Even the summer stench had become common, though she wouldn't miss its passing as autumn took hold.

Their work, too, had grown routine, even tedious. But today had been different, memorable. Anne had found Henry, and Hattie had every reason to think that she'd soon have a new appointment doing the work of a real spy. Baltimore, and then what? In wartime, she'd learned to take each day as it came, but this went against her restless nature. She'd put her past behind her, and she felt a world of possibilities opening before her.

She turned north at 19th Street, the same neighborhood where she'd met Thom walking with Lucy last night. This evening, the sidewalks were mostly deserted. It was nearly dinnertime, she realized, feeling a pang of hunger.

The Trents' home was two blocks west on L Street. It was a solid, elegant dwelling without the pretensions of the house Hattie had grown up in. She rang the bell, and a servant answered, someone Hattie didn't recognize.

"Is Mrs. Trent in?" she asked. "Or Julia? I'm a friend of her cousin."

Anne's Aunt Patty came bustling toward the door. "Hattie, dear. How lovely to see you again! But where is Anne?"

The servant swung the door wide, admitting her. The foyer was open and welcoming, papered in a soft floral print, an oval rug covering a portion of the polished wood floor. "Anne has gone to send a telegraph to her parents, with word of Henry. He's in hospital at the Patent Office. She asked me to stop by and tell you."

Mrs. Trent pressed her hands to her cheeks. "Alive."

Hattie nodded. "He was shot in the foot and the arm. The arm's worse than the foot." She hesitated, unsure whether to mention the amputation orders. Better to convey what Dr. Greenfield had said, she decided. "The doctor thinks it's a flesh wound."

Mrs. Trent gripped her arm. "So we can hope for a recovery?"

"I think so."

"Thank heavens. Every day I pray for those boys. Tell me, is there word of Richard?"

Hattie swallowed hard. "Not yet. Henry lost track of him at Manassas after he was shot."

Mrs. Trent clasped her hands to her chest. "Well, we shall hope and pray for the best. And what of your brother, Hattie? George, isn't it? Any word of him?"

"I'm afraid not."

"Oh, your poor parents back in Indiana. They must be so worried."

Hattie could hardly respond to this honestly, knowing her parents had disowned George. Instead, she deflected. "We all worry so over our soldiers, don't we?"

Mrs. Trent nodded vigorously, the jowls of her broad face jiggling. "Indeed we do."

"A pleasure to see you again, Mrs. Trent. I must be getting home now."

Mrs. Trent grabbed her arm. "Oh, but you must stay for dinner. We've only just sat down, and there are two empty seats. Sam and Halsey are off visiting friends."

Hattie's rumbling stomach was not enough to offset the discomfort she knew she'd feel, seated around a table of half-strangers, including Mr. Trent, who ran among the highest circles in the city. "That's kind of you to offer, Mrs. Trent. But—"

"No objections, my dear." With surprising strength, Mrs. Trent tugged her from the foyer toward the dining room. "I can only imagine the sort of meals you and Anne must endure. A boarding house! My stars. I simply begged Anne to stay with us. You could have, too, you know."

"It's not so bad," Hattie said. "We've become independent in ways I'd not have imagined."

"Another casualty of war," Mrs. Trent shook her head as they entered the dining room. "Call me old-fashioned, but I hate to think of all the work women do now since our men are off fighting."

Seated around a candle-lit table amid smells of fresh-baked bread and roasted meat were Anne's relations. "Hattie!" Julia exclaimed. "It's been too long since you've visited. But where's Anne?"

Mrs. Trent gestured for a servant to seat Hattie at the table next to Julia. "Anne is telegraphing her parents with some excellent news," she said. "She's been to see Henry at the Patent Office hospital. He's safe."

"Thank God!" Tears welled in Julia's eyes. Anne had said she was sweet on Henry, who at eighteen was only two years older.

"By Jove, that's wonderful!" said Mr. Trent, known about town and also among family as the Judge, owing to the work he'd done with the Buchanan administration.

"What injuries has he sustained?" asked Charles. Julia's handsome older brother was a surgeon at the Armory Hospital, another of the makeshift facilities for treating the wounded.

Hattie slipped into the chair the servant pulled out for her. Though she'd grown up with servants, she'd always been uncomfortable at being waited on, especially since her mother was so merciless with them. "Shot in the foot and the arm," she said. "But the doctor seems optimistic."

"I'll stop by and see for myself in the morning," Charles said.

"What about Richard?" Julia asked.

"He was at Manassas with Henry. But after being shot, Henry lost track of him."

Mrs. Trent set a hand on her daughter's shoulder as she eased into her seat. "If the Good Lord saw fit to save Henry, I don't know why he wouldn't see fit to spare Richard too."

"I hope so," Julia said.

A servant presented rolls, which while not as fluffy and moist as Mrs. Sullivan's were still delightful, especially spread with apple butter. Deferring to Mrs. Trent's sense of decorum, Hattie heeded Miss Whitcomb's advice and quelled her urge to devour them in three bites.

"Isn't the apple butter magnificent?" Mrs. Trent asked.

Hattie agreed that it was.

"My dear mother's recipe," Mrs. Trent said. "It's taken years, but Cook has finally gotten it the way I like."

Hattie felt even more ravenous as the servant forked smoked mutton and boiled potatoes onto her plate. "This is indeed finer fare than at Mrs. Sullivan's," she told Mrs. Trent. "Though you mustn't let her know I've said so."

Laughter rang around the table. When it subsided, Julia said, "I know Anne says she sometimes misses home something terrible. I suppose you do, too, Hattie."

Hattie sliced into the mutton, taking care to make the piece small. The best diversion from such questions, she'd found, was to speak in general terms and hope the conversation turned another direction. "Indiana can be quite humid in August. Nearly as bad as here, but at least there, the wind blows."

"I simply don't know what we'd do without the summer house," Mrs. Trent said. "I tried to get Anne to come with us there for a few weeks, but she was committed to her work with Mr. Pinkerton."

The judge stabbed a bit of mutton with his fork. "How's the little man treating you, Hattie?"

Hattie smiled to think how this swipe at his height would enrage Mr. Pinkerton. "Well enough."

"Did Anne tell you, Hattie, how one of his spies came to our house?" Julia said.

"She mentioned something about it," Hattie said. "But she was reluctant to share the details."

Charles shifted in his seat. "I don't know that we need to be telling that tale."

"Whyever not?" said the judge, his voice booming. "It's not as if we've done anything wrong."

"It was last year, before you and Anne had come to Washington," Julia said.

"Early days of the war," the judge said.

"A rather bland-looking gentleman came to the house," Julia said.

"Black whiskers, that's what I remember," Mrs. Trent said.

The spy wasn't Thom, then, Hattie thought. His whiskers were brown, with a tinge of auburn that matched her own hair.

"The Pinkerton man made inquiries about Mrs. Rose Greenhow," the judge said. "She and her little daughter often visited here."

"Lovely woman," Mrs. Trent said. "President Buchanan used to dine at her house. Brilliant conversationalist, and she always dressed in the mode."

"Mother!" Charles said. "I shouldn't think you'd still be singing her praises."

"An individual can have many faces," the judge said.

"What sort of questions did the Pinkerton man pose?" Hattie asked, eager for any specifics on how a real spy went about his business.

"He asked whether Mrs. Greenhow seemed glad to meet the officers who visited our house," Charles said.

"And he wondered whether she'd asked about Sam and Halsey and me visiting the Lincolns," Julia said. "Anne might have told you—the boys used to play there all the time. Such grand times they had, putting on circuses and the like. Of course, that was before Willie Lincoln died."

"So tragic," Mrs. Trent said. "Poor Mrs. Lincoln has never been the same. Says she can't abide the sight of Sam and Halsey, bringing back all those memories. Poor Tad must suffer so, losing a brother and now kept from his friends." She dabbed her eyes with her napkin.

Hattie had heard many stories about Mary Lincoln, not all of them flattering. She couldn't imagine what it must be like, dealing with grief on top of the scrutiny she received from those who viewed the Lincolns as country bumpkins undeserving of their positions in Washington.

The judge cleared his throat, looking askance at his wife's display of emotion. "I pulled the man aside," he said, returning to the subject at hand. "Asked what was wrong with Mrs. Greenhow. That's when he told me he was with Pinkerton."

"And you told us we'd best take care with what we said around her from then on," Julia said. "A little while later, we learned she'd been arrested for passing information to the rebels."

Mr. Trent harumphed. "More of her associates should've been caught, but Pinkerton's men were lax. Put her under house arrest, then let her go upstairs and change clothes. Can you imagine? Of course, she burned half the evidence against her in the fireplace."

Mrs. Trent shook her head. "And the daughter—she slipped into the yard and started calling out that her mother had been arrested. So you can be sure every one of the people spying for Mrs. Greenhow got away."

Hattie leaned back in her chair, her stomach filled with mutton, boiled potatoes, and rolls slathered in apple butter. She couldn't recall ever having eaten so much. Miss Whitcomb would be aghast. She patted the corners of her mouth with her napkin.

"I can't vouch for all of Mr. Pinkerton's men," she said. "But I suspect there were some lessons learned that day. Mrs. Trent, I'm so grateful for this wonderful meal. But I must really be—"

"Oh, but you can't leave without dessert!" Mrs. Trent said. "It's Mary Lincoln's white cake."

"Truly scrumptious," Julia said. As she spoke, one servant slid away Hattie's dinner plate, and another deftly replaced it with a silver-rimmed dessert plate featuring a slice of white-frosted cake.

Hattie relaxed into her chair. It would be impolite to leave before the meal was finished, and at any rate, she had a fondness for sweets that she'd rarely indulged since leaving Indiana. She took a bite and found it as delightful as Julia had indicated, moist and sugary. "Delicious," she said, nudging another ladylike bite onto her fork.

"At least Mrs. Lincoln is more generous with her recipes than with her bonnets," Julia said.

"You mustn't speak badly of Mrs. Lincoln, dear. You know she adores you, even if she won't see you now that Willie's gone. And besides, the problem with the bonnet had nothing to do with generosity."

"Except your own." The judge wiped a spot of frosting from his mustache.

"I have this bonnet, you see," Mrs. Trent said to Hattie. "Fashioned by Willian's, on Pennsylvania Avenue. Do you know it?"

Hattie shook her head. The only bonnets she wore were the three she'd brought from Indiana.

"Best milliner in town, should you ever need one. The hat in question is fashioned of straw and embellished with the loveliest purple ribbons and strings."

"You mean it *was* embellished with purple strings," Julia said.

"Hush, dear. I'm getting to that. The point is, I was quite pleased with Willian's work. Last summer, I wore the bonnet to a promenade concert on the Executive Mansion lawn."

"The Marine Band used to play there on Wednesday and Saturday afternoons," Charles explained. "Before the war heated up."

"Yes, but on Wednesdays, it was only society people who went," Mrs. Trent said. "And this was on a Wednesday, so everyone was in their best apparel."

"Mother looked stunning," Julie said. "Purple and white silk, lavender kid gloves. And the bonnet."

"We made the rounds," Mrs. Trent said. "Catching up on the latest news. Before we knew it, we were all standing at attention for the anthem, and then the music wound down."

"She tells a long story, doesn't she, Hattie?" Pushing aside his empty dessert plate, the judge winked at her. "And all over a hat." He chuckled.

Mrs. Trent swatted his hand. "As I was saying, we proceeded to the South Lawn to pay our respects to the Lincolns. I noticed Mrs. Lincoln looking intently at my bonnet. Soon enough, she pulled me aside and said that she'd ordered a bonnet with the same ribbon, but Willian had been unable to procure matching purple strings. I understood what she wanted, of course. Quite provoking, for I did love that bonnet, but I gave it to her."

"That was kind of you," Hattie said. She hated to think how her own mother would have responded, covetous with her belongings and having nothing but disdain for the Lincolns.

The servant came silently to remove her dessert plate, emptied as cleanly as her dinner plate had been. Hattie rose from the table. "And now I really must get going. Anne will be wondering what's become of me."

"I'll call for the carriage," the judge said as he and Charles rose from their seats.

"Oh, I couldn't presume," she said. "And after all I've had to eat, the walk will do me good."

"At least allow me to escort you," Charles said with a little bow her direction.

Under normal circumstances, Hattie was not opposed to a handsome escort. But Anne had reported that Charles's fiancée was intensely jealous, and she did not wish to cause him trouble. "Thank you for the offer, but it's really not far."

Mrs. Trent shook her head. "Young women these days. So independent."

"Thank you again. You're lovely, all of you, to invite a stranger to share your meal."

"Nonsense," Mrs. Trent said. "You're no stranger. The thanks are ours, that you've come out of your way to share the news about Henry."

"Tell Anne I'll look in on him tomorrow," Charles said.

"And I'll go by as well," Julia said. "Mother's friend has been after me to pay a visit to the hospital. She thinks I'd do well to assist there. Goodness knows I'm bored to tears now that there's no school, and Mother won't hear of me partaking of social events till after my coming out."

Mrs. Trent lay a hand on her arm. "War may disrupt your schooling, but we must hold to some measure of propriety, mustn't we, Hattie?"

"I suppose so, Mrs. Trent." Hattie backed away before they could raise any further objections to her walking home alone. "A good evening to you all."

As a servant escorted her to the door, she thought of how different the Trents were from her own parents. They had money and, yes, some pretension. But it hadn't made them cruel. Far from it.

She banished the thought. Her parents were the Quakers she'd conjured in her imagination, the ones who'd died in the Kansas housefire. They'd not been well-off, but they'd been every bit as kind and gracious as the Trents.

Outside, the sky was a dusky shade of blue, and crickets chirped in the grass, seeming invigorated by the cool air. More people were out now that the dinner hour had ended. It was Hattie's favorite time of day, evoking memories of when she and George used to sneak from the house to the edge of town. They'd lie on their backs on a small hill, the soft cool of evening spilling all around, and stare up at the sky, waiting for the stars to come out and talking of the grand places they'd visit one day. Ceylon. Bolivia. Africa. As far as they could get from home.

George could be part of her Quaker family, she decided, and their evening hillside part of her past.

She turned a corner, and there was Lucy. It seemed a cruel twist of fate, coming upon her two evenings in a row, until she remembered that Lucy lived not far from the Duncans.

Lucy nodded as she approached, not arm-in-arm with Thom Welton but with a slight, gray-bearded gentleman Hattie recognized as her father, though they'd never been introduced.

"Good evening, Hattie," Lucy said in a voice that couldn't have been more pleasant. "What a surprise, to see you again, and in these environs." She pronounced *environs* in the French way, having attended, as Julia Trent had, Madame Smith's French Academy before the war shut it down.

Hattie slowed, meeting Lucy's gaze. "I've just finished sharing a meal with friends," she said.

"Is that so?" Lucy said, sounding genuinely puzzled. "Oh, but I'm being rude. Hattie, this is my father, Representative Horace Hamilton. Papa, this is Hattie Logan. She's with Mr. Pinkerton's agency as well."

Mr. Hamilton tipped his hat, acknowledging Hattie. "Another mailroom girl, eh?"

"For the moment, yes," Hattie said.

He patted his daughter's arm. "Couldn't be prouder of my Lucy, doing her part for the cause. And to think she's headed for Baltimore."

Baltimore. Hattie felt as if someone had struck her in the stomach.

"Papa!" Lucy lowered her voice. "You mustn't go about telling everyone."

"She works with you," he blustered. "I assumed she knew."

Lucy glanced furtively to her left and right. "Miss Warne hasn't made the official announcement yet. And in any case, it's not the sort of thing that should be broadcast publicly. You'd make a terrible spy, Papa."

He laughed. "I suppose I would."

"Papa was worried at first, about me leaving here. But I assured him I'll take every precaution."

"And you won't be so far away, dearest, that I can't keep an eye on you. Discreetly, of course."

The day's victories—the glow she'd felt from Miss Warne's interview, the joy of Anne's finding Henry, the warmth at the Trents' table—receded. In their place came the familiar feeling that the universe was conspiring against Hattie. Inventing a new family, a new history, had done nothing to change that.

"Wish me luck." Lucy waved dismissively, then continued down the street with her father.

Numbed by Lucy's revelation, Hattie proceeded toward Mrs. Sullivan's, the closest she had to a home. She shouldn't have been surprised, she told herself. Lucy's family knew all the right people. Their commitment to the Union cause was unwavering. All Hattie had to her credit was a knack for ciphers and a made-up story. She'd had no business believing Miss Warne would choose her. But knowing that did nothing to lessen the sting.

Chapter Seven

OCTOBER 10, 1862

O ctober proved a gentle month in Washington, the weather pleasant, the skies mostly clear, the maples and oaks blazing orange and red.

To the north, in Baltimore, Hattie suspected conditions must be equally lovely. But she'd have been stifled there, she told herself, harkening back to Anne's point about the difficulty of maintaining a ruse. She told herself Miss Warne had been right to choose Lucy. She was the perfect counterpart to Rose Greenhow, the Rebel spy the Duncans had spoken of—charming, tasteful, impeccably dressed, and always with something to say, even if it was mindless. All Lucy lacked was a little daughter to inform her cohorts in the event she was caught.

Much as she disliked Lucy, Hattie didn't actually wish her to be caught. Even one's enemies didn't deserve the conditions in Rebel prisons, which were overcrowded and filthy, according to those lucky enough to have been released in a prisoner exchange. And if Lucy were caught, Thom Welton would likely be apprehended as well, and Hattie most definitely did not want that.

It was Lucy's proximity to Thom that bothered Hattie most. They were playing at being brother and sister, and that required a level of intimacy. This should have been of no concern to her, one way or the other. But each time Thom brightened the mailroom with his broad smile, dropping off another satchel of letters, she felt a twinge of envy, and that only deepened when he stopped to inquire of her work, showing genuine interest. No matter how she reminded herself that he made a point of greeting all the women, not just her, she felt as if he lingered at her side, trying to engage her even as she sought to discourage him.

Whenever he continued on to Richmond, carrying the letters the mailroom girls had inspected, Hattie found herself growing tense. Baltimore was far safer than Richmond. It might be teeming with Rebel sympathizers, but if the Rebels ever came to suspect his spying, they could do little about it there. Maryland was Union soil, and Billy Yank was in charge. Baltimoreans who sympathized with Johnny Reb no doubt rued the fact that their circumstances were not of their choosing, as Hattie sometimes did. But there was no sense dwelling on that, she reminded herself. Better to accept the facts and go about your business, as she strove to do following the disappointment of Lucy's having been chosen for the Baltimore assignment.

Mostly, Hattie achieved this frame of mind, though at first she'd clung to the hope that Lucy's father would demand her return to Washington. Despite Lucy's assurances that she'd be safe in Baltimore, General Lee had had other ideas. The day after Lucy left for her new assignment, Lee's troops forded the Potomac thirty-five miles upriver from Washington, near the West Virginia line. From there, it was a short march to the northeast to Frederick, Maryland. Along the way, the papers reported, Lee's soldiers had belted out "Maryland, My Maryland." Set to the tune of O Tannenbaum, the lyrics bemoaned despots and northern scum.

But the papers also reported that many in Lee's forces were too gaunt and weary to sing. They crowded at farmhouse doors, begging for food, complaining that they'd been subsisting on only green apples and green corn. When they reached Frederick, one observer said a stench filled the streets, emanating from the filthiest men he'd ever seen, wearing uniforms that hadn't been changed in weeks.

Lee had thought Marylanders would welcome the Rebels with open arms, but the reception in Frederick was cool. No matter. The Rebs continued north toward Pennsylvania. If they took Harrisburg, they'd be well-positioned to circle back to Baltimore, the real prize, where a large contingent of Reb sympathizers—the sort that Thom and Lucy had endeared themselves to—would welcome Lee's army with open arms. Once occupied, Baltimore would not be remotely safe for spies posing as sympathizers. The prospect could not have sat well with Representative Hamilton.

Fortunately for the Union cause, Lucy's father was spared the worry by an incident that demonstrated how a slip of paper might change the tides of war. In a field near Frederick, a Union soldier spotted a bundle of three cigars. Wrapped around the cigars was a folded paper that detailed Lee's battle plans. The find couldn't have come at a better time for the overly cautious McClellan.

It should have been a decisive turning point for the Yanks, gaining advantage from this secret. But as Constance told it, having claimed Lucy's position as mailroom rumormonger, a Secesh spy in McClellan's inner circle had learned of the intercepted battle plans and ridden hard through the night to warn the Reb generals.

There must have been some truth to the story, for when the armies clashed days later at Maryland's Antietam Creek, each commander seemed to know clearly what the other was up to. According to news reports, Antietam became one of the fiercest battles of the war. Anne and Henry had followed such reports closely, gleaning information not only from the papers but also from the wounded men who ended up in the Patent Office hospital after Antietam. One soldier said the sky had turned red as soldiers loaded and fired with the fury of demons, some laughing hysterically.

Every day for two weeks after Antietam, Anne and Hattie had checked the casualty lists, having learned that George's 14-th Indiana regiment and Richard's 19th had been part of the madness. Neither of their names appeared on the lists. It was hard to know whether to take this as good news or bad since so many of the dead had been left where they lay, nameless and forgotten by their rattled comrades. Each day, the lists of ones who had been identified had grown longer. Hundreds, then thousands.

Every night, before falling asleep, Hattie summoned the image of George as she'd last seen him, waving goodbye and wishing her luck as he boarded the train that would take him from La Conner. Every night, she whispered a prayer for his safety even as she wondered how God could be so unconscionably silent in the face of so much carnage.

Henry, at least, was safe. He'd gone through a rough patch in the days after his arrival at the hospital, with much pain and a fever that made Anne worry whether trying to save his arm, as Dr. Greenfield had recommended, was worth it. But then his fever had broken, and now he was slowly regaining his strength. He could sit up in bed, his back propped against one of the glass cabinets, when Anne came to visit. In the early weeks, Hattie had come, too, wanting to support Anne in case they arrived to find he'd taken a turn for the worse.

But as Henry emerged from the worst and began to show an interest in his surroundings, Hattie noticed his gaze fixing more on her instead of his sister, and his smiles, however feeble, seemed more and more often directed at her. Anne noticed this too. Teasing, she'd remarked how if Henry had his way, they'd be real sisters before long. Hattie had brushed aside the suggestion, saying that what Henry saw wasn't her so much as the comfort of home and hearth, and a distraction from the guilt he felt at not being strong enough to return to battle.

Henry was a good lad, though young. Under other circumstances, Hattie might have been more receptive to his attentions. But knowing he'd likely never regain enough use of his arm and foot to return to soldiering, he spoke continually of returning to Indiana, and Hattie wanted no part of that. So as he'd gotten farther removed from danger, she'd begun begging out of the hospital visits. Eventually, Anne quit trying to persuade her to come.

One crisp October day, Anne went off to the hospital as usual at the end of their workday. As usual, Hattie had declined to go along, telling Anne she wanted to stay behind and finish going through the stack of mail in front of her before she went home. Constance had stayed late, too, with her own shorter stack of letters to finish. It was a new little challenge they'd inserted into their often tedious work, seeing if they could read every letter that had been steamed open before quitting for the day.

"I don't know why we bother," Constance complained, unfolding the last letter in her stack. "There's always more where these came from."

She had a point. One of Pinkerton's couriers came through nearly every night, slipping in a back entrance and depositing new stacks of mail to be opened. "I'll say one thing for the Seceshes," Hattie said. "They're faithful correspondents."

"True enough," Constance said, perusing the letter in front of her. "I swear I read this same letter earlier today, from the same sender, but addressed to someone else. Drivel about pound cakes and bonnets. She must have a good deal of time on her hands."

"It's a plot to lull you into complacency," Hattie teased. "Are you sure *bonnet* isn't actually General Lee, and *pound cake* a reference to Mr. Lincoln?"

Glancing sideways at Hattie, Constance refolded the letter and slid it back into its envelope. "Unlikely," she said.

Constance wasn't a bad sort. Since Lucy's departure, she'd become more fun to be around, bantering back and forth with Hattie and the other women. Charlotte, too, seemed to have come out of her shell, and Agatha smiled far more than she used to. Lucy had been like a hot August sun, Hattie realized, dominating their patch of sky, demanding notice.

Constance stood, arched her back slightly, and reached for her cloak. "That's it for me. You'd best get going soon, or you'll be walking home in the dark."

"I've only got three more." Hattie held up the envelopes, fanned in her hand.

"They'll be there in the morning," Constance said.

"By morning, they'll be in the finished stack," Hattie said.

Constance shrugged, fastening the cloak over her shoulders. "Suit yourself. But a finished stack of letters won't help you fend off a drunken soldier in the dark."

"Three letters," Hattie said. "They'll only take a few minutes."

Constance let herself out, closing the door softly behind her. Hattie started in on the top letter. Variations on pound cake and bonnets, she thought, though in this one there was at least mention of the Potomac Army being slow to advance. That was hardly noteworthy, though. Every child in Washington knew that McClellan was dragging his feet.

The next letter had not even that small insight, the sender making only perfunctory reports of the weather—pleasant days, cool nights—and giving a long-winded description of her attempts to hire someone to paint the front porch before winter set in.

Hattie reached wearily for the last letter, her stomach growling with hunger. A brisk walk back to the boardinghouse would hold off the hunger pains until she reached the boarding house, where she'd be greeted, she hoped, by the peppery aroma of Mrs. Sullivan's mulligatawny stew.

She slipped the letter from the envelope and unfolded it. Then she sat up straight. No bonnets or pound cake here, only a nonsensical jumble of words:

DAISY MULES LOGAN CLEVER COTTON KICK
BARNES INDIANA WATSON ADVISE AND MISSOURI
HAS WILL DELIVERY RUNNERS HAS CORN
BROKER LOCATIONS RANDOM MEAT KISSING FOR
HAIRBRUSH PRAYER

It was a route cipher, not so difficult to decode as a Vigenère's, but not so simple either. Carl Cunningham had shown her how to work route ciphers, too, but this was only the second one she'd encountered. Route ciphers were transpositional—the sender arranged the message in columns, which on its own wouldn't be hard to reconstruct, but you had to know how many columns and how many words were in each. You also had to figure out the proper order and whether to read the columns up or down. For additional confusion, senders added in nulls, or nonsense words.

She set the letter aside. Decoding the message was up to Pinkerton's team. She hadn't taken any letters home after Thom Welton warned her against it, and at any rate, her decoding attempts clearly hadn't won her any favors from Miss Warne.

She started to stand, then sat down again. *Logan*, she read from the jumble of words. *Indiana. Corn.*

Her father, Edgar Logan, owned some of the largest grain elevators in Indiana, not only in La Conner but in other Indiana towns along rivers large enough to accommodate barge traffic. He made his money in corn.

There were other Logans in Indiana. Other men who made their money in corn. But she doubted any were as wealthy as her father or shared his affinity for the Confederate cause.

She took a deep breath and read the coded message again. There was no way of knowing exactly how critical the message might be, but the fact that someone had gone to the trouble of encoding it placed it a notch above pound cake, to be certain. It might well reveal her father as the worst sort of traitor, making money hand over fist while aiding and abetting the enemy.

She had no desire to protect him from punishment. But if the message proved as damning as she feared, her position at Pinkerton's would be over, and then what would she do? Even Anne might disown her, and Hattie wouldn't blame her. Northern soldiers were dying by the thousands for the Union cause, and anyone who aided the South was adding to the casualties.

Why, oh why, had she not changed her name before coming to Washington? It would have been the ultimate break with the past. But it would have broken a tie with George, too, and with him off fighting, she couldn't bear the thought of that. Besides, what would she have told Anne and her father, who'd gotten her the position with Pinkerton's? That she'd simply tired of the name Logan and chosen another?

She stared at the message. It would take time to decode it. If she brought it home, she'd have to work on it only when Anne wasn't around, and it might take weeks. But the alternative...She looked again at the jumbled words. Nothing about troops or generals. Nothing about battle positions. So there weren't lives in imminent danger. She could take some time. Figure out what it said, and then decide what to do with it.

The door swung open. Hattie startled, one hand flying to her chest, the other splayed across the coded message.

Thom Welton entered. "Sorry," he said in his soft Yorkshire accent. "Didn't mean to startle you. He swung his satchel onto the table, looking a bit rattled himself. "I thought you'd all gone home for the evening." Then he smiled, and she relaxed a bit. "Glutton for punishment, are you?"

She shifted where she sat, moving the letter toward the edge of the table. "I was just finishing up. But of course you've brought us more."

"Sisyphus and the rock." He opened the satchel and upended it, spilling envelopes over the table. "Done any more work with the Vigenère's?"

"Not - not lately." She returned his gaze, hoping she sounded more confident than she felt. "I don't think Miss Warne takes kindly to me spending time on decoding when Mr. Pinkerton has a team of men devoted to the task."

"I'm not sure devoted is an apt descriptor." He tipped his head. "Might I ask a favor, Miss Logan? Hattie, I mean."

Her palm on the paper felt damp. "What sort of favor?"

"There's a chance, albeit a small one, that I've been seen coming in through the back entrance by a rather unsavory character seeking to discredit me. If I were to leave in the company of a pretty lady, that would provide some cover. Especially if that pretty lady were to join me for dinner."

She hesitated, not out of concern over the unsavory gentleman but because she'd been trying to think less about Thom Welton, and dining with him would have the opposite effect. But she also very much wanted to exit the mailroom before he spotted the message beneath her hand. "It would be my pleasure."

"I appreciate it." He turned, reaching for her mantle. Seizing the opportunity, she deftly folded the letter and slipped it into her bodice.

She stood as he turned, holding open her cloak. "No cigars, no whisky," he said. "Though a glass of sherry may be in order."

He set the mantle on her shoulders. His fingers lingered at the clasp as if he meant to fasten it, but she raised a hand to do it herself, and he moved away. Smoothing the front of the mantle, she offered a smile. "There's a chill in the air these days," she said.

"Winter can't come soon enough," he said. "Every change of season has got to be bringing us closer to the end of this bloody war."

They left the building through the front entrance, passing through the War Department, which never slept, clerks and telegraph operators lingering through the night. The evening's chill promised frost. She clutched the mantle tightly beneath the clasp, the edges of the hidden letter pressing into her skin beneath her dress.

Scarcely turning his head, Thom glanced to either side. She wondered whether the unsavory gentleman was watching them, but she did not want to draw attention by looking. "I thought we'd dine at the Willard, if that suits," he said, returning his attention to her.

She nodded, and they set off. The Willard Hotel was only a block away, but Thom set a brisk pace. Hattie had passed by it dozens of times but never had a reason—or the budget—to go inside. All sorts of dignitaries stayed at the Willard, including the Lincolns when they'd first come to Washington for the inauguration.

When they reached the entrance, a doorman admitted them, nodding slightly at Thom.

"You stay here often?" she asked.

He dipped his head, and she felt the warmth of his breath on her cheek. "Never," he said softly. "There are limits to Mr. Pinkerton's purse strings. But for a fine meal, there's no exceeding the Willard's dining room. And it's such a Federal stronghold that, minus some rather cheeky exceptions, Johnny Reb would rather cross the gates of hell than the threshold of Willard's."

"Ah, Mr. Welton." The white-coated maître d'hôtel greeted them with a bow. "It's good to see you again. I have the perfect table for you and your lady friend."

He led them directly to a screened table in a back corner of the dining room, making Hattie suspect that she wasn't the first lady friend to dine here with Thom.

"Jack will assist you," the maître d' said as he pulled out Hattie's chair. "Enjoy your meal." Hattie wasn't sure, she thought he winked at her as he left them to study the menus.

The setting was indeed private, separated from the rest of the dining room by an ornately carved wooden screen that looked almost Byzantine. Candles flickered on the linen-covered table, the only source of light besides what filtered through the cutouts in the screen.

"Acceptable?" Thom asked.

"Quite. Although I don't see Mrs. Sullivan's mulligatawny stew on the menu."

He laughed. "My, but you have expensive tastes. As an alternative, I recommend the fricassee or the capon. Both exquisite, in my unrefined assessment."

The waiter, Jack, was a handsome, broad-chested Negro with a brilliant smile. He teased Thom about Hattie being better looking than his last dinner guest, took their orders, then brought the sherry Thom requested.

"They tell me a lady is permitted a glass of sherry after putting in a day's work for the cause," he said. "That is if the lady so chooses."

"The lady chooses," Hattie said. Her mother drank juleps, her father bourbon. As long as it wasn't one of those drinks, she was game to try.

The crystal decanter glittered in the candlelight as Thom poured the sherry. He raised his glass and offered a toast. "To victory," he said.

"Sooner rather than later," Hattie added, and they clinked glasses.

The sherry, smooth and sweet, warmed her from the first sip. She allowed another sip, then set down the glass, reminding herself that spirits were among the tools of Thom's trade, and that her best defense against him asking too many questions was to pose a few of her own. "How is it that you ended up in this line of work, Mr. Welton?"

He frowned. "I'd thought we'd agreed on addressing one another by our Christian names."

"I didn't want to...presume."

He waved off this concern. "No presumptions among friends. As for this line of work, I left England under what I suppose you might call pressing circumstances."

She raised an eyebrow.

"Not of my own making," he hastened to add. "Family matters that were best resolved by some distance. An ocean helps."

She nodded. "Families can be challenging."

"To say the least. At any rate, I'd done some police work in London, so I hired on with the New York City Police shortly after my arrival. But there are some on the force who don't take kindly to foreigners."

"I thought the British were an exception. The headmistress at my school would've given her eyeteeth to have come by an accent legitimately."

He flashed a boyish smile. "No such admiration at the NYPD. When Mr. Pinkerton came along seeking recruits, I jumped at the opportunity. I have only two talents, really. I'm a fair shot with a pistol, and I can act almost any part. That was sufficient to impress Mr. Pinkerton."

"He seems to rely on you heavily."

"I suppose he does." In the soft light, Thom's face looked more relaxed than in the mailroom, his brown eyes welcoming. He leaned in, closing a bit of the gap between them, and turned the glass in his fingers. "Enough about me and my rather uninspiring background," he said. "Tell me about the Logans of Indiana."

She felt a moment's panic at him asking so directly. Had he seen *Logan* and *Indiana* through her splayed fingers back in the mailroom? Forcing calm, she held his gaze. "There's not much to tell. Corn. Lots of corn."

"So I hear." He cocked his head, inviting her to say more.

"In your line of work, I should think you'd have been to Indiana. From what I hear, you've been nearly everywhere else."

He laughed. "Hardly a world traveler, I'm afraid. When I'm not back and forth between Baltimore and Richmond, it's mostly Kentucky and Tennessee where Pinkerton sends me. Kentucky has been trouble from the start. They claim to be neutral, but for a Union state, there's a good deal of rallying around the Southern cause. Ever seen the Mississippi?"

She shook her head, sipping again from the sherry. Growing up, she'd traveled the river every summer, going to and from her grandfather's Louisiana plantation. But that was exactly the sort of information she'd rather no one know.

"I'd like to see it sometime," she said.

"You really should. Makes the Potomac look like a little creek. The Rebels are doing their best to hold onto their control of the river. They've heavily fortified its banks. It's their main thoroughfare for supplies. Guns, grain, cotton. Last time I went through Memphis, I swear there were thirty thousand bales of cotton piled up at the wharf."

His gaze, though soft, was also penetrating. *Cotton* was another word from the letter hidden in her dress.

"No wonder they call it King Cotton," she said.

"Quite so." He refilled his glass, but only halfway. "There's a sense in the South that all one needs for a thriving economy is cotton—and the enslaved persons to plant and harvest it. That's why, up till now, they've welcomed the North's blockade."

There he was, dropping another word from the message, *blockade*. But these were words of import to the war generally, Hattie reminded herself, and not necessarily any reference to the message she'd hidden.

"I don't understand," she said. "I should think the Rebels would want such a valuable commodity brought to market."

Jack approached the table, a large silver tray balanced on his hand and shoulder. In one steady motion, he lowered the tray to the table's edge and set a wide bowl in front of Hattie. "For madam, the fricassee," he said. He set a plate containing a fat, roasted miniature hen in front of Thom. "And for Mr. Welton, the capon. May I assist with anything else?"

"Not at the moment, thank you," Thom said.

Hattie smoothed her napkin in her lap, her mouth watering at the smells of butter and cream rising from the sauce. She dipped a spoon in it, tasting only a small portion as Miss Whitcomb said was befitting a lady.

"Satisfactory?" Thom asked.

"More than satisfactory," Hattie said, savoring the peppered creaminess on her tongue. She'd had no idea such foods could still be had in wartime. "Outstanding."

He picked up the thread of conversation where she'd left off, wondering about why the South would welcome blockades. "You're right that the South wants their most valuable commodity to reach markets. But before it does, they want to inflate the price as much as possible. That's why, even though they've made a fuss over our naval blockades, they've also put an internal embargo on shipments of cotton. They hope to create such a demand in England and France that those countries will eventually side with the South, just to get their cotton."

She pondered this over a tender bite of fricassee. If the Rebs didn't want cotton brought to market, then perhaps whatever the message said was of less concern than she'd thought. "Has their strategy worked?" she asked.

"Not entirely. As it turns out, King Cotton is a bit less powerful than Johnny Reb would like. There are other suppliers, like Egypt and India. Plus some in Europe haven't taken so kindly to the Rebs' strongarming. But it remains a fact that cotton is worth far more now than before the war."

"You mean the cotton that's smuggled out?"

He sliced into a bit of leg meat. "Exactly. Blockade running is great sport for the Rebs, not to mention the profits to be had. Our best bet is really to starve them out."

She frowned. "How?"

"The Union has control of the great grain-growing states. Illinois, Tennessee, Indiana." He stabbed a bite of capon, then held it poised in the air. "That's where you're from, isn't it? Indiana?"

Had she told him she was from Indiana? She didn't think so. "My parents moved there when I was young," she said, referring to the Quaker parents she'd invented. "It never really felt like home." This part at least was true. "But I don't understand," she added. "What does grain have to do with cotton?"

"To be blunt, it's a starvation strategy. The Rebs can keep running blockades, but their people can't eat money."

"Starvation." She glanced at what was left of the fricassee. "That sounds harsh."

"No more harsh than the brutality of the battlefield, I assure you. We put the pressure on New Orleans, and they gave in. Now General Butler has been ratcheting up the pressure, though he's stalled out at the moment, near Vicksburg. Whoever controls Vicksburg controls the Mississippi, and whoever controls the river has a good chance of winning the war."

"Because of cotton and grain." She ate a last bite of fricassee, then nudged the bowl aside, her stomach warm and pleasantly full.

He mopped up a bit of gravy with a dinner roll. "It's true what they say. You're a quick study. And you show a good deal more interest in these matters than your friend does."

At the compliment, color rose in her cheeks. "Anne is keenly interested in the war. She keeps up on all the news. Most of what I know comes from her."

"I recall you saying as much. She has a brother fighting, doesn't she?"

"Two, actually. One wounded at Manassas, the other unaccounted for."

"And your brother? George, is it?"

Behind Thom's disarming charm was a steel trap of a mind. She wondered if he ever forgot anything. "Yes, George. He's with Indiana's 14th," she said.

"What do you hear from him?" Thom asked, having swallowed the last of the roll.

"Nothing lately. I tell myself that doesn't mean anything. Anne and I check the casualty lists, hoping for news."

He wiped the corners of his mouth with his napkin, then set the napkin aside. They fell silent as Jack came and took away their plates.

"I should clarify," Thom said when Jack had gone. "When I said you showed more interest in war news than your friend does, I was speaking of Lucy."

"I don't count Lucy among my friends," she said bluntly. "Not that I'd want that to color your thoughts about her." As soon as the words left her mouth, she realized how self-important this sounded, as if her opinion weighed on his judgments. She was only here, after all, because he'd needed a decoy. "I know Lucy has the right background for the Baltimore assignment."

"I suppose she does. Miss Warne seems quite pleased. Lucy has endeared herself quite nicely to several of Baltimore's Secesh women."

She told herself she should be happy that Lucy was doing good work for the cause. "Building on the groundwork you've laid. It sounds as if everyone in Baltimore trusts you," she said, wanting to turn the conversation away from Lucy.

He folded his hands, setting them on the table. "Not everyone. Just last week, a man accosted me in a Baltimore saloon, saying he was sure he'd seen me here in Washington, chatting with Mr. Pinkerton."

"Oh my," Hattie said. "Whatever did you do?"

"I declared—rather loudly, I'm afraid—that he was a liar and a scoundrel. Then I landed a punch between his eyes to make sure he and everyone watching knew I meant it. He shut up after that. Still, the whole thing was unfortunate. I don't imagine he'll be trusting me with any more of his Secesh secrets."

She wondered if the man Thom had spotted hanging around the War Department was connected in some way with this incident. "I do hope you'll be careful, Mr. Welton."

The candle on the table flickered. "Thom," he reminded her. "And thank you. Your concern means a good deal to me."

She felt a rush of warmth at these words. Even as she reminded herself that this was only a gentlemanly expression of gratitude, a plan began taking shape in her head.

"The thanks are mine," she said. "For the meal and the conversation."

"Ah, but it's getting late, isn't it?" He pressed his hands to the table and stood. She did likewise, too quickly for him to come around to assist with her chair, a lapse that would have dismayed Miss Whitcomb.

He reached for her mantle and set it on her shoulders. "For the record," he said, his voice barely more than a whisper. "I wish it were you rather than Lucy Hamilton sharing a house with me."

Chapter Eight

NOVEMBER 28, 1862

It had taken Hattie two weeks to decipher the message about corn, cotton, blockades, and her own surname, Logan. She worked on it in secret, not wanting even Anne to know.

Fortunately, Anne was often at the hospital with Henry. Occasionally, so as to not arouse suspicions, Hattie went with her, though she still worried over how Henry brightened whenever she came in the room. Naturally, Julia Trent took a keen interest in his progress as well, and Hattie kept hoping he'd pivot his attentions toward her.

Julia had become a regular volunteer with the Sanitary Commission, requesting placement at the Patent Office hospital, where the harried doctors and nurses were happy for the help. Julia had wanted to be taken on as a nurse, but the woman in charge of the Sanitary Commission, Miss Dorothea Dix, wanted no nurses under thirty years of age. Of those, Miss Dix preferred plain-looking women who wouldn't distract the soldiers as they healed. Julia's brother, Charles, was of a similar mind, so Julia had to content herself with lesser tasks like reading to the patients, writing letters for them, and—for those whose religion allowed it—playing cards to pass the time. She visited Henry every day, lessening Hattie's guilt over her own short, infrequent visits.

While Anne was at the hospital, Hattie had filled page after page in her notebook with attempts to decode the route-ciphered message. She reasoned that the first word, DAISY, was significant only because it had five letters, a clue that the remaining words should be arranged in five columns, with five words per column.

Next, she had to determine how the words in the rectangle were meant to be read. Clockwise going inward yielded only nonsense, as did counterclockwise. She tried reading up each column, then down each, then alternating up and down. Again, she got only nonsense. Finally, by trial and error, she landed on a reading that made some sense. The first and fourth columns she read from top to bottom, and the others she read from bottom to top.

She sifted out the nulls—words like *kissing* and *hairbrush*—and arrived at something that approximated sense:

BARNES MISSOURI HAS MEAT LOGAN INDIANA HAS CORN WATSON WILL BROKER FOR COTTON ADVISE DELIVERY LOCATIONS AND RUNNERS

RUNNERS were most likely blockade runners, she thought. Who Barnes and Watson were, she had no idea. But LOGAN INDIANA HAS CORN—that had to be her father, involved in some sort of illegal arrangement to line his pockets while prolonging the war. There would not be another New Orleans, where a Rebel city fell for lack of food and supplies, as long as men like him were aiding the Rebels.

Next, she'd had to decide what to do with the message. She assumed the deals it mentioned, involving meat, corn, and cotton, had already been made. Her father was generally smart enough to cover his tracks, and she suspected his associates were too. Still, they should be watched going forward, so future deals could be stopped.

But if anyone at Pinkerton's learned of her father's traitorous activities, Miss Warne wouldn't trust Hattie with so much as cleaning the teapot, much less opening and reading Secesh mail. She surely wouldn't consider Hattie for any future assignments, a prospect that seemed even more appealing since her dinner with Thom.

Following their dinner at Willard's, Hattie had found she trusted Thom. If he felt the same about her, he wouldn't hold her father's actions against her, especially since he'd hinted that his own family circumstances had spurred his leaving England.

With this in mind, she'd devised a plan. At the first opportunity, she'd hand the message over to Thom. She'd explain her decoding and ask him to deliver it to the right people without compromising her position with Pinkerton's. In the meantime, she'd borrowed a needle and thread from Mrs. Sullivan, then folded the deciphered message and stitched it into the hem of her petticoat. This was how Thom carried his most important messages, she'd been told—not stitched into a petticoat, of course, but into the lining of his jacket.

Then she'd waited for an opportunity to pass the message to Thom. Frosts came at night, and chill winds blew from the north, signaling winter's approach. The mailroom girls now coveted their turns at the stove and iron, for their closet-like room, with an exterior wall to the north, was cold, especially when the wind blew.

But Thom didn't come. Instead, other couriers brought the mail. Constance said she'd heard he'd gotten stuck in Virginia. Then one cold November morning, with breathless excitement that would have made Lucy proud, Constance updated her report, saying she had it on good authority that Mr. Welton had been arrested.

Hattie's heart sank. "In Virginia?" she asked.

"In Baltimore," Constance said.

"That can't be right," Hattie said. "The Rebels aren't in charge there."

"I'm simply passing along what I've been told," Constance snapped. The wind and cold seemed to be making all the women testy.

"Who arrested him?" Hattie asked. "For what?"

Constance threw up her hands. "How should I know?"

"Maybe some Rebs sneaked in during the night and carried him off," Agatha said.

"Maybe he's in jail," Charlotte said. "That would be simply *horrid*."

Hattie refused to speculate. But that night, she'd lain awake for hours, wondering and worrying and praying no harm came to him.

The next morning, Constance had come to the mailroom with the cat-and-canary look that meant she had information. "It was a Federal provost marshal," she said, looking pointedly at Hattie.

Hattie kept her focus on the envelope she was opening, not wanting to seem overly interested. "You mean that's who arrested Mr. Welton?"

"Who else?" In Lucy's absence, Constance had gotten cheekier.

Hattie had relaxed in places she hadn't realized she'd been holding tight. "So he's been released," she said as the envelope's flap gave way.

"Of course not," Constance had said with an air of superiority that made Hattie think she'd made the same assumption and been corrected. "If the Federals let him go, it would raise suspicions among his Secesh friends."

Hattie was embarrassed not to have realized this on her own. "But Mr. Pinkerton can't just let him rot in prison."

"Oh, he won't." As far as Constance was concerned, Mr. Pinkerton could do no wrong. "I'm sure he has a plan for securing his release."

Hattie didn't share her confidence in their employer. Why hadn't he alerted Baltimore's provost marshal that Thom was only pretending to aid the Rebel cause?

Finally, Constance had brought news of Mr. Welton's escape. To hear her tell it, the plan and its execution had all been Mr. Pinkerton's doing, his men intercepting a carriage that was transporting Mr. Welton from the local jail to Baltimore's Fort McHenry.

Anne found an item from a Baltimore paper confirming that Secesh sympathizer Thomas Welton had indeed escaped Federal custody. Hattie smiled to read it. Not only had Thom escaped, he'd also managed to cement his reputation as a valued and daring Rebel ally, breaking free of Federal clutches.

Day after day Hattie waited for Thom to saunter through the mailroom door. Flashing his charming smile and carrying a satchel bulging with letters, she imagined him regaling the mailroom girls with tales of his adventures. Still he didn't come.

The next report from Constance was that he was back in the South, gathering up information on artillery batteries in Norfolk, defenses at Roanoke Island, and the Rebels' ironclad, the *CSS Virginia.*

"The naval war is heating up," Anne remarked

Constance eyed Anne sharply, as if they were dueling to see who was the more knowledgeable. "Along with the submersibles."

"That's right," Anne said. "The Rebs are testing them."

"Which we know because of Miss Baker," Constance said smugly. Elizabeth Baker was a Pinkerton operative who, like Miss Warne, had been entrusted with fieldwork. "She worked her Richmond connections and got into the ironworks there. She observed a big ship under construction, and officials told her it and another vessel would be in the water within months, defending Richmond."

Hattie shook her head, smiling. Some men could be so gullible, never suspecting women of having minds of their own, much less of spying on the construction of warships.

"And that was the submersible?" Anne asked.

"Yes. One of Miss Baker's Richmond acquaintances told her he was going to witness a test of a submarine battery. She feigned ignorance of the project, and he invited her along to see it with her own eyes. After the demonstration, Miss Baker returned to her room and made a sketch showing all the details. Then tucked the sketch in her bonnet and went north to deliver it to Mr. Pinkerton."

For the rest of that day, Hattie thought of all that Elizabeth Baker had accomplished, charming men into giving away their secrets. If she could do it, why not Hattie? Richmond would be a more exciting assignment—and a more meaningful one, she suspected—than Lucy's was, keeping house in Baltimore. And in Richmond, Hattie could see Thom now and then. Perhaps they'd even share an assignment.

Lucy was a well-dressed conversationalist who could insert herself into the right Baltimore circles, and she had a British accent to match Thom's. But Hattie had learned Southern graces, like it or not, and while she'd suppressed the accent she'd picked up from her mother when she was young, she could easily dredge it up again. Thankfully, she'd had the good sense to make her Quaker parents' origins in North Carolina, giving her a ready explanation for these aptitudes. And she knew she had the pluck to gain access to Rebel secrets as Miss Baker had.

She wanted the challenge of real spy work, and there was no better place to do it than Richmond. Thom would recommend her, she was sure, and with Henry here, she wouldn't feel so guilty about leaving Anne. She resolved to broach the idea with Miss Warne at the first opportunity.

But for now, Hattie's idea would have to wait. Miss Warne was in Chicago, not due to return until after the holidays. An upheaval was underway within the Pinkerton operation. Earlier in the month, President Lincoln had relieved General McClellan of his command, hoping that his replacement, General Burnside, would act more decisively than McClellan had. Mr. Pinkerton had reported directly to McClellan, and if the rumors were true, he had no intention of shifting his allegiance to a new general.

Before departing for Chicago, Miss Warne had alerted her ladies that the Pinkerton Agency would continue contract spy work for the federal government, but whether that would include the mail operations remained to be seen. Their work would continue through the end of the year, she said, but beyond that, she could make no guarantees. The uncertainty had only made Hattie more eager to do actual spy work.

~ ~ ~

As Hattie waited for Miss Warne's return—and, less patiently, for Thom Welton's—Julia provided a distraction. Having procured five tickets to Ford's Theatre from family friends who rarely used their seats, she'd invited Anne and Hattie to attend a theatrical.

"It's the last night of The Marble Heart," Julia told them. "A tragedy, but I hear the actors are dreamy."

To Julia's delight, Henry planned to go with them too. It would be his first real outing since his injuries. Last week, he'd been discharged from the hospital, and he was now recuperating with the Trents. He walked with a limp, relying on a crutch or a cane, and he had only partial use of his mangled arm, but he was otherwise whole and reasonably well. All he could talk about was getting home to Indiana.

If the outing had been elsewhere, Hattie would have begged off, preferring—in part, for selfish reasons—that Julia and Henry spend time together without her in the mix. But she loved the theatre. When she and George were young, they'd loved staging performances, borrowing sheets from the linen closet for curtains and setting up chairs for an imaginary audience. Then her mother had caught wind of their antics and shut down the shows.

When Hattie had told Miss Warne about her imagined Quaker parents, the part about her having read every one of Shakespeare's plays had been true. The highlight of her stint at Ladygrace had been acting the part of Hamlet—only girls attended finishing school, and so all the male roles were played by girls. But since coming to Washington, Hattie hadn't been to the theatre, mostly because she couldn't afford it.

The night of the show, Hattie and Anne dressed in their best clothes. They'd be no match for Washington society girls, Hattie knew. But as she studied herself in the mirror, she noted how her gown's emerald hue drew the green from her eyes, and she saw how Anne's dark hair, offset by her white satin frock, gleamed in the lamplight. They took turns fixing each other's hair, Hattie pulling Anne's into a French twist, leaving wisps in the front that she curled into ringlets, and Anne gathering Hattie's curls up and away from her face.

"You're beautiful, you know," Anne said. "When you put your mind to it."

Hattie laughed, dismissing the compliment. "So that's the secret to looking pretty? Applying one's mental capacities?"

Anne playfully swatted her shoulder with the hairbrush. "I only mean that you never bother with your looks, and sometimes you should."

"It would be easier if you'd agree to be my maidservant. I can't pay much, but you'd have my neverending gratitude."

Anne paused in her brushing, catching Hattie's eye in the mirror. "I've been meaning to tell you—I've decided to go back with Henry, right after Christmas. To Indiana"

A knot formed in Hattie's stomach. "But you can't...I mean, how will I get on without you here?"

Anne resumed her work, causing Hattie to wince as she tugged the brush through a tangle of curls. "The same as you always do, with your quick wits and charm." The larger question, they both knew, was whether either of them could remain in Washington if Mr. Pinkerton's mailroom operations ceased.

"I intend to return," Anne continued. "But I don't want Henry to travel home alone, and I feel as if I should be there to help ease him back into things. I've gotten used to seeing him as he is now, but it will be a shock to Mother and Father."

Hattie's knotted stomach relaxed a bit, hearing Anne say she planned to return. But she also knew that if Mr. Pinkerton closed the mailroom, Anne would likely never come back.

"You must promise not to fall in love with some gallant Indiana gent and stay there forever," Hattie said.

Anne fastened the curls in place, then wove in a hairpin. "There are gallant Indiana gentlemen? I had no idea."

They laughed together, breaking the tension of Anne's announcement. A fine carriage arrived a few minutes later, sent by

Mr. Trent and drawing much astonishment from Mrs. Sullivan, who rarely saw her boarders travel in such style.

The evening was crisp and clear, the moon low and nearly full. Julia and Henry welcomed them into the carriage, and the four of them exchanged banter as it rattled along the road to Ford's Theatre. Hattie said nothing about Henry and Anne's upcoming departure, unsure whether anyone had broken the news to Julia.

The coachman delivered them to the front of the theatre. Following Julia and Anne, Hattie took his hand as she stepped from the carriage. Standing in the night air, she gazed up at the brick building. Compared to the Crawford House, where her mother had taken her and her brother for occasional doses of culture, Ford's was a modest theatre.

She slipped her arm through Anne's, leaving Henry to offer his to Julia.

"I'm told this used to be a church," he said.

"That's right." Smiling, Julia hooked her arm around Henry's. "Folks said God would punish Mr. Ford for turning a Baptist church into a theatre. But look at all the people streaming in. If that's punishment, I suspect he's all for it."

Anne laughed. "He's got the right idea. Heaven knows we need a distraction, with our men off fighting in God knows what muddy swamp."

Even with Julia's steady arm and his cane, Henry moved slowly. They entered the theater through a door tucked beneath rows of concrete arches, then passed through the lobby into the auditorium. Hattie had nearly forgotten how magical a theatre could feel, especially in the moments before the show began. Row after row of red-upholstered seats, nearly all of them filled with well-dressed ladies and gentlemen, rose from the floor near the stage. Sconces lit the walls, lending a fairy-like glow.

With Julia and Henry leading the way, they ascended the stairs to the dress circle. Some people leaned against the back wall, others filling the seats. Hattie had forgotten, too, the smells that an audience carried with them—tobacco, perfume, and in the case of Ford's, whisky from the men who'd stopped for a drink at the saloon next door.

Their seats were in the dress circle's lowest row, with a commanding view of the stage.

"How can your parents' friends neglect such fine seats?" she asked Julia as they settled in. "I can't imagine anywhere I'd rather be."

"Magical, isn't it?" Julia said.

"Hattie has something of a theatrical background, you know," Anne said.

"Do tell," Henry said.

"It's nothing really. Just a few childhood plays."

"And the starring role in Hamlet at Ladygrace," Anne said, her blue eyes sparkling.

"Playing Ophelia?" Henry asked.

"Playing Hamlet," Hattie said. "The cast was all female."

"The opposite of how it was in Shakespeare's day when men played the women's parts," Anne said. "But heaven forbid a boy pass through the doors of Ladygrace. Miss Whitcomb would have fainted dead away. So that left Hattie as Hamlet."

They laughed. The orchestra began tuning up, a pleasant cacophony of percussion and strings.

"Look over there," Hattie whispered to Anne. She nodded to the right of the stage, where insets in the wall provided private seating, the arched openings festooned with gold curtains above and American flags beneath. "The Lincolns are here."

Anne leaned forward, and her smile broadened. "Oh my stars! It's really them."

"Mr. Lincoln loves the theatre," Julia said. "A respite from the trials of his office. Sometimes they attend here, and other times at Leonard Grover's theatre."

"Which do they prefer?" Hattie asked. She'd passed by Grover's countless times, situated right on Pennsylvania Avenue, but she'd never been inside.

Julia shrugged. "I've never heard them say, but my guess is Mr. Grover's. He's a friendly fellow—Papa knows him well—and he allows Tad, the Lincolns' youngest boy, to play backstage with his son. The two of them get into all sorts of mischief, as you might imagine. Once, Mr. Grover arranged for Tad to have a walk-on part. No speaking lines—Tad has a cleft lip and doesn't speak clearly—but the president was in attendance that night, and I heard he got a big smile on his face when he recognized the spritely creature as his very own son."

Hattie started to say how she'd spoken with Mr. Lincoln that day back in September, but then Anne leaned forward, arms poised on the balcony's railing, and said, "Nearly a full house. Half of Washington must be here."

Hattie scanned the auditorium. In the center section, a man turned his head, and she saw what looked to be a familiar face. She tugged Anne's sleeve. "There, in the center." She paused, counting rows. "Nine rows up from the stage, three seats in from the aisle. It's Mr. Pinkerton."

Anne squinted that direction. "I can't tell for sure, but isn't that Miss Warne beside him?" she said, her voice low.

"Maybe there's truth to the rumors," Hattie said, matching Anne's low voice. "But isn't Mr. Pinkerton married?"

Anne nodded. "His wife came over with him from Scotland when he supposedly had only a few coins to his name. I met her once, in Chicago. Rather plain-looking and short of stature, like him. A dour sort of woman. Nothing like our elegant Miss Warne."

The lights came down for a moment, warning that the show was about to begin. Hattie leaned back. It was only an evening at the theatre, a diversion for Mr. Pinkerton and Miss Warne. It meant nothing. And yet she couldn't help thinking that Miss Warne of all people must be fully aware that the best way to hide certain secrets was to flaunt them.

The lights came down for good, and the actors took the stage. For the next hour and a half, Hattie found herself swept up in the tale of Raphael, a sculptor who wooed a woman as cold and unresponsive as one of his creations. In a dream, he found himself among the ancient Greeks. His beautiful statue came to life, but even as a living, breathing woman, she spurned the sculptor's affections, setting her sights on a wealthier man.

When the curtain closed on the final act, the sculptor had smashed his statue and now lay dead. Coming out of her reverie, Hattie stood and applauded the performance.

"You were right about the actors," Anne told Julia as the applause died down. "Dreamy. Especially the one playing Raphael."

"Mr. Booth," Julia said. "He is handsome."

"He struck me as rather angry," Henry said as he helped Julia on with her cloak.

"He was only playing the part," Anne said.

"It seemed like more than that," Henry said. "Did you notice where he was looking when he delivered his sharpest lines? Directly at Mr. Lincoln's box."

They started for the exit. "Papa did mention a slight of some sort involving the president and Mr. Booth," Julia said. "As I recall, it involved Mr. Booth's performance in *Fanchon the Cricket* last month. Mr. Lincoln was in attendance, and he sent Mr. Booth a note afterward indicating he'd much enjoyed the show and inviting him to the White House. Papa said Mr. Booth crumpled the paper, saying he'd rather a Negro praise him than Mr. Lincoln."

Anne's eyes flashed. "In that case, I'd happily side with any number of Negroes before I'd waste another breath on a man like that, dreamy or not,"

They exited into the night. In the brisk air outside the theatre, Hattie turned up her cloak's collar as they waited for their carriage. "Do you think Mr. Lincoln will truly free the slaves?" she asked Anne.

"He's said he will. Of course, it will inflame some Northerners who care only about the Union and have no interest in putting an end to slavery. I don't see how anyone can abide the practice.

No person should be sold like chattel and forced to do another's labor."

"Have you ever heard Frederick Douglass speak?" Henry asked, speaking past Julia to Hattie. "He's brilliant."

Hattie shook her head. Her parents had always gone to great lengths to degrade the man. "I'd like to. My brother George admires him greatly."

And then, because Julia was looking slighted, she added, "Thanks ever so much for including me tonight, Julia. It's the cheeriest I've felt in a long while."

"And from a tragedy, no less," Julia said.

"That speaks volumes about the war," Anne said. "I wish it would hurry up and be over."

"Provided the Federals prevail and the slaves are set free," Henry said.

This was what Hattie wanted, too, of course. A life after the war. She couldn't imagine exactly what it might entail, but if she were honest with herself, part of her hoped that in addition to George, it somehow involved Thom Welton.

She shook off the thought. It was nothing more than illusion, the sort of vision that came with the uncertainties of war.

Chapter Nine

DECEMBER 24, 1862

The Christmas season in Washington felt more festive than any Hattie could remember. Despite the war raging all around—or perhaps because of it—strangers in the streets wished one another good cheer and a happy yule. Evergreen boughs festooned the doors and archways of the Executive Mansion, and the city's gas streetlights added a pleasant glow to the gray dusk that fell in the late afternoon.

Hattie's holiday memories from Indiana were less than pleasant. For her mother, Christmas seemed nothing more than an excuse to become more exacting with the servants while pining for the plantation and the enslaved persons who'd been at her beck and call there. Hattie's mother had also never been satisfied with the gifts her husband bestowed. Hattie recalled her parents exchanging many sharp words beside a tall, glittering Christmas tree before her father eventually retreated to his study with a cigar and a bottle of bourbon.

Their mother had also demanded Hattie and George show the appreciation for gifts they hadn't wanted—for Hattie, fancy frocks and bonnets, and for George, mechanical banks and abacuses. Each year, it had been a relief when the gifts were all opened and they could retreat to their separate passions, George roaming the snowy fields on the outskirts of town, and Hattie curling up in the turret library with a book.

So when Anne extended a Christmas Eve invitation from the Trents, Hattie's first impulse had been to decline. Besides, the event would only underscore the fact that Anne would soon be leaving for home. Hattie hated to think of how lonely she'd be then. No matter what her friend promised, Hattie doubted she'd ever return to Washington. The only thing Hattie had to look forward to was Miss Warne's imminent return, which would allow her to make her case for a real spying assignment.

But Anne had refused to take no for an answer. She insisted that Julia's mother would be horribly offended if Hattie declined, and so it was with much reluctance that Hattie found herself seated at the Trents' expansive mahogany dining table on Christmas Eve. Mrs. Trent had placed her between Julia and Henry, as a sort of buffer, Hattie thought. The Trents liked Henry well enough—who wouldn't, kind and gracious as he was—but Julia's coming out was still months away, and her mother worried over Julia's obvious romantic interest in her cousin.

Having left most of her wardrobe back in Indiana, Hattie dressed as she had for the theatre, in her emerald gown, curls pulled back with a shiny hairpin. Across from her at the table sat Anne and a handsome young officer introduced as Lieutenant Franklin Stone, a stranger to all except the judge, who sat at the far end of the white-clothed table. Samuel and Halsey sat on either side of him, and his wife sat at the opposite end. Five white tapered candles set in polished silver holders graced the table. In one corner of the dining room stood a tall evergreen festooned with strung popcorn and decorated with tiny cakes, apples, and clove-studded oranges, which added to the delightful mix of smells coming from the kitchen, including roast turkey and mince pie.

A servant placed a bowl of soup in front of Hattie. The broth tasted of celery, onion, and some sort of meat.

"Gertrude makes a delightful turtle soup, don't you think?" Mrs. Trent asked.

"Delightful indeed," said the lieutenant. Spoon poised in the air, he smiled broadly at Hattie, displaying a lovely set of white teeth. "Does turtle suit you, Miss Logan?"

Hattie set down her spoon, thinking of the turtles George used to catch from the pond at the town's edge. He'd bring them home as pets, setting up elaborate dwellings of mud and sticks in the servant's shed out back, a secret they'd managed to keep from their parents. The creatures' wrinkled skin and sharp eyes had made them seem wise, Hattie thought.

"Turtle soup! Turtle soup!" exclaimed Halsey, hammering the table with the end of his spoon.

"That's quite enough, Halsey," Julia said, leaning forward and catching her youngest brother's eye.

He glared at her, but his hammering slowed and then stopped altogether.

"Oh, but this is mock turtle soup," Mrs. Trent said. "There's no getting actual turtle with the war going on."

Relieved, Hattie resumed eating. "It's quite delicious," she said, meeting the lieutenant's gaze.

"Uncle Joe says you fought at Antietam, Lieutenant Stone," Anne said.

"Franklin," he said, bestowing his vibrant smile on Anne. "Yes, I was there. Frightful scene. But our forces prevailed."

"And how is it that you've come to Washington City?" Anne seemed quite captivated by his smile, and indeed by all of Franklin Stone, whose broad shoulders nicely filled out his crisp blue uniform.

"By a circuitous route, I'm afraid. After Antietam, our regiment returned to Virginia, making a circuit around Harper's Ferry, Warrenton, and Falmouth. At each juncture, we saw battle. At Fredericksburg, a ball strafed my leg. A superficial wound, as it turned out, but while in hospital here, I met Judge Trent."

"What were you doing at the hospital, Uncle Joe?" Anne asked.

The judge scraped the last of his soup from the bowl. "Mr. and Mrs. Lincoln went to visit the wounded soldiers. They invited Patty and me to come along."

"Although it seems the Lincolns failed to invite you to dinner, Lieutenant Stone." Julia's eyes sparkled with mischief. "Otherwise you'd not have landed here."

The lieutenant laughed. "The Lincolns were quite gracious, but no, there was no invitation to dine with them. Your father and I got to talking about Spinoza—I studied the classics in college—and when he found out I was being discharged from the hospital, he invited me here for Christmas Eve."

"Don't get him talking Spinoza at the table," Mrs. Trent warned. "We'll all be bored to tears."

"Henry was wounded at Manassas," Julia said, catching Henry's eye. "Dreadful injuries to the leg and arm."

"Threatened to take the arm," Henry said. "But a lady doctor intervened."

"A lady doctor?" Franklin laughed. "She must be a quack."

"Quack, quack, quack," Halsey said, imitating a duck.

His brother rolled his eyes. "So childish."

The judge glared at the younger boy, silencing him.

"Dr. Greenfield struck me as quite competent," Hattie said, a bit more coolly than she'd intended.

"She told me that if I wanted to save my arm, I should raise a fuss when the surgeon came round," Henry said.

"As I recall, she specifically said you should threaten to come back and shoot him if he operated without your consent," Anne said.

"You told the surgeon you'd kill him?" Samuel asked, wide-eyed.

Henry laughed. "Not in so many words, but he must have gotten the message because I've still got my arm." He lifted his arm for all to inspect, though only halfway, having lost half its range of motion.

"That arm will come in handy when you return to the front," Franklin said.

"He's not going back," Anne said quickly.

"Not right away, anyhow," Henry said. "Anne and I are headed home the day after Christmas. We'll see what happens from there."

Anne glowered but held her tongue. Hattie knew she and Henry had argued over his returning to battle. It would kill their mother, Anne maintained, especially with Richard still missing.

"Wouldn't mind a few days home myself," Franklin said. "Rest and recuperate. Before Fredericksburg, every man in my regiment was scheming of a way to get leave for Christmas."

"And where is home, lieutenant?" Anne asked.

"Vincennes," he said. "In southwestern Indiana, on the lower Wabash."

"I had no idea you were from Indiana too," Anne said. "We Duncans are from Indianapolis, and Hattie's from a little town north of Terre Haute."

The lieutenant graced her with his smile. "And which town would that be, Miss Logan."

"Nowhere you've ever have heard of, I'm sure." She smiled sweetly, hoping to dismiss the topic.

Happily, the servants entered the dining room at that moment, disrupting the conversation. One gathered up empty soup bowls while another delivered plated meats, including roast turkey with cranberry sauce, baked ham, and chicken curry. The room filled with savory smells as a third servant ferried in oyster pie, beets, coleslaw, winter squash, salsify, and fried celery. Rarely had Hattie's mother, who cottoned in impressing others, ever put on such a feast.

As dishes were passed around the table, the talk turned to praising the food. Hattie was ravenous, the mock turtle soup having only whetted her appetite, but she took only small portions of each item, thinking less of Miss Whitcomb's lessons in etiquette and of soldiers on the battlefield, celebrating the holiday with only hardtack and canned meats.

Before long, though, Anne circled back to addressing the lieutenant. "Which Indiana regiment are you with, Lieutenant Stone?"

"The Fourteenth Infantry," he said between bites of oyster pie.

The turkey Hattie was chewing went dry in her mouth. She swallowed quickly. "That's my brother's regiment. George Logan. Perhaps you know him?"

Franklin stabbed a portion of ham. "Logan...Logan. Wasn't he taken prisoner?"

Her heart sank and raced all at once. Prisoner. That would mean George was alive, or at least the odds of it were better than if he'd been engaged at Antietam, where scores of names from Indiana's 14th had eventually showed up on the casualty lists. "I – I don't know."

Franklin frowned. "You haven't heard from him?"

"Not lately," she said, being purposefully vague.

"An unusual case. As I understand it, he was taken to Old Capitol Prison."

"Here?" Hattie said, incredulous. The rundown prison was no more than a mile away, on Washington's east side.

"Here, here!" Halsey pounded on the table with his fist, imitating a judge's gavel.

Julia reached over and grabbed hold of his wrist, arresting the action. "Isn't that where they took Mrs. Greenhow?"

"And Belle Boyd," Anne said. "The spy they call the Secesh Cleopatra."

"George is a Union soldier. He can't be imprisoned with the Rebels." But even as Hattie spoke, she thought of the message stitched into her petticoat. Maybe someone else had gotten wind of her father's traitorous actions and fingered George as a threat.

"I don't recall for certain what happened," Franklin said. "I only heard third hand. It was something involving Lafayette Baker."

The judge harumphed, sopping up a bit of cranberry sauce with a roll. "That scoundrel. I don't know what Stanton sees in him."

Lafayette Baker—no relation to the Pinkerton operative Elizabeth Baker—ran a parallel spy operation to Mr. Pinkerton's, reporting directly to Edwin Stanton at the War Department. Hattie had seen Mr. Baker a handful of times—a tall, restless man with gray eyes and a full red beard—coming and going from Stanton's office. With the shift in military leadership from McClellan to Burnside, she'd heard rumors that Lafayette Baker's spy operations would be expanding.

"Isn't Mr. Baker an Army colonel?" Anne asked. "That's how I've heard him referred to."

The judge laughed. "Lafayette Baker likes people to call him a colonel, but he has no military experience whatsoever. A vigilante, that's what he was out in California, before he ingratiated himself with the War Department."

Hattie knew Mr. Pinkerton shared the judge's dislike of Mr. Baker. More than once, she'd heard him accuse Baker of ham-handed tactics and flagrant mismanagement of federal funds, if not outright corruption. But then the two of them were competing to show who ran the more capable spy operation.

"I don't understand how or why George would have anything to do with Mr. Baker," Hattie said.

"As I said, it's an intriguing set of circumstances," Franklin said. "Assuming the rumors are true."

"Baker rarely bothers about the truth," the judge said.

"Hush now," his wife said. "Let Lieutenant Stone tell what happened."

The judge shook his head, then went back to carving his slice of ham.

"Please," Hattie urged. "Do tell."

Franklin tipped his head to one side, looking quizzical. "I'm surprised he didn't write you. Prisoners are allowed some correspondence, though letters are screened before being passed on to the recipients."

Anne smiled. "Of course they are."

Franklin's gaze remained fixed on Hattie, who struggled to come up with an explanation that would satisfy without revealing too much of her past. "I came to Washington after George enlisted," she said. "I'm sure he'd have written, but our parents have..." She paused. "They have some difficulties they're working through, and so perhaps they haven't passed along news of him to me."

Franklin offered a sympathetic smile. "The war has taken a toll on so many. Are your parents near Vincennes? I could check in on them for you. I'll be going back soon, on leave due to this blasted injury."

She returned the smile as casually as she could manage. "I appreciate the offer. But you've done plenty, letting me know about George. Perhaps you could say more about the rumors?"

He dabbed the corners of his mouth with his napkin. "Mr. Baker seems quite captivated, shall we say, by the adventurous aspects of his work."

"You mean spying?" Samuel asked excitedly.

"Hush," his mother said. "Lieutenant Stone will explain."

The lieutenant cleared his throat. "Several months ago, Mr. Baker inserted himself among our regiment, saying he had reason to believe there were traitors in the ranks. Perhaps your brother made some untoward remark, or perhaps there was something in his background that raised Mr. Baker's suspicions. I'm unclear on that part. In any event, Baker had him hauled off to prison."

A few seconds of uncomfortable silence followed as the possibilities sank in. Hattie dared not let it linger. "Clearly there was some mistake. George is no traitor. I must go straightaway to the prison and speak with the authorities there."

"A Christmas reprieve," Henry said. "How fitting."

"I doubt you'd find him there," Franklin said. "According to what I've been told, that's where the tale turns stranger still. One of Baker's cousins, in the employ of Baker's detective police, sprang George Logan free. Last I heard, he was in Canada, spying on Mr. Baker's behalf."

"Canada!" Julia's mother exclaimed. "What sort of business would Mr. Baker have there?"

"There's a strong Rebel presence in Montreal," Anne said. "I've seen mention of it in the papers."

"Niagara too," Henry said.

The larger question, Hattie thought, was why Mr. Baker would bring into his employ a man he'd formerly fingered as a traitor. But that was not an angle she wished to pursue in this setting, and she was pleased when the servants arrived just then to clear the main course and present the desserts.

"Plum pudding!" Halsey nearly levitated from his seat, his fist raised in triumph.

"And mince pie," Julia said.

Hattie felt filled to the brim already, but she accepted a small slice of pie. Savoring the taste of ginger, nutmeg, and orange mixed with diced apples and dried fruits, she could hardly contain her excitement at what she'd learned about George. His imprisonment concerned her, of course, especially because she feared the trouble had something to do with their father. But all that mattered was that he'd been freed, if Franklin's information was correct. And if George was in Canada, he must be safe, or relatively so.

As Hattie downed the last bite of pie, the buttery crust fairly melting on her tongue, Mrs. Trent called for the wassail to be served. The warm punch was poured, and the adults around the table held their mugs high and toasted the season.

"To family and friends," the judge said.

"To our brave soldiers," Julia said, eying Henry.

"To a swift end to the war," Anne said.

"To home," Henry said.

"And to Santa Klaus," Halsey said, raising an imaginary mug.

Laughter filled the room. Bourbon warmed Hattie's throat as she sipped the Wassail, which tasted of cider and vanilla and ginger. As the others discussed the latest war news, her thoughts turned again to George. The thought of Canada intrigued her. She knew little about the region except that there must be a good deal of snow there in winter—and that it was a long way from their parents.

The dreams she'd entertained of reuniting with George at the war's end took on a new cast. Could she make her way to Canada too? If Mr. Pinkerton and Mr. Baker were rivals, as everyone said, perhaps Mr. Pinkerton could be convinced he needed a female operative north of the border. She resolved to ask Miss Warne about it as soon as she returned, if only to plant the idea.

But first, she needed to confirm that George was still in Canada. It was a big country, so she also needed to know where exactly he was. Was he allowed letters? What sort of identity had he assumed? To find answers, she would need to pay a visit to Mr. Baker's National Detective Police Agency. And before she could do that, she'd need to think through what explanation she'd give about herself, George, and their family.

She realized with a start that everyone but her had pushed away from the table. Franklin Stone was at her side, offering his arm. "I believe your presence has been requested in the parlor. Something about holiday carols."

She stood, flushed and woozy from the bourbon. From the parlor, she heard Julia plunking out the first few notes of Deck the Halls. So much warmth, so much cheer. She felt acutely that she was an outsider who had no place in this bright family scene. She steadied herself, one hand on the table, and looked up at the lieutenant.

"Will you convey my regrets, please? I'm..." If she said she wasn't feeling well, he'd make a fuss. "I'm expected at a friend's house."

"Then allow me to escort you."

She glanced at the grandfather clock in the corner opposite the tree. Eight fifty-five. "That's kind of you, Lieutenant Stone. But a carriage will be coming for me at nine."

"At least allow me to help you with your wrap."

Thom Welton had been the last person to help her with her cloak, and she still clung to the memory of his fingers brushing her shoulder. "I appreciate the offer. But you've lingered long enough. The others will be wondering where you are."

He took her hand and lifted it to his lips. "I see you're a woman who's used to getting her way." He said this warmly, but she took it as an accusation, akin to what her mother used to say, though in a more derogatory manner.

She withdrew her hand. "Good evening, Lieutenant," she said, turning quickly from the dining room.

"Merry Christmas!" he called after her.

She hurried to the hall closet, where she rummaged for her cloak. From down the hall, she heard that "Deck the Halls" had concluded, and Julia was starting in on "Hark the Herald Angels Sing." If Hattie moved quickly, she'd be blocks away before anyone missed her.

Finding her wrap, she draped it over her arm and slipped outside, not wanting to delay her exit with putting it on. The night air was crisp and cold, her breath showing in little puffs as she strode swiftly to the end of the block. Only after turning the corner did she stop and fasten the cloak, a frigid breeze prickling her skin. Overhead, the sky was dark and wooly with clouds. Along the path were puddles that had formed in the afternoon's rain. In the lamplight, she saw that ice crystals had formed at their edges.

She turned up the cloak's collar and continued down the street. No one else was out and about. Why would they be, on Christmas Eve, a time when friends and families gathered in the warmth of brightly lit homes. The winter breeze cut through the wassail's haze, and as Hattie walked, she thought more clearly about the prospect of reuniting with her brother. She would go to Mr. Baker's office at the first opportunity and, once she'd confirmed Franklin Stone's story, she'd make a plan. The timing was fortuitous. If Miss Warne was not inclined to offer an assignment in Canada, perhaps Mr. Baker would send her there to spy. Her mailroom experience had to count for something, and she could tout her experience with the Vigenère's Square, limited though it was.

The sound of footsteps interrupted her thoughts. She hurried on, skirt swishing. It was only someone like herself, she thought, walking home after a Christmas feast. The neighborhood was upstanding, and she had no cause for alarm.

Yet a memory from her time in Indianapolis plagued her. One evening, she'd sneaked out of Ladygrace when the needling of an especially obnoxious girl had become too much to bear. A walk in the moonlight had restored her spirits, but then a man had begun following her. She'd run back to the school, and though he'd come after her, she'd been faster.

Afterward, safe in her room, she'd wondered if running had been a mistake. Certain men were predators, and women their prey. As with a coyote or bear, running might only heighten the urge to chase and pounce.

The deserted street before her seemed darker than ever, the homes set far back, curtains drawn. As always, she knew the city was crawling with soldiers, now predisposed to drowning their sorrows in saloons because they'd been denied passes home for the holiday.

She quickened her pace, heart pounding. Behind her, the footfalls sped up. Her boarding house was four blocks ahead. Unencumbered by skirts, a man could easily catch her before she reached safety.

Do not run. Do not run.

She stopped, motionless as a hare beneath a hawk's shadow.

The footsteps continued.

She whirled around, then kicked off one of her black beaded shoes. Swiftly, she retrieved it. Holding the heel out, she said, "One step closer, and I'll gouge out your eyes."

A dark figure raised his hands in surrender. "Commendable ferocity, Miss Logan," he said as he stepped from the shadows.

She lowered the shoe. "You might have made yourself known, Mr. Welton, instead of slinking about in the dark."

He dipped his head, touching his hat's brim, ever the English gent. "Professional hazard. My apologies, Miss Logan. You're a hard one to catch up with. Now that I've managed it, do let me escort you home."

She slipped the shoe back on her foot and took his arm. "Am I to think you've followed me all the way from the Trents?"

"Afraid so."

The pounding of her heart tapered off, and she fell in step with him. *I've missed you*, she wanted to say, but that would have been far too forward. Instead, she said, "You seem predisposed to unlikely encounters."

"Yet another professional hazard. But tonight I've a reasonable excuse, having escorted Lucy Hamilton to her home. We came from Baltimore this afternoon, and she was eager to join her family for the holidays."

"Surely they invited you in?"

"They did, but I declined. On the way there, Lucy pointed out the house where your friend's cousin lives."

"I see." Leave it to Lucy to put herself right back in the thick of things.

"Seeing it all lit up, I wondered whether their festivities might have included you. After dropping Lucy off, I may have lingered a bit on the outskirts of the property."

"Please don't tell me you were hiding in the bushes."

He stroked his beard, considering. "No, it was more a cluster of trees."

She relaxed into his arm. "I thought you'd been avoiding me after our dinner at the Willard."

He raised an eyebrow. "You're a formidable woman, Miss Logan, but I doubt I'd need to get myself arrested simply to avoid you."

So it was true, what Constance had said. "Was the prison as awful as people say?"

He shrugged. "They aren't meant to be comfortable."

"I'm glad Mr. Pinkerton arranged your escape."

"I don't know how much arranging he did. The plan was my idea. And if I do say so myself, it worked rather nicely. My Secesh friends are duly impressed that I gave my wicked Yankee captors the slip. I believe they'll trust me all the more for it."

"Had their suspicions been mounting?"

"It seems to me they're mounting all around, on both sides."

"Will you keep running letters now that Mr. Pinkerton is reorganizing his operation?"

"For a few more weeks, I suspect. Depending on how things sift out, I may end up spending more time in Virginia. I'll need some cover for that."

"Your sister Lucy?"

"That ruse has run its course, I'm afraid."

Hattie wasn't sure if that meant Lucy's had been a short-term assignment from the start or whether Lucy had failed in some way. "Would you ever consider working for Mr. Baker?"

He laughed. "Switch allegiance to the Colonel? Well, he has a good number of disreputable types in his employ, so I suppose I'd fit right in. But Mr. Pinkerton would never speak to me again. Why do you ask?"

"I've had the most extraordinary news. A guest at the Trents serves in the same regiment as my brother George. He said George has been plucked from the ranks to do spy work in Canada, overseen by Mr. Baker."

"Overseen is a generous assessment. Mr. Baker's National Detective Police Agency is a loose operation. But he's made use of military men in the past, so the story's plausible. He had three companies from an Indiana regiment tasked with raiding the homes of suspected smugglers in Maryland. My Secesh associates in Baltimore were up in arms about that."

"So you think there's a chance George might be in Canada?"

"There's a strong Secesh presence there, especially in Montreal. I've suggested to Mr. Pinkerton that he plant some men there."

"And women, too, I hope."

He smiled. "Of course. I'm quite certain the Rebs have posted women spies there already."

Her rooming house came into view, and she noticed his steps slowed before hers. "You know where I live."

"I suspect more men do than you realize, Miss Logan."

Reluctantly, she slipped her arm from his. He caught her elbow, and as he turned her toward him, she felt the night's first flakes of snow land on her cheeks. She met his gaze, his brown eyes soulful yet intense.

"I've missed you, Hattie Logan."

His words warmed her from deep within. In Indianapolis, a few men had courted her, but only in Miss Whitcomb's parlor, under her supervision. Thom Welton's attentions felt entirely different. Looking up at him, she said, "I've missed you too."

He glanced at Mrs. Sullivan's lit front window, and then with what might have been a waltz step, he edged her into the shadow of a sprawling elm. The snow was beginning to fall in earnest, and the branches offered some protection as well as a good deal of privacy.

"I'm leaving in the morning for Richmond," he said. "But I hope that when I pass through here again, you'll allow me the pleasure of your company."

She smiled. "Only if you promise not to lurk about in the bushes."

"Trees," he said, returning the smile.

An errant breeze ruffled her petticoat, and she remembered the plan she'd formed, to confide in Thom about the message and her father's involvement, in hopes that he'd convey the information to the authorities without betraying her. But not here, not now, with the wooly clouds overhead and the Christmas Eve silence all around.

Dislodged by the wind, a clump of snow fell from a branch to Thom's shoulder. She reached up, brushing it off. As she did, he drew her close, his arms encircling her waist. "You're an amazing woman, Hattie Logan," he whispered, his breath warm on her ear. He pressed his lips to hers, warm and urgent, and the thrill that ran through her as they kissed was like nothing she'd ever felt before.

Chapter Ten

DECEMBER 28, 1862

Hattie's Christmas Eve stroll with Thom Welton, capped by her first kiss, had been magical. But the days that followed were anything but. She saw Anne and Henry off at the train station, and the goodbye was more emotional than she'd braced for. Aside from her brother George, Anne was the best friend Hattie had ever had—bright, charming, and never one to pry into Hattie's secrets. The room at the boarding house felt cold and empty without her, and more than one night, tears had dampened Hattie's pillow when she lay down to sleep.

Without Anne and Lucy, the mailroom girls were down to only four, and they were all uneasy over Miss Warne's imminent return from Chicago, bringing news that would determine their future. As if that wasn't enough, Constance reported that Thom Welton had encountered trouble while crossing the Potomac on Christmas Day.

Of all the dangers Thom faced, Hattie hadn't considered him having problems crossing the river. But of course she'd know there were hazards. Hoping to deny the Federals access to the waterway, the Rebs had burned bridges early in the war. They had also built batteries along the Potomac's southern shore. These had eventually been abandoned under Federal pressure, but with the back-and-forth of the war, there was always the chance they'd be reclaimed.

"What sort of trouble did Mr. Welton run into?" Hattie asked, hoping the others didn't notice the quiver in the voice.

"He was crossing in a sailboat. You remember how that storm blew through on Christmas Day?" Constance said.

Hattie nodded. The gentle Christmas Eve snow had changed to rain and thunderstorms the next day.

"The wind blew Mr. Welton's boat off course, and it grounded on a sandbar. He carried two women and their three children to safety."

"He swam?" Charlotte asked.

"Waded," Constance said. "In waters up to his waist."

Agatha shivered dramatically. "The water must have been freezing."

"Indeed. But you know our Mr. Welton. Gallant and brave." Constance lowered her voice, signaling that she had an especially juicy fact to share. "And his efforts were rewarded. As he picked up one of the women, a packet fell from her skirt, wrapped in oilcloth. He scooped it up before she noticed. Inside were letters addressed to Secretary Benjamin."

"The Rebel secretary of war," Hattie said.

"That's right." Constance held up several letters, fanned in her hand. "Shall we see what they say?"

At the kettle, Hattie reached for the letters. "Mr. Welton brought them this morning?" she asked, hoping the query sounded sufficiently casual.

"No." Constance grabbed an envelope from the pile that had already been opened. "Another courier dropped them off. Mr. Welton has taken to bed. He's in a good deal of pain, the courier said. Inflammatory rheumatism, apparently."

Hattie held an envelope over the kettle. A desire, swift and strong, to be at his side overtook her. "I suppose he's at the Willard. At least the accommodations must be comfortable."

Constance cocked her head. "The courier said he's in Richmond. I must say, you seem awfully interested in the specifics of his situation."

She felt her face flush. "I know how valuable he is to Mr. Pinkerton."

"Maybe not anymore," Agatha said, her expression dour.

"I do wish Miss Warne would hurry back from Chicago and let us know what will become of us," Charlotte said.

Hattie was grateful that the talk turned then to speculation on what would happen with the mailroom operations now that Mr. Pinkerton no longer reported directly to the commanding general. She steamed the envelopes in silence, worrying all the while over Thom's condition. It was so like him to overlook any harm to himself while coming to the aid of a group of strangers—including a female courier for the enemy, no less. She found herself wishing he were a bit less gallant. She hated to think of him lying abed in a Richmond hotel, limbs aching.

As the women pored over the letters, they discovered just how valuable Thom's find had been. Addressed to the Reb secretary of war, all the letters were signed by an A. Calvert. In one, the sender told of the Federal provost marshal having arrested a Reb spy. In another, Calvert wrote of the marshal arresting three Baltimore residents suspected of disloyalty. Yet another included a carefully copied list of parole records—records kept by the provost marshal's office.

"Seems as if Baltimore's provost marshal is on the wrong side," Charlotte said.

"Not necessarily," Hattie said. "But someone working in his office is. A clerk would have access to all sorts of information that should be kept from enemy hands. He could even be issuing permits and passes to aid the enemy."

"It's a good thing Mr. Welton happened upon these letters," Constance said as she gathered them up. "I'll set them aside to show Miss Warne."

Hattie spent the rest of the afternoon wishing she were at Thom's bedside in Richmond. But she'd set out that morning intending to inquire with Lafayette Baker's National Detective Police about George's whereabouts, and she could not let distressing images of Thom Welton interfere with that.

An hour before their usual quitting time, she announced that she was leaving early.

"On whose authority?" asked Constance, who had somehow appointed herself in charge of the mailroom during Miss Warne's absence.

"Oh, let her be," Charlotte said. "Anyone can see how she's pining after Mr. Welton."

"For your information, I have an errand," Hattie said brusquely. "Nothing at all to do with Mr. Welton."

"If you say so," Agatha said.

Had her concern been that obvious, Hattie wondered as she left the mailroom. Even in the late afternoon, Mr. Stanton's war office was abuzz with activity. Mr. Lincoln's proclamation freeing the slaves would take effect the day after tomorrow. While no one knew for certain how it would affect the course of the war, it was sure to aggravate the slaveholding Rebs as well as some in the North, including some soldiers who were content to fight for the Union but balked at the idea of risking their lives to free the enslaved. Hattie knew both her parents would be livid at the emancipation. As far as she was concerned, there was no point in sacrificing for the Union cause if the wickedness of slavery prevailed.

And this winter was shaping up to demand a good deal of sacrifice. There was talk of the Rebels' General Bragg launching an offensive in Tennessee, while on the Federal side, Major General Grant was said to be pushing his troops through the swamps around Vicksburg, Mississippi. The Union's General Burnside, while still licking his wounds from the December battle at Fredericksburg, was reportedly assembling his troops for another try.

Outside the War Department, the air had warmed considerably since morning, when frost had covered the greenery. Hattie turned down Pennsylvania Avenue. Near the Capitol, she spotted the address she was looking for, an tired-looking, two-story brick building. There was no sign indicating the National Police Detective Agency, but she checked the address—217—and then let herself in through the front door.

The office she entered was dingy, the floors unswept and the windows so grimy as to subdue what little light remained in the day. Along one wall was a rack filled with long-barreled carbines. On the opposite wall hung pistols of various shapes and sizes. Overcoats hung on a corner rack, riding boots piled haphazardly beneath.

A rough-looking man gazed at her from behind a wooden desk, while two others, looking equally disheveled, lounged in chairs at the back of the room.

"Lost your way, miss?" The man behind the desk stood, and Hattie saw that he was scarcely taller than her.

"I'm an expert at helping ladies find the right spot," said one of the men in the back. He slapped his knee, grinning at what he clearly thought to be a hilarious joke.

The man beside him thunked the crude man's chest with his open hand. "Watch yer mouth. The colonel goes around bragging how he hires only the best and the brightest, and you're hellbent on provin' him wrong."

The man at the desk turned. "Gentlemen!" he said sharply. "Surely you both can find something to do."

"Wants the little lady to himself," muttered the first man, but he took his leave behind the other, exiting through a back door.

Hattie drew herself up. Whatever Mr. Pinkerton's flaws, he at least had the sense to hire men like Thom Welton over the dregs she'd just seen. "I'd like to speak with Mr. Baker," she told the short, round man behind the desk.

"About what?"

"My brother works with this agency." She wasn't entirely certain this was true, but she thought it best to speak boldly. "I'd like to offer my services as well."

The man grinned, showing a missing tooth that made Hattie think of a jack o'lantern. "And what sort of services would those be?"

She drew herself up. "I wish to inquire about employment as a detective for the Federal cause."

He chuckled. "Mr. Baker only hires women of a certain persuasion."

"And what persuasion would that be?" she asked, though she had a fair idea.

Red tinged his cheeks. "Nothing that bears discussion in mixed company."

"Then Mr. Baker is making a grave mistake. I understand Mr. Pinkerton employs women in his detective work, and they manage quite well without compromising themselves."

"The answer is no."

"I'd prefer to hear that from Mr. Baker himself."

"He ain't of a mind—" He turned at the sound of footsteps on the back stairs.

Following his gaze, Hattie recognized the handsome, gray-eyed man as Lafayette Baker.

"I'll be the judge of what I've a mind for, Mr. Odell," he said.

"Sorry, Colonel. It's only that—"

"Come with me." Mr. Baker gestured for Hattie to follow him up the stairs.

She hesitated. The chief detective struck her as the sort of man a woman should avoid being alone with. But she'd come to speak with him, and if that meant speaking in private, so be it. Hoping to show she was no woman of disrepute, she crossed the room and ascended the stairs, comporting herself as the sort of lady Miss Whitcomb had aimed for her to be.

In the center of Mr. Baker's upstairs office sat a massive oaken desk. Atop it lay a thin stack of papers, a shiny silver NDP badge, and an elegant gold-handled saber. Draped over the padded leather chair behind the desk was a red silken sash. On the wall behind it, next to a large curtained window, hung a framed notice reading *Death to Traitors.*

In front of the desk were two straight-backed chairs. Mr. Baker motioned for her to sit, and she took the chair nearest the door. She held herself stiffly, poised between the chair's back and its edge. Mr. Baker eased into the padded chair behind the desk, then folded his hands over the polished wood top.

"So you want to be a detective." In his voice, she detected a sneer. "Whatever makes you think you can do such work?"

"My brother spies for you. In Canada."

His face darkened. "If it's Kerby you mean, I've done him quite enough favors already, bailing him out of Old Capitol Prison."

She looked at him blankly. Would George be going by the name Kerby?

"Not that Kerby's arrest was entirely his fault," Mr. Baker continued. "Pinkerton's man at Niagara couldn't figure out that he was only feigning Secesh loyalties. But then Pinkerton's operatives are a bunch of useless amateurs. Far too lenient with suspects. You're familiar with the Rose Greenhow case?"

"I am," Hattie said, glad she hadn't mentioned her Pinkerton's experience.

"Bungled from start to finish. Allow a suspect free range of her home, and why wouldn't she burn her incriminating papers? Allow her daughter outside, and why wouldn't the child alert her mother's friends? One must be tough with prisoners. Force them by uncommon means, if necessary."

Hattie hoped George hadn't been on the receiving end of such measures. "The Rebels make good use of women spies," she said. "That's why—"

Mr. Baker cut her off with a wave of his hand. "Women can't be trusted. Only last week, I had the postmaster's niece arrested in Fairfax. The postmaster went whining to Mr. Lincoln, of course.

But the girl had over a hundred ounces of quinine stitched into her skirts, destined for Rebel troops."

"I hardly think that's reason enough to mistrust all women, Mr. Baker."

"Colonel Baker," he corrected, leaning back in his chair. "You have no idea the scum I'm forced to take on. Fools in Congress, acting as if this agency was formed with the sole purpose of granting political favors. Last month, I caught two of my men stealing from my operational funds. And yet Congress also demands to know every detail of my work, with no regard to the fact that it's secret by design. It's a wonder I'm able to bring to justice any of the state's enemies intent on plotting its ruin."

"That's precisely the effort to which I'd like to avail myself," Hattie said, hoping to steer his rambling back to the reason for her visit.

"Mine is an operation to rival Eugene Viodcq," he said, ignoring her still. "He began as a fugitive from justice, you know, before offering his services as a spy for the French police."

"I understand Viodcq was also a master of disguise," Hattie said. "I have some stage experience myself."

Mr. Baker plucked the badge from his desktop and twirled it slowly in his fingers. "The men of the NDP must be fearless. They can shirk from nothing. Last fall, I went to Fairfax to arrest a Rebel officer who'd been prowling about. He was, shall we say, unreceptive to my intervention. I was forced to carve him to pieces with his own bowie knife. Left a bit of a bloody scene, I'm afraid. Perhaps you read of it in the papers."

She shuddered inwardly but took care to show no outward sign of her reaction. "I'm afraid not," she said, meeting his steely gaze.

He pushed up from his desk and strode to the window, gesturing for her to follow. She did as he bid, though stopping short of where he stood.

He pulled back the curtain. Surveying the street below, he pointed at a man on the corner, dressed in a black overcoat and checking his pocket watch. "Recognize him?"

She shook her head.

His gaze turned on her. "That man is a Rebel spy. They take turns, keeping watch on our comings and goings here. He waved a hand at the window. "There's no end to the corruption I'm rooting out. The profiteers are everywhere. Right before Christmas, I caught a Union colonel trying to smuggle tea, coffee, and playing cards to the Rebels. He stood to pocket five thousand dollars from his treachery."

She shifted foot to foot, thinking of the message involving her own father's treasonous dealings. If tea and playing cards yielded that much money, she could scarcely imagine what he must make from dealing in barge loads of corn.

"You must be quite skilled in the means by which you entrap such nefarious sorts," she said.

His eyes lit with the compliment. "It would be no exaggeration, my dear, to say that this war cannot be won without my efforts. Last month, I apprehended the entire crew of a blockade runner. Do you know how I did it?"

Seeing the effect praise had on him, she decided to lavish more in an effort to bring the conversation back around to her desire for a post in Canada, or at least some clarification as to whether the mysterious Kerry had anything to do with George.

"Whatever you did, I'm sure it was clever, Colonel Baker."

He stepped toward her, closing the curtain. "Indeed it was. I donned overalls and posed as the engineer of a tugboat towing the schooner out of Annapolis. When I'd gathered the evidence I needed, I arrested the lot of them. Evidence, my dear, is everything."

He stepped closer still. Like a snake striking, his hand darted to her bosom, his fingers tapping along the edges of her breasts. "If you're a Rebel spy, there's a good chance you've hidden tins of quinine in your corset."

She recoiled, embarrassed and angry. "I'm no Rebel spy, sir."

He cocked his head, seeming puzzled at her reaction. "I was merely demonstrating how one must be direct in investigating one's suspicions."

She backed toward the door, grabbed the knob, and swung it open. "Good day, Mr. Baker," she said, closing the door firmly behind her.

The walk home felt lonelier than ever, as did the evening in her tiny attic room. She tried to read a volume of Dickens that Julia had loaned her, but thoughts of the encounter with Lafayette Baker got in her way. She was inclined to agree with Mr. Pinkerton. The man was a pompous arse, if not an outright scoundrel who'd delighted in running his hands across her bodice. And for her troubles, she was no closer than before to reuniting with George.

~ ~ ~

When Hattie arrived at the mailroom the next morning, the other girls were already seated. There were no new stacks of letters, she saw, only Miss Warne standing at the head of the table, her hair pulled back in the usual severe bun. She wore a gray dress so plain that Hattie wondered whether she'd come from an assignment that required her to meld into the background.

Hattie slipped into her seat, and Miss Warne began to speak. "I want to begin by thanking all of you for your diligence while I was away."

Next to Hattie, Constance beamed with the eagerness of a puppy expecting a reward for good behavior. Her countenance fell as Miss Warne continued without mentioning her by name.

"As you're aware, the Pinkerton Agency is in the process of shifting its operations now that General McClellan is no longer in command. Mr. Pinkerton intends to keep detectives and couriers in the field, but the task of sorting through and reading correspondence will be delegated to another agency."

She paused, letting the announcement sink in.

"Will Mr. Pinkerton keep us employed in some other capacity?" Constance asked.

"I'm afraid the other positions at Pinkerton's are far more hazardous than your work. They require, shall we say, a different set of skills."

A set of skills that doesn't involve ironing, Hattie thought with glee. This was her chance. "Nonetheless, if a person would like to be considered for a field post, what should she do?"

"Nothing," Miss Warne said flatly. "We're well aware of how to find each of you, should we find ourselves in need."

Agatha stood and reached for her wrap. "I withdraw myself from consideration," she said. "There's enough danger as it is just living here, what with the Rebels so close."

Charlotte stood too. "Consider me withdrawn as well. I'll go see Miss Dix about a nursing position."

The two of them donned their cloaks and left. Constance glared at Hattie as if she were intruding on some private meeting.

Miss Warne folded her arms at her chest. "You two are free to leave as well."

Constance rose from her seat. "Thank you for all you've done for us, Miss Warne. Please extend my thanks to Mr. Pinkerton as well. I remain at your service whenever the need arises."

Miss Warne smiled primly. "I appreciate that, Constance."

Hattie did not intend to grovel, no matter how much she desired a position. She stood, reached for her cloak, and started out behind Constance. Turning, she locked eyes with Miss Warne. Unsure what she might say without sounding obsequious, she only smiled and nodded curtly. To her dismay, tears welled in her eyes. First the news of Thom's disaster, then her aborted effort with Mr. Baker, and now this.

Miss Warne touched her arm. "A word, please, Miss Logan," she said softly.

"Yes, Miss Warne?"

"You've not withdrawn yourself from consideration?"

Hattie straightened, choosing her words with care. "Not at all, Miss Warne. It would be my honor to serve as you and Mr.

Pinkerton see fit. I can work as discretely and as independently as you need me to."

"Despite an element of risk?"

"Our soldiers face far greater risks, I'm sure."

Miss Warne nodded. "Indeed they do. How do you feel about crossing the border?"

"With Canada?" Hattie said.

Miss Warne looked at her quizzically. "What makes you think Mr. Pinkerton has operations in Canada?"

She thought of what Mr. Baker had told her about the Pinkerton man at Niagara. But it wouldn't do to mention Lafayette Baker. "Only rumors."

Miss Warne's brow furrowed. "One must be prudent about rumors, Miss Logan."

Hattie tamped down a surge of resentment. Passing rumors hadn't hurt Lucy's prospects. "Of course. But I believe the papers have reported on Rebel activity in certain Canadian cities." This was a guess. What little she knew of Rebel operations north of the border had come from Franklin Stone. "And I know Mr. Pinkerton would not miss an opportunity to gather information."

"He would not," Miss Warne said, not committing one way or another to the specifics of Hattie's speculation. "But it's the Virginia border I have in mind. You may have heard some—" She cleared her throat. "Some talk about the unfortunate incident at the Potomac involving Mr. Welton."

"Constance mentioned something," Hattie said.

"While he recovers, we need someone to take over as courier for the Baltimore-Richmond mail. We have reason to believe our usual substitute's credibility may be compromised. The next logical choice would be Lucy. For the most part, Mr. Welton's contacts in Baltimore trust her. But it wouldn't do for her to travel alone. I broached the subject with her, and she suggested you accompany her to Richmond if you're willing.

"Lucy wants me to travel with her?" Hattie couldn't keep the surprise from her voice.

"More than anything, what one needs in such assignments is a cool-headed companion. You seem to have her confidence in that regard."

"And your confidence, Miss Warne?" The question had to be asked. "Have I earned it?"

Miss Warne looked at her sharply. "I should inherently trust the orphaned daughter of upstanding Quaker parents, shouldn't I?"

Hattie swallowed hard, regretting she'd ever made up that story. "I shouldn't want to be judged on any merits but my own."

Miss Warne studied her, and Hattie did her best not to look away.

"Fair enough," Miss Warne said at last. "I'll have a pass prepared for you. I don't suppose you'll need an assumed name?"

Hattie would have loved a new name, but she didn't want to appear too eager. "Whatever you think best."

"It's simplest to keep your given name at the start. Assuming a new role can be challenging enough without having to answer to a new name too. I understand you've done some acting in the past?"

Lucy didn't know this about Hattie—it must have been Thom who'd told her. "I acted in plays growing up, and I had the leading role in a school production."

"What about dialect? The part we have in mind for you is as a friend of the Welton family who hails from Virginia."

Hattie summoned the dialect she'd worked hard to shed, learned at her mother's knee. "I do so miss the Old Dominion," she said, softening her vowels and drawing them out as her mother did.

A smile curled at Miss Warne's lips. "Very well. I'll tell Lucy. Have your bag packed and ready. If all goes according to plan, you'll leave within the next few days."

Chapter Eleven

DECEMBER 31, 1862

As Miss Warne had instructed, Hattie went home and packed a small bag. She wished she'd thought to ask how long she might be away, but in any event, she had brought little with her from Indiana and so had little to bring on this journey. Then she passed the time by reading the Dickens novel, and when she grew restless, by going for walks in weather that was unseasonably clear and dry.

On New Year's Day, a message arrived for her at the boarding house. *Departure 7 am* was all it said. Hattie told Mrs. Sullivan she'd be away a few days, visiting a friend of the family. She might be detained, she added, so the landlady shouldn't worry if her absence was extended. Mrs. Sullivan, from whom few secrets were safe, pressed for details, but Hattie demurred.

She slept poorly that night, as she had the night before, plagued by questions of why Lucy had asked for her company on this errand to Richmond. How would Hattie get on, sharing meals and a room with a person for whom she had little affection?

Still, this was her chance to show Miss Warne what she could do, the ultimate goal being further assignments that would either bring her closer to George or to Thom Welton. She didn't want to presume too much, having put off amorous advances from other men, but his kiss had suggested he felt much toward her as she did toward him. This thought led to a new worry as she tossed and turned, over Thom's health and when she might see him again.

As promised, the carriage arrived promptly at seven. Lucy was already inside. Hattie had dressed as if for a stage role, with a wretchedly uncomfortable crinoline beneath her blue silk frock. Lucy looked entirely at ease in a white dress trimmed with lavender ribbons.

"Hattie, dear," Lucy said, her British accent thicker than Hattie remembered. "I'm so very glad you've arranged to travel with me."

"There's no one I'd rather travel with, dearest Lucy," Hattie said as she settled into her seat. As long as she was laying on the charm—and the hyperbole—she may as well show off her Southern drawl.

As the carriage headed for the wharf district, Lucy chatted amiably, speaking first of the weather and then of war news, with a decided slant toward the Rebel cause. Uncertain why Lucy was playing this up, Hattie said little.

"We're fortunate the Old Bay Line has retained some passenger service," Lucy said, referring to the packet steamships that passengers between Baltimore and Norfolk, a route that also went up the Potomac. "It's a shame the service has become so unreliable now that the military has commandeered so many of their vessels." She lowered her voice, presumably for effect. "The Yanks, you know."

Hattie nodded, playing along, as the carriage slowed in front of a bustling wharf. The driver helped them out, and as Lucy paid him, Hattie looked around the busy scene. Troops in blue uniforms were all around, some constructing what looked like a new warehouse to house military supplies.

They proceeded to the wharf where a packet steamer was docked for passenger boarding, black smoke billowing from its smokestack. A soldier checked their passes and gestured for them to board. "It's seen better days, I expect," Lucy said as they seated themselves in chairs that had numerous scratches along the wooden arms. "But it's better than an all-day carriage ride."

Hattie didn't find the trappings so bad, especially knowing that the steamer might have been only recently released from military use transporting cargo, soldiers, and even prisoners. As the steamer left the wharf, she watched out the window as the city receded from view, grateful for the tiny flotilla of Union frigates that had wrested control of the Potomac from the Rebels early in the war.

The packet steamer deposited them at Aquia Creek Landing amid a mass of boats, railroad tracks, and warehouses. The railroad bridge, which the Union Army had taken over, was a sight to behold, tall and rickety, though it had opened only a few months ago.

Men milled about the landing, most in Union blue uniforms. Large warehouses lined Aquila Creek Dockside, where many of the soldiers were offloading crates of supplies. "A shame the Confederate terminal here fell to Burnside," Lucy said.

Showing their passes, they boarded a train car hooked to the locomotive, which sat puffing black smoke. Most of the passengers were soldiers. Shortly after Hattie and Lucy settled into their seats, the whistle blew, and the train chugged ahead, picking up speed

It took Hattie a moment to register that Lucy was staying in character, giving the Secesh perspective on how control of the landing had shifted. "Such a loss," she tutted, playing along.

Hattie settled back in her seat and closed her eyes. After lying awake the past two nights wondering how she'd manage this journey with Lucy and prove herself to Miss Warne, she felt exhausted. Within moments, she drifted into sleep.

She woke when the train lurched to a stop. Judging from the sun's position in the sky, it was nearly noon.

"Quite the sleeper you are," Lucy said. "I've been reduced to talking to myself like some doddering old woman."

Hattie couldn't tell if she was teasing or genuinely miffed. "Sorry," she said, dabbing at the edges of her mouth with her handkerchief. "Where are we?"

Lucy stood. "End of the line." She handed Hattie her travel pass. "Just south of Falmouth."

They filed out ahead of a group of soldiers. All around them were white canvas tents, some labeled with large wooden signs: Headquarters, Post Office, Officer Quarters, Mess Hall.

Hattie stepped carefully as she followed Lucy along the rutted road. Despite the cold, the noonday sun was melting portions of the dirt into mud. Without Lucy, she'd be utterly lost, Hattie realized. She didn't like depending on anyone, especially a person who'd upbraided her the way Lucy had. At the same time, she was glad Lucy seemed to know where she was going—or at least Hattie hoped she did.

"You seem well-acquainted with the route," Hattie said.

Lucy laughed. "I believe only God himself is well-acquainted with the current route from Washington to Richmond. It seems to change by the hour." Lucy nodded at a canvas tent up ahead with a gray-uniformed sentry on attention on either side of the entrance. "There's where we cross the border," Lucy said. "Have your travel pass ready."

Hattie clutched the slip of paper as they approached the sentries, who ushered them into the tent. *Enemy territory*, Hattie thought. Aside from their uniforms, the soldiers seemed little different from the Federal troops she saw every day in Washington, young and weary-eyed.

Inside the tent sat a gaunt-faced officer of low rank, judging by his epaulets. Sporting a wide mustache, he looked slightly older than the sentries.

"Passes." He held out his hand, and Lucy and Hattie complied.

The officer glanced at the papers they handed him. "Mind yourselves in Richmond," he said, waving them through. "It's becoming less and less hospitable to ladies."

"We shall." Lucy flashed a smile over her shoulder. "Thank you for your concern."

On the other side of the line, Hattie followed Lucy toward a pair of mules fastened to a wooden cart. She dropped a handful of coins from her gloved fingers into the driver's hand. He was a rough-looking man with several days' growth of whiskers.

Hattie and Lucy settled into the back of the cart, the seat nothing but a rough-hewn wooden plank. The cart smelled of hay and manure.

"It's only a short ride to Fredericksburg," Lucy said cheerily, and Hattie had to marvel at her adaptability. It was not a trait she'd have associated with Lucy before today.

The cart lurched forward. Hattie grabbed onto the side, grateful for her gloves that with any luck would help avoid a splinter. Leafless oak and elm branches spread toward the sky from fat tree trunks on either side of the road, the afternoon sun shining at a low, piercing angle.

Lucy began to jabber—a distraction, at least, from the fear of being tossed from the cart as it jostled along the road. Lulled by the rolling wheels and Lucy's chatter, Hattie spoke only now and then, making empty remarks like, "Is that so?" or "How fascinating."

Then the carriage hit a rut, jolting her to attention. The coachman flicked the reins, and the mules jerked forward. On the far side of the road, a cart full of soldiers rumbled past.

Hattie expected Lucy to rebuke the driver, but she only smiled. "Our inconveniences are trivial compared to what our fighting men endure," she said.

"Indeed," Hattie said. Maybe Lucy's time in Baltimore and Thom's good influence had softened her around the edges, she thought.

She clutched the side of the cart. The distance between Washington and Richmond was only a little over a hundred miles, she'd been told. But they'd traveled several hours already and had yet to reach Fredericksburg, the halfway point.

"I do hope we reach Richmond by nightfall," she said.

"We might," Lucy said, "depending on what we find at Hamilton's Crossing. Brother Thom told me that earlier in the war, this trip could take a week."

"My stars," Hattie said, using an expression her southern mother favored.

Finally, they crossed the Rappahannock and entered Fredericksburg. On Christmas Eve, Franklin Stone had described some details of the battle here, but Hattie was unprepared for the devastation in what had once been a charming colonial town. The Rebels had fought from the cellars and narrow streets, she recalled the lieutenant saying. Imagining the smells of blood and gunpowder and the cries of the wounded, she shuddered.

Today an eerie quiet seemed to blanket the town. As their cart rumbled along the street, Hattie noticed the haunted stares of the townspeople, reminding her of the blank eyes of soldiers who poured into Washington after a battle.

A few miles south of Fredericksburg, the cart pulled up in front of what looked like a small station house, positioned at the intersection of the road and the railroad tracks. A crew of men was loading supplies into the freight cars of a train that sat on the tracks. Nearby were a smattering of white canvas tents and a shanty labeled with a sign that said "Telegraph." A similar sign, hastily lettered with "Hamilton's Crossing," hung above the station house door.

The cart's driver, having spoken no more than a handful of words during the journey, now helped Hattie and Lucy down from the cart. Dismissing them with a nod, he turned his attention to a pair of passengers waiting to go north. Hattie expected Lucy to head straight for the train, but she went instead toward the station house, and Hattie followed.

Inside, Lucy's charming demeanor shifted. She marched up to the clerk and demanded to speak with the superintendent, stating loudly that she had a complaint.

So she can act, Hattie thought, for they had yet to board the train, a different line than the one they'd ridden earlier in the day.

The clerk tried to placate Lucy, but to no avail.

"I must see the superintendent at once." Lucy stamped her foot. "Your railroad has managed to lose our trunks."

"My apologies," the clerk said. "With the transporting of supplies for our men, a trunk sometimes—"

"Inexcusable!" Lucy's eyes flashed. "We cannot continue our journey without our trunks. We must return to Richmond at once and retrieve them."

The clerk sorted through a stack of tickets, then held out two labeled *Richmond.* "There is no charge, of course, owing to our error."

Lucy snatched the tickets from his hand. "A fortnight ago, I had the same difficulty, a lost trunk on this same route. I insist on seeing your superintendent."

"I'm afraid the superintendent is quite—"

"Indisposed?" Lucy's voice rose, and through the open doorway, Hattie saw heads turn. "Too busy to hear the concerns of a lady whose journey has been interrupted due to this firm's mismanagement?"

With this, the clerk relented, leading Lucy and Hattie out the back of the station house to a small tent with no signage to indicate its purpose. As they entered, a short, ruddy-faced man looked up from a desk made from a board laid across two barrels.

"Sorry to interrupt, sir," the clerk said. "But this lady—" He indicated Lucy. "She insists on a word with you."

The florid man dismissed him with the wave of his hand. "Whatever your complaint, madam," he said, addressing Lucy, "I assure you that the Richmond, Fredericksburg, and Potomac line is doing the best we can under the circumstances. Our first obligation, as you surely know, is to our troops. At times, their priority must by necessity inconvenience other passengers."

Lucy strode purposefully toward the makeshift desk. Trailing behind, Hattie nearly twisted her foot on the uneven ground.

Rather than stop in front of the desk, Lucy continued around. The man stood, standing nearly eye to eye with her. "Mr. Ruth, my brother Thom said I could expect better from you," she said, her voice low.

The superintendent startled at the mention of Thom's name. "Your brother—that would be Mr. Welton?" he asked softly.

Lucy nodded. "He'd be traveling with me, but I'm afraid he's taken ill," she said. "That's why I've brought Miss Logan," she added, indicating Hattie.

Mr. Ruth's face relaxed. "I do hope he'll recover soon."

"He seems to be on the mend," Lucy said.

Mr. Ruth scribbled a few lines on a piece of paper, which he folded and handed to Lucy. She slipped it into her bodice.

"Again, my apologies for your trouble," Mr. Ruth said, loudly enough to be heard outside the tent.

Lucy harumphed loudly, assuming again the role of disgruntled traveler. "We shall see, when this wretched war ends, if your railroad continues to be worthy of our patronage."

Mr. Ruth walked them to the tent's door, which he held open so they could exit. "I shall do my utmost to make it so," he said. "For now, Godspeed on your return to Richmond."

Lucy held her head high, ever the disgruntled traveler, as they boarded the southbound train, its locomotive now running.

"Well, I never!" Lucy declared as they settled into their seats. There seemed no cause for her outburst except as an excuse for her to bend her head toward Hattie and whisper in her ear. "This train line suffers some unfortunate bottlenecks and delays while transporting Rebel troops, I'm told—all under Mr. Ruth's supervision."

Hattie smiled, smoothing her skirts. It was good to know that even in enemy territory, there were friends helping the Union cause.

The ride to Richmond was comfortable enough, though the train car smelled of men's sweat and a cheesy odor, the source of which Hattie preferred not to guess. Compared with the earlier parts of their journey, it was also blessedly short, making only one stop before coming to Richmond. If Mr. Ruth oversaw acts of sabotage as Lucy's remark suggested, Hattie was glad he'd not arranged any that would have lengthened their trip further.

Uncomfortable in her stiff crinoline, Hattie looked forward to changing once they arrived at their hotel, assuming the tasks at hand allowed for it. As to the exact nature of those tasks, Lucy had offered little, saying only that she'd brought letters to deliver.

It was nearly evening when the train finally chugged into the city, the January sun slanting golden across the western sky. The bustle of activity in the Confederate capital was nearly the same as in Washington, though there seemed far more smokestacks graying the sky. The North had a big edge in manufacturing, Anne had explained to Hattie, but the Rebs were doing their best to catch up. In addition to ironworks, they'd set up factories for making tents, uniforms, harnesses, swords, and bayonets.

The train crossed five sets of tracks as it proceeded to the city's center, one for each of the five railroads that transported people and goods in and out of Richmond, Lucy said. Along the way, she pointed out Chimborazo Hospital, a sprawling complex sitting high on a hill overlooking the city, and two prisons, Libby and Castle Thunder. Both had been warehouses before the Rebel government seized them, Lucy said.

Hattie wondered how Lucy had come by this knowledge, but it wouldn't do to question her, so she remained silent.

"You're awfully quiet," Lucy said. "I hope you're not fearful of the Yanks closing in. Our boys in gray do a fine job of protecting the city. McClellan came storming at us last summer, but the good generals Lee, Stuart, and Jackson turned him back on his heels."

"Quite so," Hattie said. Knowing Lucy's high opinion of General McClellan, she was impressed with how well she was acting the part of a loyal Southern lady.

The rails carried them into Richmond's business district, where the streets were crawling with soldiers. A block to the east, on an expansive lawn, a Confederate regiment performed a military drill, marching in step as a band played a tune Hattie recognized as "Dixie's Land." Behind them rose a massive stone structure fronted by a row of stately columns.

"That's the Capitol building," Lucy said as the train slowed to a stop. "Jefferson Davis took his oath of office right there on those steps. In fact, every person of any consequence in Dixieland has graced its halls at least once. Many come and go regularly."

"How interesting," Hattie said, drawing on what she hoped was an ample supply of generic remarks.

As they got off the train at the station, Hattie studied the woman in front of her, who carried herself as Hattie's mother did, back straight, head high, her gaze fixed a tad above eye level. Hattie mimicked this posture, moving with deliberate grace.

Lucy hailed a cart driver to transport her trunk and Hattie's bag to the hotel. Hattie didn't like how reliant she felt on Lucy's knowing the ins and outs of this assignment, but she reminded herself she was the one tagging along.

Once the driver had loaded their belongings, he set off with his horses. "We'll walk," Lucy announced. "It's not far."

The street and its adjoining sidewalk were paved, which made for easy walking compared to some of the terrain they'd navigated earlier in the day. They rounded a corner, headed toward the domed Capitol. Across the street was the five-story Spotswood Hotel, a blocky brick structure that looked nearly new.

"That's where we'll be staying," Lucy said. "I trust it will suit."

"One can't expect all the comforts of home while traveling," Hattie said, though in truth, the thought of any bed at all was welcome at this point.

"When the war is ended, my brother and I may make a home for ourselves right here in Virginia," Lucy said as the doorman ushered them inside. "Who knows?" she said, and Hattie detected mischief in her eyes. "Perhaps you'll join us. I've seen how Thom fancies you."

Hattie blushed, telling herself Lucy had only said this for the benefit of the doorman, who must be wondering who she was. Lucy must have stayed here with Thom, she realized. No wonder she knew her way around Richmond.

Perhaps Thom was even here now, recuperating at the Spotswood. Hattie's heart quickened at the thought.

In the lobby, she noticed a group of people gathered around notices posted on the wall. As she and Lucy passed by them, she saw they were studying lists of names as she and Anne had done at the Treasury Building. MISSING, WOUNDED, LOST were the headings.

A young red-haired woman ran her finger along the list labeled LOST. Her finger stopped beneath one of the names. Seeing her eyes filled with tears, Hattie looked away. She'd never been good at witnessing another person's grief, perhaps because her mother spent so much time and energy pining over all she'd lost when she'd married Hattie's father and moved north from the Louisiana plantation where she'd grown up.

In contrast to the Spotswood's plain exterior, the hotel's lobby was elegantly furnished with red velvet sofas, gilded tables, and gold-flecked wallpaper that matched the heavy gold drapes adorning the windows. A fire crackled in the marble fireplace, and on the walls hung oil paintings of fox hunts and picnics.

At the front desk, Lucy signed her name in the registry and handed it to Hattie. "All the important people stay here."

Hattie smiled, befitting her role as family friend, even as she silently wondered why they were checking in to a potential viper's nest of Rebel dignitaries and military officials.

She was glad to get out of the public eye, following the bellman upstairs, where he showed them to their room and deposited their luggage. A plain white chenille coverlet topped the double bed, and gold drapes, similar to the ones in the lobby, adorned a single narrow window. The washstand, like the bedstead, was rather plain. Indeed, the room had none of the fancy fabrics and carvings that Hattie's mother had used to decorate her large, ostentatious home—an attempt, Hattie supposed, to replicate the furnishings of the Louisiana plantation she'd so dearly loved.

Following Lucy's lead, Hattie unpacked the two spare outfits she'd brought along with her toiletries. Lucy's trunk contained enough for the both of them, Hattie thought, with her several outfits nearly filling the room's narrow closet.

With that chore complete, Lucy suggested they proceed to the dining room. Though the hour was early, Hattie felt as if she could have fallen directly to sleep without supper. But her task was to accompany Lucy, and accompany her she would.

They descended a wide staircase to the hotel's restaurant, where the maître d' seated them at a corner table. Lucy tugged off her gloves as they studied the menus. The fare was nothing to rival the offering Hattie had enjoyed with Thom at the Willard, evidence that the Federals' starvation strategy must be having some effect. The only meats listed were roasted chicken and turkey, and as Hattie noticed on the plates of nearby diners, the portions were tiny.

"Three dollars for a cup of coffee," she remarked to Lucy.

Lucy shook her head. "The same price as chicken."

They both ordered soup, which the waiter delivered with a thin half-slice of bread and no butter. The broth was watery and only lightly seasoned. In it floated a few chopped carrots and a smattering of beans.

As they ate, Lucy chatted about taking Hattie to visit Cousin Belle and Uncle Harry while they were in the city, persons Hattie assumed to be recipients of the letters Lucy had brought from Baltimore. "Perhaps Uncle Harry will tour us around the armaments protecting the city," Lucy said. "I'd quite like that, wouldn't you?"

"Indeed," Hattie said. Out of the corner of her eye, she saw how the man at the next table had perked up at the mention of armaments. "I'm sure they're substantial."

"Brother Thom says they are."

Hattie spooned from her soup. "I do hope your brother is recovering."

Lucy frowned slightly. Had Hattie said the wrong thing? She wished Lucy or Miss Warne had explained more clearly what should and should not be said in public.

"It was only a cold," Lucy said. "Thom will be back to his responsibilities any day now."

The man at the next table, having listened intently to this back-and-forth, now returned to cutting his chicken.

"I'm glad to hear he's on the mend."

"The sight of you will do him good," Lucy said, and as with the remark made in the doorman's presence, this, too, seemed intended for a larger audience than just her. This must be part of the ruse, Hattie thought, that she was a family friend because of her association with Thom. "In fact, I think we should stop by and see him when we've finished eating."

Hattie smiled demurely. So Thom was indeed here at the Spotswood. The thought thrilled her, but knowing better than to act surprised, she continued spooning her soup.

Lucy took an interminably long time with her meal, seeming intent on dropping information that cemented her place as a genuine Secesh. "It is wicked, is it not, the way the Yanks are going at Vicksburg? And the gall of that ape-man they call their president, proclaiming our slaves free when he hasn't the slightest jurisdiction over them.

"What we need is a truce and a peaceful re-entry into the Union," Hattie said, parroting what she'd heard one of the rising Peace Democrats in the north say. She could not bring herself to add the rest of what the man had contended, that the north should forget about the plight of the southern slaves and concern themselves only with the future of the white race.

"Better yet, a full and complete victory for the South," Lucy said.

At last, the meal was finished. Leaving the restaurant, Lucy stopped at the front desk and asked for the number of her brother's room. The clerk scanned the registry and reported that Mr. Welton was in room 307.

The heaviness Hattie had felt in her feet and legs from the long, circuitous route they'd taken to Richmond seemed to disappear as they ascended the stairs. Thom. She would see Thom. She told herself she should not be so excited, that she should presume nothing between them, but his kiss had left an impression that was not so easily erased.

Lucy rapped softly on the door of room 307, then let herself in. A sconce lamp cast long shadows over the room, furnished similarly to the one Hattie and Lucy occupied on the floor below. In the narrow bed lay Thom, propped up on pillows. His face had thinned since Hattie last saw him, and in the lamplight, the creases in his forehead seemed to have deepened. But his smile was as bright and genuine as ever.

"Why, here come my angels of mercy," he said. "I expect I've died and gone to heaven."

Lucy swatted his arm with her gloves. "There will be no talk of dying, brother dear. I've been so worried about you, as has Miss Logan."

His eyes met Hattie's. Returning his gaze, she felt as she had the night he'd kissed her, as if they shared a deep, unspoken connection. "To what do we owe the pleasure of Miss Logan's presence?" he asked.

Hattie hoped the room's privacy allowed for a forthright response. "Miss War—" she began.

Lucy cut her off. "Miss Warner. You remember her, don't you, Thom? She and Mother were childhood friends until the Warners moved from Derbyshire to just outside Richmond. The tobacco business, if I'm not mistaken. Miss Warner is rather frail these days, I'm afraid. She wanted to move north to be with her brother in Washington City."

"I see," Thom said.

Hattie shrank with the blunder of having nearly spoken Miss Warne's name aloud. The walls here must be thinner than she'd thought. She wondered if there was reason to suspect they were being monitored, or whether the precaution was standard. They might have whispered without detection, but she supposed Thom's question, and Lucy's long-winded response, were an intentional means of diffusing suspicions.

"In her condition," Lucy continued, "Miss Warner could scarcely travel alone, and her brother is quite preoccupied these days, with the war and such." Lucy flung a hand in the air as if the details of war were far too trivial to be bothered with, a gesture that served her well, judging from the number of times Hattie had seen her use it that day. "He couldn't break away to fetch her, and of course, I needed to tend to you. So naturally I thought of our dear friend Miss Logan. I wrote her about Miss Warner's predicament, and she kindly offered to accompany her from Richmond to Washington City. I'm quite certain I told you all of this, Thom."

Hattie had to give credit where it was due. Lucy was masterful at making things up.

"You likely did tell me," Thom said. "It's only that my head's been muddled with this grippe."

"Aren't I always saying you need to take better care of yourself?" Lucy scolded. "At any rate, Miss Logan and Miss Warner can travel safely now that the dreadful business at Fredericksburg has passed."

"Dreadful for General Burnside, you mean," Thom said. "Our own boys are quite satisfied with how things turned out at Fredericksburg."

Lucy waved her hand again. "It's dreadful, all of it. Why can't the Yanks just leave us be? Any small thing that needs doing becomes such an *ordeal*. Which reminds me, we've brought your letters for delivery."

Thom smiled, though more weakly than before. "That's kind of you, bringing the letters. You can leave them with me, and I'll—"

"Oh, but you mustn't worry yourself about them, Mr. Welton," Hattie said. "Lucy and I will see them delivered, won't we, Lucy?"

"Of course. We'll have them out in short order and be on our way."

Worry showed on Thom's face. "You mustn't stay in Richmond too long. The city's crawling with pickpockets and thugs. Be prudent about where you go, even in daylight, and most certainly at night. And the doctor tells me smallpox is spreading through the less reputable neighborhoods."

"I trust the doctor's taking good care of you," Lucy said.

"He's let some blood," Thom said. "And prescribed laudanum for the pain." He nodded at a small blue bottle on the bedstand.

"Are you hurting horribly?" Hattie asked, wishing she could hold his hand, smooth his forehead. But that was impossible with Lucy in the room.

He lifted a hand, flexing his swollen fingers into a half-fist, and she saw how this pained him. "Only when I move," he said.

"We'll get you back to Baltimore as soon as you're able to travel," Lucy said.

"I'm eager for that," he said. "There's talk that Burnside's cavalry is on the move. If they cross the Rappahannock, we're all in for it."

"The wicked Yank," Lucy sputtered, playing along.

Thom closed his eyes, clearly exhausted. "It will be good to get home."

Lucy bent to kiss his forehead. "We'll leave you to your rest, Brother."

Hattie did the same, brushing her lips to his warm skin. "Be well," she whispered.

Lucy smiled knowingly, and Hattie wondered if she'd been too forward. She was only playing a family friend, after all. But friendships could deepen, couldn't they? She hoped so.

~ ~ ~

Hattie woke the next morning thinking that even though Thom was still sick, she needed to extract the message from her petticoat and deliver it to him. She hated to burden him with a difficulty of her own making while he was feeling poorly, but she had no way of knowing when the next opportunity would arise, and she felt the importance of the message more deeply now that she was here in Richmond, experiencing firsthand how each element of the Union's strategy—including the limits on food and supplies that her father was circumventing—was necessary to bring a swift end to the war.

She and Lucy rose and began dressing for the day. As Hattie went to put on her petticoat, she lifted its hem, running a finger along the stitching. "It's coming undone," she said. "I don't suppose you've brought needle and thread."

Pulling the laces of her corset, Lucy glanced her way, and Hattie quickly dropped the hem. "I haven't, but the concierge should have some."

After a breakfast of johnnycakes and chicory coffee, Hattie stopped to speak with the concierge while Lucy proceeded to the room. A thin, bespectacled man, he gathered a spool of white thread, a sewing needle, and a small pair of scissors into a red velvet pouch which he presented to Hattie.

She returned to the room with the pouch, and Lucy asked if she wanted to mend the petticoat before they left to make their deliveries. In need of privacy to extract the paper, Hattie said no, it could wait till evening.

Downstairs, Lucy hired a carriage, and they set off through the streets of Richmond, Lucy calling out one address after another to the driver. As they traversed the city, Hattie wondered whether one of the letters in Lucy's satchel might be for L. Blackstone, matching the letter she'd secreted in her petticoat hem.

At each stop, Lucy and Hattie went together to deliver the letters. When the doors were opened, usually by a servant, Lucy would ask to speak to the letter's intended recipient. If that person was out, the letter went back in the satchel.

"Can't risk letting them fall into the wrong hands," Lucy had explained when they began their deliveries. "Richmond is rife with suspicion of spies, and there's no telling what the Rebels would do if they doubted our intentions."

Whenever they were able to complete a delivery, Lucy lingered, chatting with the recipient about Thom's illness and promising to convey wishes for his speedy recovery. Sometimes, the person would drop a bit of information, like the man who mentioned the number of Rebel troops stationed at Fredericksburg and a woman who told Lucy where she bought her black market tea. Hattie made mental notes of these facts, and she assumed Lucy did too.

At one house, an attractive young woman came to the door. When Lucy explained about Thom, the woman said with a lilt that suggested French lineage, "Have you heard Mrs. Greenhow's back?"

Hattie listened even more closely, remembering what the Trents had said about Mrs. Greenhow snooping around their house and her subsequent arrest as a Rebel spy.

"Thank heavens she's secured release from that wretched Old Capitol Prison," Lucy said.

"I hope the Yankees haven't turned her allegiance," the young woman said.

"I wouldn't think so," Lucy said. "She's an ardent supporter of the confederacy."

"Nevertheless, one must be wary," the woman said. "There are those who'll switch sides if they believe they'll profit from it. Tell Thom to be careful about carrying correspondence for her."

"I will," Lucy said. "Good day."

As they strolled down the long walkway toward the carriage, Hattie whispered, "I had no idea Rose Greenhow was back in Richmond."

"Oh, yes," Lucy said. "And I expect she'll be up to her old tricks, though she'll have a hard time sneaking back into Washington now that she's become so notorious. And don't be fooled—that woman we were speaking with is no angel herself."

Hattie raised an eyebrow. "How's that?"

"Her letter was addressed to Mrs. Mason, but that's an alias. I'm told her real name is Augusta Morris. Thom says she showed up in Washington one day claiming she had the Rebels' signal plan and would sell it for ten thousand dollars. When her offer was declined, she started spying for the Rebs. At the time of her arrest, she was apprehended in, shall we say, a compromising position that involved the adjutant general's clerk. She served time in the Old

Capitol Prison too. Thom thinks she and Mrs. Greenhow are part of the same spy ring, though each pretends to detest the other."

Hattie felt a twinge of envy that Thom had shared this information with Lucy. "Don't the Federals realize Rose Greenhow and Augusta Morris, or whatever she calls herself, will go back to spying now that they're out of prison?"

Lucy shrugged. "You'd think so. But men always seem to underestimate a woman's capabilities, don't you think?"

As they traveled from Court End to Midtown to Church Hill, Lucy shared similar tidbits gleaned from Thom. One man who came to the door at a house in Shockoe Bottom wore a patch over his left eye. "He's got a glass eye underneath," Lucy confided after they'd left the house. "When he doesn't want to be recognized, he simply removes the patch, or else he pops out the eye and goes about as a one-eyed man. Thom thinks he's a double agent."

So much Thom had shared with Lucy, Hattie thought, and so little he'd shared with her.

The day dragged on, the carriage rattling beneath as it carried them from house to house. Hattie was eager to return to the hotel so she could get the hidden message out of her petticoat hem and slip it to Thom.

But Lucy seemed intent on delivering every letter in her satchel before nightfall. Did that mean they were leaving in the morning? It was infuriating that Lucy knew all the details of their assignment, parceling them out in bits and pieces to Hattie, who knew next to nothing. It seemed to Hattie a way for Lucy to flaunt her position, and Hattie wasn't going to assist toward that end unless her need to know was truly essential.

By the time they'd delivered the last letter—none had been for L. Blackstone, Hattie noted—darkness was falling. When they arrived back at the Spotswood, the lamplighters were making their rounds. She didn't have to feign fatigue when she pushed aside her plate halfway through supper and told Lucy she was going up to bed.

Engaged in conversation with a widow she'd invited to their table—the sort of befriending Thom claimed was useful—Lucy bid Hattie goodnight. With any luck, the widow would keep her talking long enough for Hattie to complete her errand.

In their room, Hattie took the needle, thread, and scissors from the little velvet bag, then ripped out the stitching in the portion of her petticoat where she'd hidden the letter addressed to L. Blackstone. Excising it, she felt as if a burden was lifted. She slipped the envelope in her bodice, then basted the hem up to hold it in place until she returned to the room and could stitch it properly.

She took the back stairs to the third floor, then went down the hall to the room she remembered and rapped quickly on the door. When there was no answer, she knocked louder. Leaning forward, she pressed her lips to the wood. "Thom? It's me. Are you all right?"

Footsteps plodded toward the door. It opened a crack, then opened wider.

"Why, I'll be a horse's patootie." A stout man stood in the open doorway, gripping the doorknob and swaying a little. Hattie smelled whisky on his breath. "Ain't you a sight for sore eyes. Dunno who you're after, but I'm right glad to see ya."

She recoiled as he reached a hand toward her as if to grab her by the waist. "Sorry," she said. "Wrong room."

She made a fast retreat for the stairwell, seething as the man called after her to come back. Why was it that when men were lewd, women were left feeling they'd been the ones in the wrong? As she descended to the second floor, her anger gave way to disappointment. She'd had the right room, she was certain—307. But Thom had said he'd be going north any day now, recovered or not. Another of Pinkerton's men—there were a handful in Richmond, she knew—must have come for him this morning, travel arrangements in hand.

She told herself it was all for the best. This was no place to be ill, in a lonely room at the Spotswood, especially when the town was awash in suspicion over possible spies. And there were also the rumors of Burnside's advance. She should be glad Thom had gotten out when he had, she told herself, but that didn't quell the ache of not having had a chance to see him before he left or deliver the message she was eager to get rid of.

She was pleased, at least, that she got back to the room before Lucy. Hoping the widow was still jabbering away, Hattie sat at the table, took the folded paper from her bodice. Grabbing the scissors, she was about to undo her basting and resew the hem with the message inside when she heard the rattling of a key in the lock.

Clutching the folded paper, Hattie thrust her hand in her lap, concealing the message as best she could in the folds of her skirt as Lucy came in. She paused a moment, looking Hattie up and down. "I thought you'd be in bed. You said you were tired."

The folded paper might as well have been a lead weight in Hattie's hand. "I was just getting ready to undress when I remembered I should fix my petticoat."

Lucy cocked her head. "Took your time with it, did you?"

Hattie breathed deep, hoping agitation didn't show in her face. Casually, she "I stopped in the washroom. And then I sat here a bit, thinking about what you might have in store for us tomorrow."

Lucy smiled, seeming pleased at this tacit admission that she was in charge. "We've done what we came here to do." She turned and sat at the edge of the bed, leaning forward to unfasten her boots. "Tomorrow we go north."

Relieved, Hattie took advantage of her turned back to pop the loose stitches in her hem and slide the paper back in its hiding place. When Lucy rose to tuck her boots beneath the bed's edge, Hattie reached purposefully for the needle and thread.

"I learned quite a lot today," Hattie said, threading the needle. "As we went from house to house."

Lucy's eyes sparkled. "I'm glad of it."

"Will your brother accompany us?" Hattie said, feigning indifference as she began to stitch.

"Brother Thom went north this morning."

Hattie felt the weight of her gaze, assessing her reaction. Along with disappointment, she did her best to look surprised. "I hope he's well enough to make the journey."

"He's a strong man of much fortitude," Lucy said smugly. "I'm sure he'll be fine."

Hattie knotted the thread and snipped off the tail. She patted the repaired hem, hoping Lucy didn't notice the large, hasty stitches. "There," she said. "That's better. Now I'd best get this needle and thread back to the concierge before we turn in."

Lucy began unbuttoning her dress. "You needn't bother," she said. "We'll be off before sunrise, and you can return it then with the key. Your time now is better spent packing your things, then getting some rest. There's no telling what sorts of obstacles we may encounter on our way north."

Much as Hattie wanted to rid herself of the last of the evidence, she relented, not wishing to rouse Lucy's suspicions. She took one of her two dresses from the closet and folded it into her travel bag. Then She undressed, folding her simple frock into her traveling bag. She hung her petticoat in the armoire beside the blue and gold morning dress she intended to wear tomorrow.

As Hattie climbed into bed, Lucy was still fretting over which of her own frocks to wear tomorrow and which to pack in her trunk. Sometimes, Hattie thought, having fewer clothes was a blessing. Exhausted, she closed her eyes and fell into a sleep that lasted straight through to morning.

She woke to Lucy rocking her shoulder. "Rise and shine," Lucy said, chipper as a sparrow in springtime. "The train leaves in an hour."

Lucy went to fetch the bellman as Hattie rose, still groggy with sleep. She retrieved her clothes from the closet and layered them on, stockings, corset, camisole, petticoat. She put on her traveling dress and fastened the bodice buttons, then sat at the edge of her bed to button her boots. Reflexively, she felt in her petticoat's hem for the folded paper containing the message that implicated her father, as she'd done every morning since stashing it there.

But the letter was gone.

Chapter Twelve

JANUARY 6, 1863

The day after Hattie's return to Washington, a hard rain set in. Falling in sheets against her room's single window, oozing through the caulking and dripping to the floor, the deluge mirrored her spirits. The missing message changed everything. She should never have bothered with decoding it in the first place. She should have left that to the experts and prayed no one connected her with the traitorous Logans of Indiana. Neither should she have let down her guard with Lucy who, judging from the neat stitching that now attached her petticoat's hem, had pilfered the paper while Hattie was sleeping.

Now Hattie could do nothing but pace her tiny attic room as she waited for the inevitable summons from Miss Warne. She should have confronted Lucy on their journey back to Washington. But at the time, the shock of her betrayal had only begun to set in, and Hattie's main thought was that she didn't want to give Lucy the satisfaction of acknowledging she'd been bested. Better to let her think she hadn't yet discovered the missing paper, Hattie decided. So she wouldn't be forced to converse with Lucy, she'd feigned a headache, and soon enough, her excuse became a reality.

Three restless days passed before the skies finally cleared. That's when the summons came, delivered by a messenger boy.

Miss Warne wanted Hattie to report to her at two o'clock that afternoon. The address given was one Hattie didn't recognize, on Capitol Hill.

After being cooped up in the boardinghouse, it felt good to get out and walk. Cool and brisk, the air smelled fresh. Water ran in gullies along the boardwalk, and frost glistened in the grass. Hattie stepped carefully, avoiding patches of ice that had frozen last night. But despite the clear skies, a sinking feeling plagued Hattie. Her days in Washington were surely numbered. She had no real skills, no way to support herself other than what she'd learned with Pinkerton's. She'd be forced to leave, and she had nowhere to go.

Hattie was surprised at how much affection she'd developed for Washington City during the months she'd spent there. Even with the continual threat of the Rebels closing in, the city hummed with activity that heightened her sense that whatever she'd been doing—even the mundane work of the mailroom—was making a difference for the Union.

The address Miss Warne had given led Hattie to a small, nondescript frame house in a modest neighborhood. With Pinkerton's retreat from the War Department, Miss Warne had mentioned that the agency's operations in Washington would be coordinated out of another facility, but Hattie hadn't expected that to be a house.

Hattie approached the front door and used the knocker to wrap on it twice. She expected a hireling to come to the door, but to her surprise, Miss Warne herself answered the knock. As usual, she was plainly clothed in a gray morning dress, her hair pulled tightly back from her face.

"Do come in," she said. Her cool tone was Miss Warne's usual way of speaking, Hattie reminded herself, but still it increased her feeling that nothing about this meeting boded well.

She followed Miss Warne to a sparsely furnished parlor. At Miss Warne's bidding, she seated herself on a red horsehair sofa. Miss Warne closed the door, then sat in a blue wing-backed chair across from the sofa. "How was Richmond?" she asked.

Hattie swallowed hard. "I believe we accomplished all we set out to."

"I trust Lucy was a satisfactory guide."

"She seemed well-versed in the route and the tasks at hand," Hattie said, matching Miss Warne's cool tone.

Miss Warne's gaze was intense, and it was all Hattie could manage not to look away. "Lucy has her flaws, as do we all," she said.

"Yes, ma'am," Hattie said. It would do her no good, she knew, to unleash the mental list she kept of those flaws.

"Yet Lucy has proven up to most of the tasks we've assigned. And when necessary, she takes initiative. That's an admirable quality, wouldn't you say, Miss Logan?"

Hattie nodded, though she had a strong sense of where this was going. From her dress pocket, Miss Warne extracted a square of paper. She unfolded it, smoothing it on her lap. Hattie glanced at the columns of code, the words "Logan" and "Indiana" seeming more prominent than ever.

"I trust this looks familiar," Miss Warne said.

Hattie had rehearsed in her head all the ways she might explain herself. She could insist she had no allegiance to her father, only a desire that his treasonous activities not reflect poorly on her. This was entirely true, but she greatly doubted Miss Warne would believe her. Families stuck together, supported one another. Most families, anyhow.

She'd also thought of telling Miss Warne she'd had every intention of delivering the message to Thom so he could pass it along as he saw fit. This also was true. But it would also raise questions about why Hattie trusted Thom Welton over Miss Warne.

Having no viable defense, Hattie stood. "I'm sorry, Miss Warne. Perhaps I'm not cut out for spy work."

Before her supervisor could respond, Hattie left the parlor, let herself out the front door, and walked briskly away without looking back. Reaching the corner, she turned toward the Capitol. Her pace slowed, tears welling in her eyes.

So many poor choices she'd made, destroying her best hopes for venturing out on her own. She'd been wrong to keep the message, wrong to think she could escape association with parents who cared more about wealth and prestige than preserving the Union and acknowledging the horrors of slavery.

And much as she wanted to blame Lucy for her current predicament, she had to admit she'd likely have done the same if their positions had been reversed. Spy work required a wariness even of one's closest associates. Recognizing this, Hattie realized that what she'd taken as affection from Thom Welton might only have been his attempt to get close enough to Hattie to determine whether she, with her aptitude for decoding and desire to do more than open letters, posed a threat to the agency and the Union.

With a gloved hand, she wiped the tear that had trickled down her cheek. She knew only one thing for certain—she could not return to her parents' home in Indiana. She could not endure her mother's belittling, her father's treasonous grain deals, or their mutual disdain for enslaved people.

But there was still her brother, George, assuming she could find him. Still, the hope that they could cobble together some sort of life for themselves after the war. But even if she had some assurance he was really in Canada, she had no means of getting herself from here to there. She scarcely had enough money saved to cover the next month's rent at the boardinghouse.

She needed work. But what skills did she have? Snooping at letters and some amateur decoding. That might have been enough to get her a position with the National Detective Police, her best hope of getting to George, but after meeting Lafayette Baker, she had little interest in being under his thumb, even if she could convince him to put a woman other than a prostitute or barmaid on his payroll.

What she needed was some sort of employment that would allow her to work her way north without having to worry about paying room and board. On the sidewalk, she passed an amputee hobbling along on crutches. There was nursing, she thought. The thought of it hadn't been pleasant when she'd gone with Anne to visit Henry at the Patent Office Hospital, but her circumstances were different now.

She veered east, backtracking toward the Patent Office. As on her previous approach to the facility, army carts filled the nearby streets. Inside the building, there was more activity than when she and Anne had visited, entering after hours. The cries of wounded men pierced her as they had when she'd been there before. As she passed one soldier, he reached for her hand. She stopped, allowing him to hold it as she smoothed his blonde locks from his forehead, which was hot to the touch, murmuring comfort as he called out in feverish delirium for his mother.

Hoping she'd provided the man at least a few moments' comfort, she let go of his hand and continued along the rows of beds, passing alcove after alcove as she searched for someone in charge.

"Hattie!" a woman called out. "Is that you?"

She turned in the direction of the voice and saw Julia Trent kneeling beside a man propped in a corner near the door.

Hattie hurried toward her, then stopped short when she saw that the man was unconscious, his head covered in blood. The smell of it, metallic and sickly sweet, made her woozy, and she fought an urge to dash outside and gulp fresh air.

Julia dipped a rag in a basin of water red with blood. "Saber cut to the temple," she said, pressing the rag to the wound. "The surgeon needs it washed before he can dress it. Do me a favor, will you, and get some clean water for the kitchen." She nodded toward the door.

Hattie complied, lifting the basin and holding it away from herself as she maneuvered toward the door. Though she tried to hold the basin steady, she felt her hands quiver. She'd never liked the sight of blood, and she'd never seen so much of it all at once. Queasiness roiled her stomach as blood-red water sloshed from the basin over her boots. By the time she reached the kitchen, she felt she might be sick. She thrust the basin at a man in a white uniform.

"Fresh water," she managed to say, then clamped her lips as bile rose in her throat.

The man looked at her curiously but took the basin and replenished the water. Bracing herself, Hattie returned to Julia. *Look at her, not at him,* she told herself.

Fortunately, a pair of orderlies arrived at the same time Hattie did. Julia rinsed the rag, turning the water an ugly shade of pink, and pressed it to the man's temple a final time before the orderlies loaded him onto a stretcher and hauled him off.

Julie stood, leaving pink streaks as she wiped her hands on her apron, and greeted Hattie. "Fancy seeing you here." With the back of her hand, she brushed a loose strand of hair from her forehead, which Hattie saw was perspiring. "Mama has been wondering why we haven't seen you at the house."

Mrs. Trent had made Hattie promise that she would pay them regular visits until Anne's return. But with the mail room's closing, Anne's return was less likely than ever, and besides, Hattie felt that Mrs. Trent's urging had been more from pity than anything else.

"I've been away. And Mr. Pinkerton has rearranged operations. I'm now without work." She would leave Julia to make her own assumptions about cause and effect. "I thought...I understand nurses are paid forty cents a day, plus room and board. And if I could be attached to a regiment, I might eventually be able to connect with my brother. Only..." Her voice trailed off.

Seeming to sense her distress, Julia steered her away from the blood-soaked floor and into the open section of the room, where the air, while not exactly fresh, was at least not heavy with the smell of blood. "You're too pretty to be a nurse," she said. "Miss Dix prefers plain-looking women over thirty."

"But you're young and pretty," Hattie said.

Julia laughed. "Thank you. After some days here, I feel as old and ugly as time itself. At any rate, I'm only a volunteer, so Miss Dix's standards don't apply to me."

Of course, Hattie thought. Julia had a loving family. She had no need to support herself in order to stay away from them. "You're doing good work here. I had no idea it could be so hard."

"It can be brutal." Julia blew back another errant curl. "I'll be glad when this war's over."

"As will I. Give my best to your mother," Hattie said. "And to all your family."

She turned to leave, but Julia trotted after her. "Wait, Hattie. I've just thought of something. That night at the theatre, you said how there was no place you'd rather be. And you said how you'd once played Hamlet."

"In a school production," Hattie said. "No money in that."

"Yes, but only last night, Papa said over dinner how Mr. Grover is in an awful fix. You know Grover's Theatre, don't you?"

Hattie nodded. "On Pennsylvania Avenue. You said the Lincolns have a box there."

"That's right. As I think I told you, Papa is a good friend of Leonard Grover. His box office manager slipped on the ice right after Christmas. She hurt her hip and won't be able to return to work for weeks. He's desperate for someone to fill in."

"I don't know that I'm qualified. I know nothing about running a box office."

"It's only taking tickets and counting up the nightly receipts, Papa said. It's just that the person has to be trustworthy. Papa can vouch for you on that."

Only because he doesn't know what happened with Pinkerton's, Hattie thought. "That would be kind of him, but—"

"No objections." Julia spoke as her mother often did, with assurance of a fait accompli, as she shooed Hattie toward the exit. "Go see him. Now. He's a good man, and you'll be doing him a favor."

Hattie said she'd consider it. Clearly, she wasn't cut out for nursing, at least not the sort she'd have to do here. As she left the Patent Office Hospital, she fairly gulped in the fresh air. It wouldn't hurt, she supposed, to speak with Mr. Grover. At the very least, a few weeks' work would buy her time to consider what to do next. And maybe—she hesitated to entertain the possibility—maybe she could acquaint herself with a traveling troupe of actors. She'd never heard of a female stagehand, but she might show herself worthy of handling costumes or helping with props. Acting troupes must cross over into Canada now, and if she got lucky, she might be able to track down George.

She hugged her arms to her chest, warming herself against a sudden wind blowing along the avenue. She turned down E Street, her toes prickled by cold that infiltrated her boots, and hurried toward the stately wooden structure that housed the theatre. The front doors were latched, but she went around to the back alley and found a door propped open. A slender lad, likely a stagehand, was wrestling a large armchair inside. A prop, she suspected, being carried in for the evening performance.

She waited until the stagehand cleared the door with the chair, then she slipped inside. Backstage it was dark, and she felt her way along the curtain, away from where a single spotlight lit the stage. She heard the sounds of furniture being dragged across the floor, a stagehand yelling to mind the tablecloth.

Her feet reached the stairs that led down the side of the stage. Staying close to the wall, she went softly but swiftly up the aisle toward the front of the theatre, hoping the stagehands were too preoccupied to notice her. Though the auditorium was dark, she felt the thrill that always came when she entered a theatre, the anticipation of being transported to a realm where anything was possible.

Cracking one of the exit doors only a little, she stepped into the lobby, where she blinked back light streaming in from the windows. Overhead, wide-eyed cherubs perched atop fluffy clouds on the high ceiling's painted frescoes.

A door along one side of the lobby was open. Thinking this must be the office, she approached. Behind a desk sat a round-faced, silver-haired man, engrossed in a tally of figures.

She rapped on the door, and he startled. "Good God," he said. "I thought you were a ghost."

"Mr. Grover?" she asked.

He pushed aside the ledger. "That's me."

"Julia Trent suggested I speak with you. She says you're in need of temporary help at the box office." She hesitated to say "manager," not wanting to oversell her capabilities.

He leaned back in his chair, hands locked behind his head. "That," he said, "would be an understatement. If there's a way to make last night's receipts balance, I surely can't see it. What sort of experience do you have?"

"None directly. But—"

"This is a large operation, Miss...what was your name?"

"Logan. Hattie Logan. I understand that, sir. But I've been told I'm a quick study," she said, though this assurance had only gotten her so far with Miss Warne. "And I'm familiar with the workings of the theatre." This last was an exaggeration, to be sure.

Mr. Grover leaned forward, rubbing his chin. "You say you're a friend of Julia's?"

"Yes. The judge will vouch for my trustworthiness. And my father owns a business." *An untoward* one, she thought, but a business nonetheless. "He insisted I learn to keep accounts." Which she'd hated, but the circumstances had been different. She nodded at the ledger. "May I?"

He pushed it across the desk. "Be my guest."

She scanned the columns. Ledger work was a lot like ciphering. Look for patterns, then look for aberrations. "There," she said, pointing at an entry midway down the page. "I believe you've transposed those two numbers."

He pulled the ledger back and studied the entry. "By Jove, I have." He looked her up and down. "It would only be a month or two until my manager gets back. And I'm afraid there are better-paying jobs out there."

She smiled. "The arrangement sounds perfect. Thank you, Mr. Grover."

He rose from his chair, brushing his hands together as if to fully distance himself from the distasteful work of tallying numbers. He set a hand on her shoulder. "Welcome to Grover's," he said. "Your duties begin tonight."

Chapter Thirteen

JANUARY 25, 1863

G rover's New National Theatre proved a busy place indeed. Before the holidays, when Hattie had gone to the theatre with Julia, Anne, and Henry, Ford's auditorium had been only two-thirds full. Another casualty of war, Hattie had thought at the time, with the numbers of those wishing to escape their troubles for the duration of a three-act show insufficient to offset those who could not bring themselves to indulge in such frivolity while battles raged all around.

But only weeks after that performance, fire had swept through Ford's Theatre, gutting the interior. Mr. Ford was raising money to rebuild what he promised would be the grandest theatre the city had ever known. In the meantime, the town's theatre goers were flocking to Grover's. Tallying the box office proceeds each night, Hattie saw that Ford's misfortune was Grover's good luck.

As the days went by, Mr. Grover made clear that he was pleased with Hattie's efforts, and she in turn enjoyed the evenings she spent at the theatre. More than ever, it proved a wonderful place to forget. At the theatre, no one cared where you'd been raised or where your family's allegiances lay. Patrons came to lose themselves in another time, another place, another story for which the past had been neatly constructed to produce a satisfactory outcome.

Toward the month's end, the rains returned with a vengeance, thwarting General Burnside's plan to close in on Lee's flank north of Richmond. Torrents turned Virginia roads to muddy swamps where, if the reports coming into Washington could be believed, men sank to their knees and mules to their ears. After two days of his men slogging through the muck, the general called off the march. This failure on top of his demoralizing defeat at Fredericksburg in December was enough to doom the whiskered general. President Lincoln accepted his resignation, making yet another change at the top of his ranks.

But the foul weather did little to dampen Hattie's spirits now that she had a diversion. Slipping in to watch what remained of the shows after the box office closed, she could forget her troubles for a spell. When a show stayed more than a day or two, she amused herself by picking a part and memorizing the lines, whispering them under her breath as she watched. Alone in her attic room, she'd repeat them, acting out a slice of the drama with no audience. She especially envied the actors in the traveling companies, their performance new in every location, and no one caring how they'd played it before.

An actor's life might suit her, she thought, and so she went out of her way to be friendly with the star companies passing through town. Some of the actors were haughty and self-absorbed, but others seemed happy for an association, however fleeting, with anyone other than the same ones they traveled with.

Especially satisfying was the rapport Hattie was developing with the actress Alice Gray, currently playing opposite John S. Clarke in *Our American Cousin*, a farcical tale of a boorish American's quest to retrieve an inheritance from his pompous British relations. When the cast first arrived from Baltimore, Alice had complained of a sore throat. One of Grover's stock company actresses had offered to fill in, but she'd bungled the lines during rehearsal, and so Alice had felt compelled to go on herself. Before the performance, Hattie had fetched horehound drops from the apothecary and brewed her a tea of lemon and honey.

Opening night went off without a hitch, with Alice and her co-stars returning in a curtain call to an ovation. Afterward, Alice had summoned Hattie backstage. Seated before her dressing room mirror, she'd thanked her profusely. "My throat doesn't feel half as bad as it did. I don't know what I'd have done without your assistance. Imagine if that bumbling woman had opened tonight. Why, we'd have been run out of town."

"She did seem ill-suited," Hattie said, reluctant to speak poorly of a woman Mr. Grover had selected for his stock company cast.

Undoing a hairpin, Alice studied Hattie's reflection in the mirror, her eyes a piercing shade of blue. "You've got a pretty face, Miss Logan. Earnest. And I'll bet you're whip-smart. You should be with the stock company, not stuck in the box office."

Hattie was about to refute this praise, then remembered Anne's chiding her for that habit. When a person pays you a compliment, you shouldn't feel compelled to argue the point, Anne always reminded her. It's an insult to their judgment.

So instead, Hattie told Alice, "That's kind of you to say. I've done a bit of acting, and I'd love to do more. It's just that I'm not sure how to get started."

Unpinned, Alice's hair fell to her shoulders, a mass of curls. "There's no one way. You just start."

Hattie leaned against the doorframe. "Is that how it went for you?"

Alice shook her curls, a youthful gesture, though now that Hattie saw her up close, she guessed her to be at least ten years older than she was. "I got my start by necessity," Alice said. "Living with my family outside of Buffalo, in New York. Father was a laborer, working on the Canal project. Poor people from Ireland, my folks were. He died in an accident when I was fifteen. My mother took it hard. I could scarcely get her to leave her bed. My brother was only ten. It fell to me to support them. Not much a girl could do, then or now. I didn't figure factory work paid enough to support the three of us." With a rueful smile, she shrugged. "So I waltzed into the grandest theatre in Buffalo, the Metropolitan. Whoever ran it must have had money, I thought, and so I went right up to the first person I saw and declared myself ready for work."

"That's true pluck," Hattie said.

Alice laughed. "Or stupidity. Either way, the manager gave me a shot. I couldn't read or write a lick back then, mind you. It's a struggle for me even now. I had no choice but to rely on my memory. I could hear a set of lines once and repeat them back perfectly. Still can."

"That's impressive," Hattie said. "And you must get to travel to the most wonderful places."

Alice smiled, running a brush through her hair. "Depends on what you call wonderful. And I had to prove myself with the stock company first. Got my break playing alongside Edwin Booth. "The Wonder of the Age," that was the show. We played to a packed house every night. After Booth moved on with his company, I got my first benefit performance."

"Your own show," Hattie said.

"That's right." Alice set down the brush and, taking up a cloth, began wiping stage makeup from her face. "I played the Indian maiden Pocahontas, a role I still perform now and again. I was well-enough received. I kept at it until the Buffalo crowd turned on me." She shook her head, and Hattie saw the sadness in her eyes. "I don't suppose I'll ever know why. There were some jealousies, I guess, at my having risen from such impoverished circumstances. And audiences can be fickle. At any rate, I soon tired of the hisses and boos, though I never gave them the satisfaction of knowing it. I simply quit."

Hattie understood completely. "Is that when you joined the star company?" she asked, using the theatrical parlance for a traveling troupe.

"Not directly. I bounced around a bit. New York, Charleston, Cleveland. In Baltimore, I first performed with John," she said, referencing Mr. Clarke. "He was a childhood friend of Edwin Booth, married to Booth's youngest sister. I'd impressed Mr. Booth, performing with him, and he put in a good word for me.

I've been starring back and forth with the two of them ever since, John Clarke for the comic roles and Edwin Booth for the tragic."

"You're quite versatile, Miss Gray," Hattie said.

"Please, call me Alice. And now, if I may presume on you for one more kindness, I'd be forever grateful if you brewed up another pot of that tea for me before I retire to the hotel."

Hattie happily complied, brewing tea and fetching medicinals that night and in the nights that followed until Alice had fully recovered. As the show's run neared its end, Alice began seeking Hattie out simply for the companionship, saying how tired she sometimes got of the women in the star company. Hattie gleaned much from their conversation. With each encounter, her newfound ambition of acting took deeper hold.

Forthcoming as Alice had been about her past, she never questioned where Hattie had come from or what she was doing in Washington. Actors came from all sorts of backgrounds, she pointed out one day. All that mattered was how they could reshape themselves on the stage—and sometimes, Alice said without going into specifics, a troubled past could even be helpful.

Hattie was especially encouraged to learn that Alice had spent last summer and fall acting in Montreal. The management at the Theatre Royal liked to import American talent during the summer, she said, which provided her with a paycheck between seasons.

By the final night of *Our American Cousin*, Hattie had worked up the nerve to ask Alice if she might put in a good word for her with her troupe's manager. That resolve became even more firm when Mr. Grover told her that same afternoon that his usual box office manager had fully recovered from her fall, and Hattie's services would no longer be needed.

Hattie had known this day was coming, but that didn't make facing it any easier. As she waited for the final show to begin, she listened to the rattle of carriages down Pennsylvania Avenue, the drivers pulling up one by one alongside the curb that fronted Grover's and couples emerging from the coaches in happy procession. Bustled in silk, the ladies clutched the arms of their escorts as they stepped gingerly into the February slush, snowflakes pelting their velvet cloaks and splotching their satin gloves.

Cheeks pink with cold, Hattie watched a young woman clutch her gentleman's forearm as they entered the theatre. Laughing, the woman stomped snow from her buttoned boots. For a moment, Hattie thought the woman might be Julia, and she suffered a pang of guilt at never having gone to the Trents to thank her and the judge for recommending her to Mr. Grover. Before leaving Washington, she'd do that, she told herself, though where she'd be leaving for, she had no idea.

From her weeks at Grover's, she recognized some in the crowd. There was the stout doctor whose coat buttons looked ready to pop, attending with his wife, who fluttered her fan with such enthusiasm that it seemed she might take flight. There was the one-legged soldier in Union blue, his chair wheeled by a woman who cooed at him as if he were a child in a buggy. And there were the two white-haired sisters who came every Friday, clutching one another by the wrists.

Behind the sisters came a tall man, hairline receding. At his side was Kate Warne. Hattie averted her eyes, making change as the man purchased their tickets.

"Good evening, Hattie." Miss Warne's expression was clipped and her expression unreadable.

"Good evening, Miss Warne," she said, focusing on the man's face as she handed him the coins. "Enjoy the show."

They moved on, and the line snaked forward. Hattie let go of the breath she hadn't realized she was holding. She might have expected Miss Warne, having seen her at Ford's when *The Marble Heart* was playing. Did Miss Warne enjoy the theatre, she wondered, or did attending simply aid in her many guises? Did she have any real affection for the man at her side, or was he another of her assignments, making the social rounds in Washington as she feigned Secesh sympathies?

In the lobby, the hum of voices swelled with happy anticipation. Soon the lights dimmed, signaling that the curtain would rise on the play. Between admitting stragglers, Hattie began working her tallies and figures. Twice she made errors and had to begin anew. It had been bad enough, knowing this was her last night at Grover's. Now seeing Miss Warne had rattled her too.

It seemed to take forever for intermission, when Hattie could lock up the box office and find a spot in the balcony to watch the remainder of the show. Some nights, she had to stand, but thankfully, tonight she found an aisle seat in the top row.

As with every play she'd watched here, she'd learned the first half of the plot from rehearsals. Alice played the part of Florence, a charming British aristocrat whose family learns that their wealthy great uncle has disinherited them in favor of a colorful and slightly uncouth American cousin, Asa, played by John Clarke. Rounding out the plot was a devious agent of the estate who has his eyes on Florence, who in turn falls in love with a Royal Navy officer. There were several laugh lines, including a scene in which Asa, not understanding the intricacies of the British bath, douses himself in the shower with his clothes on, eliciting roars of laughter from the audience.

Despite all the blunders, everything worked out in the end, as was the way with comedies. Alice's character got to marry the Navy man while John's got to marry the humble heiress, and the wily estate manager got caught in his misdeeds. Fully recovered from her throat ailment, Alice was spot-on tonight, registering what Hattie judged to be her finest performance of the run.

When the lights came up, Hattie stood and applauded as loudly as the rest, calling the cast back on stage for another round of recognition. These endings, a return to reality, always felt bittersweet. But now was not the time for Hattie to indulge her feelings. If she was going to solicit Alice's advice—maybe even her help—concerning how to get on with a theatrical company, she needed to do it now.

She followed the crowd downstairs as the balcony emptied, then walked the aisle to the proscenium, where a set of steps led backstage. She ducked behind a curtain, headed for Alice's dressing room, when a man stepped from the shadows.

He flashed a smile. "Looking for someone?"

She recognized him at once. Handsome and slender, he was Alice's beau, Edwin Booth's brother John Booth, the same man Hattie had seen last month in the starring role of *The Marble Heart*. Alice had mentioned he'd be coming from Baltimore for the final performance, intending to travel with the company to Philadelphia.

"I was hoping to have a word with Miss Gray," Hattie said.

Booth stepped closer, and she smelled whisky on his breath.- "Alice is changing. Perhaps I can be of help?"

"I don't think so." Despite his good looks, there was a hardness about him that made her wary.

He pressed closer still. "You must be the box office girl. Alice speaks highly of you. She believes you have a future in the theatre."

"That's..." He had her back to the wall, and she felt like a rabbit frozen in the shadow of a hawk. "That's quite kind of her."

"I trust she speaks highly of me as well."

Oddly, Alice hadn't mentioned John Booth until yesterday, but Hattie wasn't about to tell him that. She wanted out from under his gaze, out from the press of his presence.

"She speaks highly of the Booths." Chatter seemed the easiest way to ease the tension that felt tight as a wire between them. "She's told me how your father was a renowned stage actor, and how playing alongside your brother Edwin advanced her career. And she said how your sister's married to John Clarke, who—"

"A comedian!" In the dim light, John Booth's eyes seemed to glitter. "As if the world needs another of those. A true actor performs tragedy, don't you think, Miss...Sorry, I didn't catch your name."

"Logan." She said this less forcefully than she'd meant to. "Hattie Logan."

He stepped toward her, his face directly in front of hers. A handsome face, to be sure, and fine-featured, but there was an air of anger about him, similar to what she'd sensed when she'd seen him onstage.

He pressed one hand to the wall, pinning her in place. "A pleasure to meet you, Miss Logan," he said with what she supposed he intended as charm.

She was not of a mind to be seduced tonight, especially not by Alice's beau. But she could not think how to get away from him. In this backstage corner, no one was likely to spot them. And the Booths were an important family in theatrical circles. If she screamed or pushed him away or otherwise drew attention, he could unmake whatever slim chance she had at a future in the theatre.

"Mr. Booth." She struggled to keep her voice even. "Please."

He leaned closer still. "Such a pretty little filly you are."

Her fear shifted to anger. "I am not—" she began.

At the sound of footsteps crossing on the wooden floor, Booth backed away.

"Miss Logan! Miss Logan!" A figure stepped into the light, revealing a familiar face. "Is that you? I do hope you haven't been avoiding me." Hattie had never heard Miss Warne sound so agitated. "The seats you sold my companion and me were wholly unsatisfactory. I demand a refund."

It took a few seconds for this appeal's purpose to register. "I apologize, ma'am. If you'll come with me to the box office, I'll see what I can do."

Booth offered a lopsided grin, then gave a slight bow. "I'll leave you to your work, Miss Logan."

As he stepped toward Alice's dressing room, Hattie hurried toward the stairs, Miss Warne following at an even clip. Hattie had dealt with several cantankerous patrons during her weeks in the box office, but never had she been so grateful for a complaint.

When they reached the box office, Hattie ushered Miss Warne inside. The quarters were cramped, and there was only one chair, so they both remained standing. Still rattled from Booth's advances, she breathed deep, willing her voice not to betray her fear. Depending on how much of the encounter Miss Warne had witnessed, there was a good chance her opinion of Hattie had sunk lower than ever, the general assumption being that a gentleman only made such advances when a lady invited them.

Hattie opened the desk drawer, reaching for the cash box. "I'm truly sorry for your unsatisfactory experience this evening, Miss Warne. Of course, the management will issue a full refund."

"The seats were fine," Miss Warne said brusquely.

"But why did you—"

"Intercept you? I wanted a word with you this evening. I saw you go backstage, and when you didn't emerge in a timely fashion, I decided to follow. Behind the curtain, I noted that man's proximity. An actor, isn't he?"

Hattie nodded. "John Booth," she said quietly. "I'd gone backstage to speak with Alice Gray. She played Florence onstage."

"And played it well," Miss Warne said.

"Mr. Booth intercepted me. He's Alice's beau. I had no interest in his advances, but I couldn't see how to stop him."

"That was evident from your expression," Miss Warne said. "Which is why I intervened as I did."

The full impact of what the Pinkerton operative had done began to sink in. "Thank you," Hattie said quietly.

Miss Warne waved away her appreciation. "As I said, I hoped to have a word with you. That is if you'll promise to hear me out this time."

Hattie flushed. "I didn't mean to be rude the last time we spoke. It was only that I was..." Her voice trailed off. She'd felt so many conflicting things that day. Anger at Lucy's betrayal. Heartbreak because her future with Pinkerton's was over.

But that was in the past. What mattered now was admitting she'd been at fault. She straightened, squaring her shoulders as she looked directly into Miss Warne's gray eyes. "I was ashamed. I should never have withheld that letter. It was just that I feared you and Mr. Pinkerton would lose faith in me once you learned of my background." Now that she'd begun, Hattie's words tumbled out in a rush. "Sorry to say, my father's traitorous activity surprised me not in the least. He values profit above all, and my mother's loyalties have always been firmly with the South. That's why I was so keen to leave home and do some good for the Union cause."

"You wanted to redeem yourself of your past," Miss Warne said.

"I suppose so. I wanted to erase where I'd come from and focus on making a difference. Working at Pinkerton's was just what I needed. Then I came upon that message, and I felt it all unraveling. I sewed the message in my petticoat until I could figure out what to do, and then in Richmond, Lucy discovered it."

"You might have explained your predicament to her," Miss Warne said.

Explain to Lucy? Hattie couldn't imagine that. "None of this would have happened if I'd just passed along the message from the start. I hope the delay in my turning it over hasn't done any lasting damage."

Miss Warne offered a faint smile. "No, not lasting. We've had our eye on Blackstone, the intended recipient of that message, for some time. We believe he's working several schemes to benefit the South while at times feigning loyalty to the Union."

"A double agent."

"Yes. So our approach to him must be delicate. That's where you come in. Because of your father's involvement, you're uniquely positioned to earn Mr. Blackstone's trust. I expect you could glean some useful information from him. But that would require you returning to Richmond."

"You'd trust me after I withheld the message?"

"You made a poor choice," she said. "But your motivation is understandable. Most of us have things in our background we'd change if we could. You're becoming your own person now, Hattie, forging your own destiny. You've erred, and you'll err again. But I don't doubt your loyalty. What I don't know is whether what I've said is enough to persuade you to take on this assignment.

Given what we know of Blackstone, there's more than the usual risk. Still, any information you gather would be quite useful. And I believe your work at the theatre is ending, so it seems there's a window of opportunity for us both."

Hattie smiled. "You have an uncanny aptitude for knowing such details."

Miss Warne's lips turned at the edges. "It's my business to know things. If you're willing, I suggest you pack up your things tonight. You might be several days in Richmond. I'll send a carriage for you in the morning."

"I'm willing," Hattie said without hesitation. Acting could wait. This was a chance to get back in Miss Warne's good graces and do the sort of spy work she'd dreamed of.

"Good." Miss Warne set her hand on Hattie's shoulder, a tentative and unexpected show of affection. "Be ready in the morning. Instructions will follow from there."

Chapter Fourteen

JANUARY 26, 1863

T he next morning, Hattie woke to the sun rising beyond her attic window, the day breaking in slashes of pink and orange. In her excitement, she'd hardly slept, and yet she felt invigorated. She'd been given another chance, and she intended to make good on it.

Truth be told, her sleeplessness was also from worry. From what Miss Warne had said, the stakes of her assignment were high, as were the risks. Who was L. Blackstone, she wondered, and how had he become involved in a scheme that included her father? How did their venture operate, and what could be done to stop it? Her future might hinge on the answers. So might the Union's.

There was no sense speculating. She'd find out soon enough.

The carriage pulled up in front of Mrs. Sullivan's boarding house shortly past seven. Carrying her travel bag, Hattie hurried down the stairs. The smell of scones and chicory coffee drifted from the kitchen as she let herself out the side door, hoping to avert any probing questions from Mrs. Sullivan about the family emergency she'd feigned.

Young, red-headed, and freckled, the driver was a different man from the one who'd taken her and Lucy to the river last month. The carriage was smaller and less elegant than what they'd ridden in then, making Hattie think that Mr. Pinkerton's contract arrangement with the government must not be as financially lucrative as when he'd worked directly under General McClellan.

The driver was friendly, smiling and wishing her good day as he stashed her bag. He opened the carriage door and offered a hand to help her up the steps, which she gladly accepted, as the steps were rickety.

Ducking inside, she saw to her surprise that she was not alone. From the longer bench, Thom Welton tipped his hat at her, smiling warmly.

"The day is young, and already it has brightened considerably," he said.

Her joy at seeing him was so great she could scarcely speak. In the flurry of preparations, she'd given little thought to whether anyone would be joining her in Richmond. If anything, she'd expected Lucy, a prospect that promised its own set of challenges.

"You're looking much better than when we last met, Mr. Welton."

The driver shut the carriage door, and she started for the bench facing Thom. "And how much better I'd look with you beside me," he said. "I'm told my profile does the best for my meager looks."

He scooted to one side, and she settled in next to him. The carriage wheels began to roll, jostling her toward him, and she thrilled at his proximity.

With a light brush of his fingers, he touched her cheek. "I've missed you something terrible," he said, his voice husky.

She leaned toward him, not thrown by the carriage but purposely, and he drew her into a kiss.

"And I've missed that," she said when their lips parted.

As the carriage picked up speed, she looked him over more carefully. His color was better than when she'd last seen him, but his face was gaunt, and his shoulders, while still strong and solid, seemed to have shrunk a bit. "Are you truly well now?" she asked.

He shrugged. "Mostly. I thought I'd bested those Secesh women by intercepting that packet of letters when I carried them through the water. But I'll admit there have been moments during this affliction when I've felt as if they were the ones who bested me. Last I heard, though, the doctors think I've turned the corner."

She hoped they were right. His flushed face concerned her, as did his eyes, which though open and sincere seemed dull, too, as if he were suppressing some pain.

"You didn't need to come along," she said, happy as she was to see him. "I could have traveled to Richmond alone."

"Leave my new bride? Not a chance."

She stared at him. "Bride?"

"Miss Warne didn't tell you?"

Hattie shook her head. "She was scant on details."

He laughed. "That's our Kate." He reached in his pocket and pulled out a thin gold band. "It took some convincing, but I won her and Mr. Pinkerton over. You are, after all, a family friend," he said. "Or so you played with Lucy. Family friends do marry, and as I pointed out, your southern connections will prove useful to an old spy who seems of late to be under more suspicion than usual."

She pulled back, mocking affront. "Why Mr. Welton, are you suggesting a marriage of convenience rather than love?"

He pulled her toward him, and they kissed again. "It's love," he whispered in her ear. "No matter what we feign, nothing could be truer."

She blinked back tears, moved by this declaration. "Oh, Thom," she said. But she couldn't go on, afraid she might cry with happiness.

He took her hand and slid the ring over her finger. "Not the way I intended to propose to the woman of my dreams. But we are all cart before the horse these days, aren't we? So this will have to do until our work is behind us."

The band felt light on her finger, and for a moment she thought she might be dreaming the whole scene. Then a carriage wheel struck a rut, and the jolt of it was enough to assure her that this was indeed real, every bit of it, Thom and his declaration of love and the marriage they would feign in Richmond.

She felt suddenly conscious of the driver, recalling how she and Lucy had maintained their assigned roles throughout their journey to Richmond, lest someone overhear. "Is it safe to speak so frankly?" she asked, her voice low. "With the driver so close?"

"As safe as such words ever are between a man and woman," he said. "As for the driver, he's on Pinkerton's payroll, so you may be assured of his discretion. After we reach the river, we'll have to assume our roles. So now is the time to lay clear our plans. I assume Miss Warne, reticent though she has been, conveyed the crux of the assignment."

"Only that I'm to see what I can learn from a smuggler and double agent." She felt color rising in her cheeks. "You know about the message Lucy took from me?"

He nodded. "Lucy's judgment...let's just say it isn't always the best."

"In this case, neither was mine," Hattie said, holding his gaze. "I panicked when I saw my surname and Indiana. Once I decoded it, I knew for certain that my father was involved in smuggling grain to aid the South. I figured if Miss Warne and Mr. Pinkerton found out, they'd let me go."

"They'd have understood if you explained."

She nodded. "I know that now. And I didn't intend to keep the message forever. I meant to entrust it to you. In fact, I went to your room the night before we left Richmond, but you were already gone."

He set his hand over hers, and she reveled in its warmth. "Well, it has all worked out for the best, hasn't it? I've gotten myself a fair young bride without so much as lifting a finger, and between the two of us, we'll have a good chance at gaining the information we need from Blackstone."

"You'll be helping me?"

"Of course. From what I understand, he's not the sort you'd want to handle on your own." Seeing her frown, he added. "Not as your first assignment, anyhow. And you can help with the other half of our work, which is to gather information on a Rebel spy network operating near Vicksburg."

"But I only packed for a short trip."

He laughed, and for the first time, Hattie allowed herself to relish the sound of it. "We shan't be traveling to Vicksburg. But there are certain influential persons in Richmond we suspect of complicating matters for our troops there."

"Might Blackstone be one of them?"

"What makes you think that?"

"His connection with my family. My grandfather's plantation is near Vicksburg. He's my mother's father, but my own father might be a link between him and Blackstone. The way my grandfather and his overseer treated the Negroes there is seared in my memory from summers I was forced to spend there when I was young. Children separated from their mothers and husbands from their wives. Whippings for the slightest infractions." She shuddered. "And other things I'd rather not mention."

Thom rubbed his jaw at the spot where his beard ended. "Taking Vicksburg would give the Union control of the Mississippi River. That would be the primary route for the operations mentioned in the message you intercepted."

"So my father—and Blackstone—would do everything they can to maintain Confederate control."

"Exactly. Our troops are having a hell of a time there. General Grant tried approaching Vicksburg from the north, but the Rebs blew up the railroad behind him and destroyed his supply depot, forcing him to retreat to the swamps without any means of getting supplies. To make matters worse, every plan they make seems to get leaked to the enemy. Is there any chance someone from your grandfather's plantation would pretend Union sympathies and embed himself with Grant's troops?"

"It's possible," she said. "I doubt there's much my grandfather wouldn't do in order to keep his Negroes."

"What about the Knights of the Golden Circle? Ever heard your father or grandfather mention them?"

"I don't know about Grandfather, but I remember my father and mother discussing a group by that name being organized in their county. I got the idea my father was involved, but that was nearly two years ago, and I was barely speaking to them, intent as I was on leaving home. I shudder to think what they're up to."

"Your shuddering is warranted. The Knights of the Golden Circle formed nearly a decade ago with the aim of extending the reach of slavery in this country. One of their schemes was to overrun Mexico and get it admitted as a slave-holding territory. They're well-funded, and they're not afraid to use force to achieve their goals. Some of them were likely involved in the plot to kill Mr. Lincoln last year."

Hattie raised an eyebrow. "The plot Miss Warne helped uncover and thwart."

He nodded. "I played a small role as well, but she made all the arrangements and helped carry it out, escorting Lincoln under the ruse that he was her ailing brother. We have some indication that Mr. Blackstone was among the self-proclaimed Knights intending harm to the president."

"And yet he's been able to convince some that he favors the Union?"

"We suspect he reports to Lafayette Baker now and again. But we can't be certain, and Mr. Pinkerton and Colonel Baker aren't exactly friendly, so we've no way of knowing for sure."

As Hattie pondered this, the carriage rolled to a stop at the wharf district. Taking her hand, Thom helped her from the carriage. The day was gray and windy, and rain pelted her bonnet as they queued up to board the packet steamer. Worried about Thom's rheumatism, she hoped they wouldn't be left standing for too long in the weather.

"Was it the steam packet that capsized on Christmas?" she asked, eyeing the choppy water.

He brushed a damp strand of hair from her cheek. "No. The steam packet's much more stable. We were crossing upriver from here, in a pole boat."

"I wish you hadn't taken that risk," she said.

"Ah, but risk is our business, Mrs. Welton."

Her breath caught, hearing him call her this. *It's only for the assignment,* she reminded herself. He'd seemed sincere, professing his love. But he hardly knew her, and she was not so naïve as to think a man in his position, however kind he might seem, would not want to take advantage of her role. Miss Warne would have arranged everything to be proper, she knew. Separate rooms, separate beds. That was what Hattie should have wanted, too, but she wasn't sure she did.

Thom took her hand, and they boarded the packet steamer like the newlyweds they pretended to be. They sat on a bench, protected from the weather. As the boat moved away from the shore, Thom rested his head on her shoulder and closed his eyes. She brushed his cheek with the back of her hand. His skin felt warmer than it should have. She hoped he wasn't pushing himself too hard, making this trip.

At her touch, his lips turned in a brief smile, and then he dozed off. Hattie looked down at the gold band encircling her finger, marveling at the turn of events. For all her envy of Lucy, she was headed to Richmond with Thom, in a role far more intimate than what Lucy had played, and she now had an opportunity to prove herself every bit as capable, if not more, in spy work. Thom had every confidence in her, and she intended to do all she could to make good on his trust, and Miss Warne's too.

As on Hattie's previous trip with Lucy, the steam packet docked at Aquia Creek Landing. Getting off, she saw that the place was still awash in Union blue, though the level of activity there seemed less frantic than before. The Army of the Potomac was regrouping, Thom explained in terms neutral enough not to arouse suspicions, with the attentions of both sides now focused mainly on Vicksburg.

When they boarded the Richmond, Fredericksburg, and Potomac line, Hattie noticed more civilians traveling than before too. She'd dozed through most of the rail journey with Lucy, but now she felt wide awake. Surrounded by passengers of various loyalties, she and Thom improvised chatter befitting a newlywed couple. Under the pretext of telling her about places they might settle when the war ended, Thom spoke of Virginia towns he'd visited before—Manassas, Winchester, Warrenton, Fredericksburg—and she smiled, thinking how of all the people who might overhear their conversation, she was the only one who had an inkling of the true purpose of Thom's travels. In turn, Hattie talked mostly of her brother George and the collections of bugs, beetles, and butterflies he'd kept when he was young.

When the train pulled into Falmouth, Thom handed Hattie her travel pass. Reading *Mrs. Thomas Welton, Baltimore,* she felt another wave of pleasure.

"What shall I say if I'm asked how I like Baltimore?" she whispered.

"Admit you've yet to set foot in your new home but look forward to doing so once your honeymoon has ended," he said.

She cocked her head at him. "You've strange notions of how one celebrates marital bliss, Mr. Welton."

"Perhaps I do, Mrs. Welton. But you're stuck with me now."

The tent city south of Falmouth was as Hattie remembered, the battle lines unchanged from when she'd passed through before. Thom said that while Federal forces here had regrouped under another change in command, all eyes were now on Grant's attempts to take Vicksburg. Indeed, the Federal soldiers milling about on the north side of the Falmouth border seemed restless.

Hattie and Thom approached a tent flanked by two gray-uniformed sentries, they readied their travel passes for review. They were ushered inside, where a broad-shouldered Confederate officer sporting a massive beard recognized Thom from his courier work.

Thom introduced Hattie as his new bride, and the officer slapped his back, grinning. "I'd offer a celebratory cigar," he said. "But last I heard, the nearest cigar was six hundred miles west of here."

Thom thanked him for the sentiment, and he and Hattie passed through the checkpoint without question.

"You seem to make friends wherever you go," Hattie said. "I don't know how I'll ever keep track of them."

"You needn't try," Thom said. "I forget half of them myself. The names, that is. Not the faces, though. When it comes down to it, it's the faces that matter."

The cart that bore them to Fredericksburg was no chariot, but the driver seemed a shade more reputable than the one Lucy had chosen, and there was not a trace of hay or manure within. Thom chatted amiably with the driver about the troops stationed nearby. Not much action now that Burnside had called off his disastrous mud march, the driver said. He supposed some big battle was in the works, but he withheld speculation on where it might be.

When they left the cart to board the train outside Fredericksburg, Hattie asked if Thom planned to look in on his friend Mr. Ruth, the trainmaster, whom she'd met when she came through with Lucy.

"Not today," Thom said. "From what I hear, he's been busy," he added, eyes twinkling.

Busy creating bottlenecks and delays to confound the Rebels, Hattie knew. She wondered how long Mr. Ruth could keep up such activities.

As if reading her thoughts, Thom dipped his head to whisper in her ear. "I'm told General Lee has appealed to Jeff Davis to have Mr. Ruth replaced. But Davis isn't having it. He says Mr. Ruth has his full confidence."

That was what they need if they were to succeed with Mr. Blackstone, Hattie thought as they boarded the train—his full confidence. Because of her father, her presence should go a long way toward gaining it.

As she settled in for the ride to Richmond, Hattie noted only a few Rebel soldiers in their car. But she felt the other passengers had an air of suspicion about them, perhaps from being so close to the enemy line. Thom must have sensed this, too, for he chatted optimistically about the Rebels' prospects and the rosy future of the South once the war ended.

"The Yanks are growing weary of war," he told her. "They can't get past Fredericksburg. And in the west, they're stuck outside Vicksburg. Mark my words—there will be an armistice before the year's end."

Overhearing this, the elderly man in the seat in front of them turned. "There's also a good deal more sympathy for our cause in the North than the Yanks like to let on. The Peace Democrats know this is an illegal war. If that sham of a president continues to ignore their grievances, he'll have another secession on his hands."

Hattie seized the chance to practice her role. "Why, you mean more states would join our cause?" she said, drawing out her vowels in the manner of her Louisiana relations.

The man harumphed, then stood, turning to face them. "This is New England's war. I have it on good authority that folks in places like Indiana and Tennessee are none too pleased that their commerce with the South has been interrupted."

"I've got relations in Indiana," Hattie said.

"A little town—what's its name, darling?" Thom said.

"La Conner," she said. It felt odd to speak aloud the name of a town she'd tried to forget. "I don't suppose folks there are happy with the turns this conflict has taken."

The man reached in his pocket and extracted a small stack of what appeared to be tickets, printed on paper the color of goldenrod. He fanned them out, then held them at arm's length for Thom and Hattie to inspect. "Headed to the Old Northwest myself next week. Then to Pennsylvania. We're distributing these to friends of the cause, so when our brave boys march through the North, they'll know which civilians are friendly."

Thom leaned forward, squinting. "I don't have my spectacles. What do they say?"

"KGC," the man said. "Perhaps you've heard of our society?"

"Ah, the Knights of the Golden Circle," Thom said. "Bickley's group, isn't it?"

"The very same." The man restacked the tickets and returned them to his pocket. "You've got a well-informed husband, missy. I suggest you inform your Indiana relations that Mr. Bickley's Knights are amassing support throughout the state. Why, from what I hear, Mr. Bickley himself is heading to Indiana soon." The man lowered his voice. "Scout work," he said, using the military's term for spying. "That's what I hear."

"Imagine that!" Hattie grasped Thom's arm. "Dearest, my relations would be ever so grateful if we sent them one of those tickets, so they can prove their loyalty when the time comes, as it surely will. Perhaps they'd even be able to meet Mr. Bickley when he comes through the state."

The man raised a finger to his lips. "You heard none of that from me."

Thom reached for his wallet. "How much for a ticket?"

"Dollar apiece," the man said.

"We'll take two," Thom said, extracting two Confederate dollars. "One for your father and one for your mother," he said to Hattie.

The transaction complete, the man sat down again. Thom set a hand on Hattie's arm, then leaned in and whispered in her ear, "You've got a knack for this."

She smiled, pleased at how she'd engaged the man, adding details at Thom's prompting. The tickets would become part of their report to Mr. Pinkerton and Miss Warne, as would the information about Mr. Bickley's scouting—and where he was headed next.

As on her previous visit, the sky was growing dark by the time the train reached Richmond, the city's smokestacks staggered like black cannons pointed heavenward. Thom had closed his eyes again, resting during the final part of the journey. His skin now seemed to have an ashen cast that worried Hattie, but she told herself it was only the gray light.

Thom woke as they passed the warehouse which, as she recalled from her last visit, had been converted into a prison housing Union soldiers and traitors to the Southern cause. He pressed his large hands to his face, lifting and circling them over his cheeks. "Sorry," he said. "I've not been the best of company."

His voice was only weary from sleep, she told herself. "I can't think of better," she said.

He raised an eyebrow. "Meaning you prefer me silent?"

She swatted his arm playfully. "Meaning I prefer your company, asleep or awake."

They chugged past the Confederate Capitol building, its grounds nearly vacant in the waning light. The train slowed to a stop at the station, and as they got off, the elderly man who'd sold Thom the golden tickets tipped his hat at them. "You newlyweds do my heart good. A pleasant evening to you."

When he was out of earshot, Hattie said, "I don't recall telling that man we were newlyweds."

"People hear more than you think. Especially when they're eavesdropping."

She tucked this thought away, understanding it to be a simple yet significant principle for the work she was undertaking. As they left the station, she carried herself with the same grace she'd practiced the last time she was in Richmond, her head held high and her gaze directed ever so slightly above passersby as if they weren't quite worthy of her interest.

Leaning close, Thom whispered, "It seems you attract attention, Mrs. Welton."

"I surely don't mean to," she said, feigning affront.

Drizzle fell from clouds made almost imperceptible by night, and Hattie saw that Thom's gait stiffened.

"Your joints pain you," she said.

"A little," he admitted.

"Then we should hire a carriage," she said.

He waved off her concern. "The hotel's just around the corner," he said.

She straightened her bonnet, grateful for the cover against the rain, and pulled her cloak tight, slowing her gait to match his. The block and a half to the Spotswood Hotel seemed longer than she remembered, anxious as she was to get Thom inside, where he'd be warm and dry.

When they finally got there, the Spotswood's doorman greeted Thom by name. "Evening, Mr. Welton," he said, tipping his hat.

"Eddie, allow me to introduce my new bride, Hattie Welton," Thom said.

The bellman beamed with what seemed genuine delight. "Congratulations to the both of you," he said.

As before, lists of wounded and missing soldiers were posted on a wall in the hotel's lobby, though of course the names would be all new now. Even without active fighting in Virginia, there'd been the skirmishes around Vicksburg that Thom had alluded to, and there were always losses from disease and, increasingly, desertion.

A blaze burned brightly in the marble fireplace, doing much to dispel the gloom and damp. Thom removed his hat, shaking off the rain that had gathered along its brim. Had she been in another setting, Hattie would have removed her bonnet, too, ladylike graces be damned, but she knew that any behaviors that would have incurred her mother's wrath were inadvisable in the role she was presently playing.

In the lamplight's glow, Thom's pallor seemed to have lessened, his face more relaxed as he bantered amicably with the hotel's clerk, who procured a room on the third floor. But as they mounted the stairs, Hattie saw how Thom gripped the handrail, fairly dragging himself up. When they'd gotten to their rooms and he'd sent the bellman off with his tip, Thom fell onto the bed in the larger of the two rooms, not bothering to draw back the covers.

She sat beside him and felt his forehead. "You're feverish."

His eyes, though weary, looked at her with the sincerity that she'd always admired in him. "This was not what I'd had in mind when I dreamed of bedding you."

She flushed in spite of herself. Whatever Miss Warne's intentions, his were clearly of another sort. The attraction she felt for him was stronger than any she'd felt for any man. Would it be so wrong to set propriety aside and lie with a man who was her husband in name only?

In his present condition, though, there was no question of acting on their affections. "There will be time for bedding," she said. "Our journey has taken a toll on your health. Let's get you out of your wet clothes so you can rest."

Pulling away from the intensity of his gaze, she went to the foot of the bed and began undoing his boots, sensing that he lacked the energy to perform even this simple task on his own.

His eyelids closed, then fluttered open. "Have I mentioned you're a remarkable woman?"

Smiling down at him, she tugged off one boot and then the other. "Perhaps."

She removed his socks. It felt strangely intimate, holding his bare feet in her hands. She probed his ankles. "Your joints are swollen," she said.

"Is that what it is?" he said. "I thought I'd grown a pair of leg irons."

She helped him off with his shirt and trousers. She'd never seen any man so near nakedness, and she was surprised at the depth of her desire. She longed to run her fingers over the bare skin of his chest, to feel the muscles that rippled in his arms, to trace her hands along his torso to his nether parts.

He must have sensed her longing, for he pulled her close and, trailing his hand through her curls, drew her into a kiss that stirred an even deeper desire.

"Enough of that," she murmured, pulling reluctantly from his embrace. "You need to save your strength."

He gripped her wrist. "What strength I have, I'd as soon give you as hang onto."

She peeled back his fingers. "All in due time, my dear husband. For now, let's get you under these covers. You've got goosebumps."

"All your fault," he muttered as she nudged him to one side and drew back the coverlet and sheet.

"There you be," she said when he'd gotten between the sheets and she'd drawn the covers over him. "Now rest."

He looked at her, and she felt as if she'd melt in his gaze. "I'd sleep better holding you."

She pressed a hand to his cheek. Far too warm, she thought. "You seem rather adept in the ways of seduction, Mr. Welton. It makes me curious about the women you've bedded before. Perhaps I shall use my burgeoning skills in investigation to explore that question."

He smiled weakly. "At your peril, Mrs. Welton."

He closed his eyes, and she took her hand from his cheek. As she started to turn from the bed, he opened his eyes again, as if startled back to awareness. "I'm sorry...if I've assumed too much. I could have gotten a second room. That's what Miss Warne intended."

"We mustn't raise questions about our marital bliss," Hattie said. "I may be new to this enterprise, but even I know that's not the sort of attention we should be drawing right now."

Seeming satisfied, he closed his eyes again, and soon she heard him drawing the deep breaths that came with sleep.

The gas lamp hissing, she unpacked her bag and hung up her clothes, then did the same with his. Another sight she'd not have anticipated, her dresses hanging side by side with Thom Welton's suitcoats and trousers, and yet he'd helped her fall so easily into her role that she nearly had to remind herself that they were not truly married. How scandalized Miss Whitcomb would be to know her former pupil was sharing a hotel room with a man to whom she was neither wedded nor betrothed, a man who traded in secrets.

~ ~ ~

Hattie told herself that after a day or two of rest, Thom would be well enough for them to carry out the tasks they had come for—and to make good on the pleasures he'd promised, which she dwelt on far more than she should have, especially at night, when she climbed into bed beside him, with only her thin chemise separating her skin from his.

But Thom did not recover so quickly. Three days passed, then five, and his condition improved little. From the apothecary,

Hattie fetched camphor, which she rubbed on his chest, filling the room with a pungent turpentine smell. It brought some comfort, he said, for the pains that gripped him there, the simple act of breathing causing him to wince. To ease the pain in his swollen joints, she rubbed on a chloroform liniment, though its sickly sweet smell nearly gagged her. Every four hours, she mixed bicarbonate of soda in a glass of water and coaxed him to drink, another remedy the apothecary recommended, though it did little good.

She wanted to fetch a doctor, but Thom was wary. Rebel doctors, like rebel postmasters, were not to be trusted, he said. Members of both professions were known to be part of the Secret Lines, a network of Rebel safe houses, way stations, and spies seeking to unmask their Federal counterparts. Better to steer clear of them all, he said.

Hattie kept at her efforts to make him as comfortable as possible, and he in turn assured her of his confidence that this bad spell would pass. Her mood alternated between worry and restlessness. She mended seams in two of Thom's shirts, remarking that Lucy must not be too adept with a needle. To her consternation, he defended Lucy, saying that considering her privileged upbringing, she'd shown herself to be a good enough sport about the tasks she'd been assigned, and she'd performed them well enough, even if she'd made a few rather large blunders.

In what she recognized as an ungenerous interest, she asked him to expound on Lucy's mistakes, but he would only say that the harm done had been minimal. She chose not to press the point, in part because of her guilt over mishandling the coded message, and in part because she did not wish to argue with Thom, especially in his current condition.

She thought of Alice Gray, wishing she'd had a chance to say a proper goodbye before leaving Washington. She wondered how the company was doing and whether they'd moved on yet from Philadelphia. She hoped Alice would see her way to severing relations with John Booth. She deserved better than a womanizer like him, Hattie thought. But between Edwin Booth and Asia Booth's husband John Clarke, Alice's life was entangled with the Booth family, and Hattie thought she might have a hard time breaking free from John's attentions.

She thought, too, of Anne, who'd been a faithful correspondent, writing of Henry's progress now that he was back with his family and relaying news of Lieutenant Franklin Stone, the man who'd joined them for Christmas Eve dinner with the Trents. He's received his long-awaited furlough and had made a point of visiting Anne on his way to his family's home in Vincennes. His injury was giving him more trouble than he'd expected, Anne wrote, and while he was anxious to return to battle, she was happy when his leave was extended, especially when he tired of Vincennes and came to Indianapolis, where Anne's parents offered him a room. Anne was not one to get carried away with feelings, but her affections for the lieutenant seemed clear. Hattie had been less impressed with him the night they'd met—he'd seemed a smooth talker, and she'd gotten the feeling he was trying to play her against Anne—but she trusted Anne's judgment.

And of course Hattie thought of her brother, George, though now her thoughts turned less to how they might share a household after the war and more to how she hoped he'd like Thom when the two of them finally met. When Thom was awake and inclined to talk, she asked what he knew about Rebel operations in Canada. The Secret Lines, he told her, extended over the border, messages being passed from Virginia to Maryland to the District of Columbia and then on to Delaware, Pennsylvania, New York, and Canada. Beyond that, he wasn't entirely sure of what sort of scouting either side was doing there, though he'd heard there were many Confederates in Niagara Falls and Montreal, and no small number of Union scouts too.

When she and Thom spoke of such things, they did so quietly. The walls had ears, Thom said, a sobering reminder that part of the reason she'd been brought to Richmond was that Thom's credibility was growing thin in some Secesh circles. Too many trips south, too many messages intercepted, too much curiosity about Rebel troops and their movements—all of this was bound to catch up with him at some point, he said. If he was to continue his work with Pinkertons, with her at his side, she suggested he might want an assignment away from the Richmond corridor. In fact, Canada might be the perfect place for him to put his talents to use without the degree of risk he'd acquired here, she said. He seemed open to the possibility.

But first, he was determined to complete the work Mr. Pinkerton had assigned here in Richmond. Restless as Hattie felt in their present circumstances, he seemed ten times so. On their seventh day in Richmond, she returned from the apothecary to find him out of bed, dressed in trousers and a shirt, which he was struggling to button.

"You've got no business going out," she scolded.

He grinned sheepishly, like a boy caught out of school. "If I lie about any longer, I fear I'll revert to some primitive creature that lacks legs and backbone." Swaying a little, he held one arm to the wall, steadying himself. "A tadpole, maybe."

She brushed his cheek with a kiss. "I'd fancy you just the same. But right now, you look a fright."

He bent his knees, though she could see it pained him, ducking to gaze at his image in the armoire. He frowned at the reflection there, his face haggard, his hair edged up on one side from how he'd slept on it.

"Nothing a little spit and polish won't fix," he said, straightening. "We've got business to attend to, Hattie."

"Let me handle it," she said. "I've seen how it's done. I went with Lucy, delivering letters."

Plunking down on the bed, he raked a hand through his hair. "I don't fault Lucy, but she's not the most apt teacher."

This admission gave her some satisfaction, following on his earlier endorsement of Lucy. "But you said yourself, back on the train, that I've a knack for this work. Have I done something to make you change your mind?"

"Not at all. It's only that..." He lay back on the pillow. His face relaxed, and she realized how much it must have pained him, trying to dress himself.

She sat beside him and took his hand. "I know I've none of your experience. But I pay attention. I can act a part. I can cipher things out."

He shook his head slowly, and she thought it must ache. "This isn't the same, Hattie. You have to be able to turn on a dime with whatever comes at you."

She smoothed his forehead, creased with worry. "The sooner we finish the courier work, the sooner we can get you home. That is, when you're strong enough to travel. Let me help."

He closed his eyes a moment, and she hoped he was thinking as she was, of the bliss home might bring with the two of them together.

He squeezed her hand, his grip feeble compared to what she'd known. "Only the letters," he said, his voice scarcely more than a whisper. "No Blackstone. I'll handle him."

"Only the letters." She leaned to kiss his forehead, then sat holding his hand until sleep claimed him, which it soon did.

She took a stack of letters from his satchel. Not too many, she told herself. She didn't want to leave him for long in case his condition took a turn for the worse. She stashed the letters in her handbag, then slipped out the door and went downstairs, where she asked the doorman, Eddie, to summon a carriage.

"How's Mr. Welton doing today?" he asked, same as he did every time she went out.

"Gaining strength," she said, the same as she always did.

Eddie shook his head. "Not the honeymoon he'd have wanted for you."

Hattie smiled. "I reckon not. But I'm sure he'll make it up to me once he's well."

The carriage arrived, and Eddie helped her into it. She gave the addresses to the driver one at a time, as Lucy had. He seemed unfazed by the task of driving from neighborhood to neighborhood, so she assumed this was not his first encounter with courier work. Between Court End and Midtown, she attempted five deliveries and succeeded with four, the other being a residence from which the recipient had moved. At each stop, she introduced herself as Thom's new bride and explained the nature of his illness. There was much concern over his condition, some of which extended beyond the selfish interest of shuttling correspondence to what she perceived as genuine interest.

From each person, she tried to glean what she hoped would be useful information. The owner of an optical shop reported gleefully that he'd heard the whole Yankee army was leaving Aquia Creek, bound for Washington. Furloughs, he said, were being issued in great profusion to quiet discontent among the Yankee ranks. This she ascribed to mere rumor, but she made a mental note of it anyhow.

At an elegant Midtown house, a woman who alluded to her husband being a diplomat for Jeff Davis hinted that his French counterpart was trying to arrange a peace conference on neutral ground. This, too, Hattie tucked away in her memory, pleased that her approach was such that these people trusted her with the same sort of information they'd have shared with Thom. Her accent and manners, quite consciously like her mother's, though without the sharp tone and edge of superiority, had surely helped.

Over bowls of soup delivered to their room that evening, she quietly shared the information she'd gleaned with Thom, beaming when he praised her efforts. He finished nearly half a bowl of soup, which encouraged her too. After setting the dishes outside the door, she sat at the small round writing table and began to jot notes of today's efforts.

She thought Thom had dozed off, but he lifted his head from the pillow and looked at her. "What are you writing?"

"A few words to remind me of what I was told today."

His eyes widened. "You must never commit such things to paper, Hattie. Not until you're safely back in Washington."

"Oh." She set down her pen. "But I'm sure Lucy—"

"As I said, Lucy has made some substantive errors. Why do you think you're here instead of her?"

She went to him, the paper clutched in her hand, and kissed his forehead. "Because you couldn't bear being apart from me."

He lay back on his pillow. "There's truth in that, to be sure. Now burn those notes."

She wadded the paper, then tossed it into the fire, watching as the flames curled its edges, then consumed it completely. When she turned back to Thom, she saw he was sleeping. She sat back at the table and took up the pen again, along with another sheet of hotel stationery. She dated the page, then stared at the expanse of white as she listened to the fire's crackling. Warmth from the hearth crept over her, and she felt the old resentment of the home where she'd been raised being sumptuous yet cold in spirit.

She had a chance now at making a real home, one of warmth and comfort, for herself and Thom. But she knew he would never settle into such a life until they'd completed the work at hand. Toward that end, she was certain he'd approve of what she was about to commit to paper. Otherwise, a crucial part of this trip's purpose, discerning what they could of L. Blackstone, could be undone in an instant.

Father and Mother, she began. She could not bring herself to write the word "dear," for though they'd felt dear to her as a young child, her mother's bent toward cruelty and her father's indifference had erased that sentiment as she'd grown.

Miss Whitcomb has doubtless informed you that I departed Ladygrace some months ago. I have met a fine man and we have married. We are now in Virginia, my husband's sympathies lying decidedly with the South, but we shall soon be traveling to Baltimore, where I intend to post this letter.

If you've had word of George, I should like to know of it, so I might share these tidings with him.

Convention dictated that she should inquire about their health, express concerns over their wellbeing. But while she didn't wish them ill, she found it hard to wish them well, so she simply signed her name, *Hattie.*

In the flickering light, she folded the letter, slipped it into an envelope, and addressed it to the home she'd worked to forget. She had time between now and when she sent the letter to figure out what address to give them in case they sent word of George, though the main point of her writing, of course, was that if she told Mr. Blackstone she and Thom had wed, her parents needed to be able to confirm this.

Without sealing the envelope, she slipped it in the bottom of her bag, pleases that she'd thought of the need to write her parents on her own, without Thom's prompting. She was fully capable of doing this work. She only needed the opportunity to prove it.

~ ~ ~

When she woke the next morning, she reached for Thom. He stirred, and as she ran her fingers along the hollow of his throat, she felt that a rash had formed there. Upon rising, she examined it more closely, noting the pink rings and clear centers. His forehead felt feverish, as it had on the first day he'd taken to bed, and when he pulled her into a brief kiss, his breath was warmer than it should have been.

She didn't want to leave him, but he urged her to go, and she could hardly refuse, having been the one who'd begged for the chance to do his courier's work. But she took fewer letters this time, and she stopped at the apothecary on the way back to the hotel, asking for something to quell a rash. The druggist sold her a pink powder of calamine, instructing her to mix it with water and smooth it over the rash. As he had on her previous visits to the shop, he asked how her husband was faring, and when she told of the latest developments, he frowned and asked if she'd thought to call a physician.

"I want to," she said. "But you know how men can be. He believes he'll recover on his own."

The apothecary shook his head. "I hope he's right."

When Hattie returned to the room, she mixed the calamine and applied it over the rash on Thom's neck and chest. Though he admitted it itched something furious, he maintained he felt no worse for it.

In hushed tones, she brought up again the idea of bringing in a doctor. "I'd be careful," she said. "Make sure there's nothing lying about to arouse suspicions."

"Suspicions may be aroused already," he said darkly. "A Rebel doctor may pepper you with questions."

"I can manage for myself under any sort of questioning," she said.

"You don't know that. You haven't been in that situation."

"Then I'll deliver the rest of the letters tomorrow so we can go north, where we can trust the doctors. We're long overdue. Mr. Pinkerton and Miss Warne must be worried."

His face clouded. "We can't leave till I've gone to Blackstone," he whispered. "There's too much at stake. Lying here, I keep thinking about our poor soldiers dying in the swamps around Vicksburg. With what you've said about your family's connections there, Blackstone's connections may well provide the information General Grant needs.."

She set down the lotion she'd mixed and twined her fingers with his. "Then I'll go to Blackstone," she said.

"No, Hattie," he said, straining to make his point without raising his voice.

She pressed a finger to his lips. "I'll be careful, I promise."

He gripped her hand. "It's not that I don't think you're capable. It's just that you're inexperienced, and the risk is too great, especially if it's true about Blackstone working both sides."

"But you said I'm the key to getting at him because of his connection to my father. He'll only trust you because you're with me. So I'm the one who needs to convince him."

"You mustn't go alone. The risk is too great."

It was clear she couldn't change his mind, so she let the matter drop. But she saw the worry in his eyes, and she knew that in part it was because their more important work here remained undone.

The next morning, she rose early. Thom's rash had spread to his stomach and onto his back, so she mixed some more calamine and applied it to those places too. His fever seemed to have lessened, but he was terribly fatigued. As soon as he fell back asleep, she took the last of the letters from the satchel and crept from the room.

As she waited for the carriage, she saw that the weather had finally turned. All that remained of the low bank of clouds that had dumped rain for days were a few wisps on the distant horizon. The air felt crisp, though the black discharge from Richmond's smokestacks overpowered the fresh smell that would otherwise have followed the rain.

When the carriage came for her, she did not even look at the letters in her purse. Instead, she gave the driver the address she'd long ago committed to memory, the place to which the message implicating her father had been addressed.

As the driver set off across the city, she thought of the man she hoped to meet. She imagined him a businessman like her father, a twitch of impatience in his eyes, his gaze wandering away before she'd uttered so much as a sentence. He would speak brusquely, dismissively even, as if he had far more important things to do than waste away the day in idle chatter. But if the talk turned to Lincoln or the Emancipation, he'd find ample time to rant and rail about the inferiority of all but the white race and the travesty that was being set upon the Southern states, when all they'd sought was independence.

In her father, these traits had maddened her. But now she had a reason to press beyond them, forging the bond necessary to accomplish her goal. Thanks to Thom and—she had to grudgingly admit—to Lucy, she felt confident she had the skills to gain the upper hand with L. Blackstone.

Still, her heart quickened as the carriage stopped in front of a house with a centered gable, trimmed in white, and a front façade forming a covered entrance between a pair of porches. Leaving the carriage, she climbed the steps to a pair of oak-paneled doors. She wrapped hard on the knocker, determined to show confidence from the start.

A woman came to the door, her face long, her expression dour. For a moment, Hattie thought her assumption that L. Blackstone was a man might be wrong. But quickly she saw that the woman wore the plain gray of a servant.

"I've come to see Mr. Blackstone," Hattie said. "My father insisted I stop to visit while I'm in Richmond. I apologize for having come calling without a card, but as you know, such things—"

"He's gone to the cottage," the woman said in an accent suggesting she'd come recently from Ireland. Then she slammed the door.

Hattie stood a moment, unsure how to take this affront. It could be that, with her master away, the servant was at liberty to be as rude as she liked. Or it could be that Mr. Blackstone had instructed her to say as little as possible to anyone who came looking for him.

Turning, she descended the steps slowly. She hated to give up, but what choice did she have? "Cottage" was not clue enough to solve this particular puzzle. For all she knew, it was a cover for something clandestine, similar to how *scouts* were actually spies.

As she approached the carriage, she looked down the walk to where a woman was pushing a baby buggy. "Wait here, please," she told the driver. Then she walked briskly after the woman, hoping to catch up before she reached the corner. The baby must have fussed, because the woman stopped pushing the carriage and lifted the child from where it lay. She bounced the babe at her shoulder, allowing Hattie time to catch up and speak without sounding winded.

"What an adorable child," Hattie exclaimed, though the child looked anything but, its face screwed up and red with crying.

"Kind of you to say." The woman—a girl herself, actually, now that Hattie saw her up close—patted the baby's back, making cooing sounds. "Though she's not mine. I'm only the nursemaid."

"Well, you're very good with her, I must say."

This seemed to relax the girl, and the babe, too, its wails softening to whimpers. "It ain't easy, I tell you what."

"At least your household hasn't had to pull up like the Blackstones," Hattie said. She nodded in the direction of the house with the centered gable, hoping the servant was familiar with the neighborhood.

"Ach, the goings-on at that place. Carriages pulling up at all hours. To be expected, I suppose."

"Is it?" Hattie said, hoping the girl would elaborate.

The child began to hiccup, and the nursemaid turned it back on her shoulder, pounded rather too hard at its back, Hattie thought. "Missus says he's a respectable sort, but I've got my doubts, not that I'd say so to her. He's got money, no doubt of that. A shame how some folks have got houses to spare, while others of us will only ever dream of having one."

"One house was enough for me, growing up. What a bother, now that I've come all the way from Indiana to visit my cousin, only to be told he's at his cottage, and of course I haven't the slightest idea where that would be."

The girl snorted a laugh. "Miss Dridgely wouldn't tell you? An ogre in maid's trappings, that's what Carl calls her."

"Carl?" Hattie asked, reckoning by the way the girl's face had flushed, speaking his name, he must be a beau.

"Carl's a friend to me." The girl returned the hiccupping child to the buggy. "He drives for the Blackstones. Tends their horses too. He tells me the cottage is something to behold, half again as large as that house. Says he'll take me out there some Sunday when the place is empty." Her mouth formed a crooked smile. "Maybe we'll even get inside. All the way out on Old Stage Road, who'd notice?"

"Carl sounds as if he's sweet on you," Hattie said, making a mental note of the location.

The girl blushed again. "He's a good man, and handsome too. I just hope he don't go off to war and get himself killed in some lonesome field, thinking he's a hero."

She said then how she'd best be getting back, or the missus would wonder after the baby. Hattie bade her goodbye, then followed at a leisurely pace until the girl turned a corner and was out of sight. Then she hurried back to the carriage, instructing the driver to take her to Old Stage Road. She'd forgotten the house number, she told him, but she'd recognize the place when she saw it.

She very much hoped this was true.

~ ~ ~

The carriage ride to the Old Stage Road took longer than expected. As they jostled over the winter-rutted road, Hattie felt fatigue setting in. She hoped this wasn't all for nothing. If she couldn't find Blackstone, she'd have to think of some other way to convince Thom to leave Richmond. And that seemed nigh impossible with how set he seemed on trying to get information that could be passed along to General Grant.

Most of the cottages along Old Stage Road were shuttered for winter. The driver asked if she was certain this was where she wanted to go, and she assured him, with more confidence than she felt, that it was. He slowed in front of the first house that seemed occupied, a squat residence with a neglected yard and unadorned gables. "Might this be the place, miss?" he asked.

She had her doubts, but not wanting to try his patience, she said she'd inquire. She approached the house and knocked. An old man came to the door, his red suspenders slipping from his rounded shoulders. His manner was gruff, but with some cajoling, she got him to tell her that the Blackstone cottage was around the next corner. He also mentioned Blackstone's first name, Luke.

Buoyed by this useful information, she returned to the carriage and conveyed this information to the driver, who set the horses to a trot with more purpose than before. True to what the nursemaid had said, the house around the corner was a fine one. Though smaller than the house where she'd been turned away, it was of a similar type, its front porch welcoming. The curtains were drawn, but the shutters were open. A good sign, Hattie thought.

The man who answered her knock stood only slightly taller than Hattie. Fair-skinned and sandy-haired, he looked to be in his late thirties, the skin at the corners of his pale blue eyes only lightly crinkled.

"My apologies for arriving unannounced," she said, putting on her best southern airs to match her drawl. "I've come to see Luke Blackstone."

The man's gaze shifted. Wary, she thought. But as he assessed her, he spoke in a gentle, unperturbed tone. "If it's doctoring you're after—"

"Not that," she interrupted, glad she hadn't blundered by referring to the doctor as *mister*. "My father in Indiana is an associate of Dr. Blackstone's, and he very much wanted me to make contact with him while I'm in Richmond."

The man looked momentarily puzzled. Then his expression cleared. "Ah, yes. Your father's in the grain business, I presume?"

"That's right."

He opened the door wider. "Do come in."

The tension in her shoulders relaxed as she stepped inside. Lit by a tall window at the end of a hallway, the foyer was modest but tastefully decorated with rose-festooned wallpaper above the wainscoting.

"I do hope I'm not interrupting," she said.

"Not at all," the man said.

He held out an arm, and she realized he was offering to take her mantle, which she quickly unclasped. "I'd thought Richmond would be warmer," she said, handing him the mantle. "But I suppose it is winter here, same as in Indiana."

He cocked his head slightly, and she wondered if she'd somehow misspoken. "Indeed it is," he said, draping her mantle over one arm. "Right this way."

She followed him down the hallway to the parlor, which featured the same rose-bedecked wallpaper as the foyer. A fire burned in the hearth, adding a pleasant warmth to the room and a glow to the polished furnishings. The man bid her to sit on the divan. As she did, she noted the volumes lining a set of bookshelves spanning an entire wall. Not any doctor, she thought, but a learned one.

She settled her skirts, waiting for the man to fetch the doctor. Instead, he sat in a wing chair near the fireplace.

"Oh!" Her hand flew momentarily to her mouth. "I'm so sorry. I didn't realize...you are Dr. Blackstone."

He offered a genial smile, showing a row of straight white teeth. "The very same."

She returned the smile. "I might have greeted you more graciously, had I known."

"My apologies for not being clear. Just this afternoon, the household staff has removed to the city, to ready the house there for my return. I'd offer you tea, but I confess to being a bit of a blunderbuss about the kitchen. If Mrs. Firth hadn't left a cold supper, I should have none at all."

She shifted, acutely aware that she was likely alone in this house with a man Thom had deemed dangerous. But she knew her purpose, and she had her family connections to bolster it, along with Lucy's prattling example to follow.

"Dear me, I'm glad I caught you here, Dr. Blackstone. Father would have been keenly disappointed if I'd come all this way and not found you in. He sends his greetings."

The doctor crossed one leg over the other. "Given the nature of our business, I'd have thought he'd have a particular errand for you, Miss Logan."

"Indeed he has," she said. "You see, I am no longer Miss Logan, having recently wed Thomas Welton. Perhaps you've heard of him?"

Dr. Blackstone glanced to one side as if this might jog his memory. "Welton. The name rings a bell."

She sat up straighter, the proud wife. "He's a courier, running letters between Richmond and Baltimore. Father said that, in relation to your business dealings, you might have occasion to avail yourself of his services. He says a trustworthy courier can be hard to find, as they are pressed upon on all sides by those who mean to expose them. Though Thom tells me things are a bit more relaxed in Richmond than they were a few months ago."

He smiled again, but more tightly than before. "Ah, but one must never let down one's guard."

She clasped one hand in the other, which according to Miss Whitcomb signaled a lady's restraint. "Indeed. This business is all very new to me, especially coming from Indiana, where the war feels more distant. But I suppose you know that, having traveled there on occasion." She hoped this assumption was correct.

"Father seems quite encouraged by the surge of interest in the Peace Democrats," she continued. "And he says more and more people join the Knights of the Golden Circle every day."

Dr. Blackstone tapped the foot of his crossed leg in the air as if in time to some tune only he heard. "The Knights will prove useful, I suspect. Especially in the Old Northwest."

"Father is forever saying how the people must take matters into their own hands when faced with a tyrant like Mr. Lincoln," she said, repeating sentiments she'd heard often enough.

Dr. Blackstone's foot stilled a moment, then took up swinging again. "You mentioned your husband, Mrs. Welton. Did he not come with you to Richmond?"

"He did," she said. "But he's been busy about his courier work and has come down with a touch of ague."

The doctor cocked his head as he had earlier. "Nothing serious, I hope."

She caught herself starting to rub her hands together, betraying her anxiety, then squelched the impulse. "Nothing that a day's rest won't cure," she said with a dismissive wave of her hand.

"Perhaps you can bring him by when he's feeling better," the doctor said. "You know where I live in the city?"

She nodded. "Father made sure I had the address. But he said I'd best come sooner rather than later since you might be heading off soon for Louisiana to attend to some matters there. If that's the case, Dr. Blackstone, I advise you to bring your galoshes. The rains can be fierce there at this time of year, as I understand General Grant is learning firsthand."

This was her shot at learning the most vital information she'd come for. A suspicion, she'd learned, was to be floated in the most innocuous way possible. "Mr. Scarfton always says a Louisiana winter is the best answer to hell and the closest thing to it. Oh, but look how I'm prattling on, and I can see by the blank look on your face, Dr. Blackstone, that of course you have no idea what I'm talking about. My mother's people are from Louisiana, so I've had reason to visit there often. My grandfather has one of the largest plantations in the area around Vicksburg. I hate to think how they're suffering now, with General Grant closing in."

Gazing toward the fire, Dr. Blackstone pressed his hands together, fingertip to fingertip, and flexed them. "You mustn't worry yourself, my dear. Our boys there have a number of assets on their side."

"So Father tells me, and—oh!" She pressed a hand to her mouth. "I nearly forgot. From what Father said, you're acquainted with Grandfather's overseer, Mr. Scarfton. Father told me to make sure you know that if anything in that arrangement is proving less than satisfactory, you're to say so, and he'll get word to my grandfather straightaway. I trust you know what he's talking about. I surely don't."

Blackstone gave a curt nod. "You may tell your father that all is progressing according to plan."

She welled with pride at the accuracy of her guess, though she knew better than to show it. Her grandfather's wretched overseer, Isaac Scarfton, whose northern roots would allow him to pass as a friend of the Federals, must have endeared himself to Federal forces near Vicksburg. No wonder the general's plans kept getting leaked.

She suspected Scarfton was well-compensated for his efforts, no doubt from the grain-smuggling proceeds.

"I'm sure Father will be glad to learn that the arrangement is satisfactory," she said. "He says you're a skilled broker, Dr. Blackstone, and he says that if our cause had even a dozen skilled as you, we'd have our peace by now."

"How kind of him," Blackstone said. His pale eyes, Hattie realized, were hard to read.

Having gathered the information she'd sought, she stood to leave. "I've so enjoyed meeting you, Dr. Blackstone. Thank you for seeing me unannounced, especially with your household in transition. I do hope we'll meet again soon."

He stood as well. "The pleasure is mine, Mrs. Welton."

"On behalf of myself and my husband, who I hope you'll meet the next time we come through Richmond, I thank you for your efforts, Dr. Blackstone. And should you ever have need of a courier, you can leave word for Thomas at the Spotswood Hotel."

"It's good to be among friends, isn't it?" The doctor reached in his pocket, and for an instant, she thought he might produce some correspondence for her and Thom to take north, a bonus atop the information she'd already gleaned. But his hand remained in his pocket as he escorted her to the door.

It was only after they'd bid their goodbyes and she'd gotten back in the carriage that she realized she'd never explained the chain of circumstances that had led her to find him here. No matter, she told herself. Better that he accuse his dour-faced servant of giving out the address than for him to suspect that Edgar Logan's daughter had a knack for solving puzzles.

As the driver started back toward the city, Hattie leaned back in her seat, flush with satisfaction. Lucy could engage with Baltimore sympathizers, picking up bits of information here and there among the complaints about servants and the exchanging of recipes. She could even make her way around Richmond, doing a courier's work.

But Hattie had now proven she could do all that and more, engaging with the lynchpin of a lucrative arrangement that supplied the Rebels with much-needed grain and homing in on her grandfather's duplicitous overseer as the man thwarting Federal attempts to take Vicksburg. And Vicksburg, Thom had said, had the potential to swing the war in the Union's favor by handing them control of the entire Mississippi River.

She couldn't wait to tell Thom what she'd learned. He'd be proud. Better than that, he'd no more reason to linger in Richmond. She'd bring him north, and once he'd recovered sufficiently, they'd make a formidable team for the Union cause.

And to think that only weeks ago, she'd thought her work dull and insignificant. Best of all—and most unexpected—her work would now be done in love.

Chapter Fifteen

February 5, 1863

B y the time the coachman returned Hattie to the hotel, it was late afternoon. The skies, while still clear, had turned the dusty shade of blue that precedes dusk. She felt bad having left Thom alone for so long, but she knew he'd understand when he learned how she'd tracked down Luke Blackstone.

She took the stairs hurriedly, the fatigue she'd felt earlier erased by her achievement. She unlocked the door to their room and flung it open.

"You'll never guess where I've been," she said in a low voice as she shut the door. "And who I've met."

Turning from the door, she saw that Thom was sleeping. Her news would have to wait. She went to him, and as she drew close, she heard how his breaths rattled in his chest. She felt his forehead and found it hotter than ever.

She poured water from the porcelain pitcher into the basin, wishing she'd thought to set it by the window to cool before going out that morning. She wet a face cloth and wrang it out. Sitting at the edge of his bed, she pressed the cloth to Thom's forehead.

His eyes fluttered open. "I thought you'd gone off to Baltimore without me." His voice sounded tight and strained.

"Not a chance," she said. "Does your throat hurt now too?"

"A little."

"Your lips are parched. You need water."

"Thanks," he murmured as she poured him a glass of water. But when she held it to his lips, he drank only a few sips before sinking back on his pillow.

"You need a doctor," she said sharply. Maybe she should have told Blackstone more about Thom's illness. He might be a traitor, but he was also a doctor who might have shed insight into how she could help Thom.

Thom shook his head side to side, seeming to reject the idea of a doctor.

She touched the back of her hand to his flushed cheek. "This afternoon, I decided I'd go—"

He interrupted. "Eliz...Elizabeth Van Lew. She...she'll know who...which doctor to trust."

Hattie changed course, her tale of visiting Blackstone destined for another day. "Then I'll go to Miss Van Lew, straight away," she said. "If you're sure you'll be all right while I'm gone."

He nodded. "I'll be...fine." He closed his eyes.

She stood and reached for her purse, glad that Lucy had pointed out Van Lew mansion, in the fashionable Church Hill neighborhood, when they'd been in Richmond last month. All sorts of well-known people had graced its doors, Lucy said, including the famous author Edgar Allen Poe and Jenny Lind, a singer of worldwide renown. Elizabeth, who'd taken charge of the mansion following her husband's death, was incredibly brazen in making known her support for the Union cause, Lucy had confided. It was a wonder she hadn't been arrested, for the Rebels suspected her of running a spy ring to aid the Federals. In their own spywork, Lucy warned, they should at all costs stay clear of Elizabeth Van Lew or risk arrest themselves.

That mattered little now. Hattie could only hope that at this late hour, she'd be able to approach the Van Lew mansion without attracting much notice.

The coachman who had taken her to Old Stage Road had gone home for the day, so Eddie summoned a new driver, looking grave when she admitted that she needed to fetch a doctor for Mr. Welton. This driver was a young, pimply-faced lad, and she wondered as he helped her into the carriage how he'd managed to avoid recruitment, the Rebels being desperate for soldiers.

She asked him to take her to the Van Lew residence, and without further instructions, he drove directly to Church Hill, turning up Grace Street to the three-and-a-half-story mansion fronted by six columns. The place took up an entire city block atop one of Richmond's seven hills, sheltered by sprawling oaks and smaller magnolias while still affording a magnificent view of the James River.

As a precaution, Hattie asked the driver to stop not directly in front of the mansion but a block away. He pulled off on a side street, and she got out. Pulling her mantle tight against the wind, she started for the mansion. Keeping her head down, she didn't notice the Rebel officer striding in the same direction until she was nearly upon him.

"Is there trouble in the neighborhood?" she asked, thinking it best to question him before he questioned her.

"Only that this Van Lew woman and her mother's been finally caught at their sedition."

Hattie widened her eyes, expressing surprise and, she hoped, ignorance of anything untoward going on at the mansion. "I've noticed they don't fly our flag as the other good neighbors do. But I had no idea she'd come under suspicion."

"Obvious enough, ma'am, to any that's paying attention. But knowing of spies and catching them, those is two different things."

Her hands flew to her mouth, expressing horror at this revelation. "Spies! But surely the Van Lews wouldn't be doing something so traitorous."

The officer smiled wryly. "You'd be surprised what secrets women can keep if they put their minds to it. But these ones will be brought to justice, mark my words." He tapped the breast pocket of his coat. "I've got the summons right here. A grand jury's found cause to try them for dealing in Yankee currency."

"Oh my." Hattie stepped back. "That does sound vile. I don't think I should like to linger about this place, even in passing."

With that, she retreated to the side street and entered the carriage, heavy with disappointment. She'd managed well enough with the officer, she supposed, giving him no cause to suspect she'd had any business with Mrs. Van Lew. But now she was no closer than before to getting Thom the medical attention he needed.

As the carriage pulled away and she looked back at the mansion, receding in her vision, she realized how much she'd been looking forward to meeting with a woman of Mrs. Van Lew's loyalties and accomplishments. Elizabeth Van Lew had set up her very own spy ring. How had she accomplished that, and to whom did she report? Not to Mr. Pinkerton, or Hattie would have known of it. Nor could she imagine someone of Mrs. Van Lew's background reporting to the rather shady Lafayette Baker.

It was nearly dark when the carriage returned Hattie to the Spotswood. She felt a pang of hunger at the wafting smell of roast beef as she passed the restaurant, but her first concern was Thom. Tomorrow, when the apothecary was open, she'd see what other remedies the druggist could recommend.

She hurried upstairs and down the hallway to their room, her heart quickened as a man in Confederate uniform emerged from the next room. He tipped his hat to her, and she smiled as graciously as she could manage. Confederate soldiers were to be expected at the Spotswood, she reminded herself, vowing to be even more careful about speaking in tones that could not be overheard.

She started to unlock the room door. To her surprise, the knob turned freely. Surely she hadn't made such an error, neglecting to secure the door in her haste to get to the Van Lew mansion.

She slipped through the door and closed it behind her. To her delight, she saw that Thom was sitting up in bed, propped by pillows all around and looking a far cry healthier than when she'd left him. Perhaps his fever had broken.

"Ah, there she is." He managed a weak smile. "My lovely bride."

He was speaking not to her, she realized, but to the two figures standing at the foot of the bed. One was Lucy Hamilton, wearing a traveling frock Hattie recognized from the journey they'd made together. The other was a Confederate soldier. Judging from his uniform's epaulets, he was not a captain like the man in the next room but an officer of lower rank.

What was Lucy thinking, bringing a Confederate officer, even a low-ranking one, into their midst? For that matter, what was Lucy doing here at all? These were not questions to be asked in the officer's presence, of course. There would be time for that when he took his leave, which Hattie hoped would be soon.

In the meantime, they must play their roles. She brushed Thom's forehead with a kiss. "Feeling better, are you? I'm glad of it."

"These visitors roused me from my bed," he said.

"You shouldn't have gotten up, no matter who was at the door," she scolded.

Lucy laughed. "It would have caused far more disturbance if we'd forced our way in."

Hattie's annoyance rose. Did Lucy not see how ill Thom was? But it would do no good to show her distress, not with this soldier in their midst.

She approached Lucy, arms extended, while from her peripheral vision taking in the stranger, who stood not a foot away. He was not as young as she'd first judged him—it was only the fineness of his features that made him seem so. His cap sat low on his head, covering nearly all of what looked to be dark hair. His lips, thin and firm, seemed disinclined toward smiling. And yet she sensed something familiar about him. The eyes, she realized as she pressed her cheek to Lucy's. She knew those eyes.

"Dearest sister," Hattie said. "How kind of you to come all the way to Richmond to see us." Releasing her embrace, she turned to the soldier. "And to bring along such a handsome companion. Do us the pleasure of an introduction, please."

The peals of laughter that came from Lucy then were like none Hattie had ever heard. "And you think yourself...you think yourself...a spy!"

The utterance was quiet, though plenty loud for both Hattie and the soldier to hear. Had Lucy gone mad, giving them up to a uniformed Rebel, and with Thom in such a weakened state?

"Hush," Hattie hissed, putting a finger to her lips, though there was no point in it, with the soldier standing right there.

A slow smile formed on the soldier's face, and Hattie realized why those eyes had seemed so familiar.

"Miss Warne!" Hattie exclaimed.

Though nearly incapacitated with giggling, Lucy managed to lift the soldier's cap, revealing Miss Warne's shiny black hair, pulled back tighter than ever so that the cap covered nearly all of it.

"Don't feel bad," Thom said. "She had me fooled, too, for a moment."

Miss Warne loosened the top button of the uniform, which rode high on her neck. "I fear I've become too easily recognized to travel south without using a rather dramatic disguise," she said, keeping her voice low.

Now that Hattie knew the secret, she saw the clues that might have given it away—the slender shoulders, the graceful fingers, the small boots. But unless one knew to look for these, the costume's effect was as remarkable as any she'd seen on stage at Grover's National. "You were the last person I expected here," she said. "But I'm glad you've come."

They drew closer around Thom's bed, allowing them to speak more freely in their hushed tones. "Mr. Pinkerton has worried over the two of you, so long overdue," Miss Warne said.

"As have we all," Lucy said.

"He wanted to send another courier, but I convinced him that if matters were grave, it would be better if I came myself," Miss Warne said.

"In the company of your dear sister." Lucy brushed a strand of hair from Thom's forehead, and Hattie felt a pang of jealousy. Glad as she was for Mr. Pinkerton's concern, she could have done without Lucy coming along.

"I presented myself as Lucy's escort," Miss Warne said. "But now that we've reached Richmond, I dare not tarry lest I be discovered. I'll leave in the morning, and the three of you must follow as soon as Thom is well enough to travel."

There was much Hattie wanted to tell Miss Warne, especially concerning what she'd learned from Blackstone. But recalling what Thom had said about Lucy's mistakes, she hesitated to speak of such things while Lucy was within earshot.

As the two of them stepped back from the bed, Thom pulled Hattie close. Brushing her cheek with a kiss, he whispered, "What was Pinkerton thinking, sending Lucy?"

Bestowing a warm smile, Hattie shook her head slightly, conveying her own befuddlement.

Adjusting her cap in the mirror, Miss Warne caught her eye. "I'm pleased to see you faring well, Hattie."

"They are the very picture of wedded bliss, aren't they?" Lucy reached in her satchel and removed a letter. Placing it on the nightstand, she whispered, "This contains a warning that Federal agents are after you. In case any Rebs come around snooping, you may use it to gain their confidence."

"With any luck, we won't need it." Thom took Hattie's hand and squeezed it. "We'll be out of here soon enough."

"First, we must get you well," Lucy said. "And I know just the doctor to tend to you. I have it on good word that he's both capable and trustworthy." Lucy's smug smile infuriated Hattie, intent as she seemed to be on proving herself better on every front, as if Hattie hadn't been doing enough for Thom's health.

"Hattie has already gone for a doctor," Thom said. "That's where she was when you arrived."

Hattie hated having to admit defeat, but there was no getting around it. "I'm afraid my outing yielded nothing. The woman I'd hoped to see has troubles of her own."

Alarm registered in Thom's eyes. "Has some harm come to her?"

"To whom?" Miss Warne asked, her voice low.

"Elizabeth Van Lew," Hattie whispered. "When I got there, a confederate officer was approaching the house ahead of me, preparing to serve a warrant accusing her and her mother of dealing in Union currency."

Thom shook his head. "She's been far too open with her sentiments. Last I heard, the White Caps had left a message on her steps, threatening to burn her house down. The authorities won't need much of an excuse to lock her up and throw away the key."

Miss Warne straightened her jacket. "There are suspicions all around," she said softly. "Lucy, if you're bent on fetching a doctor in the morning, I urge you to proceed with caution."

"I will, Miss Warne," Lucy said. "You can count on me."

Hattie saw the flash of doubt that crossed Thom's face, quickly replaced by what could only be read as fatigue.

"And, please, all of you, depart this city as quickly as you're able," Miss Warne said. "Thom, we'll leave you now to your rest."

"There was no room for us here at the Spotswood," Lucy said, gathering her cloak. "Full up. Can you believe it? We've been forced to stay at the Monumental, and I assure you, it's not at all to the standards here."

Leave it to Lucy, Hattie thought, to complain about her accommodations when Thom was gravely ill and the authorities were closing in on a fellow spy. She supposed she should be glad Lucy was staying on to help them get back to Baltimore, but she'd have preferred her and Thom making the journey alone.

If Miss Warne knew anything of Lucy's shortcomings, she didn't let on. "Goodnight," she said. "And godspeed."

She and Lucy left, Hattie closing and locking the door behind them. She perched at the edge of Thom's bed, studying his face.

His eyes looked duller than before, and she wondered how much of his apparent recovery had been a show for Miss Warne's benefit.

She patted his hand. "Well, that was a pleasant surprise, wasn't it?"

"I should've known old Peaches would send someone after us when we were so long overdue."

"Old Peaches?"

"You didn't know?" he whispered. "Peaches was how Pinkerton referred to himself when corresponding with General McClellan."

In spite of everything, Hattie grinned. "And wouldn't we love to know where that came from."

He shrugged, and she began rearranging his pillows so he might lie back again, as he was looking fatigued. "The missus, maybe," he said.

"If that's the case, it behooves me to invent some endearing reference for you. Kitty Cat, maybe?"

He wrinkled his nose as she tucked the covers to his chin. "Not if it means I'm required to purr."

"Daddy Long Legs?"

"Better. But I can't say I'm overly fond of it."

"Sleep on it," she said, dimming the light. "You need your rest. Tomorrow, we'll have Lucy's doctor, and then—"

He caught her by the hand. "Hattie, if anything happens, I want you to know—"

"Hush," she said. "All that will happen is you'll recover, and we'll get back to Baltimore, and all will be well."

With this assurance, he closed his eyes, and in short order, drifted to sleep. She sat by him a while, and once assured his breaths were measured and deep, she gave in to hunger and went downstairs to eat. As she passed the hotel desk, the clerk waved her over.

"A note for you, Mrs. Welton."

She took the folded paper and tucked it in her purse before proceeding to the dining room. After she was seated and had placed her order for roast beef—a splurge, with the budget they'd been allotted—she took the note discretely from her purse and read it. *See me off at the station. 8:30 am, RF&P.* The note was signed simply "K," which Hattie took to be Kate Warne.

Miss Warne wasn't the sort to want any fuss made over her departure. She must have something to say. But Hattie could not think what it might be, and as the waiter set a plate before her with a thin slice of beef floating in a pool of dark gravy, she told herself she'd know soon enough what was afoot.

Chapter Sixteen

FEBRUARY 6, 1863

The morning dawned in such brilliant shades of red and orange that Hattie feared for a moment that Federal troops, quiet as they'd been, had somehow laid siege to the city, setting it afire. Seeing that it was only the colorful ushering in of a new day, she lay abed, Thom sleeping peacefully at her side, and thought of how there was nowhere she'd rather be at that moment unless of course the whole scene could be transported to a future when the war was over, and she and Thom could dispense with the whispers and subterfuge.

Thom's sleep last night had been better than any since they'd arrived in Richmond. Hattie rolled toward him, hugging his chest, and felt the deep stirrings she experienced each time they touch. Soon—very soon, she hoped—Thom would be well enough for them to consummate their love. She had little notion of what to expect, but she trusted Thom with all her heart, and she trusted he'd be tender with her.

But that lay in the future. As Thom began to stir, she pushed herself away from him and rose from the bed.

He stretched, and his eyes brightened, watching her dress. "Mrs. Welton, you may well be the only doctoring I need."

She smiled. "I wish it were so. But perhaps this physician of Lucy's can get you strong enough to travel."

His smile dimmed. "I hope her judgment can be trusted."

"I know you've questioned it before," Hattie said, fastening the top button of her bodice. "But you've never said why."

"I've caught her saying more than she should, and to the wrong people."

She waited for him to explain, but he said nothing more. He seemed protective of Lucy even as he warned of her errors.

"This seems a simple errand," she said. "She shouldn't have to say much of anything except that you need doctoring."

She finished dressing and went downstairs, returning with a mug of chicory coffee and a slice of toast from the dining room for Thom. "Miss Warne left a note at the front desk last night, asking me to see her off at the station. You'll be all right if I go?"

"Of course," he said, then sipped from the mug. "If only this illness affected my taste buds. Then it wouldn't be so hard to pretend this stuff was coffee."

"The hardships we endure," she said, brushing his forehead with a kiss.

Downstairs, she asked Eddie to summon a carriage. He procured one in short order, and within minutes, she was on her way to the train station. Even at this early hour, the city thrummed with activity, carts and carriages rattling along the streets while smokestacks from the ironworks spewed black smoke into the sky.

At the station, she asked the driver to wait while she went inside. The depot was busy, with soldiers milling about among the civilians and the air smelling of grime and sweat. At the far end of the waiting area, she spotted the narrow-shouldered figure of Miss Warne in her Rebel disguise. As Hattie approached her, Miss Warne held out a hand, greeting her as if they were acquaintances who'd happened on one another at the station.

Miss Warne suggested they move outside to the platform where her train was scheduled to depart. The morning's chill lingered there, even among the steaming engines, and Hattie pulled her cloak tight as they retreated to a far corner where they could talk, the train yard rendering their words unintelligible to anyone but them.

"Thank you for coming," Miss Warne said. To make herself heard above the rattle of engines and the squealing wheels of trains shifting into position, she nearly shouted into Hattie's ear. "There are some things I wanted to communicate out of earshot of Lucy. I'm sure you understand."

"Of course," Hattie said, leaning close to be heard. She wondered if Lucy's days with the Pinkerton Agency might be numbered. Though she knew it was ungracious, the thought gave her some satisfaction.

"The letters Thom brought along—what's become of them?" Miss Warne asked.

Hattie straightened, squaring her shoulders. "I delivered them."

"Very good," Miss Warne said.

"I also called on Luke Blackstone."

Miss Warne's gray eyes brightened. "I trust he received you graciously."

"He did. I told him my father sent me. Which reminds me." Hattie dug in her purse, extracting the letter she'd penned to her father, having sealed it shut on the way to the station. "I was hoping you could see this to the mail. I felt it only right, under the circumstances, to inform Father of my recent marriage to a man who shares his convictions."

Miss Warne fingered the envelope, then slipped it in the jacket pocket of her soldier's uniform. "That should prove useful." Her lips turned in what passed for a smile. "It sounds as if you've turned a liability into an asset."

Hattie's chest swelled with pride. "That was my intention. As it turns out, Dr. Blackstone is acquainted not only with Father but also with the overseer at my grandfather's..."

Her voice trailed off as a uniformed soldier passed, tipping his cap at the person he took for a fellow soldier. Mindful of her disguise, Miss Warne nodded, acknowledging the greeting, but kept her cap on.

"You were saying?" Miss Warne said when the soldier was gone.

"My grandfather's plantation is in Louisiana, not far from Vicksburg, just south of Milliken's Bend, near the river." Though the stranger seemed out of earshot, Hattie made her voice light and carefree, as if this were mere nattering to pass the time. "It seems Dr. Blackstone and Father have a mutual acquaintance in Isaac Scarfton, my grandfather's overseer. He hails from the North, but his loyalties are with the South." A train whistle blew, sharp and shrill. Hattie drew closer still to Miss Warne, her lips close to her ear. "Dr. Blackstone indicated that Mr. Scarfton is the one passing General Grant's battle plans to his enemies."

Miss Warne's brow furrowed. "I'll see that gets passed along." She reached in her pocket and extracted a roll of dollar bills, which she pressed into Hattie's hand. "It isn't much, but it should see the three of you through to Baltimore. Don't tarry, Hattie. You all need to leave here as soon as you can."

"We will," Hattie said. "Thank you."

She started to slip the cash into her handbag, but Miss Warne grabbed her wrist. "Keep it on your person."

Hattie wondered what sort of dire circumstances Miss Warne was envisioning, that Hattie might lose access to her belongings, but the whistle blew again, and there was no time to ask. From the northbound train, a conductor cried, "All aboard!"

Miss Warne squeezed Hattie's hand. "Until we meet again," she said.

~ ~ ~

On the way back to the hotel, Hattie basked in the glow of her accomplishments. She'd conveyed to Miss Warne the information she'd acquired from Dr. Blackstone. In turn, that should turn attention on her grandfather's overseer Isaac Scarfton, a weasel-faced man who was an ogre with the enslaved people of the plantation. What consequences he'd suffer, she didn't know, but at the very least, General Grant's plans would no longer be compromised.

All that remained was to get Thom out of Richmond. His bright manner this morning had encouraged her. Perhaps it would be only a few days before he was well enough to travel. She thought of the other good the two of them might do, teamed as husband and wife. Maybe they could even persuade Mr. Pinkerton to send them to Canada, where with any luck she could track down George.

Brightened by these prospects, she left the carriage and entered the hotel. Though the morning's red sunrise had portended a storm, the sky's only clouds were well in the distance, and the winter sun shone brightly if not warmly. Her steps felt light as she climbed the stairs. Only weeks before, her future had seemed far from certain. Now, she'd at least turned one part of her past in her favor.

When she reached the door to their room, she again found it unlocked. Lucy, she thought, with a twinge of annoyance. Couldn't she have let Thom rest? Then she remembered Lucy's plan to fetch a doctor. As she went in, she saw there was indeed a man at Thom's bedside, his back to her.

As she shut the door, he folded his stethoscope and slid it into the pocket of his dark coat. Noting his stature and the way he carried his shoulders, slightly slumped, Hattie froze in place. Standing at the end of the bed, Lucy smiled.

"There you are, Hattie. I fetched Dr. Lucas, just as I said I would. He says with the right treatments, Thom will be good as new in no time."

The man turned to face Hattie. The pale blue eyes and the sandy hair, graying at the temples, were all too familiar.

Her stomach sank. He held out a hand. "A pleasure to meet you, Mrs. Welton."

She shook his hand, her grip limp, her fingers clammy. So this was how he intended to play it, as if they'd never met. "The pleasure is mine," she said in a voice that seemed to belong to someone else.

"There aren't many like Dr. Lucas in Richmond, tending to friends of the Union," Lucy said proudly. "I was lucky to find him, as he has only just returned to the city."

Dr. Blackstone to his Rebel friends, Dr. Lucas to the Federals. Why hadn't Hattie thought to press Lucy for details on the doctor that she swore had come highly recommended?

"You know how women can be, Dr. Lucas," Thom said. "Fussing over a man when all he needs is a bit of rest."

"Ah, but their intentions are for the best." The doctor reached for a black satchel set near the foot of the bed. "Let's proceed with the leeches, Mr. Welton."

Hattie stepped close, her thigh brushing the mattress. "That won't be necessary, Dr. Lucas," she said coolly.

"Don't be ridiculous, Hattie," Lucy said. "The doctor says Thom needs leeching and emetics if he's to recover.

"Though I can't say I'm looking forward to the prospect of either treatment," Thom said.

Hattie folded her arms across her chest. "We appreciate you coming, Dr. Lucas. But we have no further need of your services."

"Hattie Logan!" Lucy said. "You seem determined to send Thom to the grave."

"Welton," Hattie said, her eyes fixed on the doctor.

"I won't stand for it," Lucy said. "Dr. Lucas, proceed with your treatments."

Thom clasped Hattie's hand. "Darling, if it truly disturbs you—"

"It does."

The doctor smiled, showing a row of bright teeth. "If you change your mind, you know where to find me."

Hattie kept her gaze on him as he left the room, shutting the door softly behind him.

Now it was Lucy crossing her arms over her bosom. "You really can't bear the thought of me—"

"Hush," Hattie hissed. "We've got to get out of here, now."

"But why?" Lucy demanded.

"Dr. Lucas isn't how you know him, is it Hattie?" Thom whispered.

Shaking her head, Hattie went to the closet and began stuffing clothes into her bag and Thom's. "Help me, Lucy."

Lucy stayed where she was. "Not until you explain what's going on."

"Dr. Lucas, with Union sympathies," she said, "is known among those favoring the South as Dr. Luke Blackstone. He's engaged in plots to smuggle goods and pass secrets that benefit the Rebels."

Lucy's face blanched. "But I didn't...I had it on good information..."

With some effort, Thom raised his head from his pillows. "You went on your own to see Luke Blackstone, Hattie?"

"Yes." She folded a pair of Thom's trousers and added them to the bag. "I knew you wouldn't leave until we learned what he's up to."

"But how did you know he was up to anything?" Lucy asked.

"An intercepted letter," Hattie said. "I tracked him down at a cottage outside of Richmond. Believing me friendly to the cause, he confirmed suspicions about a spy passing Union secrets near Vicksburg. I conveyed that information to Miss Warne before she left this morning so she could pass it along through the proper channels."

Thom struggled to a sitting position, then swung his legs over the edge of the bed "Knowing that could change everything for General Grant."

"I hope so," Hattie said. "But now Blackstone knows I was only feigning Rebel sympathies when I called on him yesterday."

Lucy wrang her hands. "What do we do?"

"Well, we can't stay here, that's for certain." Hattie stashed a folded dress in the travel bag.

"There must be a train leaving soon," Lucy said. "I'll get my things and meet you at the station."

"The station's the first place they'll look," Hattie said.

"I understand Elizabeth Van Lew has secreted fugitives in her home," Thom said.

"She may have been arrested," Hattie reminded him.

"She has a brother living there," Thom said. "Perhaps he can help."

"Can Eddie be trusted to arrange for a driver who won't divulge where he's taken us?" Hattie asked.

Thom smiled weakly. "A few coins may buy their silence."

"I wish we had time to disguise ourselves," Hattie said, thinking of the stories she'd heard of Miss Warne's many disguises.

"You and Lucy go on without me," Thom said. "You two won't be as easily recognized as me."

"I'm not leaving you," Hattie said. "You can barely walk."

"Then I'll dodder along as Mr. Lincoln did, making his way through Baltimore in the middle of the night."

"It's hardly the middle of the night," Lucy said crossly.

"Your chances would be better if we laid a shawl over you, hiding your face as best we can." Hattie dug in her bag for the black shawl she'd packed. She arranged it around Thom's shoulders, then tugged at the edges to shroud his face.

"A good effect," she said. "With the weight you've lost, we could almost pass you off as Mr. Lincoln."

"As if that would help," Lucy grumbled.

Thom shook his head, displacing the shawl. "I see why Mr. Lincoln felt humiliated in this get-up. Bring my pants and shirt."

"A little humility never hurt anyone," Hattie said, but she brought him the only trousers and shirt she hadn't yet packed.

Thom fumbled with the buttons of his bedclothes. Hattie knew he was trying to hurry, but his fingers were so swollen. "Let me help," she said, and he didn't object as she undid the buttons.

"Aren't you the cozy couple?" Lucy said, turning to the window as Hattie helped him dress.

This was hardly the time for petty jealousies, Hattie thought as she laced up Thom's boots. "Now take my arm," Hattie said when she'd finished. "Lucy, come take his other arm."

"I can stand on my own," Thom objected.

"Your legs are bound to be wobbly," Hattie said.

"You do know how to make a man feel small," Thom complained, but he allowed their assistance.

Standing, Thom was indeed unsteady on his feet, but he shook free of their hold. "Let me walk a few laps about the room," he said. "I need to think."

"About what?" Lucy asked as he took one shaky step and then another toward the window.

"About what we do if someone intercepts us."

"We have the letter Lucy brought," Hattie said. "The one that urges you not to go north again because the Federals have fingered you as a Rebel spy."

Thom nodded. "You have the letter, Lucy?"

"In my handbag," she said.

"Good. If anyone stops us, let Hattie and I do the talking," he said.

Lucy pressed her lips firmly together, clearly unhappy with this directive. At the same time, fear showed in her eyes. Spy work had been only a game for her, Hattie realized, a venturesome diversion. Now that they were in real trouble, her charm and chatter were of little use.

Thom steadied himself on the windowsill, then turned to face them. "I'm ready."

"You're certain?" Hattie said.

He nodded, and they set out from the room and down the hall. At the stairs, they met the Rebel officer Hattie had seen going into the room next door. He tipped his hat to Thom. "Good day, Mr. Welton. I see you're feeling better."

Hattie tried not to show her surprise at the officer's addressing Thom by name. "How could I not be feeling better, Captain McCafferty, with these two lovely escorts?" He swayed a bit, and Hattie took hold of his arm. "My wife, Hattie, and my sister, Lucy, visiting from Baltimore."

"Ah, you've come across the Potomac," the captain said.

"Yes," Hattie said. "Quite the journey these days."

The captain smiled. "We hope that soon those inconveniences will be a thing of the past, once our troops take Washington. I assume you ladies have reported to the military governor, General Winder?"

"Oh, but we've never had—" Lucy began.

"Never had the pleasure of meeting General Winder," Hattie interrupted. "But we'd be pleased to speak with him now that we know passes are required."

"He'll find their papers in order," Thom said.

"I'm sure he will," said the captain. "Just a formality, you know. If you like, I can make the proper introductions, as I've heard you're not in the best of health."

"A bit of ague is all," Thom said, though his gaunt face betrayed him.

"Ladies, if you'll proceed to the general's headquarters, I'll meet you there straightaway," the captain said. "We'll have no problem getting your paperwork in order."

He proceeded down the hall to his room. Only when Hattie heard the rattle of his key in the door did she let out the breath she'd been holding.

"Damn it all," Thom muttered. "We can't risk going to Miss Van Lew now. Not if he's going to be waiting for you two to show up at General Winder's headquarters."

"We'll proceed there straightaway," Hattie said, keeping her voice low. "When we've got our papers, we can plan our escape. Lucy, you know what to say?"

"I – I think so," Lucy whispered. "I've brought a letter for my brother, warning him not to come north, because the Federals aim to arrest him for spying."

"A letter from whom?" Thom said.

"From Mr. Pink—"

"From the Confederate officer to whom Mr. Welton reports," Hattie interrupted. "You must under no circumstances mention any names."

Lucy straightened. "I know. I just forgot."

"I'd best go with you," Thom said.

"No," said Hattie. "That would only raise suspicions, given your condition. Get back to the room. You look white as a sheet."

Thom shook his head. "I don't know how I managed to wed such a stubborn woman."

"I never represented myself as anything different," Hattie said. "Now go."

Chapter Seventeen

It was four o'clock when Hattie and Lucy reached General Winder's headquarters. Captain McCafferty was there to meet them. As he escorted them into the general's office, Hattie marveled at Thom's nerve, having ingratiated himself with such high-ranking officials.

The general greeted them cordially, and McCafferty explained why they'd come.

"I'm glad to meet anyone associated with Mr. Welton," the general said. "Especially two pretty women. Mr. Welton is a noble fellow, quite valuable to the Southern cause."

"That's why his Baltimore associates sent a warning with his sister," Hattie said. "Apparently, he has fallen under suspicion and should not return north anytime soon."

The general templed his fingers under his chin. "Is that so?"

Lucy fumbled in her bag for the letter. Finding it, she handed it to the general. "I believe the message speaks for itself." Lucy wasn't exactly keeping quiet as Hattie had urged, but at least she wasn't babbling.

The general's brow furrowed as he scanned the letter, then returned it to Lucy. "If Mr. Welton is in danger, he most certainly should remain here in Richmond. His services are vital. If only the rest of his countrymen would commit themselves to our cause, we could bring this war to a swift end." He eyed Lucy. "Those would be your countrymen, too, I presume, Miss Welton."

Lucy dipped her head, smiling coyly. "I do hope and pray our fellow Brits will come around. Mr. Lincoln is a despicable man. It wouldn't bother me at all to see him kidnapped or shot. This business of freeing the Negroes...why, only last week, I heard—"

Under the table, Hattie gave her a swift kick in the ankle, interrupting her tirade. "My dear sister-in-law and I know little about affairs in Washington, General Winder," Hattie said. "We are but adjuncts to the courier services my husband provides, though we of course share your sentiments, wanting victory to come as soon as possible. In the meantime, we are strangers here in Richmond, and Captain McCafferty has advised that we need some papers from you so we may avoid interference from your guards."

Winder waved his hand dismissively. "Do not concern yourselves any further with that, Mrs. Welton. No passes are necessary. Should anyone question your being here, simply tell them you've reported to me."

"Quite kind of you," Lucy said. "I can see that you're a man of good sense."

Hattie rose quickly, giving Lucy a stern look that caused her to follow suit. "We appreciate your time, General Winder, knowing you have many important matters to attend to. And now we really must return to the Spotswood and see to my husband's well-being."

She nodded at Captain McCafferty, who stepped forward from the wall where he'd been leaning. "Captain, thank you for arranging this meeting. The two of you have put our minds at ease during this difficult time."

"Oh yes," Lucy gushed. "We are forever grateful."

Hattie's smile tensed as they left the general's office. Lucy seemed constitutionally incapable of staying quiet.

They settled into the carriage. As the driver set the horses in motion, Lucy smoothed her skirts and smiled. "That went well, don't you think?" she said.

Hattie glared at her. "You were to speak only of the letter you'd brought, not blather on about Mr. Lincoln and freeing the Negroes."

Lucy jutted her chin, defiant. "My remarks were entirely in keeping with our aims."

"You were overstating the case. That's a sure giveaway that you've got something to hide."

Lucy folded her arms at her waist. "The general would have agreed with me, had you not so rudely interrupted."

"The plan was for me to do the talking, remember?"

"No harm done. We have General Winder's assurance for safe passage."

Hattie shook her head. "I don't like it. If we needed passes, the general should have seen that we got them."

Anger flashed in Lucy's eyes. "You only mean to discredit me."

"I mean nothing of the sort," Hattie shot back.

"You've never liked me. You wanted the Baltimore assignment, and you resented me being chosen. It's hardly my fault your father's a traitor. I can't believe Miss Warne went along with Thom's idea of you posing as his wife. You're a risk to us all."

"It's your propensity to say too much that puts us all at risk," Hattie shot back. "For all your fine upbringing, you've clearly never learned to hold your tongue. And then bringing that doctor. If not for him, Captain McCafferty might have left us alone."

"The one has nothing to do with the other!" Lucy protested.

"Of course they do," Hattie said. "Blackstone must have gone from Thom's bedside straight to McCafferty."

"The real trouble is that you presented yourself to Dr. Blackstone as sympathetic to the Rebel cause. You should have left well enough alone."

The accusation struck a nerve, bringing forward a thought that had gnawed at Hattie since she'd first seen Blackstone in their room. She'd have thought a doctor could be trusted not to betray a patient. But if Blackstone was angry at how she'd duped him, the meeting with General Winder might not be the end of it.

They rode the rest of the way in silence, Lucy staring out one carriage window and Hattie staring out the other as a shroud of twilight fell over the city, the streets bustling with workers going home for the evening. She tried to imagine Richmond as it was before war broke out, without Confederate flags flying from the rooftops, without gray-uniformed soldiers mingling with the civilians, without the tension of not knowing when and where the next advance might come. But she could scarcely recall her own life before the war, much less that of a city she'd never known then.

When they arrived at the hotel, Hattie asked Lucy to stop at the dining room and order dinner to be brought to the room. "Get what you like for yourself," she said. "Thom and I will have soup."

A look of defiance crossed Lucy's face, and for a moment, Hattie thought she was going to object. Then her face softened. "Very well," she said. "You go on up to Thom. It's you he wants most to see anyhow."

So she was jealous after all. Hattie touched Lucy's arm. "What he wants is for all three of us to get out of here as quickly as possible."

"I know that," Lucy said.

Feeling that all had been set as right between them as it would likely ever be, Hattie went up to the room. There she found Thom propped up on pillows. He smiled, seeing her. "You're a sight for sore eyes," he said. "Did you get your passes from the general?"

She kissed his forehead, then sat beside him on the bed. "He assured us we didn't need them. He said if anyone questioned us, we need only say we'd reported to him."

Thom's face clouded. "Then I don't know why McCafferty insisted on you going there."

"I wondered that too. At least the general acknowledged that you're a valuable courier. He took the warning about you not going north to heart."

"How did Lucy do?"

Hattie sighed. "Talked more than was necessary. But I don't think it hurt anything."

"That's our Lucy. I've warned her about that. There's a time and place for her prattle, but she seems to have a hard time turning it off. I suppose she's not had an easy time of it, coddled as she was growing up."

"I don't know why coddling would make a person run at the mouth."

"Evidently it does." He took her hand. "Those of us who've had to contend with more difficult circumstances are the warier for it. Lucy wears her heart on her sleeve. It's what makes people trust her."

"Whereas I'm heartless," Hattie teased.

"Not heartless. Guarded, a trait that mostly serves you well. Do you think it's safe now to go to Miss Van Lew?"

"I hope so. We just need to be mindful of Captain McCafferty. He seems to be keeping an eye on us."

Thom stroked his beard. "McCafferty's a detective in General Winder's employ. But that's never concerned me before. We've been on friendly terms, so I thought nothing of him taking the room next door."

Hattie smiled. "In the citadel of the enemy, as it turns out."

Lucy arrived with two waiters carrying trays of food. Hattie cleared space on the little table for them to place the dishes. After they left, she removed the covers from the plates, pleasant smells of baked trout, leg of mutton, and prairie chicken filling the room. In addition, there were plates of chicken salad and spiced oysters.

"Quite the feast," Thom observed.

"I couldn't decide what to get," Lucy said. "It all looked so good."

There was no soup, the only item Hattie had specifically requested. But she said nothing of this, not wanting to raise Lucy's ire. Besides, it all looked delicious, a veritable wartime feast. She only hoped their allowance from Mr. Pinkerton could be stretched to cover the charges. Then again, if Elizabeth Van Lew could help them get out of Richmond, they wouldn't have to worry about their budget.

The food was as tasty as it looked. Even Thom ate heartily, and Hattie had to admit that Lucy had been right to be so indulgent.

Hattie was stacking the empty plates on the trays when a knock sounded at the door. Lucy started for it, but Hattie shot her a warning look and went ahead of her. She opened the door to a lean, long-faced man dressed in a black overcoat.

"I've come to see Thom Welton," he said.

From his bed, Thom turned toward him. "George Clackner," he said, beckoning the man in. "What a surprise. What brings you here from Baltimore?"

Clackner strode past Hattie and Lucy into the room. "May I offer a chair, sir?" Hattie asked, mindful of her southern manners.

"Only if you allow me to get it." He crossed the room, grabbed one of the straight-backed chairs, and plunked it down beside the bed. "I heard you were ailing," Clackner said to Thom. "So I thought I'd look in on you while I'm in town."

"That's right kind of you, George. I don't know that you've had the pleasure yet of meeting my wife, Hattie."

Clackner dipped his head. "A pleasure," he said.

"The pleasure is entirely mine, Mr. Clackner. Any friend of Thom's is a friend to us both, especially as you've so kindly thought to call on him during his illness."

"George Clackner is one of the best detectives you'll ever meet," Thom said. "General Winder would be lost without him."

Thom's easy tone aside, this warning made Hattie's skin prickle. The last thing they needed was another of General Winder's detectives hovering about.

"Your courier work is just as vital, Thom," Clackner said.

"I'm afraid I'm not much use, lying abed," Thom said. "Though I'm feeling much revived by the splendid meal my sister brought up. George, you remember Lucy."

Thom gestured toward the door, where Lucy was standing a moment earlier. But she was gone. Evidently, she'd slipped out when Clackner came in.

Hattie laughed, covering her alarm at Lucy's disappearance. "Gone to fetch dessert, I suppose. Lucy has been mooning after the luscious-looking pound cake displayed in the dining room. Oh, but Mr. Clackner, you must join us for a slice."

"I wouldn't want to impose."

"No imposition at all," Hattie said, heading for the door. "I'll run catch her, and we can enjoy our dessert together, perhaps with cordials to celebrate Thom's renewed health."

She slipped out before either man could object. Down the hallway, at the head of the stairs, Lucy leaned against the wall.

"Our goose is cooked," Lucy said, her brow knitted with worry. "George Clackner is General Winder's star detective."

"Thom's handling him well. Perhaps it's nothing but a social call as Mr. Clackner claims. Though your rushing from the room like that may well have aroused his suspicions. I told him you'd gone for pound cake and offered to fetch him a piece too." Grabbing Lucy's forearm, she started down the stairs. "We'll go together to the dining room, and when we return with dessert, you'll keep quiet. Understand?"

Lucy nodded, but Hattie saw how her bottom lip quivered. "I need you to be strong, Lucy. Thom needs you to be strong."

She nodded again, this time biting her lip to stop its quivering. Hattie took the stairs slowly, hoping to calm her. At the landing, she turned and saw Captain McCafferty and three armed men waiting for them at the bottom of the stairs.

Lucy turned, trying to tug Hattie back up the stairs. But as Hattie glanced that way, she saw George Clackner come out of the room.

Hattie clutched Lucy's arm tighter. "Down," she said through a clenched smile. "And whatever you do, don't let on that anything's amiss."

They took the stairs slowly and carefully, as would any southern lady. "A pleasure to see you again, Captain McCafferty," Hattie said when they got to the bottom.

"The General wishes to see you again," he said, mustache bristling.

Hattie smiled charmingly. "Of course, we'll be happy to accommodate the General's wishes. Tell him we'll be there first thing in the morning."

The captain shook his head. "That won't do, Mrs. Welton. He wants to see you now."

Hattie glanced at Lucy, who'd frozen like a rabbit in a hawk's shadow. At least she was keeping quiet.

"Surely the general wouldn't have us going at such a late hour," Hattie said.

"His concerns are urgent," the captain said brusquely.

"This all seems highly irregular," Hattie said. "I need to check with my husband."

She turned and saw Winder's star detective, George Clackner, standing on the landing. Two armed men stood beside him. They must have come up the back stairs, Hattie thought.

Lucy paled, seeing them.

"Very well," Hattie said, turning back to face Captain McCafferty. "We'll go with you now."

~ ~ ~

In a small, windowless room adjacent to General Winder's office, Hattie and Lucy met with the general for the second time that day. This time, he wasted no effort on a smile.

"How are the two of you, and how is Secretary Seward?"

"I don't understand your meaning," Hattie said.

"I've never in my life seen Secretary Seward," Lucy said, her expression reeking of desperation.

"You two are smart enough, I'm sure," the general said. "Otherwise, they wouldn't have sent you here to collect information on Richmond's fortifications. But we are smart enough for you this time, and Mr. Welton too. I've suspected the three of you all along."

Hattie straightened, determined to bear up under this pressure even as Lucy seemed on the verge of crumpling. "I came here with my husband to look after his health. He has risked his life carrying letters for the Confederate States of America. His illness is a direct result of that work."

The general's lips turned in a half-smile. "I believe Dr. Blackstone can speak with some authority on those claims."

Anxiety roiled her stomach, but she squared her shoulders and said, "Then bring Dr. Blackstone here, and allow me to look him in the eye, and you shall see whose account in more credible."

Lucy stepped forward then. "General, you should know that my father is a man of some influence in the north."

Hattie's heart sank. Of all the things to say, when Lucy was supposed to be Thom's British sister.

The general laughed. "Is he now? Well, if you're looking for intervention on your behalf, it would be better coming from a man wearing gray."

He turned to the officers who'd brought them in. "Take them to Castle Thunder to await trial for espionage."

Chapter Eighteen

FEBRUARY 10, 1863

G eneral Winder had commissioned the Castle Thunder prison out of three buildings on Richmond's Cary Street—Greaner's Tobacco Factory, Palmer's Factory, and Whitlock's Warehouse. It was in the former Whitlock's Warehouse that Hattie and Lucy were confined, a space designated for women and colored prisoners.

The prison was a wretched place, the cells filthy and crowded. Rations were paltry, Hattie soon discovered, the bread little more than a mix of water and flour, the peas infested with worms and the rice with vermin. What little meat they were given—bacon, mostly—was usually rotten. The ventilation was poor, and the stench of bodies held in crowded conditions mixed with the lingering odor of tobacco from the warehouse's past.

They often heard musket shots, some coming from firing squads carrying out executions in the brickyard behind the prison. The notoriously brutal Captain Alexander, who had charge of the prison, made daily patrols with his fierce black boar hound, Nero. It was hard to say which one, man or beast, struck more terror into the prisoners' hearts.

From the moment Hattie entered the prison, she'd resolved to find out what had become of Thom. General Winder had said he suspected the three of them, giving her reason to think that Thom, too, had been arrested. She believed her best chance of learning where he was being held was by acting to the hilt her role as a true southern lady. Hattie's decision to comport herself with dignity was in marked contrast to Lucy, who alternately groveled and begged and demanded release.

Thom would want her to be strong, Hattie knew. But at night, alone on the straw pallet that served as her bed in a cell shared with a dozen women, shivering in a thin prison-issued shift, she gave herself over to sorrow, her tears flowing as much for Thom's uncertain fate as her own.

She vowed not to cry openly, as Lucy did, wailing her discontents. Such displays of sorrow did nothing to move the guards, who seemed a hard lot following Captain Alexander's harsh example. A woman could be punished as well as a man, one of them warned when Hattie objected to the maggots in her soup. For such an indiscretion, a prisoner might be sent to the dungeon, a six-foot-square cell without windows or heat. Her hands might turn black from being tied behind her back for hours, or she might be forced to wear a barrel shirt, consisting of a flour barrel with armholes cut in the sides.

The guards also warned against prisoners poking their heads out the windows, an offense for which some had been shot. But on Hattie's second day in prison, she and her fellow prisoners were forced to the windows to watch an execution. One of the guards, swarthy and with a swaggering manner, jeered that any one of them, especially if charged with spying, could be next. "Jeff Davis don't tolerate no such activity," he said, "so don't be thinking your skirts will protect you."

The man at the gallows had been charged as a spy, though the women whispered that he'd sworn his innocence at a sham trial. Some of the women crowded at the windows laughed and made crude remarks as they watched the proceedings. But Lucy's face blanched as the executioner placed a hood over the man's head, so Hattie turned her by the shoulders so neither of them saw as the prisoner met his death. She noticed that a second guard, smaller than the first and with a disquieted look in his hazel eyes, also turned his head.

The execution was botched, Hattie gathered from the women who'd seen it. The rope broke, and when the drop was released, the prisoner fell to the platform. Cursing, the executioner had to be called for a new rope. There seemed few limits, Hattie thought, to the cruelty men would afflict on one another.

Long after the ordeal, Lucy remained shaken. She sat on her pallet, knees pulled to her chest, head bent at the neck.

Hattie knelt beside her. "Lucy, we've got to stay strong. You know that's what Thom would want of us."

"I don't care what Thom wants. It's because of him that I'm facing the gallows." She began to sob.

Hattie tried to put a hand on her arm, but she pulled away. "You're not facing the gallows," Hattie said. "They've got no evidence against us."

"That horrid doctor!" Lucy wailed. "He's the one who turned us in."

"I'm sure he is," Hattie said. "But that doesn't mean he'll prevail."

"And that wicked General Winder," Lucy said between sobs. "He wouldn't believe me about my...about my father."

With this, she dissolved fully into tears, and Hattie could think of nothing more to comfort her. Lucy had grown up getting her way, her confidence vanishing at the first taste of true deprivation she could not talk her way out of.

Hattie stood, becoming aware that a few pallets away, a small group of prisoners had gathered around a dark-eyed woman who gesticulated wildly as she spoke.

"It's all an error that will soon be corrected," the woman was saying. "I am a British citizen."

"She don't sound like a limey," one of her audience said.

The woman straightened. "I'll have you know I was born in the Bahamas, a British colony."

Hattie approached the group. "Who is she?" she asked one of the prisoners.

"Loreta Williams. Or Loreta Velazquez. Or Lieutenant H. T. Buford. Depends on who's asking."

Hattie studied the woman, who was addressing her fellow prisoners with a flourish and an air of independence. She wore the same prison shift as the rest of the women, but with her high cheekbones and spirited eyes, she managed to look elegant

"I dressed as a man and fought for the South," Loreta said. "I fought at the First Battle of Manassas. I was wounded at Shiloh. And for this heroism I'm imprisoned?"

Murmurs of objection at this injustice sounded all around.

"I thought the South was short on soldiers," Hattie said to the prisoner beside her. "I should think they'd welcome anyone willing to fight, even a woman dressed as a man."

"There's some that say she ain't all she claims," the prisoner said as Loretta bellowed on about her heroics when she'd assumed the guise of Confederate Lieutenant H. T. Buford.

"How's that?" Hattie asked.

The woman smiled, showing a gap where a bottom tooth should have been. "Might have got herself in trouble same as I did, distracting the soldiers, as they say."

Hattie nodded, thinking how it would shock Miss Whitcomb to know her former pupil was using her conversation skills to chat with a common prostitute. "So you're saying that's the real reason Loreta was arrested."

The gap-toothed woman shrugged. "Like I said, depends who you ask. This ain't her first dog and pony show, that's for sure. Got herself arrested for parading around Lynchburg dressed like a soldier. Nabbed some jewels in New Orleans, and that got her more attention in the papers, which she don't seem to mind one whit. The Yanks don't seem to want her around, and neither does Winder, I reckon."

Hattie nodded, then retreated to her pallet. Lucy had quit sobbing and was now staring at the ceiling in what seemed a near-catatonic state. Hattie lay back, then turned toward the wall. She couldn't worry about Lucy. She needed to find Thom.

That night, as the guards made their rounds, Hattie approached the hazel-eyed one who, like her, had refused to watch the gruesome scene in the courtyard that afternoon.

"Something eating at you, lass?" he asked in a thick Scottish brogue.

"My husband, Thom Welton. I believe he's been arrested." She reached discreetly into her sleeve, where she'd moved two dollar bills from her bodice, taken from the roll of money Miss Warne had pressed upon her at the train station.

Without looking away, the guard deftly palmed the bills, sliding them into his pocket, quick as you please. "You want to know where he is."

She nodded. "And if possible, I want to see him. Or the British consulate. He's a British citizen, so he shouldn't be held here at all." Whatever stories she'd spun, Loreta Velazquez had at least raised the idea that a British citizen might have protections others lacked.

The guard cocked his eyebrow. "Ain't asking much, are you?"

~ ~ ~

Two days later, the hazel-eyed guard with the Scottish brogue came for her. "Follow me," he said.

Thinking she might have been called in for questioning, Hattie glided with as much dignity as she could muster over the filthy floors, ignoring the stench of excrement as she followed the guard past the next large cell. Her heart sank as they approached the warden's office.

But to her relief, the guard led her past the warden's office and out the front door. The day was dreary, the skies gray and cold, but Hattie reveled in the fresh air, breathing in great gulps.

The guard grabbed her by the wrist. "Don't you go getting ideas about running off, or I'll have to clamp on the cuffs."

She fell in step beside him. "Where are you taking me?"

"You asked for your husband, didn't you?"

"Thank you," she whispered.

He raised a finger to his lips. "Enough."

Her step felt light. Thom was alive. And he wasn't in Castle Thunder, for they were headed away from those three buildings. They walked two blocks, then turned north. In front of a four-story, flat-roofed brick building, the guard turned and led her inside.

As at Castle Thunder, the smell of tobacco permeated the building. There was also the stench of unwashed bodies that she'd grown accustomed to at the prison, along with a sickly-sweet smell that reminded her of the Patent Office wards.

"Is this a hospital?" she asked.

The guard nodded. "For prisoners and the deranged."

As the guard led her through a maze of cots and pallets, a man cried out with a banshee-like wail, and she shuddered to think that this was where Thom was confined. But at least he was safe. She hoped he was getting much-needed medical attention, though she saw few attendants and only one man who might have been a doctor. One of the attendants wore prison garb, and when she asked her escort, he informed her that prisoners might, on good behavior, volunteer to tend the sick and in doing so, be allotted extra rations.

"There's ones that get themselves to the hospital other ways too." The guard chuckled under his breath as he led Hattie up the stairs. "Had us a smallpox outbreak last year. Turns out the men been smearing their faces with croton oil. I dunno where they got such an idea, but it did give them a passing resemblance to the pox."

"They wanted to come here because conditions are better?" Hattie asked hopefully.

He shook his head. "Nay, lass. They figured they'd get sent over ta the pox hospital, and along the way, they'd jump from the cart. Us guards won't go risking our lives chasin' after men with the pox. Aye, but the warden caught onto their scheme soon enough, and he put a quick stop to them shenanigans."

On the second floor, the guard stopped, shielding his eyes with his hand as he surveyed the patients lying about. "I'm told your man's here somewhere."

Hattie wasted no time, moving past cots and pallets that were crowded together without any semblance of order. For the most part, there weren't many bloody wounds among these men, and Hattie was glad for it, recalling how her stomach had roiled as Julia tended a bleeding man. But the vacant stares here reminded her of the Patent Office patients, though the despair felt even thicker here.

Finally, she spotted Thom in a far corner. She hurried to him, pulling the guard along with her. When they arrived at his cot, Thom's face lit up. "A sight for sore eyes," he said. "For sore everything."

The guard let go of her wrist, warning her to mind herself if she ever wanted to see Thom again. Then he stepped back, hovering nearby but giving them some privacy.

Hattie crouched beside Thom and took his hand, which felt warm—too warm, she thought, but she held it tightly anyhow. "Are they treating you well?"

He shrugged, and she saw how even that small movement pained him. "The men around here have warned that admission to Castle Thunder Hospital is more or less a death sentence. I'm still alive, so that's something. You and Lucy—Winder said he'd sent you to the women's facility. How are you faring?"

"Well enough." She didn't want to trouble him with Lucy's despondency. "We're treated better than the men, I hear." She pressed her hand to his cheek, glad at least that he was protected here from the sorts of punishments Captain Alexander meted out. But there seemed no good outcome for him. If his condition improved, he'd be transferred to the prison proper, and then what would become of him? And if he got worse—well, from the looks of him, gaunt and haggard, she couldn't see how he could get much worse and continue to live.

He clasped her hand, searching her face with a gaze so intense she felt as if she were melting. "Hattie, you've got to make sure Mr. Pinkerton knows what's happened to us. He'll do everything in his power to get us out of here. There are prisoner exchanges. He just needs to grease the wheels. Others have been freed, even known spies. Plus they've got no proof against us."

None save the testimony of Dr. Luke Blackstone, she thought, despising the doctor for passing himself as a Union sympathizer when she knew him to be so clearly of the Secesh persuasion, and for doing it with the charm and smile that led folks to trust him, a genial doctor who should have had only the best interests of the afflicted in mind.

"I'll find a way to get a message to Mr. Pinkerton," she assured Thom. She had no idea how, but she still had some of the bills Miss Warne had given her, and now she knew a cooperative guard.

"How did you convince the guard to bring you here?" Thom asked.

She smiled. "I have my ways." His eyes widened, and she added, "Nothing untoward, I promise. Just a little old-fashioned bribery."

"Have they brought you for questioning yet?"

She shook her head.

"When they do, deny everything."

"Everything?"

He smiled weakly. "Not that you're my wife. Because you are, you know. In all but the ceremony. But you must tell them that you know precious little about my work, only that I run letters for the South."

"What about what I told Blackstone, concerning my father?"

"Stick with that, too. Emphasize his grain smuggling for the Confederates, his organizing with the Knights, anything you can think of to convince them they'd lose his services if any harm came to you."

"But that won't help you get out."

"You can't help me much, can you, if you're locked up? So worry about yourself first. And Hattie, you've got to talk with Lucy.

Make sure she knows what you'll be saying so your stories align. At this point, her best chance is leaning on her father's influence. He may be a Union man, but if he's as well-thought-of as she claims, they won't want to risk antagonizing him. Back her up on that when they bring you for questioning."

The guard approached, his gaze darting nervously toward the stairs. "Time to say your goodbyes, lass."

Thom reached beneath the bedclothes and brought out the gold pocket watch he carried with him everywhere. He pressed it into her hand. "This belonged to my grandfather. I want you to have it. It's not much, but if you get in a jam, you might be able to trade it for—"

"I can't take this," she said.

"No arguments." He kept his hand pressed to hers, the disc of the watch warming under their touch. "Know always that no matter what anyone says, you are my one true wife. Do whatever you need with this to get to safety. Be strong, Hattie. For all of us."

She pressed her lips to his, willing herself to remember the warmth of them, not embarrassed in the least to bestow as passionate a kiss as she could manage with a host of strangers looking on.

Chapter Nineteen

FEBRUARY 10, 1863

When the Scottish guard—Hattie learned his name was Jake—returned Hattie to her cell, Lucy was sullener than ever.

"I thought you'd gone and left me, like everyone else."

Hattie almost blurted out that she wouldn't mind leaving her, if such a thing were possible, but she checked herself. As Thom had pointed out, it was crucial their stories matched when they were called in for questioning. To ensure that, she couldn't risk antagonizing Lucy any more than she already had.

"I went to see Thom," she said as simply and evenly as she could manage. "He's in the Castle Thunder Hospital, a few blocks from here."

Lucy pressed her lips in a thin line, offering no response. She turned her gaze to a corner of the cell where Loreta Velazquez was holding court.

"I've never passed such a miserable night as that one I spent in Tennessee, dressed as a Confederate soldier," she told the women gathered around her. "Rain fell in torrents over the living and the dead alike. I could have withstood the cannon better than that awful weather. Between the booming of thunder and the shells exploding all around, launched by Yankee gunboats, not a person slept, I assure you. I was lucky to escape with my life. The shrieks and groans of the wounded haunt me still."

"How'd you manage to keep your wits about you?" asked a plump woman, her eyes wide with admiration.

"It wasn't easy, I'll grant you that," Loreta said. "In such a situation, the most singular ideas run through a person's mind. The past seemed to me but a happy dream, and the future as far off as a child's rendering of heaven. The mental and physical engage in a contest for control, and more than once I felt myself slipping from fantasy into madness.

"But I managed, and the next day, in the fiercest of fighting, I held my own as the bravest of men did. It was undoubtedly one of the most terrible battles of the war. At every lull, the enemy advanced. Such a sickening spectacle of suffering I hope never again to witness. And yet Providence rewarded my bravery, for I encountered my very own father there on the battlefield, fighting for the same cause as I."

Hattie caught the eye of the gap-toothed woman, who shook her head in disbelief. Like Hattie, she hung back from the group. There was no need to stand close, for Loreta's voice projected as much as a preacher delivering a fiery sermon. She certainly did not lack for confidence.

"You and your daddy had a reunion, right there on the Shiloh battlefield?" the gap-toothed woman asked.

"Oh no," Loreta said, sweeping her hand for effect. "My father didn't recognize me. How could he, when I was dressed in the noble gray of our troops, with a dark mustache secured to my upper lip. It was enough to survive the day, though I became quite ill from exposure and fatigue. Yet my spirits soon regained their elasticity, and I found I could not remain inactive while so many exciting scenes continued to unfold around me."

Lucy, who'd been staring blankly in Loreta's direction, moved toward her. "Exciting scenes, you say."

"Oh yes," Loreta said. "It is not in my nature to brood over misfortune. Soon enough, I was ready to resume—"

Lucy lunged at her, fists flying.

"Lucy!" Rushing toward her, Hattie grasped at her flailing arm, but Lucy yanked away, grabbing hold of a chunk of Loreta's gleaming black hair and tugging with such force that Hattie flinched.

Loreta twisted away from Lucy, yowling in pain. "Bitch!" she screamed, dark eyes flashing.

Jake came running. "What's this hubbub?"

"She tried to kill me!" Loreta cried.

Her face red with anger, Lucy scowled. "She won't shut up."

"Calm down, Lucy." Hattie touched her shoulder, but she flinched and ducked away.

Entering the cell, Jake took hold of Lucy's wrists, pinning them behind her back as he led her away. The women gathered around Loreta began muttering over what they'd seen. "Thinks she's queen of all she surveys," one of the women muttered. Hattie supposed that meant Lucy, though it might have been said of Loreta.

Hattie wished she'd immediately done as Thom said, convincing Lucy that they both needed to tell the same story when they were questioned, instead of waiting until Lucy was in a better mood. She hoped it wasn't too late.

All afternoon, Hattie waited for Lucy's return. She was glad, at least, that Captain Alexander and his dog Nero hadn't been the ones to respond to the altercation. She'd heard of him turning the dog loose on prisoners and the dog tearing them within an inch of their lives. Which of the captain's punishments might be meted out on women, she didn't know. She only hoped Lucy was able to compose herself once she got away from Loreta. If she was truly unhinged, she posed a danger not only to herself but to Thom and Hattie too.

It was almost evening when Jake returned. "You're to come with me, Mrs. Welton. The captain wants a word with you."

Following Jake, Hattie felt as if she was walking into a trap that was ready to spring. She pressed her hand to her bodice, feeling for the ticking of Thom's watch that she'd stashed there, the metal warmed by her flesh. *Be strong,* he'd said. *For all of us.*

Jake led her to Captain Alexander's office. He rapped twice on the door.

"Enter!" The voice from the other side of the door was booming, theatrical.

Jake swung the door open. "Mrs. Welton," he announced.

Captain Alexander rose from his desk, and his dog Nero rose from where he lay on the rug. Nero snarled at her, baring his teeth.

"Good boy, Nero." The captain patted his head, and the dog sat as Jake left the room, closing the door.

When Captain Alexander made his rounds, Hattie had done her best to ignore him. Now she met his gaze. His black hair fell nearly to the nape of his neck, and his black beard straggled nearly to the top of his chest. Across his black shirt, he wore a red sash, and the holster around his waist held two pistols and two pairs of handcuffs.

"Nero is keen on enforcing the rules," the captain explained.

"I've broken no rules," Hattie said.

"I'll be the judge of that. Sit, Mrs. Welton," he said, indicating a straight-backed chair facing his desk. "Or is it Miss Logan?"

Holding her expression so as not to show surprise, she sat. "My parents are the Logans of La Conner, Indiana, if that's what you're getting at. I hate to think of their distress upon learning I've been so unjustly apprehended."

He cocked an eyebrow as he sat back down in his leather chair and Nero resumed his place on the rug. "Your parents would be upset to know you're in a Confederate prison?"

She breathed deep. Thom was right, she knew. Her best hope lay in evoking the past she'd been desperate to forget. "My father is a loyal supporter of the Southern cause. My mother's loyalties also lie squarely. Her father is helping fend off a Yankee attack on Vicksburg."

The captain stroked his beard. "So I've heard. But then how is it you've associated yourself with Thom Welton, who has betrayed our trust through and through?"

"My husband has done no wrong, Captain. He has risked his life running letters for the South."

"Your husband, if that's who he is, has admitted to working for the US government. He claims he recently became disgusted with the job and has decided to leave it." The captain shrugged. "And he's got every right to, I suppose, as a foreigner."

Hattie tensed. The captain was testing her. Thom wouldn't have so easily admitted to working for the Federals, not after telling her to deny all charges. "Thomas Welton is indeed a British subject, falling under the Queen's protection. I'm certain the British consul will vouch for him."

Captain Alexander laughed, an ugly sound. "Her Majesty's envoys will be of little help to him. The consul dispatched to Richmond hates Americans and is not inclined to intervene on behalf of British subjects who endear themselves to the Federals."

"What evidence do you have that Thom is one of those subjects?"

He grinned, revealing small, yellowed teeth. "That's not something I'm at liberty to reveal. Suffice to say I've got my sources."

Blackstone, of course. It all went back to the doctor's word against theirs. Having reached a dead end, Hattie changed tack. "What have you done with Thom's sister?"

"Me? Nothing at all."

"She was taken from our cell only hours ago."

"Ah, you must mean Lucy Hamilton. She and I conversed earlier in the day. I believe you were at the hospital, visiting Mr. Welton."

Dread spread from the pit of Hattie's stomach. Her absence had given the captain a chance to catch Lucy off guard. "What did she tell you?"

With a light groan, Nero lay down on his side. The captain reached down and patted his belly. Withdrawing his hand, he opened his desk drawer and took out some papers written in what appeared to be his own hand. "Do you like poetry, Hattie?"

She shifted, uneasy at the familiar way he addressed her. "I like it well enough, I suppose."

"Then indulge me, if you will, in listening to a bit of the verse I've penned." He shuffled through the papers. Selecting one, he held it up in front of his face. Squinting, he read in a bellowing voice, "For whom shall men fall, for whom shall they die, but for the love of a woman true. But suffer the lady bent on deceit, and the wrath that will be her due."

He watched her face for a reaction. She had heard rumors of prisoners gaining favor with the captain by flattering him for what he perceived as his talent for writing verse. And she'd pretended her way this far, so praising a bit of doggerel did not seem out of line, though the lie somehow felt harder than the others she'd told. "You're quite a skilled poet, Captain Alexander."

He returned the paper to the stack, then straightened it. "So I'm told. With that prelude, I'll admit that your friend Lucy had quite a story to tell about the three of you being on Allen Pinkerton's payroll, working on behalf of the US government."

So Lucy had betrayed them completely. Fury rose in Hattie's throat. On its heels came discouragement. But she could not indulge either feeling. She owed it to Thom to stay the course. "My husband's sister and I disagree on any number of things."

"Truly, Miss Logan, there is no sense in you maintaining this ruse. Lucy Hamilton has disavowed relations of any sort with you and Thom Welton."

"What have you done with her?" she asked again.

"Nothing nefarious, I assure you. You might say she's under observation in the citizen's room. Perhaps you've heard of it?"

"I have." Another prisoner had told Hattie about a spacious area where certain male prisoners with access to money were allowed to sleep on actual cots and eat meals purchased with their own funds, provided they first shared a portion of those funds with Captain Alexander. "I hadn't realized you allowed women there."

He folded his hands, large and pawlike, atop his desk. "Lucy is the first. I've arranged for separate sleeping quarters, of course, but she may mingle with the men during meals. Once I drew her out of her melancholy, your friend became quite free with her speech, though with women like her, there is always the tedious matter of sorting fact from fiction. She made some rather incredulous claims about her father being an important figure in the US government, saying he'd stop at nothing to secure her release. I don't suppose you know anything about that?"

Hands in her lap, Hattie worried her thumb over her palm. So this was how it would end. Lucy would be set free based on her father's influence while she and Thom were left at Castle Thunder to rot, or worse. And yet, angry and disappointed as Hattie was with Lucy, she'd at least owned up to her origins instead of running from them as Hattie had. Not that Lucy had much to own up to. And yet her privilege hadn't served her well. No matter the pain of Hattie's upbringing, she'd learned from it. She'd become her own person, equipped to grapple with adversity rather than sell out those around her to save her skin.

In Hattie's silence, Captain Alexander leaned back in his chair, fingers laced behind his head. "Of course, I wouldn't expect you to come to Lucy's defense. Not after she's exposed the lot of you. This business about her father is all a ruse, I'm sure. To tell the truth, it angers me. She will find a very unpleasant experience awaits her upon her release from the citizens' room."

Hattie took a deep breath. "Lucy Hamilton is exactly who she says she is, the daughter of a man of some influence in Washington. Even if, as my own father dearly hopes, we achieve a peace that recognizes the sovereignty of the Confederate State of America, I can't imagine what consequences might unfold if Lucy's father pursued an investigation into the circumstances of her arrest and imprisonment without substantive evidence. And truly, sir, I don't know how long she can last here, even in the citizens' room. She hasn't the fortitude for it. I beg you to release her, sir. For her own good and your own."

He slapped his palms flat on his desk, startling her. "Lucy Hamilton betrayed you. Now you want me to show her leniency? That won't do a thing to help you or Thom Welton."

Letting go of her worrying hands, she straightened. "I'm not expecting it would. But I urge you to consider Lucy's background. In a prisoner exchange, she'd be worth quite a lot."

He shook his head. "You're a puzzle, Miss Logan. An enigma. I can't reconcile your concern for someone who betrayed you, nor can I reconcile what I've been told about your duties with Mr. Pinkerton with what you say about your own family's background. But that, of course, is subject to verification."

She jutted her chin. "You might speak to Dr. Blackstone."

"Dr. Blackstone has gone north, I'm afraid. And while he certainly confirmed before departing that you knew more than you should about Edgar Logan's assistance to our cause, we have no way of knowing how you came upon that information. You can pretend to be his daughter as easily as you pretend to be a courier's wife."

An idea seized her then, a way to possibly secure her release and perhaps even Thom's. "If you have a sheet of paper to spare, Captain Alexander, and if you'll see fit to lend me your pen, I'll write a note to my father, asking that he confirm our relationship. Your most reliable courier is indisposed at the moment, but there must be others running letters by now."

He raised an eyebrow. "Others with clearer loyalties, I should hope." He reached again in his desk drawer, then presented her a paper and pen. "Write your note. I'll address it to Chester Logan, and we shall see how he responds."

She took the pen and, willing her hand to stop shaking, wrote as firmly and directly as she could manage.

Father,

I am in a bad place, being held at Castle Thunder prison in Richmond. Captain Alexander, the warden here, knows of your work and asks that you confirm that I am indeed your daughter.

I assured him that whatever our past differences, we are indeed bonded by blood, but he wants your word on it.

She hesitated, holding the pen slightly above the paper, trying to think how to close. Well wishes would come off as insincere. Forgiveness, if it came at all, would take time. One day, perhaps, she and her father might speak of love, but it was too soon for that now.

The captain drummed his fingers on his desk. "I haven't got all day."

She simply signed *Yours, Hattie,* then handed him the note and hoped for the best.

Chapter Twenty

FEBRUARY 25, 1863

People spoke of making peace as if it were something that could be crafted, like a tunic or shawl. But it was not so easy, not for the nation and not for Hattie. From the snippets of war news that trickled into Castle Thunder, the month of February was ending in relative calm. But on both sides, everyone realized that this was an illusion. Many battles and much sacrifice would be required before anything resembling peace could be achieved.

After meeting with Captain Alexander, Hattie had no idea where to put her energies. She'd turned so much anger on Lucy, inwardly if not outwardly, and what good had it done? Lucy had betrayed both her and Thom, putting herself in the captain's favor and gaining the best accommodations Castle Thunder offered.

Still, she didn't regret speaking on Lucy's behalf. What she'd told Captain Alexander was true. Lucy's father would raise Cain if anything happened to her. When he'd allowed her to pose as Thom's sister, he'd assumed, as she had, a little lark from which she'd emerge unscathed. When things had gone your way your whole life, when you had wealth, power, and influence, it was probably hard to imagine anything different.

Hattie hadn't come around to liking Lucy, but during the days they'd spent together in the women's cell, she'd come to understand how pointless it was to resent her circumstances. Nor was there any sense in trying to best Lucy, especially not now that adversity had gotten the better of her. No wonder she'd snapped under questioning.

Three days after Hattie met with the captain, Jake pulled her aside at the end of what passed for the evening meal. "Your friend Lucy has been swapped for two boys the Yanks was holdin'. Had some value, that one did."

"Does Thom know?" she asked quietly.

Jake looked to his left and right. "I dunno, lass. Capt'n's keepin' close watch on that'un."

"It can't be that close. There are so few staff at the hospital."

"He ain't there anymore, lass. Captain had him hauled out for questioning, and now they got'im over to this side, in the Greaner's Warehouse." Greaner's was the largest of the three warehouses that made up the Castle Thunder block, a three-story brick structure with barred windows and a row of dormers along the roof.

Hattie hugged her arms to her chest. Thom was so close and yet so far. "Is he well?"

"I canna say for sure, but from what I'm hearing, he's right frail."

"Can you take me to him?" She reached into her bodice and pulled out the roll of bills Miss Warne had given her. She peeled off three of them and offered them to Jake. "Tonight, if you can manage it. Please."

He shook his head. "Ain't so easy as that. Like I said, he's being watched."

She offered another three bills, nearly the last of what Miss Warne had given her. "You can share this with whoever's guarding him."

Jake hesitated, then pocketed the money. "I canna promise anything, lass. Could take some time, but I'll try."

Worries kept her up half that night. She was certain Captain Alexander had lied to her about Thom's confession, and she had no doubt he'd have lied about her while questioning Thom. She trusted Thom would see through that. But did he know that Lucy had given up the fact that they all worked for Pinkerton? What if Captain Alexander had said nothing to Thom about Lucy's confession until Thom dug himself a hole? What if he'd resorted to torture or turned Nero loose on Thom, with no regard for his frail health.

In the days that followed, she waited for Jake to bring word of Thom while she tried to focus on other concerns. One was whether Lucy, once freed, had gone to Miss Warne and Mr. Pinkerton with the details of their imprisonment. It seemed the least Lucy could do, but Hattie suspected her shame at having betrayed them might be keeping her silent.

Hattie waited, too, for her father's response to the letter she'd entrusted to Captain Alexander. Her father's allegiance to the South was beyond question. He only had to affirm that she was his daughter, and the officials would be compelled to let her go. Then she'd go directly to Elizabeth Van Lew and seek her help in freeing Thom. According to him, Elizabeth was a clever spy with a network of like-minded friends in Richmond.

So much hinged on her father. Hattie despised nearly everything her parents stood for, despised the way they'd chided George for his love of nature and his gentle ways with animals, despised how they'd always found fault with her, despised them for the privilege and greed that made even their children pariahs in their small Indiana town. And yet now, with time and distance between them, she also saw how deeply unhappy her father and mother were—or, more accurately, how deeply unhappy they'd made themselves.

She relished her happy memories of George—how he'd nursed a broken-winged bird to health, how he'd spirited off a litter of kittens before their mother had them drowned. But her memories of her parents were mostly of harsh judgments and stony silence. The closest she'd seen her mother to happiness was during visits to the Louisiana plantation where she'd grown up. Lydia Logan relished the carefree days she'd spent there as a child, drinking lemonade on the veranda and singing along as Hattie's grandmother played the piano. Then Hattie's grandmother died, and even the memories of these small joys had leaked away, replaced by bitterness.

Hattie liked to think there had been some good in her mother, some levity at least, that had made her father fall in love with her. But perhaps it had been only a marriage of convenience, tied to the wealth that was always her father's first concern. And yet despite the success of his grain storage business, Lydia complained incessantly of the deprivations she suffered, living in a small Indiana town where no one rose to her expectations, least of all her husband.

Hattie wondered if it was her unhappiness, hardened into bitterness, that had hardened her father too. She remembered a few happy moments with her father when she and George were young. A hot August night when he'd taught them to catch blinking fireflies on. An afternoon on the porch when he regaled them with his escapades as a hand on a riverboat when he was only sixteen. She hoped that when her father got her letter, he'd think of these happy memories, too, and not the fact that Hattie had snuck away from Indiana without their permission.

Each time Jake passed by on his guard rounds, Hattie caught his gaze. Each time, he only shook his head. Despair curled at the edges of her existence, threatening to overtake her. Peg, the gap-toothed prisoner charged with debauchery, seemed to sense Hattie's waning spirits and tried to cheer her with stories of her childhood encounters with fairies and leprechauns back in Ireland. Hattie believed little of what she said, but the accounts did make her smile.

Loreta, too, was nothing if not entertaining. From her fabulous tales of battles and narrow escapes from danger as she fought with the Confederates while disguised as a man, Hattie derived a sort of mental exercise, making mental notes of the inconsistencies. And what harm was there in Loreta's fabrications? They were all tale-tellers of one sort or another.

One day, Peg shared another impossible-sounding tale, this one gleaned from a Castle Thunder guard who was friendly with her in ways Hattie preferred not to speculate on. According to Peg, a prisoner on the men's side, Sidney Hanover, liked to entertain his fellow prisoners after the evening meal with cheerful tunes belted out in his off-key baritone voice.

Yesterday, in the middle of one such performance, he'd thrown his hands in the air and then fell to the floor. After a moment of shocked silence, an uproar ensued, the inmates calling for the guards to summon a surgeon. At that hour, the surgeon was none too happy about his summons, and after a quick examination, he pronounced Hanover dead as a doornail.

"Tossed him in a wagon, they did," Peg said, eyes twinkling. "And the wagon driver sets off for the hospital, 'cause that's where they keep the coffins. But when they get to the hospital, Hanover's gone. So the driver turns back, thinking the stiff's somehow rolled outta the cart, but there's nobody to be found. Turns out he was only pretending to be dead."

Hattie had seen some fine acting during her time at Grover's National, including some who'd acted out death on the stage, but she didn't know that any of those performances would fool a doctor. But the hospital staff was certainly overworked, and perhaps the surgeon had done only a cursory examination before declaring Hanover dead.

Whether because of the Hanover debacle or some other cause, Captain Alexander seemed especially out of sorts when he made the rounds with Nero the next day. As usual, Peg retreated to a far corner of the cell as they passed. The scar on her cheek, she'd told Hattie, had come from a dog's attack when she was a child, and she'd been deathly afraid of dogs ever since. Nero seemed to sense her fear, for he always stopped and raised his nose, sniffing in the direction where she cowered.

Today, the captain's face twisted in a smile as he observed Nero sniffing in Peg's direction. He turned a key, opened the cell door, and let go of the dog's leash. In an instant, Nero was lunging for Peg.

Seeing her terror, Hattie stepped between her and the dog. Long ago, George had taught her that the best way to deal with an aggressive animal was to face it down without showing your fear, making yourself as large as possible so it sensed you were in charge. She breathed deep, filling her chest and swelling her shoulders as she raised her arms, palms out.

"No!" she yelled firmly. "Go away!"

Nero snarled at her, teeth bared.

Hattie stamped her foot. "Be gone!"

Stepping back, Nero barked loudly at her. He seemed to have forgotten Peg.

The captain scowled. "You have a way of inserting yourself where you don't belong, don't you, Miss Logan."

"Mrs. Welton," Hattie hissed, keeping her eyes on the dog.

The captain shook his head. "Never met a woman who so clung to a story." He clapped his hands, and Nero trotted back to him.

Hattie clasped her hands at her waist to calm their shaking. "I am the courier's wife."

The captain laughed heartily as he secured Nero's leash. "Your courier has made his final delivery."

Panic seized her chest. "Explain yourself, Captain Alexander."

The captain cocked his head, and Nero barked menacingly. "If I didn't know better, Miss Logan, I'd think you were a man dressed in women's clothes, with the way you assert yourself."

He turned then and, without another word, went on with his rounds. Hattie helped Peg to her feet. "You saved my life," Peg said.

"He only meant to scare you," Hattie said with more confidence than she felt. "Never let them see your fear."

~ ~ ~

That evening after supper, Jake came for Hattie.

"Is there word of Thom? Can I see him?" she asked.

"'Fraid not. That's a hard lot, guardin' him."

Her shoulders relaxed. "He's alive, then."

Jake nodded curtly, his expression grim. "For the time being. You're to come with me, lass. Capt'n wants to see you."

She followed Jake out of the cell, dreading the encounter that lay ahead, knowing the captain's mood had likely only turned fouler from her intervening on Peg's behalf.

Nero snarled as she entered the captain's office, which smelled even more strongly of tobacco than it had before. In the glow of the sputtering wall sconce, the hound looked fiercer than usual. Captain Alexander offered no greeting, only grunted and gestured to the empty chair.

Hattie held his gaze as she perched on the chair. *Never let them see your fear.* Men who acted like animals had to be handled the same way.

"I'm told my husband has been moved from the hospital to this block," she said. "I wish to see him."

The captain sneered. "Your wishes are none of my concern. Your husband, if you insist on maintaining this charade of being his wife, is a damned liar. Our highest officials and their supporters trusted him to bring sensitive letters and documents over the border, and all the while he was working for the Federals."

"What evidence do you have against him?"

He laughed, an unpleasant chortle. "Have you forgotten how easily your friend Lucy turned on you both? She made clear that your employer, Allen Pinkerton, gave her the letter she brought to Richmond."

The letter that was supposed to have protected Thom. That, too, had gone awry. "If Mr. Pinkerton employs my husband, why isn't he trying to get him released?"

"Oh, but he is. You've been in the papers ever since your friend's release. And that damned Allen Pinkerton gets the Richmond paper nearly as quickly as I do. From what I hear, he went straight to Secretary Stanton, pleading for a team of emissaries to come under a flag of truce and arrange the release of you and your husband. But apparently the secretary of war has other things on his mind besides the two of you."

At least Mr. Pinkerton had tried—and was still trying, she hoped. "This is all a mistake," she said.

"So Mr. Welton claims. But nothing he's told us will stand up in court."

There was a court of sorts here, a military tribunal to hear the cases of Castle Thunder's more prominent prisoners. The proceedings would no doubt be unfair, but at least they would buy Thom some time. "When will my husband's case be heard?"

Alexander's eyes narrowed. "You ask more questions than is befitting a lady, Miss Logan. I am the interrogator here.'"

She flattened her hands on her lap. "I'm merely concerned over my husband's welfare, as I'm certain Mrs. Alexander would be if she were in my position."

"Unlike you, my wife is a lady. She knows better than to assert herself." He shrugged. "I always say, if a woman insists on acting like a man, she deserves to be treated like one. Which in the case of a spy means hanging. Unless, of course, there are extenuating circumstances. Certain payments, perhaps, made on a prisoner's behalf."

"A bribe, you mean."

"Crudely stated, yes. And your father would have the money for that, wouldn't he?"

"He's quite successful in his business if that's what you mean. And loyal to the South."

The drawer of the captain's oaken desk creaked as he slid it open. He reached inside, extracting an envelope. He tapped it on the desktop. Then he turned it over, and she saw her father's familiar slanted script.

Hattie Logan, c/o Castle Thunder Prison, Richmond, Virginia, CSA

She reached for the envelope, but Captain Alexander pulled it away, waving it enticingly under Nero's nose. The hound sniffed the envelope with much interest, a string of drool forming at the corner of its mouth.

"Get it!" Captain Alexander said.

The dog chomped at the envelope, but the captain yanked it from his reach.

"A small amusement for Nero," he said. "He performs so many vital services here. Perhaps you'd like to pat his head, Miss Logan, and tell him what a good boy he is. He'd appreciate that, especially after how you got in his way this afternoon."

She kept her hands in her lap, knowing there was little to prevent Nero from chomping off her fingers if his master ordered it. "He'd be a more likable creature if he wasn't turned loose on frightened women," she said.

The captain ran his fingers along the edges of the envelope. "I doubt Nero cares who likes him," he said. "No more than I do."

He reached for a letter opener on the edge of his desk. He held it up to the light, admiring the scrimshaw handle. "A fellow sailor gave this to me. Did you know I was in the US Navy, Miss Logan? Then the war broke out, and I abandoned my commission to join a band of Confederate pirates, seizing Yankee ships in the Chesapeake and sailing them for Richmond. Ah, those were the days."

He lowered the letter opener and wedged it in the corner of the envelope, all the while locking eyes with her. "I was captured, you know. Fort McHenry, in Baltimore. But I made my escape. Leaped from a rampart and swam to freedom. That's why so few escape from here. I know the tricks." He sighed dramatically. "Most of them, anyhow."

He ran the letter opener along the envelope's sealed edge. The sound of its slicing pierced the silence. Hattie's breath caught. The captain held in his hand her chance to leverage her family ties to get herself out of here, and Thom too.

The captain withdrew a folded paper from the envelope. Holding it by the top edge, he flicked it open, keeping it at arm's length as he read the message. "Direct," he said. "I like a man who's direct."

He turned the letter, then flattened it on the desk, pushing it toward her. She leaned in, reading her father's words.

Hattie Logan is no daughter of mine.

Her breath left her. She felt as if her chair had been yanked away, leaving her with nothing solid beneath. All the years she'd yearned to be free of her parents, all her time in Washington, pretending they were someone else. Now the cords were cut, the ties severed. Not by her but by them.

She felt gut-punched. Surely her father understood that her life was on the line. Was his anger at her leaving that great? She'd never thought her running off would hurt anything but their pride. Was that enough for her father to reject his own flesh and blood.? And yet she'd done the same.

Captain Alexander slid the letter away from her, then refolded it and slipped it back in the envelope. "The matter is settled. You are not who you claim to be. Or if you are, your people have written you off. Either way, it's time you quit pretending."

There was some truth in this, she realized. Pretending as part of a spy's work was one thing. But there was no point in pretending as a way to forget.

"Edgar Logan is my father," she said. "Lydia Logan is my mother. They may not claim me, but they can't erase me any more than I can erase them."

The captain tossed the envelope to the side of his desk. "You know, Miss Logan, you've become quite an annoyance to me. I'm told you've been badgering the guards for access to Mr. Welton. And he's doing the same, begging to see you. And begging never sits well with me. Just ask Nero." He kicked the dog in the haunches. Nero cowered as if he were only a pup. The confusion in his eyes made Hattie pity the beast.

The captain took his pen from his inkwell and jotted a note. "I'm transferring you to Libby Prison, Miss Logan. Let Major Turner deal with you. Welton's the prize here, and I don't want him distracted while we extract whatever information we can from him." He smirked. "To ensure a fair trial, of course."

Her heart sank. She would be across the city from Thom, with no way to see him. "There's no women's cell at Libby Prison," she said.

Captain Alexander shrugged. "Not my concern. Turner will find a way to accommodate you. He's a clever fellow, they say, despite his youth." He gestured toward the door. "Out with you, Miss Logan. Gather your things for transfer in the morning."

"Please, Captain Alexander. I implore you to reconsider."

He stood suddenly from his chair. Nero rose to his side, flecks of spittle forming at his mouth as the sharp sound of his barking filled the room. "Out, I said. Now."

She got up, gathering her skirts as she locked eyes with him. "You're a cruel man, Captain Alexander." *And a wretched poet,* she nearly added, but she didn't want the insult to come back on Thom.

Jake was waiting for her in the hallway. He looked miserable.

"I'm being transferred," she said. "In the morning. To Libby Prison."

He shook his head. "I feared as much." He steered her by the elbow down the hallway, away from the captain's office. Night was falling, the windows dark.

Hattie stopped, turning to him. "Take me to Thom. I've got to see him."

"Capt'n would have my hide. I got a wife and three young'uns still at home. I cain't lose this post."

"Point me to him, then. I'll go on my own. If anyone asks, you can say I ran off."

"I told you, lass, they've got a guard on him."

"You could distract him. I only need a minute."

Jake rubbed his chin. "You get caught, and it's curtains for the both of us."

"I won't get caught."

"No offense, lass, but your record on that account ain't much to brag about."

"I'll be quick," she insisted. "All you need do is talk with the guard. One minute, and I'll slip away, and we'll meet back up, and you can return me to the women's cell. No one will be the wiser."

Jake steered her forward, his hand on her elbow. "You're a persuasive one, Mrs. Welton."

She offered a weak smile. "And you're a good man, Jake."

"A man who had best keep this post or he'll get sent off to fight," he muttered.

He guided her to a back door. He looked left and right. Satisfied no one was watching, he chose a key from the ring he carried and turned it in the lock. He pushed the door, opening it only wide enough for her to slip through. Across the courtyard, she made out the shape of the Greavor's building, a hulking shadow in the night. Over its dormered roof hung a half-moon, glowing faintly behind a curtain of clouds.

"Hug tight to the walls," Jake said. "Stay in the shadows. You reach that far door, you hang back till I get there. I'll head for the women's cell, like I'm droppin' you there. Then I'll switch back and come after you."

She nodded, then slipped through the opening. The night air filled her lungs, damp and carrying only a trace of the choking smoke that often settled over the city. Though surrounded on all sides by Castle Thunder's buildings and walls, she felt a sense of freedom. How often she'd taken for granted the brush of evening air on her skin, the stars popping out overhead. And the quiet—here there were no guards' footsteps, no keys rattling, no raucous laughter from women whose whimpering filled the silence when they thought their fellow inmates were sleeping.

She hugged close to the wall as Jake had instructed, the bricks cool against her back as she made her way slowly along the shadows. Reaching the door, she hung to one side of it, pressing herself to the wall. She heard voices inside, and a moment later, the door opened.

Squinting at the burst of light through the doorway, she held her breath as two guards emerged, laughing. They stopped on the stoop, one guard gesticulating wildly as he recounted last night's foray at a saloon.

Hattie closed her eyes and willed herself to blend with the night. Finally, the guards went on their way, crossing the courtyard to the Palmer's Factory building where Union deserters and prisoners of war were held. Only when they'd entered that building did Hattie allow herself to relax.

Moments later, the door opened again. This time, it was Jake. She scurried up the steps and through the opening.

Jake pressed a finger to his lips, then pointed to the far end of the hall. In the dim light, she made out the figure of a stocky man leaning against the wall. "Wait till you see I've got 'im lookin' my way," Jake whispered. "Then you can go to your man. But only for a minute, mind you."

She nodded, staying in the recess of the door as Jake strolled down the hallway, whistling a tune she recognized as "My Bonny Boy." He reached the cell farthest from her, and she saw a figure stir on the cot. Thom, she thought, and her heart quickened.

Jake paused, speaking to the guard in a voice too low for her to hear. The guard pushed away from the wall and turned to face Jake, his back to Hattie. She glided toward Thom's cell, glad for once that Miss Whitcomb had insisted on her pupils moving as noiselessly as deer in a forest.

As she approached, she saw that Thom had sat up on his cot. At least he wasn't forced to sleep on a pallet. He glanced toward Jake and the guard, then turned, watching her approach. He started to rise, but she shook her head, and he stayed seated.

She crouched beside him, reaching through the bars to take his hand. How pale and gaunt he looked, she thought as he wrapped his fingers around hers.

"I've missed you so," he whispered.

"And I you," she whispered back. "I haven't much time. I'm leaving in the morning."

Even in the dim light, she saw how his face brightened. "Pinkerton got you released?"

She shook her head. "I'm being sent to another prison."

His smile faded. At the end of the hall, the guard shifted. Hattie drew back. Then, seeing that he was only taking something Jake offered—a pinch of tobacco, perhaps—she threaded her fingers back through Thom's.

"I've got to go. But I promise, I'll do all I can—"

"Save yourself, Hattie," he said in a whisper so gruff she feared he was on the verge of tears.

She forced a smile. "What kind of wife would I be, thinking only of myself?"

He squeezed her hand. "Whatever happens, know that I love you, Hattie Logan."

"Welton," she corrected, fearing that if she said anything else she might burst into tears.

She let go of his hand and studied his face, wanting to remember forever the crinkles at the corners of his eyes, the jut of his chin, the smooth skin of his forehead, the longing in his gaze. "Even as I leave, my love will stay with you."

The guard started to turn. Jake grabbed his arm, pulling him back around. Hattie slipped back into the darkness, leaving Thom behind.

Chapter Twenty-One

FEBRUARY 26, 1863

Hattie's nerve held until Jake got her back to the women's cell. But when he pressed the bills she'd given him back into her hand, saying she'd be needing them more than he, tears welled in her eyes, and it was all she could do to whisper her thanks.

Hattie went to her pallet hoping no one would notice the tears streaming down her face. But Peg had been watching for her, and when she saw Hattie was crying, she rushed to her side. "Wot's that man done to you?"

Hattie shook her head, sobbing so hard she could hardly speak. "I'm...I'm being transferred. To Libby."

"Libby?" Peg made a face. "That ain't no place for a lady."

Hattie wiped her tears with the back of her hand, collecting herself. "There's some who say I'm no lady."

Peg leaned back on her heels, her chin in her hands. "You could pretend you're dead."

Hattie managed a smile. "I doubt that trick would work twice."

"Well, there's gotta be something you can do."

They sat a moment in silence. She'd miss Peg, Hattie realized. She'd even miss Loreta and her wild stories. They'd been good company, keeping her going when all hope seemed lost. At Libby, she'd have no one. As the only woman, she'd be kept apart from the other prisoners.

Peg stood abruptly. "You wait here," she said, as if there were somewhere Hattie could go. "I've got an idea."

She crossed the cell and crouched beside Loreta's pallet, the two of them whispering in the dark. Then Loreta got up and opened the satchel of belongings she'd been allowed to bring with her since she was a Confederate supporter. She withdrew something from the satchel, then followed Peg to Hattie's pallet.

Loreta held out a hand to Hattie. "Come with me," she said. "I'm going to fix you up."

Puzzled, Hattie took her hand, following Loreta to the window. "I'll watch for Jake," Peg said, and she went toward the cell's entrance.

"What's this all about?" Hattie said.

Loreta set down the item she'd taken from her satchel, then positioned Hattie in the swath of moonlight that was shining through the window now that the clouds had parted. She drew herself up, squaring her shoulders. "You're going to be among men, you need to fit in," she said in her clipped accent.

"But I don't see how—"

Loreta shook her head, wagging a finger. "That's a woman's way of objecting." She stamped her foot and swore under her breath. Hattie drew back, having never heard such language from a woman.

Loreta grinned. "That's how a man does it. I can give you the appearance. You must provide the bravado."

The plan came clear then. If Hattie was forced to leave Castle Thunder, Peg and Loreta meant for her to do it as a man, shedding her identity as a spy who might otherwise be hung for treason.

"A man," she said. "You really think I can pull it off?"

Loreta shrugged. "I did. They've sent so many young boys into battle that a woman can pass for one."

Hattie studied her in the moon's thin light. "In a dress?"

"Peg will get Jake to bring a man's uniform." Loreta took a small pair of nail scissors from her dress pocket. That she'd smuggled them into the prison was a testament to her cleverness, Hattie had to admit, though the blades were so tiny the scissors could hardly be used as a weapon. "We start with the hair," Loreta said.

Hattie reached instinctively for the curls that fell to her shoulders. "I don't see how this could work."

"You have a better idea?"

"No," Hattie admitted.

Without another word, Loreta began snipping away at her curls. As tendrils fell to the floor all around her, Hattie tried to consider the merits of the plan. Loreta's stories might be exaggerated, but Hattie had heard of other women who'd gone into battle dressed as men.

The snipping went on for a long time, Hattie's neck feeling more and more exposed as her locks fell away. Finally, Loreta was done. She turned Hattie by the shoulders to face her. "Very nice," she said. "The lips are a bit too pronounced, but I've met boys with girlish lips like that. Kissed them too." She laughed.

Hattie had new sympathy for sheep that went from wooly to naked in a single shearing. Now that Loreta had turned her from the window, Hattie saw that several of the other women had propped themselves on their elbows, watching the spectacle.

Hattie looked down at her figure, taking in the curves of her breasts, her waist, her hips. "Even in men's clothes, I don't see how you hide all—this."

Loreta grabbed the garment she'd taken from her satchel and held it up to Hattie's shoulders. "Should fit," she said.

Hattie fingered the material. It was unlike any fabric she'd ever worn, almost like a window screen. "What's this for?"

"You wear it under your clothes. See this padding? It thickens your waist. And the top part holds your breasts in. An old French army tailor in New Orleans fashioned it for me. Made three of them, actually, so it won't hurt me to let go of one. With any luck, it keeps you from getting found out."

~ ~ ~

The day dawned clear and bright. Jake came for Hattie right after sun-up, near the end of his shift. He looked up and down, taking in her short hair and men's uniform, but his face betrayed no surprise as he clamped irons over her wrists.

Several of the women tittered. "Do naugh mind them, lass," he said. "You make a fine-lookin' lad."

"Kind of you to say, sir." Hattie's voice wouldn't go quite as low as Loreta wanted, but in her role as Hamlet, she'd learned to drop it a bit.

Awkwardly, she lifted her joined wrists and waved goodbye to Peg and Loreta. They'd both gone out on a limb for her, and she had no idea how she could ever repay them.

It felt strange, walking beside Jake as she'd practiced last night with Loreta, with a bit of swagger but not so much as to challenge authority. Wearing trousers, she'd never felt her legs so keenly.

As Jake led her to the end of the corridor, she heard shouting from the women's cell—Loreta's voice, then Peg's, raised in heated argument. Alarmed that her co-conspirators had so quickly had a falling out, she turned in the direction of their voices.

Jake tugged her forward. "Distractin' the capt'n," he said in a low voice. "He'll be coming round soon, and we don't want him seeing your cart off."

Hattie couldn't believe Peg was risking another encounter with Nero so that she could make her escape without the captain catching on. "But he'll find out soon enough, won't he, when the cart arrives at Libby Prison and they see there's no woman?"

"Once the cart leaves here, those prisoners are Henry Turner's responsibility. Aint' likely he'll admit the only woman he was transporting slipped away before reaching his prison."

Hattie hoped he was right. They reached the exit, and Jake thrust open the door. Hattie squinted into the sunlight. On the street was a cart filled with standing prisoners, each cuffed to its railing by the wrists.

Jake led her to the cart, and she stepped inside, head held high, shoulders back. "After that last man escaped, they're taking no chances," Jake said ruefully as he cuffed her to the rail. Then he closed up the back of the cart.

"Hatfield Logan," he called to the driver. "That's the last of 'em."

The driver flicked the reins, and the cart rolled down the road. Jostled, Hattie lost her balance but recovered it quickly. She'd never stood so close to so many men at once, the smell of their sweat strong, hygiene not being among Captain Alexander's priorities.

The cart circled the block, and she thought of Thom, still trapped inside. He'd laugh to see her now, but he'd also admire the cleverness in what she and Peg and Loreta had accomplished, transforming her from Hattie to Hatfield.

As the cart continued down Cary Street, she saw a man pacing in front of what she knew to be a slave auction house. "Twenty-three able-bodied Negroes," he called out. "Twenty-three workers on sale today!"

She knew all too well what that meant—the separation of families, the lashings, the forced labor. Lincoln's proclamation had changed little for Virginia's enslaved people. Her own circumstances, desperate as they were, were trivial by comparison. As Hatfield Logan, she at least had the assurance of freedom if she could hang on until the hostilities ended. But if the Confederacy prevailed, there was no hope for the people enslaved in plantations all around the South.

Their freedom was a cause worth risking her life for, even if others wanted only to see the Union restored. She knew Thom felt the same. He'd told her as much, that first glorious night in Richmond, before his illness worsened, before the heinous doctor and Lucy had betrayed them. An immigrant from Britain, he held fast to the founding principles of the nation they spied for, as did she. Every man, woman, and child had a right to life, liberty, and the pursuit of happiness.

The cart continued down the street toward the enormous brick building that was Libby Prison, whitewashed on the bottom, brick on top. Hattie savored the sun's warmth on her face, the gentle breeze on her skin, hoping to recall those sensations through whatever trials awaited her.

She would prevail, she told herself. She would don a hundred disguises, if that's what it took, not to expunge her past but to redeem it.

THE END

Thank you for reading *The Courier's Wife*. If you enjoyed this book,
please take a moment to share your thoughts with a review.

MORE BOOKS IN VANESSA LIND'S CIVIL WAR SERIES

Lady in Disguise (exclusive to newsletter subscribers)

Enemy Lines
Gray Waters

Be the first to know about new books and giveaways—
sign up for Vanessa Lind's newsletter and get a free copy
of *Lady in Disguise*, prequel to *The Courier's Wife*

Author's Note

This book is inspired by Pinkerton operative Hattie Lawton, who posed as the wife of another Pinkerton spy, Timothy Webster. In Baltimore and Richmond, they endeared themselves to Southern sympathizers, passing on valuable information to Union commanders. As part of this effort, Pinkerton operatives also opened mail carried by couriers like Timothy Webster, though not exactly in a mailroom as described in this book.

Kate Warne joined the Pinkertons in 1858. Soon she was overseeing the work of the other women detectives Allen Pinkerton hired. She and her colleagues excelled at their work in part because the men they spied on so often underestimated them. Stationed in Baltimore in 1861, Warne alerted Pinkerton to a plot to assassinate Abraham Lincoln when he passed through the city on the way to his inauguration. After Pinkerton managed to convince the reluctant president-elect of the danger, Warne posed as his sister, escorting him through the night on a secret itinerary that got him safely to Washington.

Beyond Allen Pinkerton's often hyperbolic accounts, little is definitively known about Warne, and even less about Hattie Lawton. Webster is better remembered in history, and I've drawn on some of that material in shaping Thom Welton's character. I've also borrowed some details of their capture from the firsthand account of Pinkerton operative Pryce Lewis. Dispatched by Pinkerton to check on Lawton and Webster in Richmond, he and fellow spy John Scully were arrested and jailed. According to Lewis, Scully cracked under pressure and gave them all up. For the sake of the narrative, I've placed my account of Hattie and Thom's arrest and imprisonment a year later than the actual arrests of Lawton, Webster, Lewis, and Scully.

Elizabeth Van Lew, a well-known figure in Richmond, conducted spy operations for the North. She also helped escaped prisoners. Captain Alexander was in charge of Castle Thunder, and accounts of him and his dog Nero are much as he's presented here. He fancied himself a poet, and the bit of doggerel included in this book is said to be his work. Sidney Hanover's escape is a historical anecdote, though it may be hyperbolic. The same can be said of accounts given by Loreta Velazquez of her exploits while dressed as a man serving with the Confederate Army, though she did do time at Castle Thunder after authorities arrested her for impersonating a man.

For readers who want more of the history connected with several of these fascinating people, Douglas Waller's book *Lincoln's Spies* gives an excellent account.

Wondering what happens to Hattie next? You'll find out in *Enemy Lines*, Book Two of the historical fiction series Secrets of the Blue and Gray.

Printed in the USA
CPSIA information can be obtained
at www.ICGtesting.com
LVHW040300240824
788989LV00005B/1019